# PRAISE FOR BRITTAINY CHERRY BOOKS

"Readers will be drawn in by the complex characters, snappy pacing, and believable portrayals of both small-town life and the music industry. Cherry's fans will be pleased."

—*Publishers Weekly*

"Brittainy Cherry has the ability to shatter our hearts and heal them in the same story."

—*The Bookery Review*

"This is not just your ordinary romance. It is completely addictive and intensely consuming. Heartbreakingly real in all its entirety."

—*Kitty Kats Crazy about Books*

"Full of heartbreak and loss and pain. But also so full of love and hope and sweet and happy moments. I adored every single word in this book!"

—*BJ's Book Blog*

"As usual Brittainy wrote a stunning story that will touch your heart and stay with you."

—*Mel Reader Reviews*

"I'm speechless and completely overwhelmed by the beauty of this story."

—*Two Unruly Girls*

"As always Cherry aims straight for our hearts and hits a bull's-eye!"

—*°ook Bistro Blog*

# The
# Mixtape

# OTHER TITLES BY BRITTAINY CHERRY

## The Elements Series

*The Gravity of Us*
*The Silent Waters*
*The Fire Between High & Lo*
*The Air He Breathes*

## The Compass Series

*Southern Storms*

## Other Titles

*The Wreckage of Us*
*Landon & Shay, Parts 1 & 2*
*Eleanor & Grey*
*A Love Letter from the Girls Who Feel Everything*
(coauthored with Kandi Steiner)
*Disgrace*
*Behind the Bars*
*Art & Soul*
*Loving Mr. Daniels*
*Our Totally, Ridiculous, Made-Up Christmas Relationship* (novella)
*The Space in Between*

# The Mixtape

## BRITTAINY CHERRY

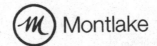 Montlake

Text copyright © 2021 by Brittainy C. Cherry
All rights reserved.

Published by Montlake, Seattle

www.apub.com

Amazon, the Amazon logo, and Montlake are trademarks of Amazon.com, Inc., or its affiliates.

ISBN-13: 9781542018364
ISBN-10: 1542018366

Cover design by Hang Le

Printed in the United States of America

*To my family. My favorite mixtape.*

# AUTHOR'S NOTE

This story came from a place of compassion and love for women around the world who go through so much day in and day out. I wanted to write a story full of heart and meaning with an authentic feel.

For those reasons, I'd like to note that parts of this story may be sensitive to a few readers due to the subject matter, which includes substance abuse, depression, verbal abuse, and rape.

# PROLOGUE

## OLIVER

*Six Months Ago*

I came from a family built of extroverts. Me? Not so much. It didn't bother me any. I was one of those lucky bastards who knew who he was at a very young age, and my family loved me for exactly who I'd always been. I thrived in my introverted ways. If I had a book, a jam-packed playlist, and a dog companion, I was a happy guy.

My brother, Alex, was the complete opposite of me—more like my parents. He flourished at social gatherings. If there was a party, Alex was there on center stage. When it came to having a twin, self-discovery almost seemed impossible because everyone compared you with your literal other half. Yet I never really struggled with that when Alex was involved. Even though we were best friends, we were extremely different in a million ways. While he was the extrovert at gatherings, I was the observer.

Alex preferred to engage in groups, while I loved to study them from afar. I knew I was a people person, but I worked best with them on a one-to-one basis. Crowds overwhelmed me, because the energy of the space always felt chaotic. Even though my brother and I never fell victim to thinking we were less than one another, the world had its own opinions of us both.

Alex and I were a musician duo, Alex & Oliver, who'd found more success than we probably deserved. With every pair of siblings in the spotlight, there was one who people preferred over the other. It was even worse with twins. People loved to compare us all the time in the media. From our looks and our personalities, to the way we dressed and handled interviews. Alex was extremely charismatic through and through. He could meet a stranger in the subway station, and after five minutes, they were seemingly the best of friends.

Me, on the other hand? I took my time getting to know a person. I didn't open up right away, which sometimes made me appear cold. It was truly the opposite, though. I wanted to know what made a person tick. I wanted to not only see them in the sunlight, but I wanted to see their rain clouds too.

I didn't care who their favorite football team was or how they celebrated New Year's Eve with friends. Who were they on their worst days? How did they treat animals when no one was looking? When they were dealing with depression, how dark were their overcast skies? Unfortunately, we lived in a world where going deep wasn't very common anymore. People lived on the surface level, showcasing the happy highlights of themselves. It sometimes took years to discover someone's shadows, and most people didn't stick around me long enough to go that deep.

Therefore, even in the duo, Alex and I had different fanbases. The Alexholics were the life of the party. They were the ones in our crowds who brought the energetic energy that my brother had. The Olives—their fan-name choice, not mine—were much more subdued. They were the ones who wrote handwritten letters and sent me long messages on social media, describing to me how our songs affected them.

Both the Alexholics and Olives were the best. Without equal parts of each, Alex & Oliver wouldn't have been celebrating our third album release with our record label.

## The Mixtape

That evening, the nightclub was packed with the music industry's finest to celebrate the release of our new album, *Heart Cracks*. The room was crawling with talent, egos, and implausible wealth. Everyone who was anyone was there—at least that was what was being alleged across the internet.

All I wanted to do was go home. Don't get me wrong: I was thankful for everything that had come my way. I had more than enough gratitude for my record label and my team, but after a few hours of me being "on," my energy craved solitude. I wasn't very much into parties of any sort. I was much more interested in going home, putting on sweats, and binge-watching documentaries on Netflix. I had an odd obsession with documentaries. Did I ever plan to be a minimalist? No. Would I watch a documentary on it? Hell fucking yes.

There were so many people at the party that night. So many people who smiled in my face but probably didn't truly know me. People who laughed and made plans to meet up again, even though they were certain they never would commit to those future plans. People who were shoulder to shoulder in conversation, chitchatting about drama within the industry.

Alex was to my left, socializing like no other. He was being the Prince Charming he'd always been, and there I was, grazing the table filled with food, stuffing my face with too many crab bites.

The only things Alex and I had in common were our taste in music and our looks. From our curly, dark-brown hair to our caramel eyes, which we didn't get from our parents. Dad often joked that Mom must've run off during their relationship. For the most part, though, we looked identical to our father, a well-built Black man with welcoming eyes, a rounded nose, and a wide, impressive smile. If our parents weren't smiling, they were laughing; if they weren't laughing, they were dancing. Most of the time, they did all three actions at the same time. We were raised by two of the happiest, most supportive people in the world.

While I cruised the appetizers table, I tensed up when I felt someone place their hand on my shoulder and thought I had to put my socializing cap back on. Turning around quickly, I breathed out a sigh of relief as I saw Alex standing behind me. He was wearing all black, with a Hermès gold buckled belt, which I was almost certain he took from my closet. His shirt collar was pressed and smooth, and the sleeves of his button-down shirt were rolled up to his elbows.

"You need to slow down on your socializing, brother. People are afraid you're going to hop on a table and start dancing," Alex joked, grabbing my fiftieth crab bite from my hand and popping it into his mouth.

"I said hi to Tyler," I offered.

"Saying hi to your manager isn't really being social." He glanced around the space and rubbed his hand against the back of his neck as his necklace swayed back and forth from him hitting the chain. It was half of a heart necklace—I had the other half. Mom gave it to us years ago, when we went on our first tour. She said she was leaving her heartbeats with us.

Corny as hell, but then again, that was our mother, corny as hell. Sweetest woman you'd ever meet, and a big crybaby. The woman still couldn't watch *Bambi* without tears flooding her eyes.

There wasn't a day when we took off those necklaces. I was thankful for the reminder of home.

"I'll go talk to Cam. How's that?" I offered up. Alex tried his best to hide his grimace, but he suffered from a lack of poker face. "You can't hold a grudge against her forever."

"I know. I just don't appreciate how she did that interview and threw you under the bus in an attempt to get exposure. That's not how your girl should be acting."

When my brother and I formed our duo, we performed in a lot of small venues. It was then that we crossed paths with small-town Georgia peach Cam—the up-and-coming country star.

Even though we were both different kinds of performers—I was the soul/R&B musician and she the country singer—we found common ground. It wasn't every day you came across two Black people who found success in an industry where we were the minority.

Even though we were both successful, Cam's rise to fame had happened within the past year. She was finally getting the credit she deserved for her talents, and I loved to see it. The only problem was, with success came ego. She glowed in the spotlight, but the same glow seemed to become addictive to her. Over time, it was clear we were growing in different directions, which I knew for a fact when we went out for lunch one afternoon and she reached out to the paparazzi to have us photographed together.

The fame became all she craved. More, more, more. It was never enough for her, and her need to be at the center of the spotlight damaged her common sense. She made rushed decisions without thinking of the consequences of her actions. She trusted the wrong people. She acted out of character from the sweet woman I'd met years before.

Still, I knew she wasn't all bad. I'd been in the limelight for the past few years; I knew how that could mess with someone's head. When we first met, we connected in the deep ways that I loved. She was a young girl with a dream, and I was a boy with the same. I knew that goodness had to still live inside of Cam. Success had come so fast for her over the past year, so I was certain she just had to find her footing. Sometimes when I looked in her eyes, I still saw innocence. Other times I saw her fear. So what kind of asshole would I have been to turn on her when she was just figuring it all out?

When she went to do an interview a few weeks ago and spoke about our personal relationship—something I never wanted the public to be involved in—Alex got pissed. Cam knew that I didn't want our relationship in the public's grips, because we'd watched time and time again how the media ripped apart people for entertainment. Cam told me she meant no harm and the interviewer had tricked her into answering the questions about our relationship. I believed her. Why wouldn't I?

"She didn't mean any harm," I muttered, looking at my highly annoyed brother.

He shrugged. "Of course not. But she did mean to use it as a way to get clout. I know you both have been together for a long time, and I don't want to say that she's using you—"

"Then don't," I said through gritted teeth.

He frowned. "All right. Dropping it."

"Appreciate that." I knew he meant well. He was an overprotective brother, and when it involved who he was dating in the past, I was the same way. We just wanted the best for one another. I pushed out a smile and patted him on the back. "My introvert senses are tingling, so I think I'm gonna head out."

"Leaving your own celebration early? I wish I could say I was surprised, but . . ." He smirked. "Cam going with you?"

"Yeah, we came together. So I'm going to go grab her."

Alex patted me on the back before grabbing a meatball on a stick from the table. "Sounds good. Text when you make it home, all right? Let me know if you need anything. Love you."

"You too."

"Oh, and brother?"

"Yeah?"

"Congrats on yet another album. Here's to fifty million more!" Alex exclaimed, his eyes glassing over like Mom's. *Emotional ass.*

"It's only the beginning," I agreed, pulling him into a hug and patting his back. I blinked a few times to keep my eyes from glassing over too. *Emotional ass.*

I guessed being emotional ran in the family. But hell, we'd worked hard over the past fifteen-plus years to build our career. Some people tagged us as an overnight sensation when our track "Heart Stamps" hit the Billboard charts, but what the media seemed to miss was the count-less years of struggle that had come before.

I grabbed one more crab bite before moving in Cam's direction, and my thoughts began racing to acknowledge that I'd have to greet the people she was interacting with. My socializing tank was nearing empty. The nerves began to work up my throat as I grew closer and closer, but I tried my best to push them down.

If there was one known fact about Cam, it was that she was stun-ning. Everyone in their right mind could agree on that concept. She looked like a goddess with her light-brown eyes, long, straight jet-black hair, and curvaceous body. She moved like music, and her smile could make any grown man crave her attention. It was that wide grin that captured my attention all those years ago.

That night she wore a tight-fitted black velvet gown that looked as if it'd been sewn directly on her body. Her hair was pulled into a high ponytail, and her lips were painted crimson as she stood tall in her red-bottom heels.

Tonight, I placed my hand on Cam's lower back, and she melted into me a bit before looking over her shoulder. "Oh, Oliver! Hi. I thought you were someone else."

Who else would be touching her on the back like that? Who else's hand would she be melting into?

"Naw, just me." The two men she was engaging with nodded and smiled my way, and I gave them the same basic greeting before turning back to Cam. "I was going to head out. I figured you'd want to come, too, since we rode together."

"What? No. The night is just getting started. Don't be a buzzkill," she seemingly joked before turning to the two men. "Oliver's always a buzzkill at these things."

They all laughed as if I was the comic relief of the night. My chest tightened, and I dropped my hold before I moved in to whisper against her earlobe. "You don't have to do that, you know."

"Do what?"

"Perform all the time." She was putting on an act in front of those people to appear light and playful, but in turn, she was throwing me under the bus, just like Alex said.

Cam's eyes locked with mine and a flash of disgust flew across her face before she recovered and gave me a fake smile and softly spoke back. "I'm not performing. I'm networking, Oliver."

*There she is.*

The woman I no longer knew. The side of Cam that I didn't like very much. Each day I longed a little more for the Cam she used to be.

*Come back to me.*

I didn't say another word, because I knew getting through to her while she was in character wasn't going to work. The men had smirks on their faces as I turned to walk away from the three of them. I didn't bother saying goodbye. Fuck them and their smart-ass smirks. All I knew was, when Cam came home that night, she was coming home to me.

Walking through the crowd of sardines, I kept my head lowered, not wanting to make eye contact with anyone in hopes of avoiding any kind of social interaction. My brain had reached its limit of engaging, and I simply needed my driver to meet me outside to take me home.

I shot my way to coat check and muttered a thank-you as the guy handed me my jacket. Then I headed to the front of the building, where paparazzi had been waiting all night on the left, behind barriers, for a chance to get a shot of any and every celebrity leaving the club.

"Oliver! Oliver! Over here! You came with Cam! Is there trouble in paradise?"

"Why isn't Cam leaving with you?"

"Is it true you two have been secretly dating for years?"

"Why lie about your relationship? Were you ashamed of her?"

And that was exactly why I didn't want those assholes in my business.

8

Instead of engaging with them, I turned to my right, where another barricade was set up. Behind the barricade were the people I truly cared about. The fans.

Even though I was exhausted and had mentally checked out, I headed over to them and smiled. I'd spend as much time as I could taking pictures with the fans, because without them, Alex and I wouldn't even have an album-release party to be celebrating.

"Hey there, how's it going?" I asked, smirking toward a young girl. She couldn't have been over eighteen, and she held a sign up that said OLIVE4LIFE.

"Oh my gosh," she muttered, her colorful braces spreading into a wide-toothed grin. Her eyes flooded with tears as her body trembled. I placed my hand against her shaky hand.

If it weren't for her friends holding her up, I was sure she was going to collapse to the ground.

"Y-you're my h-h-h-ero," she spat out, making me smile.

"You're mine too. What's your name?"

"Adya." The tears began flowing down her cheeks, and I wiped them away for her. "You d-don't understand," she stuttered, shaking her head. "Your music helped me through my depression. I w-was bullied a lot and wanted to e-end my life, but your music was there for me. You saved me."

Fucking A.

Don't cry, Oliver. Don't you dare fucking cry.

I squeezed her hand and leaned in close. "If only you knew how much you've saved me, too, Adya."

She was why I did it. Her along with all the others who showed up and showed out for Alex & Oliver. Fuck the paparazzi. I showed up for the fans, because they always showed up for me.

"Taking photos without me?" Alex chimed in, patting me on the back. He had his jacket in his hand, as if he was leaving too.

"Where are you going?" I asked.

"I got tired." Alex glanced down at his watch.

"That's a lie." Alex was always one of the last ones to leave a party.

He smirked. "Kelly texted me saying she was hungry. I figured I'd bring her some chicken noodle soup, since she wasn't feeling good."

Now, that made sense. Kelly was my assistant, and Alex was like a lovesick puppy about her. She was currently staying in my coach house while her loft was being renovated. Therefore, it seemed that Alex was around my place a lot more than normal—and he definitely wasn't visiting me. "Figured I could catch a ride with you," he said, nudging me. "After a few more pics with these guys."

I always had a feeling that the two of them had a connection, and it wasn't shocking that they'd begun talking. Honestly, they were a perfect match. For a while, Kelly suffered from an eating disorder, trying to keep up with Hollywood's beauty standards. Alex was the main one who helped her through her hardships. He would sit with her and eat meals every single day without fail, making sure she knew she wasn't alone in her struggles. What started as friendship slowly began to transform into something with more meaning.

We took a few more photographs with the fans while ignoring the vultures on the other side asking us insane questions, then climbed into the back of the black Audi that was waiting for us.

"Hey, Ralph, you all right with me smoking in here?" Alex asked as he leaned forward toward the driver.

"Whatever you want to do is fine by me, Mr. Smith," Ralph replied, being the laid-back driver he'd always been. Alex always found the need to ask him about the smoking thing, even though Ralph always said it was fine.

Alex sat back as he lit up a joint. He wasn't a big smoker or anything, but he always had a joint after some kind of event. Maybe that was his way of unwinding from social gatherings. I would've taken up the habit if I thought it would've helped with my social anxiety. Instead, pot made me more paranoid of what people were thinking of me.

Hard pass for me.

"You hear this song?" Alex asked, pulling out his phone and hitting play. "'Godspeed,' by James Blake. Shit. His voice is so fucking dope, man. Smooth as whiskey. Reminds me of our old stuff, before the record deal." He plopped back in his seat and closed his eyes. "Whenever I hear music like this, I feel like a sellout. This is the music we wanted to make, you know? Music that fucked with your soul in a good way. That made you feel alive."

The song was powerful in such a chill way, which wasn't shocking for James Blake. He made me feel to the depths of my being. Alex wasn't wrong—our music used to feel like that too. Like it mattered. When we signed with our record label, they changed our direction a lot, which brought us fame and millions of fans along with millions of dollars. Sometimes we wondered at what expense, though. How much money and fame was enough to sell one's soul?

Many days I wished I could go back to the days of small venues and tiny crowds.

Felt more authentic back then.

I reached for my phone and opened my current playlist routine to share my current favorite track from James Blake. There wasn't a day that Alex and I didn't send each other music. We used music to express how we were feeling day in and day out. Sometimes we were too exhausted for true conversations, so songs were our way to communicate.

Had a great day? "It Was a Good Day," by Ice Cube. Felt down? "This City," by Sam Fischer. The world getting on your last nerve? "Fuck You," by CeeLo Green. No matter what the feeling was, there was a song that could express it.

"You heard this one?" I asked, turning on "Retrograde," by James Blake. First time I heard it, I knew it was important.

Alex opened his eyes and leaned forward. His brows knitted as his head began to slowly nod to the beat of the song. "Shit," he said, smirking as the lyrics laid their seed in his head. His eyes glassed over as the

11

joint sat between his lips, the end of it lit with reddish-orange heat. "We need to get back to this kind of stuff." He rubbed a thumb against his watery eyes, and I smirked.

My sensitive brother always got more in his feelings when he was getting high.

"For real, Oliver. We need to get back to—"

His words were cut short as the car came to a sudden halt, jerking Alex and me forward in the back seat. "What the hell was that?" I asked.

"Sorry, you guys. Some assholes came rushing down the road like idiots," Ralph said before pushing his foot against the gas to start again.

Just as we were sitting back in our seat and beginning to relax again, the world began to shatter around us, along with the windows that busted from the impact of a car slamming against the left side of the car. There wasn't any time to react or comprehend exactly what was going on. All I knew was everything ached. My phone flew from my hand. My chest burned as my vision blurred.

The sound of horns blasting surrounded us. The sound of people shouting echoed in my eardrums.

I couldn't move no matter how hard I tried. I felt . . . upside down? Was I upside down? Was the car upside down? Was Alex . . . ?

Fuck.

Alex?

I looked to my left, my neck aching from the slight movement. There he was, his eyes closed, his face covered in blood, his body not moving in the slightest.

"Alex," I choked out, the word burning my throat as tears flooded my eyes. "Alex," I repeated, over and over again until my head began to ache in an unimaginable fashion.

I had to close my eyes.

I didn't want to close my eyes.

I wanted to check on Alex.

I wanted to make sure he was okay.

I wanted to . . .

*Fuck.*

I couldn't breathe. Why did my throat burn? Was Alex all right? My eyes began to fade as "Retrograde" echoed in my eardrums.

### A Star Is Gone

By Jessica Peppers

It looks like the music world has to say goodbye to another musician. Lead guitarist Alex Smith of Alex & Oliver is dead at 27. After a deadly car crash, he was raced to Memorial Hospital, where he was announced dead on arrival.

Insiders are saying that Alex was leaving the party due to his brother. Is it too early to put this fault on the shoulders of Oliver? Oliver was left with a few injuries but nothing too serious. Still, with such a big loss, who knows what that will do to the artist.

Stay tuned for more updates as they roll in, and remember, you read it first here on W News.

### BREAKING NEWS

The Curse of the 27 Club

Alex Smith, Dead at 27

By Eric Hunter

Jimi Hendrix, Janis Joplin, Jim Morrison, Kurt Cobain, Amy Winehouse.

What do all these musicians have in common—other than being legendary masterpieces? They all left the world at the early age of 27. Sadly, they have another joining the club at the same tender age. Alex Smith was announced dead last night after a tragic car accident took place. Rumor has it that there were drugs in Alex's system. We reached out to Oliver's team for a statement but have heard nothing back from them as of yet.

Questions are arising in the wake of such a tragedy. What does this mean for Alex & Oliver? Will Oliver continue on without his brother by his side? How will Oliver ever be able to come to grips with such a personal loss?

Only time will tell.

Keep a close eye on our site for all incoming updates on this tragic event.

Tragedy Strikes Alex & Oliver

By Aaron Bank

Alex Smith, of Alex & Oliver, was pronounced dead late this evening after a car crash. One of the music industry's brightest stars is gone too soon.

With the loss of Alex, the world didn't simply lose a talented musician. It lost a great advocate for human rights. From his voice in the Black community, to being on the front line of marches for equality, Alex Smith did a lot of good for this world. He is definitely gone too soon.

**Twitter Trending Hashtag**
**#RIPAlexSmith**
**ShannonE:** That awkward moment when the wrong Smith brother is killed. #RIPAlexSmith

**HeavyLifter:** Oliver is nothing but a fucking loser. If he didn't have Alex leave early, he'd still be alive. His death is on Oliver's hands. RIP to the best guitarist this world has ever seen. #RIPAlexSmith #FuckYouOliverSmith

**BlackJazz4235:** Who the fuck is Alex & Oliver? Sounds like an emo band who cries in their mother's basement #RIPAlexSmith #BullshitMusic

**UptownGirlz:** How is it only January 6th and one of my idols is already dead? Fuck you, new year. I want a restart. #RIPAlexSmith

**UntitledSoul:** And this is why you say no to drugs, kids. Fucking addicts. #RIPAlexSmith

**Brittainy Cherry**

The Fate of Oliver Smith Is at Risk

By Eric Hunter

It has been six months since the passing of Alex Smith, one half of the powerful duo Alex & Oliver, and time has not been kind to Oliver Smith. We saw how his stay at a mental health clinic was tainted by the paparazzi and jaded employees who exposed Oliver's treatments, which led to him leaving the facility before getting the help he probably needed. Since then, he has been a recluse, hardly ever leaving his home. An insider says he's on the verge of a mental breakdown.

Many fans were hoping to see Oliver come around and bounce back from the tragic loss, yet as time passes, we might as well pack up our hopes, kids.

It seems that Oliver is hanging up his guitar strap for good. Besides, let's be honest. Who wants an Oliver without an Alex?

# 1

## OLIVER

**Present Day**

I woke up lying beside a woman I loved yet didn't like very much anymore. It wasn't always like that. There was a time in my life when Cam Jones wowed me. We inspired one another. We had deep, meaningful conversations. I adored her. I even thought that someday she'd be my wife. Over time, though, she was becoming more and more of a stranger to me.

Days after Alex passed away, rumors began to circulate that Cam had been cheating on me, yet she swore they weren't true. That was the exact reason I never wanted our relationship to be publicized, because when the vultures got their claws in your life, they weren't going to let go until they ripped you apart.

After she told me the rumors weren't true, I didn't dig deeper. It was the paparazzi's job to spread lies. Besides, my mind wasn't in a good place. My soul couldn't even face the idea of having a fallout with Cam, because I needed her. Cam was there most evenings to lie beside me, and maybe I was a little bitch for needing that, but I hated the idea of being alone.

My thoughts were too heavy for loneliness.

Cam yawned beside me and stretched her arms out, smacking me in the face. I groaned from the movement and turned my back toward her chilled fingertips. It amazed me how someone could be so cold, even though they were wrapped in a million blankets.

As I shifted to my left, Cam yanked the comforter to the right, pulling it from me and wrapping herself into it. I grumbled to myself a bit and moved to sit up on the edge of my California king–size bed as my hands massaged my temples. Leaning forward to stand, I paused as the world began spinning faster and faster behind my eyes.

Coffee.

I needed coffee and about fifteen more years of sleep. I couldn't remember the last time I'd had a good night's sleep, outside of blacking out. I couldn't sleep while I was sober; my thoughts were too loud.

"Rise and shine, princess," a voice chirped, making me tilt my head up a bit in the direction of my bedroom door. My left eye slightly opened as the figure in front of me slowly came into focus.

Tyler stood there with a cup of coffee and a bottle of ibuprofen. Thank God for him and his ability to know what I needed before I even stated the fact. Tyler was a short, bald guy in his late thirties who was built like a superhero. He had a thick Bronx accent that he didn't leave behind in New York when he moved to the West Coast.

He always dressed in the best designer outfits and ruined his look with the worst set of sunglasses in the world. Honestly, they looked like something someone from the seventies would wear. I was almost certain I saw the same set of glasses on reruns of *Welcome Back, Kotter* that I used to watch with my dad. If Tyler was a dog, he'd be a mix of a Chihuahua and a pit bull. Built strong with a hell of a lot of bark, and a look that was all kinds of ridiculous. Somehow, it worked for him.

I grumbled some more to him and kept kneading my fingers against my forehead.

Cam moved within the sheets and yawned loudly as she sat up and rubbed her hands over her face. "Is that coffee for me?" she questioned, turning in Tyler's direction.

"Never," he huffed, picking up her bra and tossing it her way.

"It's good to see you, too, Tyler."

"How about you piss off, Satan," he replied, completely unentertained by my reoccurring mistake. It was no secret that the two of them hated one another. Even before the cheating rumors, Tyler deemed her unworthy of his attention. He and Alex had had the same viewpoint on her: she was using me to further her name.

I couldn't bring myself to believe that. Somewhere inside of her was the kind soul I knew years before. At least those were the lies I'd told myself to get through each day.

"I'll get my own coffee. I have to get going, anyway. I need to find a charity to donate to in order to get some good press," Cam stated.

"You don't give to charity for good press," I muttered.

She rolled her eyes. "That's the only reason we do charity work. Otherwise, what's the point?"

Cam slithered her body around in my bed until she was placing her bare chest against my back. Her cold brown skin pressed up against the darkness of mine, and for a second we make-believed that our bodies connected, even though we both knew we were forcing the pieces together from two mismatched puzzles.

"Did you talk to your management about letting me perform during your show tonight?" she asked me, reminding me that I had a show that night.

"I am his management, and the answer is hell to the no," Tyler remarked.

Cam released an annoyed huff. "When are you going to fire him?"

"Never," I replied.

"You hear that? Never. I'm just waiting for the day that he fires you," Tyler said.

She hissed in his direction, and he hissed right back at her.

She moved her lips to my ear, and my body slightly revolted from her simple touch. I was almost certain her eyes were locked on Tyler to prove some kind of point to him. That she had control over me, not him. "Last night was fun," she commented, her voice smoky and dry. Fun? Was it? I'd drunk too much to truly recall. Her hair swayed back and forth, brushing against the nape of my neck. "I have to get to some meetings. I'll see you tonight."

I didn't say anything to her. She didn't expect any form of communication from me. Cam and I didn't talk. Well, she talked, I didn't, which was fine for her. All she ever wanted was to have someone sit and listen to everything she said. While she needed someone to listen, I needed someone to stay. At night she'd lie beside me, and for a few moments in my life, I'd pretend that the world wasn't crashing around me and I'd feel less alone.

Crazy how loneliness led people to places they probably didn't belong anymore.

Cam tossed on her dress with a smug expression and a look of control over me. "Bye, Ty," she said, snatching the coffee from his hand and working her hips left and right as she exited the room.

Tyler looked disgusted from the sight of her leaving my room. "This is your daily reminder that you don't need to share a bed with the devil," he commented. "Anyway, get a move on. We got to get going. You should've already been showered."

He moved over to my closet doors and swung them open, revealing a massive space filled with more designer clothes than any person should've ever possessed. There was a huge kitchen-style island in the middle of the closet with pullout drawers revealing expensive watches, designer socks, and jewelry that was worth more than most people's house mortgage.

"I was thinking, maybe we should reschedule the concert."

"You're joking, right?" he asked, exiting my closet with an outfit for me. "You're the one who agreed to this performance tonight."

That wasn't a lie. The concert was my idea. After reading so many articles about how I was falling apart and a complete mess, I felt as if I had to prove I was doing okay—even though I wasn't. My career wasn't simply my own—I had a team of people depending on me to keep making music. From my manager, to my PR team, to Kelly, to Ralph, who thankfully had survived the car crash with only minor injuries. People's livelihoods depended on me. When my record label gave me the option to become a solo artist, it was a chance to make sure my team all stayed employed.

Still . . . I didn't know how to be a solo artist.

Hell, I didn't know how to exist without my brother.

"This is a good opportunity, Oliver," Tyler said, as if he could read my troubled thoughts. "I know it's not gonna be easy, and if I could take your place on that stage and perform, I would. But the best I can do is be backstage with you, cheering you on with Kelly—who, by the way, is getting you some breakfast as we speak. So, go shower and wash the seed of Chucky off your body."

I headed to the en suite shower, which had three showerheads—rich people problems—and did as Tyler told me. I wanted to argue more about why the performance that night didn't matter, because I honestly didn't see the point. I was part of a duo, and ever since Alex had passed away, it was apparent to me that Alex & Oliver was over and out.

Like the many articles had stated, who would want Oliver without Alex?

As I stood in the shower, I hoped it would wash away my buzzing headache, but it didn't. I thought it would wash away my loud thoughts, too, but it didn't. I wasn't lucky that way. I hadn't found a way to quiet my mind without alcohol in a long time.

When I got out of the shower, I didn't look in the mirror. Most of the mirrors in my house were covered with sheets. I hadn't looked in mirrors in such a long time, because in every single one, Alex was staring back my way.

# 2

## EMERY

*What's for breakfast?*

I scrounged through the cabinets in search of something—*anything*—to make for Reese. We used our last eggs and sausage links for dinner last night, and we wiped the side of the peanut butter jar nicely with a spatula to have an after-dinner snack while we read books from the library.

*Think, think, think, Emery.*

I pulled out a loaf of bread along with an almost emptied jar of jelly and set it down on the countertop.

We had one piece of bread left in the loaf along with the two end pieces, though Reese refused to eat the end pieces, no matter how much jelly I'd slap against them.

"That's not real bread, Mom," she'd argue again and again. "Those are the butt ends. That's what the birds by the lake eat."

Though she had a point, she didn't have much of a choice that morning. I had only $12.45 in my bank account, and payday wasn't until tomorrow. Half that money would go toward rent, while I'd use the other half for budget-friendly meals. We didn't have much wiggle room in our lives at the moment, since I'd lost my one job at the hotel as a line cook.

Ever since then, I'd been working nights at a sporadically busy hole-in-the-wall bar called Seven. Needless to say, the job hadn't been pulling in the money much, and I was still waiting to hear back from the unemployment office about income from losing my job.

I took out a knife and shaved off as much of the "butt end" as I could to make it look like a normal piece of bread. Then, I covered it with grape jelly.

"Reese, breakfast!" I called out.

She hurried out of her room and came rushing to the kitchen table. As she slid into her chair, she wrinkled up her nose and grumbled. "This is the end piece, Mom!" she sassed, completely unimpressed by my gourmet meal.

"Sorry, kiddo." I walked over and messed up her wavy charcoal hair. "Things are a bit tight this week."

"Things are always tight," she groaned, taking a bite before tossing the rest of the sandwich down on the plate. "Hey, Mama?"

"Yeah, sweetie?"

"Are we poor?"

The question echoed in my ears and hit me in the gut. "What? No, of course not," I answered, a bit shocked by her words. "Why would you even say that?"

"Well, Mia Thomas from camp said that only poor people shop at Goodwill, and that's where we get all of our clothes from. Plus, Randy always gets McDonald's for breakfast, and you never let me get McDonald's breakfast. *Plus, plus, plus*," she exclaimed excitedly, as if she was getting ready to list the biggest bit of proof to showcase our poverty level, "you gave me the butt ends!"

I smiled her way, but my heart began to shatter. It was something my heart had done over and over again for the past five years, ever since Reese came into this world. It shattered because every day I felt as if I was failing her. As if I wasn't enough, and I wasn't giving her the life she truly deserved. Being a single parent was the hardest thing I'd ever had to do in my life, yet I didn't really have a choice in the matter. The father was definitely never going to be in the picture, so I'd learned to handle everything on my own.

Even though I'd worked hard to make ends meet, lately it seemed that the struggle bus was driving down the road faster and faster. Each day it felt as if I were seconds away from crashing.

I hated that things had gotten so tight lately, but business was slow at the bar I worked at, which meant less tips. Plus, every job interview I came across never led anywhere. Rent was also late, and I hadn't yet informed Reese that I wouldn't be able to make her next camp deposit that was coming up; therefore, no more summer camp. She'd be devastated, as would I for breaking her heart. I wondered if kids knew that when parents had to break their hearts, ours shattered more.

I didn't know when we'd catch a break.

I stared at my girl, who looked so much like me. Some characteristics I was certain belonged to her father, but I was thankful I didn't see them. I only saw a beautiful little girl who was perfect in every way.

And her smile?

That smile was kind of like mine. More like my mother's. Along with the deep dimple in her left cheek.

*Thank God for that smile.*

She was also blessed with my bad eyesight, which was the reason those thick-framed, round glasses sat against her face. I loved that face so much. It was almost impossible to remember a day when she wasn't in my life.

You know how my heart shattered daily due to feeling like a failure? Each time Reese smiled, the cracks began to heal. She was my Earth angel, my reason for existing, and every broken crack that my heart suffered, her love fixed.

I moved over to her and ruffled her already messy, tangled brown hair. I'd need to give her loosely coiled hair a deep conditioning session along with a twist-out sooner rather than later, but my urgent concern was dinner that night and how it would come to be. It was a private concern, a secret mental struggle I couldn't let touch Reese. "You can't listen to everything everyone says at camp, Reese."

"Including Ms. Monica and Ms. Rachel and Ms. Kate?" she exclaimed, excited for almost getting permission to ignore her summer camp instructors.

"Everyone *except* the camp instructors."

"So," she said, cocking an eyebrow and picking up her sandwich, "we're not poor?"

"Well, let's see. Do you have a bed to sleep on?"

She nodded slowly. "Yeah."

"And a house to live in?"

"Uh-huh."

"A car to get us around?"

"Yeah . . ."

"And even if it's the butt ends of a sandwich, do you always have food to eat?"

"Yeah."

"And do you have a mama who loves you?"

She smirked her little shy smirk. "Yeah."

"Then there is no way we are poor. We have clothes on our backs, a roof over our head, a car to drive, and each other's love. No one can be poor if they have love." I said it, and I meant it too. When Reese came into my life, I learned that true wealth was wrapped in her love.

And with her love, I was rich. With her love, I'd never lose hope in tomorrow.

Reese lowered her eyebrows and gave me a stern look. "So, you're saying Mia and Randy are both full of baloney?"

"Oh yeah, lots and lots of baloney."

"Mmm, fried baloney sounds good," she said, biting into her sandwich. "Can we have that for dinner?" she asked.

"Maybe, honey. We'll see."

There was a knock at the front door, so I stood to my feet and headed over to answer it. As I opened it, I saw a familiar friendly face standing there.

"Good morning, Abigail." I smiled at my neighbor. Abigail Preston had lived in the apartment across from me ever since Reese and I moved in over five years ago. She was in her early sixties, lived on her own, and had been nothing but a saint to both Reese and me. On the days when I had to work the night shift, she was more than willing to watch Reese for me. She never asked for anything in return either. Even when I tried to pay her for her kindness, she told me that people shouldn't be kind in order to reap rewards.

"You do good for the sake of good doing, Emery. That's how the world keeps on keeping on—because there are good people doing good things for the simple sake of doing them."

Abigail was a good thing—a great thing, even.

Not only was she kind, but she was a retired therapist, which came in handy five years ago when I was a new mother. Abigail was there to help talk me through my anxiety, through my fears, all free of charge.

I once asked her why she stayed in our apartment building when it was clear that she had plenty of money to live in a nicer location. The story behind her choice was more than enough reason to make my heart smile. It turned out the apartment was the first place she'd ever lived with her now-deceased husband. After he passed away, Abigail went searching for a new place to live, and when she saw that the old apartment was up for rent, she knew she had to get it back.

She said it wasn't just an apartment, it was her life's story, and without that life story, she would've never crossed paths with Reese and me.

Thank goodness for a person's life story and how it sometimes intermixed with others.

"Hey, darling." She gave me her sweetest smile. She was decked out head to toe in vibrant forms of yellow. Her silver hair was pulled back into a ponytail, and her glasses hung on a chain around her neck. She also held a box in her hands. "I thought I'd stop by with some extra doughnuts I had for dinner last night. I had a craving and couldn't eat a whole dozen on my own, so I thought I'd leave the extras for you two." She opened the box for me to see the sugary treats.

She never knew it, but her door knocks were always right on time.

"Doughnuts!" Reese hollered, hurrying over to the door and taking the box of miracles from Abigail's hands. I knew most people wouldn't consider a box of doughnuts a miracle, yet when the refrigerator was empty and payday was still a few days away, a box of doughnuts was a gift from the heavens above.

Reese dashed off toward the living room sofa to dive in, and I called after her: "What do we say, Reese?"

"Thank you, Abigail!" she hollered, her mouth stuffed already with the sugary goodness.

"Only eat one, Reese. I mean it."

Those doughnuts would be enough to get us through until my check came in tomorrow night.

I turned back toward Abigail and narrowed my eyes. "For someone who had a craving for doughnuts last night, it's odd that there is still a full dozen in that box."

She gave me a sly smile. "They must've put an extra one in the box."

*Yeah, sure.*

Just a good woman doing good things.

I shifted around a bit and crossed my arms. "Thank you for that. You have no clue how much we needed that this morning."

She frowned a bit. "I think I have a bit of a clue." She pulled a piece of paper from behind her back and handed it to me. "This was placed in my mailbox instead of yours by mistake."

I took the folded sheet of paper from her and read the notice.

Rent was late.

*Again.*

27

I'd been behind for the past two months, due to losing my job and Reese having a few health issues, and luckily the apartment manager, Ed, had been nice enough to let it slide, but by the wording of his letter, it seemed that I was dangling from the end of his hospitality rope. I couldn't blame him, really. He had a job to do, and the fact that he allowed me to be two months behind without eviction was baffling to me.

I'd seen Ed send people packing for being a few weeks behind. He was a cutthroat kind of guy, all bite and no bark. Except for when it came to Reese and me. I was completely aware of the murky legalities here, and I knew the situation couldn't go on forever. Plus, there was no worse feeling than knowing you owed a person something. I wanted no debt against my name, for me and for Reese. For the time being, I was thankful for Ed's generosity. He had a bit of a soft spot for Reese, and he always said that I reminded him of his own mother. She had been a single mother, too, so perhaps Ed saw himself in Reese.

He couldn't take pity on us much longer, though, and I had to come up with a way to get him almost $2,000 in two days. I wouldn't have the money until Friday, and even then, rent would take up most of our check for the upcoming two weeks, leaving little room for gas and food.

I took a deep breath and tried to keep from breaking. It felt like an everlasting battle. If I caught up on one thing, another was falling out of place.

"If you need money, Emery—" Abigail started, but I shook my head quickly.

I'd taken a loan from her in the past, and I couldn't bring myself to do it again. I couldn't keep relying on others to give me a break in life. I had to stand completely on my own two feet. I just wished I knew how to walk better.

"It's okay, really. Everything will work out. It always does."

"You're right, it does. But if you ever need an extra inch to get yourself to tomorrow, I'll be here."

Just like that, my heart cracked and healed all at once. The tears I'd fought daily to keep from falling began sliding down my face, and I turned away from Abigail. I was ashamed of myself, embarrassed by our struggles.

Yet Abigail wouldn't allow any such thing. She wiped away my tears, shaking her head. Then she said five words that were so simple, yet so meaningful. "You're not weak; you're strong."

*You're not weak; you're strong.*

How? How did she know what I needed to hear?

"Thank you, Abigail. Truly. You're a saint."

"Not a saint, just a friend. Which reminds me, I better get going to meet a friend for coffee. You have a good day!" She turned and skipped away like the fairy godmother she'd always been.

I hurried over to Reese and took the box of doughnuts from her grip. Two and a half were missing from the box, and honestly, I was surprised it wasn't more.

"Sorry, Ma. I couldn't stop it. They are *sooo* good! You should have one."

I smiled and almost got a sugar high from the smell of deliciousness. But I refused, because if I didn't eat one, she'd have more for later. I'd learned quickly that motherhood meant saying no to yourself so you could later say yes to your child.

"I'm good right now, babe. Now, go wash up. We have to get you to camp on time."

She hopped off the sofa and raced to the bathroom to clean herself up.

While she was gone, I studied the rent notice in my hand, and my mind began swirling around, trying to figure out what could fall behind so we could fall ahead on rent.

*Don't overthink it, Emery. Things will work out. They always have and always will.*

That was a concrete belief I held in the deepest parts of my mind, because I was a woman of statistics, and the stats were on my side. When I thought back to the hardest times of my life, when I thought I wouldn't have made it through, somehow I had done exactly that—I survived.

Our current situation was nowhere near as bad a place as I'd been in before, so I wouldn't mope; I'd keep moving forward. It wasn't a dark cave I was in—I was simply dealing with an overcast sky.

At some point, the clouds would shift and the sun would shine again. Statistics never lied—at least that was my hope.

Plus, there was some comfort knowing that the sun never truly left; it just stayed hidden some days. Until those clouds shifted, I turned to music. Some people turned to yoga or working out to clear their heads. Others went for walks or wrote in a journal. But for me? My key to breathing was music and lyrics. Music always spoke to me in ways that nothing else ever could. Song lyrics always reminded me that my feelings were worthy of being felt, and I wasn't alone in my fears. Somewhere out there, another was feeling the same woes.

That was comforting in more ways than I ever could've described— just the idea of knowing that sadness wasn't only felt by me. Or that my happiness wasn't mine alone. There was a beautiful stranger somewhere across the world, listening to the same song as me, feeling both happy and sad all at once.

As we headed out the front door, I found a paper bag resting on my welcome mat. Inside were random food items, with a note on top. "Just thought you guys could play *Chopped* later this week, Chef." A note, clearly from Abigail. It wasn't the first time I'd received a paper bag with random food items beside my door from my neighbor. *Chopped* was a show that Reese and I watched often with Abigail. The concept was to take items that seemed random and create a meal from said items.

Abigail knew that my dream was to become a chef someday, and those little bags of food she left for us were not only to feed us physically, but to feed my soul too. I glanced into the bag and saw a baguette, a small honey ham, four sweet potatoes, and peanut butter.

Then, there was a note with one of Abigail's therapist thoughts: *Asking for help doesn't make you a failure.*

Just like that, the sun peeked through the clouds a bit.

"Reese! Let's get a move on!" I hollered, checking the time. I hurried and put the ham in the fridge. No time for tears of gratitude. My only mission was to get Reese to camp before nine a.m.

Each day on the drive to drop Reese off, I put on Alex & Oliver's first two albums. I only ever played the first two, though, because in my mind they were the best ones. There was an authenticity to their sound before Hollywood wrapped its money-grabbing hands around the duo. Alex and Oliver Smith were lyrical geniuses, though their record label hadn't allowed them to showcase their true gift. They'd just forced the guys to become cookie-cutter superstars. The majority of their fans loved the new stuff; again, there was a huge market for cookie-cutter music. If there wasn't, it wouldn't be a thing.

But us original fanatics? We saw the change. I wouldn't have been surprised if Oliver was a host on some TV music contest soon enough.

I wasn't the biggest fan of their new sounds, but I had quite a personal connection with the first two albums. Those albums felt as if they told the earliest chapters of my life.

*Faulty Wires* by Alex & Oliver was the soundtrack to my youth, and it meant the world to me. It was sad to think after the tragic events a few months back that we wouldn't get any more true, authentic music from the duo. I'd been holding my breath in hopes of Oliver returning to his true core, but from the headlines, it seemed as if, after the tragedy he'd experienced, Oliver was on a downward spiral with no real drive to ever come back to life.

Last time I heard, he hadn't left his house in the past six months, having become a complete recluse.

I couldn't blame him, really.

I, too, would've spiraled.

As I played Alex & Oliver in the car, Reese sang along to the lyrics she had yet to understand. Lyrics of first loves, and hopes, and demons. Lyrics of struggles and triumphs. Lyrics of truths.

I sang along, too, and like every other woman in the world, I pretended Oliver wrote the lyrics solely for me.

# 3

## EMERY

After spending all day looking for a job, I picked up Reese from summer camp, had dinner with her, and then dropped her off by Abigail's so I could head to Seven for my shift. The bar was pretty much a hole-in-the-wall. You could walk right past the building without even knowing it was open. Still, people somehow seemed to always notice it.

I told the owner, Joey, that he should've invested in more signs and lighting fixtures outside the building, but he always just huffed and puffed about how business was fine—which it was. But it could've been so much better.

The bar didn't have many people crawling in it that night. There was one guy sitting in the back-corner booth with a baseball cap on and a leather jacket. His hands were wrapped around a glass, and his shoulders were hunched forward. At the bar sat a younger couple who couldn't have been over twenty-two, and it was obvious that this was their first or second date. The awkward exchanges and almost touches made me wonder if another date was a possibility.

Then there was another guy who sat down at the end of the bar—good ol' Rob, the regular.

I swore, Rob had been sitting on that same barstool since Seven opened. He always had his coffee, which he brought in himself, with a few shots of whiskey that we added in for him. He'd do the crossword puzzles in the paper, or read about current events, but he never really spoke much.

I liked that about Rob—how he kept to himself and never minded anyone else's business.

"A lively crowd tonight," Joey said to me as I walked behind the bar to join him. He was just finishing up on his shift, and he nodded my way. "You think you can handle the wildness of this all on your own?"

I snickered. "I'll do my best." Tuesdays were the slowest days at the bar, and even though I would hardly make any tips, I figured it was better than nothing. On average about twenty to thirty people would wander in that night, which meant at least fifty dollars in tips if I was having a good Tuesday.

"Just a heads-up, there's a big concert happening at the arena. So you might get a more lively crowd after the show."

"A concert? Who's performing?" I asked. Normally I tried to keep note of when big shows were happening, because I knew it meant busier nights in the bar, but I hadn't seen anything over the previous days about a concert.

Joey shrugged. "I don't know, some Oliver and Adam, or Adam and Oliver, or something?"

"Alex and Oliver?" I breathed out, stunned by his words.

"Yeah, that's it. Sans one of the brothers, I guess. I heard it on the radio. One of the brothers was killed earlier this year. Sad."

No way. Alex & Oliver were our favorite musicians. Their music defined my childhood. Not to sound like one of *those* fans—but my younger sister, Sammie, and I loved Alex & Oliver before they found fame. Even Reese knew every lyric to every single song. After Alex passed away, I cried for a good solid three days as I played their records on a loop.

After the third day of tears, it felt a bit silly to feel so much for someone I'd never truly known, but a part of me felt as if I had known him, through his music.

How was there a concert happening that night? How was Oliver going to perform without his brother by his side?

Joey seemed less interested in the fact that tonight was such a major night for Oliver Smith. "All right, then, I'm on my way out. Have a good one."

"You too, Joey."

After he left, I wiped down the bar and imagined the magical sounds that were gracing thousands of people's eardrums as I listened to the same CD that Joey had played over and over again for the past forever years. The only way to get better music would be if someone put a dollar in the jukebox, and it seemed that the only ones to ever do that were drunken college students who loved to flash dollar bills like they were hundreds.

I wondered what song Oliver was opening with that night.

I wondered what song he'd end with.

I wondered how scary it was for him to get back onstage after the incident that had happened months ago. If it were me, I'd be so traumatized and heartbroken that I'd probably never perform again.

But Oliver's voice . . . it needed to be heard. In every duo, a fan had a favorite. Sammie loved Alex, but me? I was an Oliver girl. Most of the world thought he was the less interesting twin, but I didn't think that was true at all. Yeah, Alex was the heart of the duo, but Oliver was the soul. His voice dripped with emotion in a way that most performers only dreamed of discovering. His talent was almost surreal.

I should've been there to hear him, to see him wear his heart on his sleeve. I should've been singing his lyrics alongside him and all the others.

"Another one," the man in the hat in the back corner muttered, holding his finger up in the air and waving it around for a while before he put it back down. He didn't even glance toward me, and I wasn't even certain what it was that he was requesting. I must have taken too long to walk over to him, because he held his hand up once more and shouted, "Another one!"

For a moment I considered whether it was DJ Khaled sitting in that corner booth of mine. Soon enough he'd be yelling, "We da best!" and telling everyone how he was the father of Asahd.

Normally, I would've ignored his request and had him walk over to the bar like every other normal customer to order another drink, but it was a slow night, and anything that would keep me busy so time didn't feel like it was standing still was worth it to me.

I walked over to him, and he kept his head lowered.

"Hey there. Sorry about that. I just got in for my shift, and I'm not sure what you were drinking exactly."

He didn't tilt his head up so I could see him, but he nudged the emptied glass toward me. "Another one."

*Okay, Khaled, another what?*

"I'm sorry—" I started, but he cut me off.

"Whiskey," he hissed, his voice low and smoky. "Not the cheap shit, either."

I picked up his glass, walked over to the bar, and poured him a glass of our best whiskey—which wasn't really saying much. It was definitely not something DJ Khaled would shout, "Another one!" for, but it was the best I could do.

I went back to the table and set it down. "Here you go."

He mumbled something, and I was 90 percent certain it wasn't "Thank you." Then he lifted the glass and took the whiskey as a straight shot. He held the glass out toward me, and my gut tightened at his rudeness. "Another one," he muttered.

"I'm sorry, sir. I get the feeling you might have had enough."

"I'll tell you when that happens. Just bring the fucking bottle over if you are too incompetent to do your job and pour it yourself."

*Wow.*

Just what my day needed: a major drunk asshole.

"I'm sorry, I'm going to have to ask you to—"

Just then groups of people came walking into the bar, loud and rowdy. They were young, probably all under thirty, and dressed as if they had just left Coachella. Within seconds, there were at least twenty-five people walking into the space.

The chatter grew and grew, and it was clear that they were all annoyed beyond understanding. I glanced outside the window, and it looked as if the streets were littered with people—something that only happened after a concert or a game ended, but it was only eight thirty. The late-night crowd shouldn't have been out already.

"I can't believe that. I paid over four hundred bucks for those tickets!" one hollered.

"What a piece of shit. I can't believe he didn't show," another barked. "They better be giving refunds."

"Oliver Smith is complete trash. I can't believe you talked me into even thinking about going to that lame show."

At the name "Oliver Smith," the man's head tilted up, and I caught his eyes. Those caramel-colored eyes that I'd been obsessed with in my past. His eyes widened and looked a bit panicked as he heard his name mentioned. Then he curved his shoulders more, tugged on his baseball cap, lowering it even more over his eyes, and wiped his finger against the bridge of his nose.

I was frozen in place.

More people entered the bar, and still, my feet were superglued to that very spot.

"Don't stare," he whisper-hissed, his voice becoming even more clear. That deep smoky sound was something I'd listened to over and over again on his albums. Oliver Smith was wasted in my bar, and a storm of upset concertgoers were surrounding him without any idea that it was him they surrounded.

"I'm, I'm sorry. I, it's just . . ." I was stuttering like a lunatic. Holy freaking crap. I'd had dreams like this. Dreams where I'd run into my idol in a very low-key way and pour my heart and soul out to him while we shared a drink. Then, of course, we fell in love and he wrote a song about me, which I shared with our great-great-grandchildren years down the road.

Though this wasn't exactly the perfect dream.

*Reality never is.*

That night Oliver was unwelcoming.

And maybe sad?

Most people who drank that much alone often had a little bit of sadness in them. I couldn't blame him for that. I'd be sad all the time if I'd gone through what he had, especially in the public eye. After Alex passed away, I read some of the hateful comments people made about Oliver. If it were me, I would've wanted to die myself. I was sure he blamed himself enough—the last thing he needed was the whole world to blame him too.

"I'm sorry, I just . . . how can I help you?" I asked with my shaky voice.

His shoulders rounded forward even more as if weight was being placed against him every few seconds. He nudged his glass in my direction.

"Right, of course. Another one. I'll be right back."

I hurried over to the bar and grabbed the bottle of whiskey, then took it back to his table, set it right down, and poured a glass. "There you go."

He didn't reply, so I awkwardly stood there, gawking like a fool.

It wasn't until he looked up toward me with a cocked eyebrow of confusion that I shook out of my stance.

"Right, of course. Okay."

I hurried off back behind the bar, flustered and nervous as I tried to get all the new customers their drinks. Business was busy to the point that it was almost impossible to keep up, and I would've killed to have

Joey there to assist me. But then again, I powered through as I thought about the tips I'd receive. Plus, Oliver freaking Smith was fifty feet away from me. Drunk, sad, and still, somehow perfect.

The fangirl in me wanted to ask him a million questions about what made him write certain songs, but I kept myself together. The last thing I needed was to make a scene.

As the night went on, people started putting their dollars into the jukebox machine. Even though it was refreshing to hear different music, I wished the crowd didn't have such awful taste for bubblegum pop.

Each time I glanced over to Oliver's booth, more of the whiskey in the bottle was missing.

What happened to him that night, and how did he end up at Seven?

The crowd kept talking complete crap about Alex & Oliver—mainly Oliver—and I couldn't imagine what it must've felt like to sit there and listen to the putdowns. If it were me, I would've snapped—or, well, cried. The more and more Oliver drank, the more tense he became. Hours passed, and people still kept bringing up his name.

It was as if they had nothing better to talk about than the superstar who'd crashed and burned.

"Honestly, it pisses me off that Alex died and Oliver didn't," a big, broad-shouldered man commented as he took a shot. "He was the better brother. I always thought Oliver was odd. Besides, their music was trash."

"As if you know shit about good music!" Oliver barked before he downed the remaining brown liquor in his glass.

The big man tilted his head toward Oliver. "What did you just say?"

"I said"—Oliver stood up, rolled his shoulders back, and stumbled a bit before removing his hat and wiping his hand across his lips—"that you don't know shit about good music. You've been playing the same clichéd bar songs for the past two hours."

*Oh boy. This can't be good.*

The room instantly broke out into shouts as people realized the drunken man in the corner booth was indeed the very Oliver Smith they'd been shitting on for the past two hours.

"I mean, r-r-really," Oliver slurred, picking up the whiskey bottle and taking a long swig. He walked in the direction of the guy, who was at least twice his size, and poked him in the chest. "I'm s-sick of listening to your bullshit."

Oliver was smashed, and him approaching the guy talking to him made me nervous. The man was a freaking rock. He had muscles on muscles that were probably growing baby muscles. The guy was a beast, and if Oliver had been a tad bit sober, he never would've challenged such a man.

People stood around on their cell phones, recording the whole interaction, and I hurried from around the bar because I knew things were about to get worse before they got better.

"You're sick of me? I'm sick of you, asshole!" Big Guy shoved Oliver, who went stumbling backward; the only reason he didn't hit the ground was because the table caught him. "You must think you're a big deal, huh? Because you're rich and famous, you think you can fuck all of us out of our time and money, man?" he hissed at Oliver.

Oliver scrambled to his feet and shook his head as if he was trying to unblur his vision. Yet, based on the amount of liquor flowing through his body, I doubted any amount of head shaking would make things clear.

"I don't"—he pushed Big Guy—"appreciate"—shove—"being pushed." Both hands landed on Big Guy's chest, and Oliver pushed with all his might and got nowhere. "Geez, what are you made of? Steel?"

"Muscle, you dick."

"Oh. Well, fuck. You got me beat on the fighting avenue," Oliver concluded, which made me happy. The last thing I needed was to tell Joey how a brawl broke out in his bar between a rock star and a rock.

I was glad Oliver was stepping down and that he realized the fight wasn't worth having.

At least that's what I thought.

Oliver nodded toward Big Guy's lady, and a smirk hit his lips. "You might be stronger than me, but I bet I'd screw your girl better than you."

My jaw hit the floor.

The woman should've been offended by the comment, but I swore I saw a small grin find her lips. I bet there were a million women who would effortlessly leave their boyfriends and husbands for a night in Oliver's sheets. Even though he was the more closed-off and quiet twin, he was still Oliver Smith. "Handsome" wasn't a strong enough word to describe him. He was remarkably attractive, and with his normal mellow demeanor, he appeared that much more beautiful.

When he was sloppy and drunk, though? Not so much.

"I mean, honestly," Oliver said, sounding cocky as ever as he nodded and winked toward the woman, "I bet she's a great—"

Before Oliver could say another word, Big Guy slammed his fist straight into Oliver's face, knocking the rock star off his feet and straight to the ground.

People shouted and crowded around the fallen star with their cameras in hand as Oliver tried his best to get to his feet but couldn't accomplish standing up at all.

"All right, all right! That's enough! Bar is closed! Everyone get up and out!" I shouted, but no one listened. I had to physically start shoving the customers toward the front entrance, and when they were all gone, I glanced over to Oliver. The Oliver Smith. The man of my made-up dreams. My biggest celebrity crush lying there drunk, dazed, and confused like a broken puppy.

It didn't take long for the paparazzi to get word that Oliver Smith was at Seven that night, and they were swarming the outside of the bar, banging on the door.

It looked like they weren't ready to leave anytime soon.

*Great.*

"Here, let me help you up," I said, combing my hair behind my ears as I walked toward Oliver, who was still struggling to stand on his own. His left eye was already turning deep shades of black, with purplish tones beneath his eye. With one hit, Big Guy had messed him up terribly. He looked as if he'd been beaten over and over again, pounded until he was nothing. Yet it was one tamed, controlled hit that had sent Oliver flying.

"No," Oliver muttered, waving me away but still allowing me to help him. I got him into the booth, and he slumped over as the paparazzi pressed their bodies against the window and flashed their cameras nonstop like freaking crazed maniacs.

I hadn't a clue how celebrities dealt with it all. Fame seemed more like a curse than a blessing to me.

"Another one," Oliver muttered, putting his finger up in the air.

"Yeah, okay," I mumbled, walking over to the bar and grabbing him a big glass of water. I returned to the booth and sat on the edge of it. "Here you go."

He didn't sit up because, let's be honest, he couldn't. But he allowed me to place the glass in his hand, and he lowered it to his lips. The moment he tasted the water, he huffed and tossed the water out of the glass—straight onto me.

"Jeez!" I hissed, shooting up from the booth, drenched. "What the hell?"

"I wanted w-whiskey," he stuttered.

A big part of me wanted to push him out to the hyenas standing outside the building. I wanted to get rid of him and start cleaning up the bar, pretending that the whole night hadn't taken the most dramatic turn in the history of turns.

But I knew better. I'd worked in the bar scene long enough to know that sadness mixed with liquor was a dynamic duo. When the two were combined together, people acted out in ways they never would when they were sober. And I knew that if I gave Oliver to those monsters outside, they would destroy him more than ever. They would rip apart the small part of his soul that still remained intact and feed their families with his struggles.

I walked around to the windows and shut all the blinds so the animals outside couldn't get any more shots of Oliver's meltdown. I knew what it was like to go through dark days. I couldn't imagine doing it with cameras flashing in front of my eyes.

"All right, come on now," I said, moving over to Oliver and lifting his body up. He grumbled but didn't argue too much as I got him to his feet. He leaned against me, feeling like pounds of exhaustion, and I managed to get him to the back employees-only entrance of the bar. I unlocked my car door and slid him into the passenger seat, where he slumped into a ball. And passed out.

I hurried back to the bar, locked it up, and then headed to my driver's seat, hopped in, and turned on the engine. Before I drove off, I reached over Oliver to put on his seat belt, because I swore to God, I wasn't going to kill a rock star in my 2007 Honda Civic.

"Don't touch unless you suck," Oliver muttered as I brought the seat belt across his crotch area to buckle.

Good lord.

There was a point in my life when that statement from Oliver would've made me giddy. Currently it made me want to sober him up, because clearly he wasn't himself that night.

"Don't worry. No one's touching you tonight," I said, but he didn't even stay conscious enough to hear me.

As I put the car into drive, Oliver tilted his head toward me.

His eyes were narrowed, and I was certain he was seeing three versions of me swaying with his whiskey goggles on.

Then, he paused. His lips parted, and a rough word rolled off his tongue. "Whiskey?" he murmured.

I froze.

My foot sat against the brakes as he stared my way, a level of disconnect from reality floating around his pupils.

Was he asking me for whiskey? In his current state?

His lips parted again, but before he could speak, he lurched forward and decided right then and there that violently vomiting all over my dashboard was the right thing to do.

# 4

## EMERY

"Come on, Oliver. Just give me an inch," I muttered, trying to drag him up the front steps of my apartment building. Bringing the rock star to my apartment was my last resort. I tried to get him to tell me where he lived, but he couldn't even form a coherent sentence. All he did was mumble and drool. Then I grabbed his phone to see if I could get a number to call, but his phone was dead, and I didn't have the type of charger needed to charge his. Therefore, all I could think was to bring him to my apartment for the night. Getting him out of the car was a headache of its own kind, and now trying to get him to move his feet was a nightmare.

"I'll give you a few inches," he mumbled back.

I wondered how horrified the shy, distant Oliver would've been by his comments that night.

I wrapped his arms around me and pulled him to the best of my ability. He had the hiccups, and he kept muttering something under his breath, but it wasn't clear what he was saying. Honestly, I wasn't even interested in his words. I just wanted to get him onto the couch and let him pass out so I could go into my bedroom and do the same thing.

I called Abigail on my way home to ask if she could keep Reese overnight. Most of the time when I worked late shifts, I used the key

Abigail had given to me for her apartment, went inside, and grabbed a sleeping Reese to take over to our apartment. Yet that evening, I thought it would be best to keep her away from the drunk celebrity.

When we finally got inside the building, we headed for the elevator. The moment Oliver's feet hit the elevator floor, he leaned hard against the railing and began singing one of Alex & Oliver's songs with his eyes closed.

Even though he was drunk, he sounded like perfection. It wasn't the concert of my dreams, and Oliver definitely smelled like old cod, but he was singing, and I didn't hate it all that much.

My mind went straight to my sister, Sammie. I wondered how she would've enjoyed this interaction with Oliver. I wondered if she would've been irritated or completely smitten with the drunken man in front of me. I wondered if she would've sung along with him.

When we entered my apartment, I was finally able to let him go. He stumbled back and forth, running into side tables and lamps—which I caught before they shattered to the ground.

"Okay," he muttered, as if someone had said something to him.

"What's that?" I asked, confused.

"Bathroom," he said, swaying back and forth.

"Right, of course. It's right over—" I started to gesture toward my bathroom, but my words were cut off by the sound of a small waterfall happening behind my back. I whipped around at the speed of light to find Oliver, my idol, my celebrity crush, peeing straight into my houseplant. "What are you doing?"

"It needed water," he mumbled.

My breath caught in my throat as I stared in shock. Even in his drunken state, Oliver Smith wasn't lacking down below. My cheeks felt as if they'd been set on fire.

I turned my stare away from his body, trying to shake off the awkwardness of the whole situation. "Well, uh, perhaps we should get you to sleep. You can crash on the couch if you want and—" I glanced back toward him, and my eyes widened when I saw that now not only was Oliver showing me his lower half, but he seemed to have taken off his T-shirt, too, revealing his shredded abs. It turned out even whiskey couldn't take those away.

And somehow, Oliver managed to slip completely out of his pants and boxers, so now there he was. Standing butt-ass naked in my living room with his hands on his hips like Superman, still swaying back and forth.

Just how I envisioned my first-ever night alone with Oliver—having him stand as a drunken, naked superhero.

"What are you doing?" I gasped, trying not to look at his penis, but still, kind of looking at his penis.

"Let's do this," he hiccupped, wiping his penis hand against his mouth again.

"Do what?"

"The sex."

The sex?

He actually said "the sex."

"What? No. We aren't having sex, Oliver. Put on your clothes."

"Why are you naked in my house if we aren't having sex, then?" he asked, hiccupping as he gestured toward me.

"Um, what?"

I legit had to look down at my body to make sure I was still fully dressed and hadn't accidentally tossed my clothes to the side of the room due to my idol standing before me.

It was clear that he was so far gone that he hadn't even a clue what he was saying. I wondered how embarrassed sober Oliver would be when morning came and he realized his actions—if he'd even remember them.

I cringed at the uncomfortable sight taking place in front of me. "Please just put on your clothes, Oliver."

"You put on your clothes first," he argued.

Brittainy Cherry

I glanced back and forth around my apartment, somewhat thinking I was oddly being *Punk'd*. Or perhaps I'd slipped into a coma somewhere along the line, and all of this was a very weird manifestation of my mind.

Either way, I needed Oliver to put on his clothes, because the longer he stayed naked, the more uncomfortable it all became. Yet he seemed determined to not get dressed until I put on my clothes first.

So, like a complete weirdo, I began putting on invisible clothing in front of him.

"Okay, all dressed," I stated, placing my hands on my hips.

"All right, I'm going to bed." He lifted up all of his clothes and headed to Reese's bedroom. Before I could stop him, he was already crashed headfirst into her twin-size bed.

And there he was, folks. My Prince Charming, butt naked, passed out on my daughter's Disney princess bedsheets.

Oh, was it a sight to see. I had to say, his butt was quite plump in all the right ways.

I closed the bedroom door and headed straight for my kitchen for the bottle of two-buck wine I kept in the top cabinet for emergencies.

After that night, I needed a drink.

Or maybe the whole bottle.

# 5

## OLIVER

*Fuck, fuck, fuck.*

I awakened with the strongest pounding to my head, completely unaware of what had taken place the night before to get me to that level of pain. I groaned as I felt a repeated poking feeling in my left side.

I groaned again as I sat up on my elbows. My head felt as if it was splitting into two from the simple sitting-up motion, so I lay back down. Why did my face hurt so much?

"Hey, mister, are you dead?" a voice asked.

A small, tiny voice.

Why would I be in a place with a small voice? I opened my eyes and looked over to the tiny figure standing beside me. A young girl stood there repeatedly stabbing me in the gut with a Barbie doll.

"What are you doing?" I muttered. "Where the hell am I?" I asked, swatting my hand toward the doll for her to stop.

Her mouth dropped open. "You owe a quarter to the swear jar!"

"What the hell are you talking about?"

"That's *two* quarters!" she exclaimed before stepping back a little. "Hey, mister. Are you dead?"

Based on how my body felt, there was a solid chance I had died at some point the previous night. The verdict was still out if I'd gone to heaven or hell. "If I were dead, would you be able to talk to me?"

"I don't know, maybe. I never talked to a dead person before."

"What is this, *The Sixth Sense*? Am I Bruce Willis?" I groaned, pinching the bridge of my nose. As I touched my face, more pain shot through me. I'd had rough nights before, but never one so painful.

"I don't know what any of that means," the kid remarked.

"Then, yes. I'm dead."

She gasped and then hollered, "Mom! The man in my bed is dead!"

I opened my eyes once more and looked around. Why was I in a child's bedroom? What happened to me the night before? What was going on? Who would put a stranger in their child's bed?

Then it all started flooding back to me. The show last night . . . the show I abandoned. I ditched the performance last minute and wandered off to some random hole-in-the-wall bar to get plastered. Everything after that was a blur, including how I ended up in the bed of a child.

"Reese! What are you doing? I told you to stay out of here," a woman's voice whisper-shouted as she walked into the room. She grabbed the little girl by the shoulders and ushered her out as she complained the whole way.

"But Mom! There's a dead man in my bed!"

"He's not dead!" the woman remarked; then she glanced at me with a raised brow. "You're not dead, right?"

I shook my head slightly.

"Oh, thank goodness. I couldn't survive being responsible for that." She breathed a sigh of relief. "See, Reese? He's not dead. Now go brush your teeth. I don't want to be late dropping you off at camp."

She complained the whole way out of the bedroom. Seconds later, the woman reappeared in the doorway with a plate and a glass of water. On the plate sat a doughnut and a bottle of ibuprofen.

I pushed myself up to a sitting position and gripped the side of the twin-size mattress. The back of my hand brushed against my mouth as

I looked up at the woman. She was stunning. Beautiful, without any effort at all.

Her dark kinky hair was pulled up in a thick messy bun with a few strays framing her face. Her eyes were wide as a doe's. Her skin tone was a deepened brown that glowed all on its own. She was in an oversize Elton John–concert T-shirt and yoga pants. Her socks were mismatched, and she appeared as if she hadn't slept a wink the previous night. The bags beneath her eyes revealed that fact.

Her brown eyes were beautiful. They were the best feature on her face, with a close second being her full lips. It was a shame I didn't remember those lips sitting against my own.

Still. I hoped I hadn't slept with her. Even though Cam and I weren't a thing except on a surface level, I didn't want to be that guy who stepped out on her—even if she stepped out on the regular. It wasn't in my character. At least when I was sober.

"Here you go. I figured you could use this," she said, handing the plate and water to me. "I would've made you coffee, but I'm all out right now."

Without thought, I tossed the pills into my mouth and swallowed.

I cleared my throat. "What happened last night?" I pushed out, my throat dry and hoarse.

The woman raised an eyebrow. "You don't remember anything from last night?"

"No, and other than my face feeling like complete shit, I have nothing to go on. I'm sorry—uh—I forgot your name."

"No, you didn't," she mentioned, walking over to her daughter's desk, where she picked up a handheld Disney princess mirror. "I never gave it to you." She walked over to me and passed me the mirror, but I shook my head and pushed it away.

"I'm good," I muttered, not wanting to face my reflection. I hadn't looked in the mirror in the past six months. I didn't want to start now. "I'll take your word on what happened. So . . . what exactly happened?"

"Well, you got a bit wasted last night. A crowd formed. You got into a fight with a giant. You lost. Which explains . . . ," she said, gesturing toward my face. "Speaking of, do you want ice for your eye? I have an ice pack I can grab if you need—"

I shook my head. "Do you have my phone?"

She walked over to a dresser drawer, picked up my cell phone, and then handed it over to me. "It's dead. I tried to turn it on last night to call someone to get you, but it had already died."

"Do you have a charger?"

"No. I have an iPhone, not an Android."

Of course she did. Not that it was her fault. I put myself in this position, being a complete dumbass. I bet my manager and publicist were having meltdowns.

I massaged my temples, hoping the medicine would kick in sooner rather than later. "Listen, about last night, and, well, us . . ." I looked up toward her, and she had the blankest stare as she waited for me to continue. "Did we . . . ?"

She nodded. "Did we what?"

"You know."

"I know what?"

"You know," I urged. "Did we have sex?"

"What? No! Of course not!" she whisper-shouted again, slightly closing the bedroom door so her daughter wouldn't hear too much. The way she grew flustered made me feel like an idiot.

"We didn't?"

"Trust me, you weren't in any shape to perform any kind of act like that. Plus, I'm not going to take advantage of a person who's that messed up. *Plus plus*, my biggest concern was to get you to stop peeing in my houseplant."

I peed in her houseplant? *Way to be a drunk idiot, Oliver.* "If we didn't sleep together, then why am I at your house?"

"Like I said, you got wasted at the bar I work at, and the paparazzi crashed in and tried to bombard you. I was your only saving grace to get you out of that place after you got your butt kicked by the Incredible Hulk for being a smart-ass."

"I was a smart-ass?"

"You told a guy you could screw his girlfriend better than he could."

So, I was the complete opposite of myself. Wonderful. Sober Oliver could hardly gather his thoughts to form a sentence. Drunk Oliver had enough courage to get into a bar fight.

I narrowed my already swollen eyes as I tried to piece everything together, and still, it all blurred over. I stood up and scratched the back of my neck. "Can I use your bathroom?"

"As long as you don't go peeing in my plant again, sure. First door on your left. And eat the doughnut. You need to soak up some of that poison you took in." She definitely was a mother. She walked out of the room and shouted, "Reese! Shoes, now!"

The moment I reached the bathroom, I closed the door behind me, turned on the faucet, and splashed water against my face. Tyler was going to give me hell for missing the performance. I should've played the show last night. No, I never should've agreed to performing the damn thing in the first place. It was all too much, all too soon, but I thought it might help me to get out there and face the reality that Alex was gone.

*You fucking idiot. You should've just performed.*

All I remembered from the night before was sitting back there in the dressing room trying to get up enough nerve to walk out on the stage and perform songs I'd been performing for the past ten-plus years. All I had to do was get out of my own head, but I wasn't good at that shit. My thoughts swallowed me whole every time I was sober, and like an idiot, I hadn't had a drink that evening. I thought I could perform sober, like Alex.

Alex never walked onto that stage with a drop of liquor in his system. He didn't need anything else to get him going. His preshow tradition was meditation and prayer—that's all. No vodka, no whiskey, no temporary fix. Alex spent most of his life grounded. I was the opposite of my brother. I spent my whole life trying to float away as my anxiety spun me around at full speed.

Last night I tried to be more like my brother. I sat in my dressing room with nothing but a ceiling fan running. I needed to have complete silence, except for the sounds of the blades running around in circles. That was how Alex did it. That was how he prepped before a show. I tried to pray, but I felt as if no one was listening. I tried to meditate, but my mind was too loud.

How had Alex done it? How did he silence his mind when mine was always so loud?

As the ceiling fan spun above me that night, and my heart kept racing, I gripped the heart-shaped piece sitting around my neck. When I was younger, I thought it was kind of a dumb thing, but the older I got, the more I missed my parents and their gentleness when I was in a harsh, harsh world.

I didn't get home to Texas nearly enough to visit my parents, so every time I held that necklace close to my chest, I thought of them both and their love.

Though, that night before the show, without the whiskey, without Alex, my thoughts were eating me alive. I hated thinking so much. I hated the silence. Sometimes my mind got so dark I wondered why I was even still breathing.

Then I thought about Alex. That shit only made me sadder.

When it was almost time to perform last night, I told Tyler I was going to run outside for a quick breath of air. Once I started running, I just kept going. Which brought me exactly to my current situation.

I sat in the bathroom of a stranger that morning, completely ashamed of who I'd become. The worst part of it all was I made the mistake of looking up into the mirror. I saw how faded my existence had become, I saw how troubled my life had been, and worst of all? I saw my brother.

# 6

## OLIVER

**Five Years Ago**

"Our first sold-out show! This is fucking amazing," Alex exclaimed as he marched back and forth in our dressing room. It was a tiny venue with the smallest dressing room that we had to share, but we didn't care. This was the first show we'd ever had where tickets sold out—all three hundred. Which was a huge deal to us. The venue was all standing space, and I could hear the crowd from the dressing room.

My nerves were shot.

"And did you see this?" Alex said, excited as ever as he held a paper in front of me. "'Alex & Oliver are the Black Sam Smiths of this day and age,'" he said, reading the quote. "I mean, sure, that's a bit racist bringing our skin color into the situation, and sure, it's annoying to be compared to another artist, but shit! I love Sam Smith. If there's not a somewhat decent compliment in that sentence, then I don't know what's good," he joked.

Our race and sound always seemed to be a big topic in the tabloids. We were always being compared to other artists, and it was both annoying and flattering, all at the same time. The oddest comparison we'd received was when they said we were like Dan + Shay—which made no sense. We didn't sing a lick of country, and the only thing we had in common were our names being in our duo titles.

"It's like a backhanded compliment," I agreed, fidgeting with my hands.

Alex looked my way and snickered. "You're doing that thing again."

"What thing?"

"Overthinking. Listen, you're talented as fuck, Oliver, and those people came tonight to see that talent. We got this. You got this. This is about to be the best show we've ever done. Now come here." He held his arms out wide as he looked my way, nodding.

I cocked an eyebrow. "What are you doing?"

"I'm giving you my bear hug of comfort. Now come on, little brother. Come hug me."

"You can't call me 'little brother.' I was born three minutes after you."

"Which, in fact, makes you my little brother. Now come on. Bear hug."

I rolled my eyes. "Shut up, Alex."

"Fine. If you want to act all tough like you don't want a hug, then fine." He shrugged, giving up on the idea. I was thankful for that.

I stood up and moved to the full-length mirror, and as I began to smooth out my outfit, Alex rushed up behind me and pulled me into the tightest bear hug known to humankind.

I couldn't help but laugh at my idiotic brother, who was swinging back and forth with me tied in his grip.

"Boys!" Tyler came bursting into the dressing room and cocked an eyebrow in our direction. He didn't for a moment seem freaked out by our brotherly embrace, because he knew we were weird assholes. "Hate to break up the warm embrace, but you got a meet and greet to handle before the concert."

Alex and I looked toward one another, and then at Tyler, before we silently agreed, bum-rushed him, and pulled him into a tight hug too.

"For the love of all good things, let me go, you little emotional shits," Tyler groaned.

"Did you hear that we're the Black Sam Smiths?" I joked.

"Yes, I heard, and I called the paper for the insult. Now, pull yourselves together. You got a big night ahead of you. Tonight might be the night you play for the right person and we get the chance of a lifetime."

Good ol' Tyler had been saying that for the past ten years. It hadn't happened yet, but I wasn't giving up hope.

We headed to the front of the venue, where all those for the meet and greet were waiting in a line. There were about forty or fifty people. That was insane. For the longest time, our biggest fans were our parents. Mom and Dad were still our biggest fans, but now there were at least forty-some people who felt the need to wait in line simply to meet us.

We met with the fans and autographed whatever they brought our way—including a few tits—and it was a fantastic time. When two women walked up to us, I realized how dedicated our fans were, because one of them looked at least fifteen months pregnant. That baby was going to fall out of her sooner rather than later. The other woman, her sister maybe, based on how much they looked alike, was grinning.

The pregnant woman rested her jittery hands on her stomach. Even though she shook, I couldn't get over the fact that there was a small smile on her face, which to me felt like the biggest victory in the world. Seeing people excited to meet us made me feel beyond blessed.

The two women took a step forward, and I noticed that their legs began to tremble as they linked arms and came closer.

"Hi there, I'm—" I started, but the squeaky-clean voice of the non-pregnant one cut me off.

"Oliver Smith, yes, we know, hi. How are you? And you're Alex Smith. Oh my gosh. You're amazing. You both are. You're everything good and inspirational and meaningful in the music industry. People don't create music like you do. I think you're both the best. And amazing. And amazingly the best and and and—" And she was full-blown fangirling. I never in my life thought Alex and I would have fangirls.

Hell, we were lucky.

The other woman reached forward and pinched the chatty one's elbow, making her halt her words.

"Sorry," she muttered, turning slightly red. "I'm just—*we're*—excited to meet you both," she said, gesturing toward herself and the other woman, who hadn't spoken a word at all. She held out two concert tickets for Alex and me to sign. "Sorry, I wish we had something better for your autograph, but money is tight, so these are our souvenirs."

"That is beyond good enough for us," Alex said. "It means the world to us that you even came out." He turned to the pregnant woman and shared his smile her way, which made her cheeks blush over. "It's nice to meet you both. How far along are you?" Alex asked.

She parted her lips, and as she was about to speak, I watched her nerves overtake her. No words left her mouth.

The other woman placed her hand on the other one's forearm. "She's due next week."

My eyes widened. "Really? And you're here at an Alex & Oliver concert? That's dedication."

"Like I said, we're your biggest fans," she joked.

I smirked. "Well, if it's a boy, Oliver is a great name."

Alex added, "I hear the name Alex is better. Alexander works too. Plus, if it's a girl, Reese is a good choice, too, which is my—"

"Middle name," the women said in unison with him.

He laughed. "You are our biggest fans." He winked their way, and I was almost certain the women were going to explode into a million pieces of joy from their giddiness. "Are you two sisters? You look like twins."

"We are sisters, not twins. You two look like twins too. I mean, obviously," the nonpregnant sister said bashfully. She was so beautiful, in her shyness.

"Would you guys like a photograph?" I asked.

"Oh yes, please," she replied, pulling out her cell phone and handing it to Tyler, who was in charge of snapping the photographs.

She jumped to the left side of me, and the other placed herself right in between my brother and me. I went to place my arms around her shoulder, and without hesitation the other sister snapped. "Wait, no, my sister doesn't like to be tou—"

"It's okay," the pregnant sister said, shaking her head. She smiled wide and nodded toward Alex and me, giving us permission. Right as my arm landed against her shoulder blade, everything was flipped upside down.

"Oh my gosh!" she gasped. Seconds later a splash of water hit my shoe. I was so completely thrown off by hearing the sound of her voice that I almost missed what had happened to pull the sound out of her. Her water had broken, leaving all four of us with pale expressions.

"Oh my gosh," she kept repeating, holding her hands against her stomach as she looked back and forth between my eyes and his shoes. "I'm so, so sorry," she muttered, humiliated by what had taken place. She kept clearing her throat repeatedly as her voice shook with nerves.

"Oh my gosh, don't worry about it. Are you okay?"

Before she could answer, her sister went into panic mode and rushed to her side. "We have to get you to the hospital. I'm sorry, but we have to go. I'm sorry about your shoes."

I smirked. "As long as you keep considering using my name for the child, we'll call it even. I wish you the best of luck, and congratulations."

Alex's light-brown eyes were bright and filled with care as he added, "You got this."

Her eyes watered over as her smile returned to her lips. They thanked us both one more time, and the sister grabbed her phone from Tyler, who was still snapping photos with a mocking smirk on his face.

As the women began to walk away, the pregnant one looked back toward us. "Alex? Oliver?"

"Yes?"

"Your music . . . your albums . . . your music gives me light. I hope you know how important what you're doing is to the world. You've saved me more than you know."

Alex's eyes glassed over before he blinked back his emotions and gave a halfway grin. He always was the emotional one out of us. "Without you all, our music doesn't exist. You've saved us more than you know too."

I nodded. "Without you, we're singing in the dark. You bring us the light."

They hurried away, and I looked down at the puddle sitting in front of us, then turned to Tyler. "I'm going to need a new pair of shoes."

Alex smirked at me, cheesing harder than ever. "The puddle on the ground kind of makes me think of a good theme song for today."

"What is it?"

"'Float On,' by Modest Mouse."

I gave Alex the same kind of grin he was shooting my way because the song was too perfect. We did exactly that, too, after the most awkward yet somehow perfect interaction between two fans.

We floated on and went ahead to play one of our best shows to date.

# 7

## OLIVER

*Present Day*

"Hey, mister! Hey, mister! Number one or number two?" that small voice asked, breaking me away from my thoughts of the past as she pounded on the bathroom door.

I almost smirked at the nosy kid. I wasn't big on children, but I had to say, the girl was forward and bold.

"Number three."

She gasped and dashed away. "Mommy! That guy has explosive diarrhea!" she hollered, making me wide eyed. I didn't even know number three was an actual thing that other people knew about, and now the girl's mother thought I was exploding my insides into her toilet.

*Smooth, Oliver.*

Not much later, another knock came at the door, only this time it wasn't a tiny voice. "Uh, sorry to interrupt, but can you hurry it up? I have to get my daughter to her day camp, and I have a busy day ahead. So . . ." Her words faded as I opened the door. "I mean, only if you're okay. If you're sick, we can be late. Or if, well, if you have number three and—"

I swung the door open. "Sorry. I'm ready," I said, trying to bury the embarrassment building inside. Wonderful. She thought I was blowing up her toilet.

"No, you're not! You didn't flush or wash your hands!" the little girl hollered my way. Again with this girl and her hollering. Did she not know what an indoor voice was?

I walked over to the toilet, flushed it, then went to the sink, quickly washed my hands, and dried them. "There," I said, smiling a fake grin. "Happy?"

She placed her hands on her hips like the sassiest girl alive. "You're supposed to wash your hands to the song 'Twinkle, Twinkle, Little Star' to get rid of all the germs."

"Yeah, well, you know what? We don't have time for this. Come on, let's go," the woman said, hurrying toward the front door.

We walked the hallway and then rode the elevator down in complete silence. When we hit the first floor, a man was coming out of the main office, and he shouted toward us.

"Emery! Emery! You're late on the rent," he said.

Emery was her name. I liked it. It fit her, from what I could tell.

Her shoulders tensed up as she grabbed her kid's hand and started walking faster. "I know, Ed, I know. I swear you'll have it by the end of today. I get my check from Seven."

"I hope that's true. Honestly, Emery. You know I like you, but I'm busting my ass here. I can't let you keep sliding."

Emery's eyes shifted to the ground as embarrassment washed over her entire body. She seemed fragile, as if she'd shatter if life hit her one more time. I sensed a stern shift in her energy as she lowered her voice. "Can we talk about this later, Ed? Just not in front of my kid?"

Ed's eyes shifted to Reese, and he gave a pathetic frown. "Yeah, all right. Just get me the money, will you?"

"Will do."

Reese pulled on Emery's sleeve. "Mommy, I have money in my piggy bank you can have."

And just like that, I knew the kid had a heart of gold, even though she was sassy. Emery looked as though she was going to cry from her daughter's offer.

Before she could reply, Ed looked over to me, and his eyes widened. "Holy shit! You're Oliver Sm—!"

Emery gripped my arm with her free hand and pulled me closer to her in a protective manner. "Okay, we'll chat later—bye, Ed!"

The woman handled me better than my own security team.

We hurried out of the front door and headed around the corner. Emery walked up to her car and glanced toward me. "You're going to have to get out of Dodge before people start realizing that you are in this neighborhood. Ed has a big mouth."

I rubbed the back of my neck and nodded. "All right. I'm sorry for any trouble I've caused."

She smiled, a genuine curve to her lips, and it was clear that I was wrong—that smile was the best feature on her, not her eyes. Still, her eyes took a very close second.

But those eyes plus that smile? Phenomenal.

After seeing that pairing, something tightened in my gut. A sense of familiarity.

"Thank you for the apology." She opened the back door of her car and helped her daughter into her booster seat. She turned back to me after closing the car door. Her hands landed on her hips, and she narrowed her eyes as the sun shone directly into her line of vision. "Well, it was nice to meet you. Even though it wasn't the most normal night of my life."

I nodded once.

She walked around to the driver's seat and glanced over toward me. I kept looking up and down the street, trying to familiarize myself with the neighborhood, but of course, I was completely lost.

Emery cleared her throat and tapped the top of her car with the palms of her hands. "Do you need a lift?"

"That would be great," I breathed out, walking to the passenger door of her car.

She snickered low and shook her head. "Um, I actually meant like, the app, Lyft. Like, the car service where they pick you up. Or even Uber . . ." Her words faded off, because she probably saw how damn idiotic I appeared.

*Of course that's what she meant, Oliver, you dumbass.*

"Yeah, right. That's what I meant. I would, uh, yeah. Okay."

She must've taken pity on me, because she glanced up and down the street, then at her watch. "Or I can drop you off to wherever you're going."

I lowered my brows. "You'd do that?"

"Sure. It's no big deal."

"I'm sure you're busy . . ."

"No, she's not. Mama lost her job at the hotel, so she doesn't do anything during the day," Reese said matter-of-factly from her rolled-down window.

Emery's eyes widened. "How did you know that?"

Reese shrugged. "Heard you talking to Ms. Abigail about it when you dropped me off at her house the other day."

Emery embarrassedly smiled my way. "Kids have a way of talking too much. But it's true. My day's pretty open, so I can give you a ride."

"I appreciate it." I went to open the passenger door again, and she held her hand up.

"Whoa, whoa. What do you think you're doing?"

"I thought you said you'd drive me."

"Yes." She nodded. "But after driving you last night, you've lost your front-seat privileges. Back seat."

What did that even mean?

"Now, hurry up, will you? Reese can't be late."

She hopped into the driver's seat. I slipped into the back seat and sat down beside Reese, like a damn child. All that was missing was my booster seat.

"Good God, what's that smell?" I barked out.

"That, my friend, is the smell of your vomit," Emery replied.

"I threw up in your car?"

"Yes, and all over me."

*Note to stupid self: you owe this woman a deep cleaning of her car, a houseplant, and probably a million dollars for babysitting your ass.*

Every self-hating thought I could muscle up filled my brain all at once. I was shocked Emery hadn't pushed me out on the curb and left me for the vultures to finish off. Them or the paparazzi—same thing, really.

She turned the key in the engine. The car roared, hiccupped, coughed, and spat before she put it into drive.

"Eww, you puked in Mama's car?" Reese hollered, making a grossed-out face. "That's gross."

"An accident, I'm guessing." I looked forward toward Emery. "I'll pay to have it cleaned."

Emery shrugged. "Don't worry about it. I'll figure it out."

She rolled down the windows to air out the vehicle as Reese covered her nose with her hand and asked, "Mama, can you put on our music?"

Emery glanced back at her daughter as she began to drive. "Not today, honey."

Reese dropped her hand, appearing shocked. "But Mama! We listen to it every day!"

"Yes, so we'd better take a break from it."

"But, Mama!" Reese cried, and in that moment, I was 100 percent certain I wasn't cut out for fatherhood. Alex, on the other hand, would've been a fantastic father.

*Stop thinking about him, Oliver.*

I wished turning off your brain was like turning off a faucet. Easy and painless.

"Fine." Emery finally gave in and turned on a very familiar track, making it extremely hard to get my brother out of my head.

It was the song "Tempted," from our very first album. I hadn't heard it in years, and when it began to play, I felt the chills of yesterday vibrating through my system. That seemed so long ago, when the days were shorter and the music came easy.

It was one of Alex's favorite songs.

Emery glanced back at me through the rearview mirror. "I'm not like some fanatic fan," she commented, looking back to the road. "We just really enjoy this song."

"It's fine. You're allowed to like my music."

Reese's eyes narrowed. "This isn't your music."

"Yes, it is."

"No, it's not! This is Alex and Oliver Mith's music!" she stated matter-of-factly.

"Smith," I corrected. Her "Mith" sounded like "myth," and for some reason that made it seem as if I didn't truly exist. Funny enough, I felt like that on the daily.

"That's what I said," she said, agreeing. "And that's not you."

"I'm pretty sure I know who I am, kid."

"You have no clue who you are," Reese argued back at me, and fuck, if that wasn't an emotionally damaging statement, I didn't know what was.

"It's true, Reese. That's Oliver Smith. This is his music," Emery chimed in.

Reese's mouth dropped open in shock, and her eyes bugged out farther than I thought eyes could ever bug. She then whispered. Who knew this little girl understood the art of whispering?

"You . . . ," she started, her voice a bit shaky now. "You're in Alex & Oliver?"

"Yes, I am." I paused. "I was."

I caught Emery's saddened eyes in the rearview mirror before I looked back to Reese.

"Oh. My. Bananas," she muttered, stunned, as her face turned pale and she slapped the palms of her hands to her cheeks.

"Oh my bananas?" That was a new one.

Emery snickered. "It's clear we're both fans of your music. Anything you want to say to Oliver, Reese?"

"Yes." Reese wiggled around a bit in her booster seat before clasping her hands together and looking my way. "We only like your first two albums because the other ones are recycled mainstream garbage that was made to only sell records instead of art. We don't listen to those ones, because even if it's recycled garbage, it's still kind of like trash."

"Reese!" Emery gasped, shaking her head back and forth. "That's not nice at all!"

"But, Mama, it's true, and you said a person is always supposed to be honest. Plus, you're the one who told me it was recycled garbage. Remember, Mama?"

I couldn't help but smile at the kid. Shit . . . when was the last time I smiled? I should've started keeping a journal about the times I found a split moment of happiness. Maybe that would help me stop drowning every single day, if I knew there were moments of happiness too.

"Sorry about that," Emery said. "You know what they say: 'Kids say the darndest things.'"

"Hey, Mr. Mith?" Reese asked, tugging on my shirtsleeve.

*"Smith."*

"That's what I said. Hey, Mr. Mith, do you think you'll ever make good music again?"

"Reese!" Emery gasped again, embarrassment written across her face.

I rolled with it and shrugged. "That seems to be the question of the year, kid."

Reese crossed her arms. "Stop calling me 'kid'—I'm five years old. I'm a big girl."

"I'll stop calling you 'kid' when you stop calling me 'Mith.'"

"Okay, Mr. *Mith*!" she snapped back in the sassiest tone ever.

"Well, all right then, this morning chatter has been nothing but amazing, yet perhaps it's best if we are quiet the rest of the way and listen to the music, okay?" Emery cut in.

About twenty minutes later, we pulled up to the camp, and Emery put the car in park. "I have to walk her inside. I'll be right back."

As Reese climbed out of the car, she made sure to give me one more jab as she put on her backpack. "Bye, Mr. Mith. I hope you find good music again."

*You and me both, kid.*

"Oh, and Mr. Mith?"

"Yeah?"

"I'm sorry about your brotha," she said with a slight lisp. "He was my favorite."

I didn't know why, but hearing that from a little girl hit me harder than anything before. There I was, seconds away from tearing up in the back seat of a vomit-scented vehicle.

"He was my favorite, too, kid."

She smiled so big, and for a split second it was as if that smile was enough to take away an ounce of my pain. "Don't call me 'kid,' Mr. Mith."

She hurried away with her mother, and without thought I went to check my phone, which was still, indeed, dead. I wondered if the world was thinking I was somewhere dead in a ditch. I wondered how much that would please some people. *Stop being so negative.* It was almost morbid how often those kinds of thoughts flew through my mind. I supposed losing someone who meant the world to you would do that to a person.

*I don't want to be here.*

Fuck.

My parents.

Every time I thought about how I didn't want to be living, my mind wandered to my parents.

They were probably worried sick about me. I was almost certain they'd seen the articles that the paparazzi had run about me, and it wouldn't have shocked me if Mom was trying to book a first-class ticket to Los Angeles to make sure I was okay.

"Sorry about that," Emery told me, slipping back into the driver's seat. She turned to face me and gave the smallest grin. Somehow that smile healed an ounce of my pain too. "Where to?"

I gave her my address and she took off.

I tapped my fingers against my legs as I listened to the music still playing through the stereo. Every time I'd hear Alex's guitar riffs come through the speakers, my chest would tighten more and more.

"Can we not do the music thing? I don't really like listening to my own stuff. Or, well, any of my music since . . ." My words faded, and her brown eyes softened in the rearview mirror as guilt filled her stare.

She quickly shut off the music and muttered something under her breath, but I couldn't hear her. If it was her condolences, I didn't want to hear them. I'd received enough of those from people, to the point that they seemed ungenuine.

We drove a few blocks not speaking a word, until her soft voice filled the space again. I wondered if silence drove her mad too. I wondered if other people lived inside their heads as much as I did.

"You're a whole different person today," she said, starting up a conversation that she hadn't even known I needed to have. "Last night you were the complete opposite of who I'd imagined you to be. I always thought you were more reserved."

The nerves in my gut tightened as I tried my best to gather flashbacks of the night prior. I must've made a complete ass of myself and humiliated myself in front of that poor woman.

"I wasn't myself last night." I didn't know the last time I'd been myself. "If I did anything to offend you—"

"Don't apologize," she cut in. "Honestly, I get it. I've been there before. Once, I got so wasted that I passed out at some random person's house and woke up with a puke bucket next to me and a Taco Bell Crunchwrap smushed against my cheek. So, we all have those days."

For some odd reason, that gave me a moment of comfort. I didn't know Emery, but there was something about her that made me feel less self-aware.

"Did you pee in someone's houseplant?" I asked.

"No, but you know what they say—there's always tomorrow."

I chuckled slightly, and she looked back, appearing almost surprised by the sound that came from me. Every time she glanced back toward me, I felt a heat rush against my skin.

Strange.

"You're much quieter today," she said.

"I'm a quiet person. I'm not myself when I drink."

"Then why do you drink?"

"Because I'm not myself when I drink."

She swooned, seemingly moved by my comment. "I don't know if you meant to do that or if it's just natural for you, but sometimes you speak, and it feels like you're creating lyrics to my next favorite song."

If only it were that easy to create someone's favorite song. My record label would've been thrilled.

"Oh! Oh!" Emery gasped, pointing out of her window as we drove. "If you were wondering, which I doubt you were, that's the best Mexican food you'll ever have. It's called Mi Amor Burritos, and your life will be forever changed when you get their food." She nodded her head in pleasure as she thought about it. She was the opposite of me—more like Alex. Conversation came easy to her mind, while I struggled to gather my thoughts. "It's such a hole-in-the-wall place. I only knew about it because my sister, Sammie, stumbled across it years ago when she came to stay with me for a little bit. She has a gift of finding the best things in random places."

"Are you and your sister close?"

There was a hesitation in her before she swallowed hard and stared forward. "We were."

*For fuck's sake.* "I'm sorry."

"No worries. She didn't pass away or anything. She's just . . . I haven't seen her in a few years, since she went off to find herself. We still talk every now and again, but it's not the same as it used to be. She's on an adventure across the States, trying to find where she belongs."

"You think that's a thing? Having a place where someone belongs?"

"Belonging comes in different forms, I think. It can come from a place, a person, an object, an occupation."

"What makes you belong?"

"My daughter," she said without hesitation. "She's my safe place. What about you?"

I stayed quiet. I noticed the small frown that landed against Emery's lips as I stared in the rearview mirror. She didn't push on to force me to give her an answer, and I was thankful for that.

About twenty minutes later, we rounded the corner of the street I lived on and pulled up to a gated community. Steven, the guard, walked up to the car with a clipboard in his hands and a walkie-talkie on his hip.

Emery rolled down her car window and smiled at Steven. Steven didn't smile back, probably because he dealt with hordes of fanatics and paparazzi trying to crash through those metal gates.

"Can I help you, ma'am? Are you lost?"

"Well, I'm not in Kansas anymore, that's for sure," Emery muttered, looking toward the massive homes behind the gates. She then nodded to the back of the car. "I'm dropping off one of your prized possessions."

Steven looked in the back seat at me and still didn't smile back. He nodded once. "Hello, Mr. Smith."

"Hey, Steven."

"You created quite the buzz around these parts today."

I smirked, tossing my hands up in the air. "You're welcome for the entertainment."

"Keeps me on my toes," he said.

Steven walked away, and not long after, the gates began to open. As Emery drove, her mouth hung open, and I swore flies were seconds away from shooting straight into her throat.

"So, there's really people out here living like that?" she asked, stunned.

"Yeah." I nodded, looking around at the multimillion-dollar homes. Demi Lovato was rumored to have bought a property a few spots down from me. Alex would've loved that; she was his celebrity crush. "This is what we are wasting our fortunes on."

"Holy crap," she breathed out as we went up a hill and passed two people on a walk. "Was that a Kardashian? Holy crap, that's a Kardashian!" she whisper-shouted with her windows still down.

"A Jenner," I corrected.

"Potato-patahto," she sighed, seemingly a bit starstruck. I wouldn't have taken Emery as a Kardashian fan, but I guess people had a way of surprising you sometimes.

"I would give my left boob to have Kylie's lipstick from her makeup line."

"I think priorities need to be checked when giving away body parts for makeup."

"You just don't understand how good the makeup is."

As we approached my house, she pulled up the driveway, and I saw two people sitting on my front porch, and I knew I was in for a handful after my night's event.

"Is that your PR team or something? To do damage control after last night?"

"Worse. My parents."

She put the car in park, and I hopped out and walked over to her driver's door and leaned forward on the window frame. "Thank you for helping me out."

"No worries, really." She combed her thick, beautiful hair behind her ear and whispered, "Oddly enough, this was kind of a dream come true for me." I studied her as she bit into her bottom lip and nervously nuzzled against the skin. "Can I ask you something?"

I nodded.

"If it's too personal, you don't have to reply."

I nodded again.

She leaned toward me, growing closer as she placed her hands right beside mine on the window frame. "Are you okay? Like, overall. Are you okay?"

Her question was so gentle and packed with care. That's what it felt like that morning, ever since I'd crossed paths with Emery. She felt like a weighted blanket of protection that was keeping me from crumbling. In her brown eyes I saw the concern for me that she held.

Why would she care about me?

I was no one of real importance. Then again, perhaps she only cared about the Oliver Smith who was a performer, not the Oliver Smith I truly had been. If she knew my truth, she probably wouldn't have cared as much.

I knew what I wanted to tell her. I wanted to tell her what I'd been telling the rest of the world. I wanted to lie. I wanted to say I was fine and that everything was okay, but for some odd reason, my lips parted, my voice cracked, and I said, "No."

*No.*

That felt good to say.

No, I wasn't okay. No, I wasn't going to be okay. No, nothing was getting better.

*No.*

She smiled a smile that looked as if it were dripped in tears. I never knew smiles could feel so sad. Oddly enough, the sadness in her grin made me feel more at peace with my own despair.

Her hand moved on top of mine, and she lightly squeezed. Her touch was warm and soft, like I'd imagined it to be.

"I'm so sorry, Oliver. I'm going to pray for you to find better days. You deserve better days."

Was she even real? Or was she just a figment of my imagination that came to tell me the words I so very much needed to hear? I wanted to tell her the truth about prayers, about how they never came true. Before Alex was pronounced dead, I prayed for him to come back, but it never happened. I prayed for healing, and nothing got better. I prayed for the universe to take me instead, yet it'd left me behind to live.

I wasn't living anymore, though. I was a dead man walking, quietly wishing that the sun would fade forever, and I wouldn't have to hurt anymore.

*I don't want to be here.*

When Emery pulled her hand away from mine, the warmth she'd given me faded away too. Before I could reply to her, my parents were rushing toward me.

Emery's warmth ebbed from my hands as she pulled away, and she nodded once toward me as if it were our final goodbye as Mom rushed toward me and drew me into a hug.

"Oh my gosh, Oliver! Are you okay?"

"Yeah, Mom. I'm fine," I lied.

Sometimes it was easier to tell the truth to strangers. Your truth wouldn't hurt them as badly. I knew if my parents knew I wasn't okay, it would eat at their souls. I didn't need them worrying about my well-being after I'd been the cause of them losing the other half of their hearts.

When I glanced back at Emery, she gave me a halfway grin, noting the lie I'd told my parents, and I gave her a lopsided, weak smile back.

When she looked my way, it was as if she was saying, *I see you, Oliver, and you'll be okay.* Then she nodded once and put her car in reverse and drove away. Unlike how I'd crashed into her world, she slowly retreated from mine in a much classier fashion.

"Why did you fly out here?" I asked as Dad pulled me into a briefer embrace than Mom had.

"Well, we heard last minute you were doing a show, so we figured you could use some family support," Dad said. "Then, when we landed, we weren't able to get ahold of you, so we got worried."

Mom's eyes watered over as she hugged me again. "I was so scared that something happened to you."

The heaviness of her words and the fear that was in her made me feel like the worst son in the world. "Sorry, Mom. My phone died, and I haven't been able to make it back home until now. I'm sorry for the stress. I didn't mean to worry you."

She placed one hand against the half heart around my neck and her other hand against my cheek as she smiled at me with tears. Then she smacked my cheek and sniffled. "Don't ever do that again, or so help me, I'm putting a tracker in your phone. Now let us inside. You look hungry. Let me make you some food." Mom headed toward the front door of my house, and Dad lingered behind a bit.

My father wasn't as chatty as Mom. He didn't really say much, except for when words were needed. I was like him in that way, while Alex was more like Mom. He placed a comforting hand against my shoulder and squeezed.

"You all right, son?" he asked, his voice deep, low, and calm as ever. I couldn't remember a time Dad ever raised his voice. He may have been the most down-to-earth person I'd ever come across.

"Yeah, I'm good."

He nodded in acceptance of my answer. "Who was that who dropped you off?"

"Just a woman who was kind enough to help me out last night."

"A good-looking woman," Dad said with a smirk plastered on his face as he nudged me in the shoulder.

"Really? I didn't notice. I was just trying to make it home."

He chuckled. "Liar."

True. It was almost impossible to not notice Emery's beauty. If I were a different man with different struggles, I would've asked for her number. But the world I lived in didn't really match the world where she resided. Her world seemed more stable.

Plus, there was Cam.

I wondered how many messages I'd received from her on my dead cell phone.

"You want to talk about what happened yesterday?" Dad asked as we walked up the stairs of my porch.

"Not now."

"Okay. When you're ready, we'll be here."

If patience were human, it would be my parents. They never pressured me to talk about the thoughts that were flooding my mind. Most of the time, they simply randomly showed up and cooked me a lot of food as we listened to music and talked about anything and everything outside of my career and emotions.

I knew that the day I was ready to open up to them, they'd be there for me. There was a comfort in knowing that even when one was lost, home was always right there around the corner. As I ate my meal and chatted with my parents, I felt a little less alone.

Then, without my permission, my mind wandered to Emery. She was one of the better places that my mind had wandered as of late, and I didn't hate the fact that she was there.

# 8

## EMERY

My sister and I used to be best friends.

We used to tell one another every secret and comfort each other whenever our parents were too harsh on us. Too harsh on me. My parents were never hard on Sammie. Maybe because she was the youngest. Maybe because they loved her a little more. Maybe because she was the golden child who'd never done anything wrong.

Over the past five years since Reese was born, our relationship had shifted. We didn't talk like we used to, and when we did, the conversations felt forced. Though sometimes we'd chat, and it would feel like the old days when she had my back and I had hers, and we'd tell one another all the best secrets in our hearts.

That afternoon when she called me, for a small amount of time, Sammie and I felt like my favorite memory of us. We felt like best friends again.

"*Ohmygoshhhh!* Tell me everything! Every. Single. Thing! Don't leave a single bald spot out," Sammie squeaked over the phone as I walked into my apartment with a stack of résumés in my grip. Coming home felt like returning to a closet after dropping Oliver off at his oversize mansion. The moment I got a second to breathe, I texted Sammie and filled her in on everything that had gone down with Oliver the previous night.

Needless to say, she was having a panic attack about it all. If anyone loved Alex & Oliver as much as I did, it was my sister.

Her voice shook with excitement as she continued talking. "What did he drink? How was his hair? Were his eyes as dreamy as ever? What did he smell like? For the love of all things righteous, please tell me what he smelled like."

I snickered. "Um, whiskey and vomit?"

She swooned over the idea of whiskey vomit like it was top-of-the-line cologne.

"You lucky girl," she sang through the phone receiver. "I would give anything to smell Oliver Smith's vomit."

"You're insane," I laughed.

"Maybe, but oh my gosh, Emery. This is wild! I cannot believe you ended up front row and center at the Oliver Smith show—kind of. It's like your biggest dream came true."

"This wasn't exactly the way I dreamed about hanging out with Oliver." In my mind, I figured we'd randomly cross paths in Venice, where we just so happened to get on the same gondola by accident, then laugh at the same moment due to the mistake. Then our eyes would lock, our bodies would respond, and he'd sing to me as we traveled down the endless stream of love. We'd have five children, the first being named after Oliver. Then, somewhere along the line, E! Entertainment would offer us our own sitcom, yet we wouldn't accept because I'd see how power couples had been destroyed time and time again due to reality shows. *RIP Nick and Jessica, Jon and Kate, and Kendra and Hank.*

Then, we'd spend our fiftieth anniversary taking that same gondola ride, only this time surrounded by our children and grandchildren.

That's how the dream romance went between Oliver and me.

The reality? Not so many swoon-worthy moments. Definitely more gag-worthy situations.

"So, are you seeing him again? Was there some kind of connection?" she asked, as if she didn't hear me mention his aroma of vomit.

"The only connection was I learned that celebrities are just regular people who are messed up, with paparazzi and money. It wasn't as dreamy as you're imagining it to be."

"Yeah, okay, I get it. I'm sorry it was such a letdown." She cleared her throat. "But like, before the vomit, what did he smell like?"

I smirked, shaking my head. "You really want to know?" I asked, walking over to my couch and plopping down.

"Yes, yes, a million times yes!"

"Like a smoky forest oak that burned for just the right amount of time."

"Oh my goodness, I knew it," she blew out, "pleased" being an understatement. "Did you cut a piece of his hair for memories?"

I giggled. "You're ridiculous. But I have to say—"

Before I could finish my thought, I heard a voice in the background of Sammie's phone.

"We'll be ready for you in a few minutes for the fitting," they said.

I arched an eyebrow. "Who was that?"

"What?"

"I heard a voice."

Sammie snickered. "I'm just leaving a coffee shop; it was a woman coming in. But enough about that. Tell me more. What happened when you were with him? I need all the details."

"Well, he peed in my plant."

"Oh my. Um, is that some kind of sexual code word?"

"What? No. He legit peed in my houseplant."

"Did you ask him to do that?"

"Why the hell would I ask him to pee in my plant?"

"I don't know. Fangirls are weird sometimes."

I laughed. "Well, no, I didn't. He was so drunk that he thought he was peeing in the bathroom but went straight into my houseplant."

I could almost see Sammie's frown through the phone. "I'm going to be honest, that's pretty disappointing."

"I'm sorry to disappoint," I chuckled, shaking my head at my sister's comment. Man. I missed her. I could've really used her around me as of late, but I knew I wasn't able to ask her to come visit. If I did, the phone calls would get more distant. Sammie had a way of pushing things away when they became too much for her.

As I was talking to her, I received a message from Joey at Seven, telling me to come down to the bar as soon as possible. "Sammie, I have to get going. We'll talk later, okay?"

We said our goodbyes, and I hopped into my car to drive over to Seven. I tried my best to completely shake the past twenty-four hours from my brain. If I could go back in time, I would've never gone in to work that night. Then, my fantasy of the man who made the music that had saved me through my darkest days would still be fully intact. I'd still be a crazed fanatic, and I wouldn't have to face the reality that he was merely human after all. I remembered when I met him at a meet and greet years ago; I still felt as if he was Superman. Now I understood he was just a man who struggled like everyone else in life. I couldn't blame him for his struggles. He literally lost his other half.

My mind kept betraying me by wandering back to Oliver, the man who'd destroyed my fantasies. In a way, he'd been such a big part of my life growing up. A huge part of my sister's story too. His music is what got Sammie and me through our parents' strict rules. We'd sit in our bedroom, listening to the songs quietly with our earbuds in, because as Mama often said, "Satan's music does not belong in a house of God."

Just to be clear, any music that wasn't Mama approved was Satan's work.

Did people really get to listen to One Direction growing up? I sure didn't.

Mama said the only direction those boys were going was down to the devil's cave.

Growing up and listening to Alex & Oliver's music was our dirty little secret. They were the key to our strong sisterly bond. So, to face the reality of who Oliver was nowadays, versus the person I'd thought him to be when Sammie and I met him years ago, was such an emotional whirlwind. I didn't know how to feel about Oliver being the complete opposite of the person who'd made my sister smile all those years ago. Those smiles were the last ones I remembered ever getting from her.

I wanted to believe that the man I'd seen was a big departure from who Oliver really was deep to his core. I wanted to believe that he was just temporarily damaged, and not forever this way. I wanted to believe that somewhere within him lived the man who'd written the words that had saved me time and time again.

I craved the idea that he was still my hero, and not just a fallen star who'd burned out his light. Yet I knew there was going to be no way to prove his truths. We'd probably never cross paths again. The worst feeling in the world was coming to the realization that your idols were merely human themselves.

When I headed into Seven, still thinking about Oliver, I was completely thrown off.

"You're fired," Joey barked out as I walked into the bar through the back entrance. A group of paparazzi was outside the building, wanting to get an exclusive. They stood around like psychopaths waiting to attack. Joey hadn't even unlocked the front door yet, which seemed odd. It should've been opened for business hours ago.

"What?" A knot formed in my gut as I stood there, flabbergasted by his words.

He crossed his arms and nodded toward me. "I said you're fired."

"Joey, why . . ." I blinked, trying to get rid of the panic and turmoil that were rising up within me. Numbers started formulating in my head, bills skyrocketed across my mind, the struggles that I'd face without working at Seven. I was already struggling *with* the job. I couldn't imagine the hardships without it. "I . . . I can't lose this job. I can't."

"But you did. I've been here all day cleaning up the mess you made, and counting up the register, trying to make ends meet, and do you know what? Ends don't freaking meet because you pushed dozens and dozens of drunk people out of the bar without closing their tabs! When whatever went down, people stole bottles from behind the counter. And you gave a top-shelf bottle of whiskey to some celebrity who you didn't charge."

"I can cover the costs . . . ," I said, my voice becoming shaky.

"Oh, trust me, you already are. I took your check from the past week and am using that to recoup some of what has been lost. Outside of that, we'll call it even. You can go now."

My body shook at his words, because I couldn't walk out of that bar without my check in hand. I couldn't face Ed without actual cold hard cash to hand over to him. I knew if I showed up without a check to give him that evening, I'd be kicked out in an instant.

"No, no, no. You don't understand, Joey. That check . . . that's my rent, and it's due today. It was due a week ago, actually. Please, you can't do this."

"I can, and I did. Now go!" he barked, pointing toward the exit.

I wanted to keep arguing with him. I wanted to fall to my knees and beg for him to reconsider, but I'd known Joey long enough to know that he was stubborn in his ways, and it was almost impossible to change his mind. Besides, I'd seen him fire people for far less than what I'd done.

The tears kept rising to the corners of my eyes, but I tried my best to keep them locked in tightly. I didn't want to fall apart in front of Joey. I didn't cry in front of people. I couldn't remember the last time someone had witnessed me losing control. I kept my sadness and emotional breakdowns to myself, in private, where no one could try to give me comfort. I didn't want people's pity; I just wanted to be strong enough to keep myself from falling apart.

But I wasn't there yet. The moment I hit my car, the tears began to flow. I gripped the steering wheel, and I didn't even try to keep from allowing my heart to shatter. There were a million reasons why my heart was breaking, a million reasons why I was falling apart, but the main reason was because of Reese.

My beautiful star who deserved so much more than I'd been able to give her. She deserved the world, and I was giving her crumbs.

I didn't know how I'd do this. I didn't know how I'd be able to provide for her. All I knew was I couldn't put her in a position where she didn't have a place to lay her head. I couldn't put her life in jeopardy because of my failings. There was nothing more important in this world than my daughter.

*When it rains, it pours.*

About a year ago, I heard those words from a homeless person who was standing outside a grocery store, panhandling. It didn't rain much in Los Angeles, but that afternoon it was a downpour, making it hard to even drive through the streets.

The woman stood in the rain with a jacket covering her head, and she was swaying back and forth, chilled to her bones and holding up a sign for some help. Reese seemed completely unaware of that woman's struggles; her only mission in life was to jump in every puddle she crossed.

When I looked at the woman, my chest felt tight. Sure, things weren't perfect for Reese and me, but our struggles could've been worse. I reached into my purse and pulled out the few dollar bills that I had and handed them her way, along with my umbrella.

"Oh no, you keep the umbrella," she ordered, as she thanked me for the money. "I don't need it."

"It's coming down pretty hard. My daughter and I can just rush to our car to get dry. You need it more."

"When it rains, it pours," she sang, looking up at the sky as her face became drenched, yet still, she was smiling. The biggest smile on her face. "But the rain always stops, and the sun comes out again. Thank you for your kindness. May God bless you."

I was certain that interaction didn't resonate with the woman as much as it had with me, but her thoughts got me through some of my hardest times. Especially the ones I was currently partaking in.

*When it rains, it pours, but the rain always stops, and the sun comes out again.*

Funny how strangers could affect a person without even knowing it.

I was having a terrible day, going through my own deluge, and I couldn't even fully process it because, before I could be fully human, I first had to be a mom.

As I picked up Reese from camp, I was determined to show some of my best acting skills in front of her. Inside my soul, I was cracking due to the storm; outside I smiled like the sun.

"How was camp, sweet pea?" I asked after climbing back into the driver's seat of my car as Reese hummed some song she'd learned that day.

"It was good! We are making the biggest, biggest, *biggest* piñata ever, and Ms. Kate said we get to break it on the last day of camp! Mama, it's the size of the moon!" She gleamed, making me laugh. Even on the worst days, that little girl could make me smile.

"Wow! That must be really big."

"It is. It's the biggest thing ever. Plus! They are putting candy in it, and we all got to pick a candy we wanted in it, because Ms. Kate and Ms. Rachel said that all of our opinions mattered and I picked Skittles, because they are my favorite candy, and my best friend Mia said 'Eww' because she thinks Skittles are gross, and my other best friend Randy said I picked a bad one, so I changed it to Blow Pops." She said it so nonchalantly, as if those two other kids weren't freaking bullies.

It didn't go unnoticed by me that Mia and Randy were the same two kids who had Reese questioning if we were poor.

Tomorrow, I'd be having a very stern conversation with the camp instructors to make sure that they were truly watching over my daughter to keep her from being bullied by those two.

"Reese, you know better than changing your mind because of what someone else says. You love Skittles. Don't let these kids make you think you don't like what you like."

I glanced back at her to witness her shrugging her shoulders. "It's just because Mia and Randy are cooler than me, that's all."

"Reese Marie, don't ever say something like that again, okay? You are the coolest person in this world, and don't let anyone make you think differently."

Was it too dramatic to think that I really wanted to give those two five-year-olds a piece of my mind? Or at least their parents. I would've been horrified to learn that my child was a bully. And I truly despised the idea that Reese was surrounding herself with those types of people. I didn't want her to (A) start doubting herself in any way, shape, or form or (B) become like those two and bully others.

She was at that stage in her life where everything had an impact on her thoughts. I needed to fix the problem sooner rather than later, before it really affected her growth.

"Okay, Mama," she said, going back to her humming as if nothing major had taken place.

"I mean that, Reese. You are the coolest person I've ever met in my life. Don't forget that."

She agreed with me and went back to singing "Background Noise," by Alex & Oliver, obviously. As we drove, I fell into their music, too, somewhat forgetting the craziness of my life and allowing myself to breathe for a moment in time.

Thank goodness Abigail dropped off those groceries for Reese and me the other day. I could make that stretch for a while, and if worse came to worst, I could sell the car.

*There's always a way, there's always a way, there's always a way.*

My mind was filled with the affirmations that I spoke to myself on a daily basis. They kept me from crumbling and spiraling too far away from myself.

"Hey, Mama?"

"Yes, Reese?"

"Who's my dad?"

My heart sank into the pit of my stomach as I looked back toward her as she played with one of her dolls that was always left in the car. That was the last question I'd expected to come from her. I knew down the line I'd have to address that question. I'd played that conversation over and over again in my head for the past five years.

"What makes you ask that?" I responded, trying to sound as calm as I could, even though my heart was beating as if it were ready to burst from my chest.

"Well, at camp we are making Father's Day cards for everyone's dads, and I told Mia and Randy I didn't have a dad to make a card for, and they told me that everyone had a dad, and I didn't know that. I thought some people just had mamas, so now I'm just wondering who my dad is if everyone has dads."

Freaking Mia and Randy. The two devil children.

"That's a very good question, sweetheart, and we should talk about it later when we get home, okay?"

"Okay, Mama. I hope I get to meet him one day. I want to tell him I love him like I love you."

My already shattered heart crumbled into even more pieces than ever before.

"I love you, Reesey Pieces," I choked out, fighting the tears that were sitting at the back of my eyes.

"Love you, too, Mama."

Thankfully, she didn't bring the topic up again that night. After dinner, she headed to her bedroom to play with her toys, and I cleaned up the kitchen and gathered the garbage to take out to the trash bins outside.

As I walked outside, Abigail was walking in and gave me the brightest smile. "Hey, Emery. How are you—" Her words faded when her eyes met mine. "Oh no, what's wrong?"

The mother shield I'd been carrying on my shoulders began to crack as my shoulders dropped and my chest burned. "Just one of those days."

"What happened?"

"I lost my job today due to the craziness that took place at the bar last night. I don't know how I'm going to keep things together. We were already living paycheck to paycheck, and I made the stupid decision to spend a big part of my savings on summer camp for Reese. Now, things are even tighter, and I'm out two jobs and it seems like the world is spiraling."

"Oh, sweetheart. If you need help—"

"No, truly. It's fine. I'll figure it out. Thank you, though. To add flames to the fire, Reese asked about her father today."

Abigail grimaced and nodded in understanding. She knew my life story inside and out. Heck, she was there for me more than my own mother was when my world turned upside down five years ago.

"She's getting to that age where she'll start wondering about these kinds of things," she said. "Especially if she's surrounded by other kids who are living different kinds of lifestyles."

"Better lifestyles," I sighed.

"No life is better than another. They are all just uniquely different."

"I don't even know what to say to her. How to even bring it up. Heck, I can hardly bring it up to myself without getting emotional about it."

Abigail placed a comforting hand against my shoulder and gave me one of her sincere smiles. "Speak when you're ready. Your daughter will be willing to listen when you're able to tell it. Until then, just let her know that she has a mama who loves her. You're doing great, Emery. Just know that, even on the days when it feels like you're not."

I thanked her for her kindness, and she gave me the hug that I hadn't even known my soul needed. I continued on my way to throw out my trash as Abigail headed up to her apartment. On my way up, I ran into Ed, who of course was in search of his rent.

"Emery!" he called out, walking my way.

"I know, Ed, I know. I'll have you the rent tomorrow," I said, not exactly sure if it were true, but I'd do what I had to do to make it happen. Even if that meant taking out loans for money that would cost me double to pay back.

"You said that you'd have it tonight!" he argued, fuming as his fuzzy brows sat low. "I can't keep doing this, Emery. This is it!" he barked. His face was a deep red, and I could feel his annoyance. I didn't blame him. He'd put up with my struggles long enough, and he didn't have any reason to keep allowing me to slide.

"Just twenty-four hours more, Ed. I swear. I'm selling my car tomorrow to get you the money. Please," I begged, wiping away the stubborn tears as they danced down my cheeks.

The moment he saw my trembles and shakes, his body relaxed a bit as he grumbled to himself and pinched the bridge of his nose. "Twenty-four hours. After that you and your kid are out, all right? That's it, Emery. That's the deal."

"Deal. Thank you, Ed."

He muttered something under his breath and waved me off before he walked away.

That night after Reese and I got down on our knees and said our prayers, I kissed her forehead, tucked her into bed, and went to my room for my own good session of falling apart. After I'd had a lengthy private cry, after I'd cracked, I knew I needed something. No. I needed someone. I needed my sister.

As I dialed her number, tears sat at the back of my eyelids.

"Hello?" Sammie answered. Just from the sound of her voice, I began to break, and she must've sensed that. "Em? What's wrong?"

"I lost my job."

"Oh my gosh, Emery. I'm sorry."

"Do you think you can come here? I just . . . I need you."

"Emery . . . ," she sighed.

"I need you, Sammie. This is all too much. I'm drowning, and I need you here with me. I can't do this alone."

The line went silent for a split second, and I felt an overwhelming sense of dread as I went back to begging. "Please, Sammie. I'm struggling. I can't do this alone. I wouldn't ask unless I really needed the help and—"

"I can send money," she offered, her voice cracking now.

"No. I don't need money, Sammie. I need you. I've always been there for you at your lowest . . . please . . . I need you at mine. It can be quick. You don't even have to see Reese, I swear. I just need you."

Again, the silence filled the receiver, and I felt a spark of betrayal as Sammie whispered, "I'm sorry, Emery. I just can't be what you need me to be. I can't."

"Sammie—"

I didn't get to finish my sentence. She hung up, leaving me to feel unbelievably alone. How could she do that? How could she turn her back on me when I'd shown up for her time and time again? The hardest truth to learn in life was that not everyone loved the same way you did. I'd given my sister everything in the past, and all she'd given me was a dropped call.

# 9

## OLIVER

My parents stayed the night and flew out in the early morning. Even though I was certain they were hurting, they didn't show an ounce of their pain in front of me. If anything, they brought their bright, bubbly personalities that I grew up around and shone their love over my darkness. I was grateful for their light.

Cam had no interest in coming over, as she was still pissed at me for not answering her calls the day prior. She was even more upset that I hadn't performed at the show, saying she was ready to do a surprise song for the audience. "You didn't even think of the exposure it could've brought my new album," she scolded. "You never think of me, Oliver."

Not once did she ask why I wasn't able to perform.

Not once did she question if I was okay.

Not once did I think that we were destined for happily ever after.

Still, I selfishly needed her. When no one was with me during the nights, I crumbled and gave myself to the bottle. I didn't want alcohol to be my fix anymore, because it always swallowed me whole and I'd wake the next morning feeling worse off than I had the previous evening.

So, I leaned on Cam coming home each night.

The Mixtape

Our whole relationship was based on selfishness. She stayed with me because it made great press for her to be the sweetheart who stayed by my side during my storm, and I stayed with her so I wouldn't lose myself in the dark.

Toxic? Yes.

Terrible coping mechanism? Also yes.

I sat in my bedroom with large headphones covering my ears. I was home alone, so I turned to music to drown out the noise that was echoing in my head. I had a playlist with over six hundred of my favorite songs that meant something to me—half of which I'd probably learned about from Alex when he'd send me a song a day. I missed getting those songs.

I missed sharing my songs too.

"Oliver? Are you here?" a voice hollered through my house. The voice was loud enough to cut through the music playing in my headphones. I slid them down and placed them around my neck.

I listened to Kelly's heels click-clacking through my hallways as she grew closer and closer to my bedroom. "Just a wellness check-in! Your mom called and asked me to stop by, and well, I just wanted to stop by, too, after what happened with the show." She kept her voice loud, and there was a slight tremble in it as she searched for me. "So, if you are here, can you just make a loud noise? Because the idea of walking in on you and finding you not okay is too much for my anxiety."

I swallowed hard and cleared my throat. "Here!" I shouted. "In my bedroom."

I swore I heard Kelly's sigh of relief rocket throughout the space.

She hurried over to my bedroom and gave me a slight smile as she stood in the doorway with a coffee in her hands. Her hair was in a messy bun, and she looked as if she hadn't slept in days. The puffiness under her eyes showcased her exhaustion.

"Hey, Oliver."

I nodded once as I sat on the edge of my bed. "Hey."

91

She walked over to me and sat down. She handed me the coffee. "Coffee, no whiskey."

"Then what's the point?" I joked.

"You okay?" she asked me.

"Yeah, I'm fine."

"Liar."

"Maybe."

I lowered my head and fiddled with my fingers. Over the past few months, I'd told myself what I was dealing with wasn't depression but just a temporary sadness that would go away over time. When time passed and it didn't shift, I knew it was something I'd have to deal with for the rest of my life. Somehow, after Alex passed away, I felt . . . emptied.

I didn't even know if "depressed" was the word for how I felt. Yet all I knew was that there was an emptiness inside of me and I hadn't a clue how to fill that vacant place. I felt as if I were walking on broken glass, and I didn't even feel the pain from the cuts. Everything was numb, everything was mute, everything was meaningless.

I wanted the pain of losing my brother to go away. That was why I drank, to keep those thoughts from surfacing, but the whiskey didn't kill the struggles; it only temporarily hid them. When the whiskey faded, the pain came back stronger than ever.

"What makes you happy, Oliver?"

My mouth parted, but no words came out. Hell. I had no clue.

Kelly frowned. "What about music? Does music make you happy?"

I stayed quiet.

"Do you really not want to do music anymore? Like, if that is something you're not interested in, then fine, let it go. But I've known you for so long, and I feel like music is the biggest part of who you are."

"Yeah, it is."

"Then why are you pushing it away?"

I shrugged my shoulders and cleared my throat. "I don't know how to do music without having Alex doing it beside me."

Her eyes glassed over, and I felt bad for making her feel bad. Kelly missed Alex in a different way than I did, and I knew she was struggling. She was still going through the grieving process, but she'd never voice it to me. Maybe because she felt it would be too hard to talk about. Maybe because she hadn't yet found the words to express her pain.

She pushed a smile through her lips and nodded her head once. "Do you know what would make Alex the saddest person?"

"What's that?"

"Knowing you pushed your music away. He'd want you to embrace it, not run from it. He'd want music to be what fueled your tank after running for so long on empty. So, honestly, I think the best way you can honor your brother is by doing what you love the most. Oliver, you gotta let the music in. I think it's the only thing that is going to heal you. I don't know what happened at the concert, Oliver, and you don't have to go into it. All I want to say is, be easy with yourself. You're still mourning a big loss."

"I thought I could trick myself into doing the show, but I panicked. I couldn't bring myself to do it."

"No one blames you for what happened. At least not anyone that truly matters. Tyler and the PR team already did damage control and fixed the narrative. I'm just thankful for the woman at the bar who brought you to safety. It could've ended up much worse."

*Thank goodness for Emery.*

"I feel bad for her, though," Kelly continued. "The paparazzi has been at the place trying to get an exclusive interview with the bartender from that night, but it was reported that the owner fired her for the disruption that happened."

"She was fired?"

"Yeah. At least that's what's being reported."

*Shit.*

Emery was already struggling with life in her own ways. Leave it to me and my demons to make her life even worse off.

"I gotta go handle something," I said abruptly, shooting up from my bed.

Kelly arched an eyebrow. "Is everything okay? What's wrong?"

"I have to make something right, that's all."

"Okay, well if you need anything, let me know. I'll get back to answering these emails for you and all that jazz."

"Thanks, Kelly." I started to head out of the room but paused as I looked back to my assistant. Behind her organization and kindness, I saw it. Her pain. I wasn't the only one mourning the death of my brother, that was for sure.

It was no secret that she and Alex had been getting closer and closer each day before the accident. I wondered what they would've been if they'd had more time. I wondered if they were supposed to be a love story with a happy ending. I wondered if she blamed me for his death like the rest of the world did.

She was his type to a T too. A beautiful woman with a heart of gold. During her free time—which was limited—she was either volunteering at food shelters, giving back to the inner city, taking part in equality protests, or meditating for better tomorrows. They were so much alike—she and my brother. Shit, she and Alex were probably meant to be, up until life got in the way.

Kelly never showed her sadness in front of me over the loss of Alex. She simply handled every angle of my life with care and tact. She never brought up the shit that the rest of the world brought up and did her best to make my life easier. I wished I could do something to make her life easier too. Because I was sure when she did grieve, she crumbled on her own.

"How are you doing, Kelly? You know, with everything. How are you?"

"I'm fine."

"Liar."

She laughed. "Maybe." She brushed her hand against the back of her neck and gave me a smile that was soaked in sadness. "I'm still breathing, though, and I'll call that a win."

That seemed so simple, but oddly enough I'd found breathing to be one of the hardest things as of late.

"All right. Keep breathing. Did you eat breakfast today?" I asked.

She shifted a little in her seat, which was enough of an answer for me. "I have time before I have to handle this. Let's get breakfast."

"Oliver, I'm fine," she said warily. I wondered how many times a day humans lied to one another about being okay.

"Yeah, I know you are. Now come on. Let's go get breakfast."

# 10

## EMERY

When morning came, I awakened to my doorbell ringing. My body ached from exhaustion, and my eyes were probably still swollen from the amount of crying I'd taken part in, but still, I was able to get out of bed. Silver lining.

I headed toward the front door and was shocked to see Oliver standing there when I opened it. He gave me a slight smile that looked more like a frown, and in his hands was a giant houseplant, along with a card.

"Hi," he breathed out, making me confused as ever. His eyes were heavy, as if he hadn't slept much the night prior, either.

"Hi?" I rubbed my hand up and down my arm, nerves rocking throughout my entire system. "What are you—"

"I owed you a houseplant," he said, cutting in. He held the beauty in my direction, along with the card. "Figured I'd toss in a card too."

"You didn't have to do that, but she's beautiful," I said, smiling down at the new plant.

"She?"

I nodded. "Plants are alive, just like humans."

"Do you name them, too?"

"No, I leave that up to Reese. That one on my coffee table is Bobby Flay. The spiky one in the bathroom is Guy Fieri."

He gave me a half grin and nodded but didn't say anything else. His brows pulled in as he rubbed his hand against his cheek.

"Is there . . . something else?" I asked, not sure what was keeping him standing in my doorway.

"No. I mean, yes. I actually heard the news that you lost your job."

My mouth fell open as I winced. "Oh. Yeah."

"I can't stop thinking that it's because of me. So . . ." He scratched at his neck and cleared his throat before raising an eyebrow. "I want to hire you?"

He said it like a question, as if he wasn't completely sure of his statement.

I laughed because clearly, Oliver had lost his mind. The more I laughed, the more bewildered he appeared. "I'm sorry," I chuckled, shaking my head. "Why are you really here?"

"I mean it, Emery. I want to hire you."

"Hire me for what?"

His brows lowered and he pushed his thumb against his nose. "Well, what do you do?"

"What do I do?"

"Yes. Other than bartend."

"I don't know what you're getting at."

"You were fired because of me."

"Not directly because of you—"

"I made a scene. You were let go because of me."

"It's okay," I lied.

"It's not." His guilt didn't fade away as he looked up toward me and locked his eyes with mine. "I want to fix this mistake. Therefore, I want to hire you for . . . whatever it is you do. Or like to do. Or want to do."

I laughed. "Oliver, that really isn't necessary. You don't have to—"

*"Please,"* he begged, his voice cracking. "Let me help."

"Why is this so important to you?"

His eyes flashed back to mine, and every ounce of hurting that lived within that man was staring back my way. I didn't know why it was so important for him to hire me, but I could tell it was deeper than anything he was going to tell me.

He stood as if he was trying to get his thoughts out. As if his mind was running faster than he could handle. His hands were stuffed into his jeans pockets, making his toned arms flex slightly. His eyes blinked a few times as he took in a deep breath, yet still, no words.

I nuzzled my bottom lip. "I'm a chef. Well, kind of. I went to culinary school for a few years but had to stop when Reese was born."

A flash of hope hit his stare. "You're a chef."

"Using the word loosely, yes."

"That's perfect. I need a chef."

I doubted he needed a chef. "You honestly want me to work for you?"

"Yes."

"To . . . cook for you?"

"Yes."

"Again, I didn't finish my culinary degree."

His brows knitted as he fell into deep thought. I wondered if he knew how cute he was when he seemed so far away from reality.

"Does every chef need an education in order to make great meals?" he asked.

"Well, no, but . . . how do you know if you'd even like what I make?"

"I'm not picky. I'll eat anything."

"Should I submit a résumé?"

"No."

"Do you want me to do a test run? To make sure that I'm good enough."

"Emery."

"Yes?"

"You're good enough."

"Oh." I bit my bottom lip. "I just think there might be someone more qualified."

"I don't want someone more qualified. I want you."

When he said that, butterflies fluttered in my stomach.

Oliver didn't realize how hard it was for me to simply exist within his space. He was painfully handsome, to the point that whenever he was in close proximity to me, my cheeks felt a flash of heat. He looked so much like his brother, but also different in many ways. Alex was always smiling, from the interviews I'd seen between the two of them. Oliver was always the quiet one, with a somber stare. He didn't look rude or cold to me, as so many people had stated about him—he simply looked to be in thought. As if his mind was always wandering deeper than the surface level.

I liked that about him—how he seemed to take everything in before adding his own thoughts.

Oliver rolled his shoulders back and stood tall. He had to be well over six two, because when I stood beside him, I felt extremely small in my five-six frame.

He flicked his finger against his neck a few times. "It's a five-day-a-week position. You can have weekends off, of course, unless there's some kind of event. I know you're a mother, and those responsibilities always come first. Therefore, if there is any kind of conflict, we'll shift. The position pays a hundred and fifty thousand a year, and—"

"What?" I gasped.

Surely he couldn't have been serious. Was he drunk again?

He repeated the number, and I was certain I'd become Alice and I'd fallen deep down the rabbit's hole.

"Are you serious?" I asked.

"What would make you think I was joking?"

"Uh, the one hundred and fifty thousand a year."

"Is that not enough? Because we can work to find the right amount."

I laughed. "Are you kidding? That's more than enough. And I just have to prepare some meals for you and stuff?"

"That's it."

There was no way I could turn down an opportunity like that. That kind of money could change Reese's and my life forever. I'd be able to provide for my daughter more than I'd ever been able to before. I could get her into a better school next year. We could move to a nicer apartment. I could start saving for her future and putting money toward mine.

He held his hand out toward me. "Deal?"

Butterflies fluttered in the pit of my stomach again as I placed my hand against his chilled palm. Was he always so cold? "Deal. When do we start?"

"Monday. You remember where I live?"

"Yeah, I do."

"I'll add you to the approval list for access to the community. What's your last name?"

"Taylor."

"Emery Taylor."

Him saying my name sounded like a song that I'd wished he'd sing over and over again.

"In the card is the phone number to my assistant, Kelly. She'll get you set up with everything before Monday. She'll also let you know what's needed. Just give her a call."

"Thank you, Oliver. Truly. You just saved me more than you know."

He nodded once, and only once. "I'll see you Monday."

He disappeared down the hallway, and then I raced over to my living room window to see him climb into his car. I watched that car until it faded away down the road. After that, I headed to the card he'd left for me, and I gasped when I opened it and saw hundred-dollar bills sitting by a simple note that read: *Thanks for the ride—OS.*

There was enough for me to go downstairs to pay Ed the rent. There was enough to get me through the weekend and to have food for Reese to not only eat, but to enjoy.

I quickly checked in on my sleeping daughter and allowed her to sleep in a little longer so I could rush downstairs to give Ed the rent that was behind. The moment I stepped into his office, he looked up, seemingly fifty million times calmer than he'd been when we'd run into one another the night before.

"Good morning, Emery," he said, nodding my way with . . . was that a smile on his face? His desk was a complete mess, and he shuffled through the paperwork in front of him as if he was on a mission to make it neater.

"Hi, Ed. I just wanted to bring you the rent. I apologize for it being late, but it won't happen again."

"I know it won't. Oliver Smith handled it for the rest of your lease."

I cocked my head. "What?"

"Oliver Smith . . . you know . . . *the* Oliver Smith. The one you were running around with yesterday. He showed up a few minutes ago and paid for your rent for the next seven months. He wrote a check for each month. He even signed my notebook." Ed gleamed, showing me his autographed paper pad. "Cool guy."

The oddest thing about life was how something could show up out of nowhere and change everything in a split second of time.

# 11

## EMERY

"You can do this, Em. You are a fantastic cook. Sure, you have no personal-chef experience whatsoever, and sure, working for one of the biggest musicians of our time can seem overwhelming, but you raised a kid on your own. You've kept her fed. You're pretty fast on obtaining new techniques. You can do this; you got this," I muttered to myself over and over again as I drove to Oliver's for my first day.

I was put into contact with Kelly, who informed me that I should go grocery shopping for the week, and I'd be reimbursed for the charges, so the back of my car was filled with groceries for Oliver. I'd overthought the weekly menu a million times. Heck, I'd written out over ten different menus, with ten different styles of cuisine. It wasn't every day you prepared meals for a celebrity.

Also in the back seat of the car was my knife roll I still had from culinary school. Why? I had no clue. It just felt weird to show up to the job empty handed, even though I was sure he had top-of-the-line knives already. I had to admit, it felt nice carrying my knives again. I'd missed using them as much as I had when I was in school.

Needless to say, I had a big job to take on, but the outcome of it would be worth it. Not only was I being given the opportunity to work for a celebrity, but I was also being given the chance to give Reese a better life—a life that she deserved.

We'd have enough money to move to a different state—a cheaper state—with more opportunities. Maybe I'd even go back to school and finish my degree and start my own restaurant someday. Maybe I'd be able to enroll Reese into a private school. Or put her in gymnastics, or theater arts. The possibilities were endless.

As I pulled up to the gated community, I gave my name to Steven at the gate. He opened the gates for me, and I drove straight to Oliver's home. It was even more beautiful than I remembered. That morning, a team of people was doing yard work to keep the property in top-notch shape. They were trimming the bushes that, to me, already looked perfect and watering the fully blossomed flowers that were vibrant shades of yellows and reds.

I wondered how many people it took to keep a house that size up to par. I could hardly keep my small apartment clean for a day. I wouldn't even know what to do with a property the size of Oliver's home.

I approached the front door and took a moment to catch my breath before I wiped my sweaty palms against my smoothed-back hair. After I rang the doorbell and waited a few moments, the front door swung open, and a beautiful woman stood tall in her heels. "Hi! You must be Emery. I'm Kelly. We talked on the phone. Come on in," she said, opening the door wider.

Taking the first step into his mansion felt surreal. My whole apartment was the size of Oliver's living room, if not smaller. A huge crystal chandelier sparkled in the foyer, creating specks of light that danced across the room from the beams of sunlight coming into the space. The house was well lit with natural light due to all the floor-to-ceiling windows. To the right of me was a spiral staircase made of wooden beams, and my mind couldn't stop imagining where that staircase led to. The floors were made of a natural wood, too, and seemed polished to a T.

I was glad I didn't tell Oliver I was a housekeeper, because keeping a home that size would've been the death of me.

"It's a beautiful home," I said, glancing around in awe. It looked as if I'd stepped straight into a home-decor magazine. *Lifestyles of the Rich and Famous.* Everything was perfectly in place. A clear sign that Oliver didn't have children.

"Isn't it? Wait until you see all of it." She smiled. There was something so kind about Kelly's spirit. She seemed extremely welcoming, which made my nerves somewhat falter. She led me to the living room—the living room with *white* furniture. I couldn't ever imagine such a thing. Reese would have Cheeto dust and Play-Doh all over it in a heartbeat.

"So, it's my job to get you all squared away with your tasks and paperwork that needs to be filled out. I'll show you around the property, too, one of our last stops being the kitchen, which will be your playground."

Kelly was more than willing to take her time with explaining all the ins and outs of being a personal chef for Oliver. She went over how he'd need three meals a day, but dinner could be early so I could pick up Reese from camp. She told me that my spending for groceries was unlimited, and I'd be reimbursed for whatever I spent. Lastly, she informed me that if Reese ever needed to tag along for the day, that was fine, by all means.

"Oliver wanted me to make that very clear to you. He said you're a single mom, and he never wants you to feel as if you have to leave your daughter somewhere else during the day. He even offered getting a nanny for her while you're both here too. So that's an option."

He wanted to get help for the help?

Kelly smiled at my somewhat stunned expression. "He wants you to be as comfortable as possible. Which brings me to my next point." She pulled out a check and handed it over to me. "Your first paycheck."

I raised an eyebrow. "I haven't done anything yet," I said, stunned by the amount written on that piece of paper.

"It's a hiring bonus. To help get things going before you're paid in two weeks."

Five thousand dollars.

Simply because.

I didn't want to look like an emotional wreck, but man, did I want to burst into tears and cry. "I can't take that."

"Oh, you can, and you must. Otherwise I won't hear the end of it about how I didn't do my job. So, help a girl out," she jested.

"Thank you. This is just . . . thank you."

Kelly smiled. "I'm glad I could pass on the news, but trust me, it's all Oliver."

When we finished a lot of the main tasks that needed to be covered, plus NDAs and contracts, Kelly sat down with me on the sofa and gave me a halfway grin. "I'm going to say this now, just so you go into this situation with an open mind and heart. Oliver's a bit different than he used to be. He's always been a bit of an introvert, but now, after . . ." She took a breath and blinked away the emotions sitting at the back of her eyes. "Some days he walks around as if he's so far away from reality. If he has his headphones on, he's probably working through some of his emotions. If he walks into a room and ignores you, or if he comes off as cold or rude, don't take it personally. He's just trying his best, day in and day out, to be okay."

"I understand."

"Also, Cam might be lingering around in the mornings before she takes off for her day."

"Cam? As in Cam Jones?" I breathed out, stars in my eyes. "Really?"

Kelly didn't seem as impressed. "Yes. Really."

"Oh my gosh. I'm such a fan!"

Cam always seemed like the sweetest person whenever she did an interview. She was the only reason I'd even listened to country music. I couldn't wait to meet her in person.

"I can't wait to meet her!" I exclaimed.

Kelly cocked an eyebrow and parted her lips as if she had her own thoughts on the subject, but she shook her head and pushed out a smile. "Yeah. Totally. Also," she said, shifting the topic, "don't mind the covered mirrors throughout the house. Oliver's working through some things. If you have to use a mirror, say in the bathroom or something, just make sure to re-cover it before you leave, please."

Celebrities and their odd quirks.

Kelly proceeded to give me a tour of the property, starting outside. She showed me the tennis court and an insanely beautiful swimming pool outside, with an attached hot tub, of course. There was a grilling station and an area for entertaining with a stereo system, lounge chairs, and a firepit. If Reese were with me, she'd probably think we were at Disneyland or something. I wouldn't have been surprised if Prince Charming came from behind the bushes for a photo op.

Kelly showed me all the rooms in the house, including Oliver's bedroom suite. The teenage version of me would've freaked out at the idea of seeing Oliver Smith's bedroom. The grown-up version of me tried my best to keep my cool.

Then, there was the kitchen.

The kitchen was made for masterpiece meals. Not a tool was missing from the cabinets. There were even some gadgets that I was certain I'd have to google to figure out how to use. "What are the guidelines on meals?" I asked as my fingers ran across the marble countertops.

"Oh, you can cook anything and everything. He has no allergies at all, so everything is fair game. Trust me, he's very laid back."

The last space she took me to was the west wing of the house, where Oliver's studio was located. As we walked down the hallways, we passed glass windows looking into the studio space. At first, I assumed he wasn't in the room, since he was nowhere to be seen.

"Oh, he's hard at work," Kelly commented, making me raise an eyebrow. She then pointed to the floor, where Oliver was lying down with crumpled-up pieces of paper surrounding him. His headphones were set against his ears, and he had a grumpy look on his face.

"Sometimes he'll stay in here all day, so don't be afraid to interrupt him and get him to eat something. It's more than okay to do that," Kelly explained.

I stared at the artist lying on the floor, and a small smile fell against my lips. I wondered if that was how he lay when he wrote my favorite song, "Heart Stamps." Was he spread out on the floor with crumpled pieces of his mind scattered at his sides? Did he close his eyes and move his lips as he mouthed something to himself? Did he cover his eyes with the palms of his hands and tap his feet?

I wondered what his next creation would be.

I wondered if I'd love it too.

———— ✺〜✺ ————

After getting a tour of the house, I unloaded all the groceries and filled up the refrigerator pretty quickly. I had a few hours until lunchtime, so I started chopping up some vegetables that I'd be able to use throughout the week.

A few minutes passed before Oliver appeared in the doorway of the kitchen with his headphones on. I looked up from my cutting board and smiled his way. When his stare found mine, he seemed a bit startled.

"Emery. Hello," he said, formal as ever. He removed his headphones and let them sit around his neck. "Kelly got you settled in?"

"Yes. I'm getting used to the beautiful space. Honestly, I'd kill for a kitchen like this. It's so open, and the appliances are out-of-this-world fantastic."

"I'm glad you're pleased."

"I am." The nerves that I'd often felt around him began to build up again. "Can I make you anything? A smoothie? A snack?"

"No. I was coming for water, that's all. I'll be out of your hair," he said, moving around me to the fridge to grab himself a bottle of water.

"There is something else I wanted to talk to you about, though, if that's okay," I started.

He cocked an eyebrow. "Is everything not okay?"

"No. It is. I mean, it isn't. What I mean is . . ." I walked over to my purse and pulled out the check that Kelly had given me. "I can't take this."

"It's a starting bonus."

"No, it's not. Plus, I found out what you did for my rent, and while I appreciate the gesture, I'd like to pay for that on my own too. So, if you could take those amounts out of my check each week, I'd appreciate it."

Confusion swirled in his eyes. When he blinked, a flash of regret hit his stare. "I offended you."

"No. It was really thoughtful, but I can't accept these kinds of favors. I don't want anything that I didn't work for."

He didn't say another word, yet he took the check from my hand and then placed his headphones back on. As he began to walk away, he paused and looked back toward me. His lips parted, but no sound came out. He took a deep inhalation and flinched a little as he tried again.

Was it always that hard for him? To gather his thoughts?

"Can you do me a favor?" he asked.

"Anything you'd like."

"When you make me a meal, can you make enough for Kelly, too?"

"Yes, of course. Not a problem."

He slid his hands into his pockets and thanked me.

"If there's anything else you need from me, I'm all ears. Truly, Oliver. I know I've said it before, but this job is more than I could've dreamed of. Thank you for the opportunity."

He almost smiled, and I almost loved it.

His full lips parted again to speak, but no words escaped him. Instead, he continued to walk away, leaving me wondering what it was that he'd planned to say.

—— ❧~⟋⟋⟍ ——

Later that afternoon, a voice snapped as I was preparing lunch for Oliver.

"Who are you?"

I looked up from the chicken breast I was slicing and smiled at the woman standing in front of me. Cam Jones. *The* Cam Jones.

Oh my gosh.

I loved Cam Jones.

She looked even more beautiful in person. She was wearing a sports bra, leggings, and a honey-colored wig, and her makeup was done flawlessly. Perfect winged eyeliner, top-notch lipstick. Cam looked like a goddess, and she was standing only a few feet away from me.

I dropped the knife quickly and hurried over to her side, wiping my hands against my apron. "Oh my gosh, hi! You're Cam Jones. It's so nice to meet you." I beamed, holding my hand out toward her for a shake.

She glanced down at my hand and then back up toward me. "And you are?"

"Oh. Right. You asked me that when you came in. I'm Emery, Oliver's new chef."

"Chef?" she huffed, narrowing her eyes. "I've been asking Oliver to get a chef for years, and he said it was ridiculous. Who have you worked for?"

"Um, well, no one, really. I've worked at restaurants and hotel dining rooms in the past, but—"

"You've never worked with another celebrity?"

"No."

"None? Not even a C-list celebrity? Like one of Alec Baldwin's brothers or something?"

"No . . ."

"Jesus. Where did Oliver find you? On Yelp?"

"Close." I snickered. "In a bar."

"You can't be serious." I blankly blinked her way and she gasped. "Oh my gosh, you're serious." Cam pursed her lips together. "Are you truly a chef?"

"I am. Kind of."

"Kind of?" She looked at me as if I had a horn growing from my forehead before turning away from me and shouting, "What school did you go to?"

"Well, I didn't exactly finish my degree. But you know what they say: 'Does every chef need an education in order to make great meals?'" And by "they" I meant Oliver.

Cam stared, looking horrified. "Yes! They do! Oliver!" she hollered, marching away from me and my extended hand that she never shook. "There's a strange woman in our house!"

# 12

## EMERY

Oh my gosh.

I hated Cam Jones.

It didn't take long for me to realize that Cam Jones wasn't the sweetheart I'd seen online. "Cruella de Vil" seemed like a more fitting title for her. I wouldn't have been surprised if she kicked puppies during her free time. Each day she came to me with an even more bizarre request. When I made her eggs, she'd tell me she didn't want them scrambled. When I cooked her hard boiled at her request, she'd toss them out and order me to make scrambled.

Each time she ate my food, she grimaced and only took a few bites. "This is why it's important to not just hire anyone from the street," she muttered once, after spitting out my chili-lime chicken salad—which, by the way, was fantastic. She was just too much of a jerk to admit that I'd created something delicious.

Oliver, on the other hand, devoured every meal I'd created, and he'd compliment me on them in his very few words way. "Fantastic." "Brilliant." "Great." "Seconds?"

That was a chef's dream word—"seconds."

What bothered me most about Cam wasn't how she treated me; it was how she treated Oliver. I had thick skin growing up with the parents I had—not much bothered me, especially from Cam, because it wasn't personal. It couldn't have been personal because she didn't know me. Her hatred and crude remarks said more about her than they did me. Yet with Oliver things were different. They knew each other—at least they should've. They'd been together for years.

He seemed so far removed from her, yet whenever she interacted with him, it was as if she were speaking down to him, as if he was the scum on the bottom of her shoes. She made comments on his appearance, on his vocals, on his talent. She judged the way he drank water, the way he wrote, the way he wrinkled his nose when he seemed displeased. Everything Oliver did, Cam seemed to have a complaint for. I was shocked she didn't mention the way he breathed as an annoyance.

Or the way he fiddled with his hands.

Or the way his eyes looked so lost whenever he blinked.

Or the way his soul seemed drenched in despair.

I didn't know Oliver personally yet, but I did notice all those things. I didn't find them annoying in the least. All I wanted to do when I saw the lost man in front of me was wrap him in my arms and tell him everything was going to be okay.

That might've been the mothering instinct in me—wanting to protect all the broken souls and let them know that they were loved. That was what I tried to do for Sammie. It didn't really work out in that situation, so I decided to keep my distance from Oliver.

Oliver never questioned her rude remarks or judgmental ways. He simply took them on as if he deserved her negative commentary. Or maybe he'd gotten to the point that he tuned her out so well that her comments didn't affect him. Either way, it wasn't okay, especially with everything that Oliver had been through over the past few months. If anything, she should've been his strength for when he grew overwhelmed.

She'd belittle him in front of me, too, which felt even more demeaning. Luckily, whenever she felt sassy toward me, it was always just the two of us. Yet a part of me did wonder how Oliver would react if he witnessed it.

"Why didn't you tell me?" I asked Kelly one afternoon as she sat in the living room, going over some paperwork.

"Tell you what?"

"About Cam," I grumbled, hating that I had to speak her name.

She stopped her work and looked up with a sparkle in her eyes. "That she's a terrible human?"

"Oh my gosh! Yes! You knew?"

"Oh, absolutely. I just figured I was too sensitive, though, so I kept it to myself. Plus, you seemed so excited to meet her that I didn't want to kill that dream for you."

"Consider the dream killed. She's evil."

"Yeah. She's not really my favorite person, that's for sure."

"So, she's really always like this? Flat-out mean? I'm stunned by the way she treats Oliver too. And he just takes it."

"The past Oliver would've stood up to her for some of her latest comments. I think he's holding on to a version of her that doesn't even exist anymore. Plus, now, after losing his brother . . ." Her words faded off again after bringing up Alex. It seemed that every time Kelly mentioned him, a part of her spirit began to crack. "He's just not fully himself anymore. It's like he's not even completely here, so Cam's comments hardly affect him."

"That's too bad. He shouldn't have someone making his life harder right now."

"Nothing about Cam is making Oliver's life easier, that's for sure."

"Is she rude to you, too?"

"All the time. She isn't nasty to me in front of Oliver, though. She's not that stupid. Because while Oliver won't stand up for himself toward her, he will stand up for others. That's just the person he is. So, Cam is very sneaky with her attacks. She knows exactly what she's doing."

Which made her that much more dangerous, in my mind.

# 13

## EMERY

As the days moved forward, Cam only became worse. Her sense of entitlement was so insane to me.

"Honestly, it's embarrassing how bad you are at your job," Cam remarked one Friday afternoon right before I was about to leave to get Reese from camp. My gosh, I was looking forward to the weekend away from her. "This juice tastes like dirt!"

*Well, you did ask me to only put beets and celery in it, but okay.*

I pushed out a fake smile. "I'm sorry to hear that. Would you like me to make you another one? Maybe one with apples and watermelon?"

She shivered at the thought. "No. That's too many carbs. I can't believe you messed this up. It's literally two ingredients."

"I did what you asked me to do."

"And still, you failed. I swear, it's hard to find good help these days. I should have Oliver fire you."

My chest tightened from the threat, but I wasn't scared. If anything, I was annoyed by her constant threats of having Oliver remove me from my position. She'd been saying it since my first day on the job. Kelly said it was because Cam was intimidated by how beautiful I was, which made no sense to me. She was one of the most beautiful women I'd ever seen.

On the outside, at least. Her insides very much resembled the devil.

"Here." She frowned in disgust, holding the cup out in my direction. "Get rid of this trash."

Geez. She sure had a Grammy-winner attitude, for never having had a Grammy nomination.

*Bite your tongue, Emery. Bite your freaking tongue.*

I kept that same fake grin against my lips as I walked in her direction. The moment I reached out to grab said cup, Cam flung the juice in my direction, coating me from head to toe in the red beverage.

"Are you fucking kidding me?" I shouted, my voice filling the space. I was never in the nature of snapping, but my gosh, she was pushing all of my buttons.

"Oops, sorry," she cooed, smiling innocently. "It looks like you've made a mess."

"Me? I didn't do this!"

"Yes, you did. You spilled it all over you as I tried to hand it off. Truly, you should be more careful. You probably shouldn't wear a white shirt, either, as a chef. It seems like a messy job."

The mirth in her face pissed me off that much more. "You're a, a, a, a—"

She stood to her feet and walked closer to me, standing as tall as she could in her red-bottom heels. "I'm a what?"

"A *bitch*!" I screeched, my rage boiling over and falling off my tongue.

"What's going on in here?" Oliver asked, walking into the space to find both Cam and me standing there in the heat of our argument. The juice dripped down my chin as anger forced my whole body to tremble.

"Did you hear that, Oliver?" Cam remarked. "She called me a bitch! Fire her this instant!"

Oliver looked at Cam and then toward me but didn't say a word.

She marched over to him like a prima donna, pouting. "Did you hear me, Oliver? Fire her."

Oliver moved in my direction, and my heart started racing faster as a heavy grimace sat on his face. He looked beyond irritated at the situation at hand, and since it was impossible to read his mind, my thoughts began to go to the worst-case scenario. I couldn't lose my job. Not at the hands of some wannabe superstar.

*Fire me because I burned the toast last week, fire me because my casserole came out a bit dry a few days ago, but please, don't fire me because of her.*

That would've given Cam too much pleasure—being able to watch my pain.

Oliver's brows lowered as he studied me and the mess that dripped from my clothing. His frown deepened. He reached for the towel hanging from the oven door, moved closer to me, and began wiping the mess from my face.

"What in the world are you doing?" Cam barked. Barking seemed to be one of her favorite pastimes. "Don't touch that thing."

Oliver ignored her and kept his eyes locked with mine. "Do you need a change of clothes?" he softly spoke, his voice low and controlled.

"Please."

He nodded once and turned to leave the room, and I followed, leaving Cam to throw her tantrum. "Are you kidding me?" she cried out, but Oliver didn't look back toward her for a second. I didn't, either. My eyes were focused on him.

He led me to his bedroom and walked to his closet. I stood as still as possible, not wanting to ruin his carpeting. Within moments, he came back with a pair of sweatpants and a plain T-shirt.

"Does this work?" he asked.

"Yes, thank you."

"You can change in my bathroom." He opened his mouth to speak more, but no words came, so he shut his lips together.

"What is it?" I asked, wanting to know what it was that was running through his mind.

"Nothing. I mean, well . . ." He took a breath. "Did she do that to you? Throw the drink at you?"

"Yes."

"Has she been rude to you before today?"

"Since day one."

The pained expression on his face made me almost frown too. "I'll speak to her about it."

"Don't apologize for her. She's a grown woman who is responsible for her own choices."

"Still. You work for me, and she shouldn't be treating the staff like that."

"I don't even understand. Is she like this with everyone? I've never done anything to her. I honestly went out of my way to be kind and give her whatever she requested. Like freaking beet juice." *Who drinks beet juice?*

"She's jealous of you."

"I don't know why she'd have anything to be jealous about."

"It's because you're a good person," he softly said. "That makes her uneasy because it highlights her flaws."

I was stunned by his comment, because it didn't make any sense to me. "Wait, you know she's not a good person?" Also, did he just call me a good person?

"Yes."

"Then why do you put up with her? I see how she treats you. She's mean, Oliver."

"She wasn't always like this," he confessed. "She used to be different."

"People sometimes change, and it's not always for the better." That was something I'd learned with Sammie. "I know love can make people do crazy things, but—"

"I don't love her anymore," he confessed.

Those were the easiest words that'd fallen from Oliver's mouth since I'd met him. He said it without an ounce of hesitation.

"Then why are you with her? Why would you stay with someone like that?"

His thumb brushed against his nose. "You wouldn't understand."

"Try me."

"If she wasn't here, I'd be alone."

"And what's so wrong with that?"

He paused for a moment and fumbled with his hands before sliding them into his pockets. "My mind doesn't do well when it's alone."

I felt that. True, I couldn't understand the thought completely, but I felt how much he meant it. Oliver Smith feared being alone, because that was the time when his mind spiraled the most. My mind used to do that when Reese was a baby, and I'd be awake late at night while she was sleeping. I'd fall apart and lose myself, but truthfully, it was in those moments when I learned to find myself.

"I'd rather sit in my loneliness than be lonely with someone who doesn't care for me at all. Are you truly that afraid to sit with your own thoughts?"

He rubbed the back of his neck as he told me his deepest truth. "You don't know how dark my thoughts can get."

The Monday after Beetgate, I showed up to Oliver's house and walked in on him and Cam in a shouting match. Well, Cam was shouting. Oliver was standing calmly in the living room with his arms crossed.

"I swear to you, Oliver, if you don't get rid of that wannabe chef today, so help me I will make your life a living hell!" she hollered, apparently not noticing that I'd walked in. I stood frozen in place, unsure of what my next steps should've been.

Did I turn around and tiptoe out like I hadn't been seen until the fighting came to a halt?

Before I could even think about leaving, Oliver glanced up and spotted me. I stood as still as possible, as if I were going to become invisible.

"Good morning, Emery," Oliver said, forcing Cam to whip around and look my way. The hatred that flashed in her eyes was almost intense enough to cut me. Still, I didn't move. I felt as if any form of movement would've given Cam a reason to snap at me.

Instead, she looked back to Oliver, who hadn't moved, either. She stepped closer to him, took her finger, and poked him hard against the chest. "Do it, or else."

Oliver didn't do anything. He brushed his palm against his stubbled chin and looked back toward me. His eyes seemed apologetic, and for a moment I didn't know why. I didn't know if I'd just walked into a conversation that was going to lead to my termination.

Oliver cleared his throat and kept his caramel eyes locked with mine. "Emery. Can you . . ." He blinked his eyes closed and took a short breath before looking back at me. "Make me an omelet?"

The pressure in my chest slightly faded as those words escaped his lips.

"Yes. Of course," I mumbled, nothing more than a whisper.

"Unbelievable," Cam spit out, shaking her head. "When you get a pair of balls, call me, Oliver. I'm taking a girls' trip."

With that, she grabbed her purse from the couch, then marched off in my direction and shoved past me, with her shoulder hitting mine. I stumbled a bit but didn't fall.

Oliver's eyes were still on mine. We both opened our mouths to speak but paused when we noticed the other about to talk.

I nervously laughed. "You go ahead."

"I'm sorry . . . for her."

"Like I said, you don't have to apologize for her. I do apologize to you, though, if I caused any trouble. I really don't want to come between you two. I'm just the chef, after all."

He narrowed his eyes and looked confused by my words, but he didn't say anything. He nodded once and spoke again. "I'll be in my studio. You can bring my breakfast in there."

"Will do. Any special toppings requests?"

His lips slightly turned up into an almost smile. "Whatever you make is good enough for me."

My heart did that skipping thing that it had done every now and again around Oliver. He was such a strange individual. He had a way of not saying much but saying so much at the very same time.

"Okay." I shifted in my shoes as Oliver began to walk away, and without thought I called out to him, finally asking him the question that had been running across my mind each and every day since I'd begun working for him.

He raised an eyebrow, waiting for my question, so I took a deep breath and asked, "Are you okay?"

His mouth twitched slightly before he gave me his answer. "No."

# 14

## OLIVER

I felt as if I'd been spending the past few months existing but somehow not being fully alive. Most of the time, the only thing that I'd been able to focus on was my music, because it was my safety net. Without it, I would've probably drowned.

Yet now, after seeing what had gone down between Emery and Cam, I couldn't help but wonder how much I'd been blind to over the past few months. I felt as if I'd been blind to Cam's actions over the past few years.

Which was exactly why I needed Kelly to tell me the truth. We sat in my office for our weekly meeting to go over sponsorship deals that I had coming up, but my mind couldn't truly focus on anything she was talking about.

I sat back in my chair and grimaced. "Is she rude to you?"

Kelly arched an eyebrow. "What?"

"Cam. Does she talk down to you? Is she rude?" The hesitation in Kelly and the flash of concern that flooded her eyes answered my question. I pinched the bridge of my nose. "Why didn't you ever tell me?"

"I figured it wasn't my place. She was around before you hired me. I didn't see it as my right to speak about your relationship when I was your assistant."

That made sense, but Kelly had since become more than my assistant. She was like family in my mind. The fact that Cam would treat family that way made my skin crawl.

"You know you're like a sister to me, Kelly," I said.

She frowned. "At one point, I thought that would actually be true . . . ," she muttered, speaking of her relationship with Alex. Shit. I was making things worse. She shook off her emotions, the ones she hardly ever displayed around me, and smiled. "It's okay. Really, Oliver. If you are happy with Cam—"

"I'm not," I confessed. I couldn't think of the last time I'd been happy with her. Even before Alex passed away, I felt as if Cam and I were becoming more and more like strangers. I was holding on to a Cam Jones who no longer existed.

"Then why are you still with her?"

That was the same question that I'd been asking myself over and over the past few days.

I shrugged. "Familiarity."

"Is she truly familiar to you, Oliver? Or are you just hoping the old version of her comes back one day?"

I knitted my brows as I clasped my hands together. "I feel as if I've lost so much this year already."

"Yeah, I know. I'm not here to tell you what to do. But if you're not happy with Cam, that's something worth exploring. You don't have to stay where things are familiar all the time. Sometimes the best way to move forward is to leave some things behind."

I nodded in agreement and thanked her for giving me her true opinion. We went back to discussing business, and in the conversation, Emery came up as Kelly was critiquing all the people I currently employed.

"And what are we thinking of Emery?" she asked. "I mean, I personally love her, so if you fired her, I'd be shattered. But what do you think? Do you think she's working out?"

"Yes," I replied, sitting back in my chair. "She's good."

"What do you want to talk about? I have a nail appointment in an hour, so let's make it quick," Cam said later that afternoon as we sat in the living room. The more I studied her, the more I realized she hardly ever looked at me. She was always attached to her phone, or she was staring toward me and ordering me around.

"Do I make you happy?" I flat-out asked.

She raised an eyebrow. "Excuse me?" I figured it was an easy enough question, yet Cam seemed baffled by it. "What do you mean do you make me happy?"

"I mean exactly that. Are you happy with me?"

"We're fine. Once you get your new music out, I'm sure we can take our relationship back into the public eye, which could benefit both of us. Plus, if we did a song together, the media would go wild."

How did I receive that answer to my simple question? It had nothing to do with our relationship at all. I stared her way and didn't know the person who was in front of me anymore. Even the small pieces of the old Cam that I used to witness seemed to be nothing more than a facade.

"Cam," I muttered, shaking my head. "Do I make you happy?"

"Why do you keep asking that?"

"Because you're not replying. Hell, we don't operate like a couple."

"That's because you're dealing with whatever it is you're dealing with—"

"Which brings me to my next topic . . . you never ask how I am. Which, I'm not blaming you, because I never ask you, either. We don't talk, Cam. Hell, we don't even sleep with one another. I don't have any idea what we're getting out of this relationship. If it can even be called that."

"What are you talking about, Oliver? We're building an empire together. We are the next Beyoncé and Jay-Z. If you would just—"

"I don't want that."

"Yes, I know, but I do. So, we are going to make it happen because I know how it can help us both. My career"—she paused, evidently noting her words—"our careers will take off after this, due to this relationship."

"I can't do it."

"Do what?"

"This. You, me. I can't continue in this relationship anymore, Cam. We're not happy. We're not in love."

Her eyes flashed with emotions, and for a split second I saw her. I saw the girl I once knew living behind those sad eyes. Yet before I could grasp hold of that girl, rage flashed before her.

The new Cam was back in full force. "You are really going to break up with me? Because we aren't in love?"

*Uh . . . yes?*

"I think that's a good enough reason to, yes," I agreed.

"What's love got to do with it?" she hammered. "I mean, honestly, Oliver. This is Hollywood! No one's in love!"

I felt sorry for her. I'd seen it happen to so many celebrities in the industry. Fame overtook them and swallowed their souls whole. I never thought it would happen to Cam, though. Years back, she used to have stars in her eyes. She used to daydream about performing for a crowd of one hundred people. She used to care about the music, about the art. Now, all she cared for was money and fame.

"I'm sorry, Cam. I truly hope you find what you're looking for, but it can't be with me."

She parted her lips in shock and then shook her head. Once the surprise had faded from her stare, a hardness found her as she released a weighted sigh. "You'll pay for it, Oliver. Just watch. You'll regret this decision. Mark my words."

She turned and walked out of the room, and with her went the deadweight that I hadn't known our relationship had been pressing against my shoulders.

# 15

## EMERY

Cam hadn't been back since she stormed out on Monday. I figured she was keeping her space until I left after my shifts. Oliver hadn't brought her up, but that wasn't shocking. Oliver didn't bring anything up to me. He simply thanked me for my meals, then put his headphones back on and went back to his work. Sometimes I'd ask if he was okay, and he'd reply no. Other times, I'd follow up and ask if there was anything I could do to make him better, and he'd say no again. That was the depth of our conversations.

I found myself thinking about him more often than not. When I closed my eyes, I'd see his sad stare. When I opened my eyes, I'd see his cracked frowns.

"Knock, knock," I said as I headed into Oliver's studio.

He looked up from the notebook in his hands. "Done for the day?"

"Yes. Dinner is in the fridge. You just have to toss it into the oven for forty-five minutes at four hundred twenty-five degrees."

"Thank you, Emery. I do have a request. The Fourth of July is coming up. My parents are coming into town. Kelly will be around, and Tyler will be, too, with his wife and two kids. Perhaps we could have a celebration, if you're free to cook for it. Of course, you could take part in the festivities, and Reese is more than welcome. She can use the pool, and I'll make sure to have some kind of entertainment for her and Tyler's two kids, who are around her age." His nervous fidgeting returned as he looked away from me. "Of course, if you already have plans—"

"I don't. And that sounds so fun. I've never done a Fourth of July party. I'm excited to get creative!" I exclaimed, maybe too excitedly. I was going to be on Pinterest looking up different ideas the moment I got home. Plus, I was certain that Reese was going to love the idea of having a party—even with people she didn't really know, as long as a pool was involved. "Oh my gosh, I can make minidesserts and all kinds of appetizers." I beamed with excitement.

I swore for a split second that Oliver smiled too.

"I'm glad. Thank you, Emery."

"Thank you. This is going to be so much fun." I bit my bottom lip. "Will Cam be in attendance, too? Maybe with her family? Just so I have a headcount."

He looked down to his notebook and then back toward me. "I don't think Cam is going to be around much anymore."

"Oh? Did you two . . . did you break up?"

"Yes, we are no longer seeing one another."

"Oh my gosh, Oliver. I'm so sorry. I hope it had nothing to do with me . . ."

"It had everything to do with you."

Guilt hit me at full speed. "I'm so sorry, Oliver. I didn't mean to cause any trouble for you, and—"

"Emery. I never said that was a bad thing. It was the choice I should've made a long time ago. You just helped make it clearer for me. Besides, you were right. I should learn how to sit in my loneliness for a while."

"If you ever get too lonely, you can reach out to me," I said without thought. His brows knitted at the comment, and I wanted to smack myself for saying such a thing. He didn't reply, so I took that as a "Hell no." I cleared my throat, feeling like a frog was crammed in there. "Well, you have a good night." I turned to leave the room.

"Emery, wait."

"Yes?"

"Earlier you said something that hasn't sat well with me."

"Oh?"

"You said you were just the chef." A softness flooded Oliver's eyes. "You're so much more than just the chef."

Those butterflies that Oliver delivered me every now and again? They came back intensely. My mouth parted, but I couldn't form any words.

"Good night, Emery."

"Good night, Oliver."

Later that night, I received a text message from an unknown number.

Unknown: What kinds of things is Reese into?

The mention of Reese's name made me sit up straighter on my couch.

Emery: Who is this?

Unknown: Sorry. This is Oliver. Kelly gave me your number.

The sigh of relief that hit me was strong.

Emery: Oh, sorry. I'm guessing for the party? She's really into any female superhero or Disney princess.

Oliver: Sounds good. Thank you.

Emery: Thank you!

I went back to my notebook, where I was drafting up a menu for the Fourth of July. To my surprise, my phone dinged again.

Oliver: How are you?

I was surprised by him reaching out to me again, and not only reaching out, but asking how I had been. Most of our conversations never led to much, and I couldn't think of the last time he'd asked me how I'd been. Especially at nine at night.

Emery: I'm good. How are you?

He didn't reply for quite some time. I figured that was what it was like living in Oliver's brain—a lot of overthinking going on.

Oliver: Did you come up with menu ideas for the party?

Emery: Are you avoiding my question?

Oliver: Yes.

Emery: Why?

. . .

. . .

. . .

Oliver: Because I don't want to bring down the conversation.

Emery: It's your first night without Cam, isn't it?

Oliver: Yes.

Emery: And you're lonely?

Oliver: You mentioned I could reach out if I got too lonely.

Instead of texting back, I dialed Oliver's phone number, hoping he would answer. Knowing him, it was a fifty-fifty chance. I never really knew which way he was going to travel.

"Hello?" he said, his voice seemingly deeper on the phone than in person.

There went those butterflies again.

"Hey, Oliver. I figured it would be easier to call and talk instead of texting back and forth. Are you okay?"

He cleared his throat. "Why do you ask me that all the time?"

"Because I want to know."

"But the answer's always the same."

"Yes," I said, nodding as if he could see me. "But someday it won't be. Someday you'll be okay."

"What makes you think that?"

"I just get the feeling that someday you're going to find it—your happy ending. This is just a temporary thing. Your sadness."

"I've been sad my whole life, Emery."

That fact made my heart crack a little. I wished I could hug him. "Why is that?"

He paused for a moment, in thought maybe. I could picture him with his stern look on his face. "I think some people are just born sadder than others."

I hoped that wasn't true. I hoped someday, Oliver would find his happiness. Find the place that made him feel free from all the sadness that surrounded him.

"Can we talk about something else?" he asked.

"Sure. What would you like to talk about?"

"Anything. Anything except me. Tell me about you. Or Reese. I want to know more about you." I bit my lip, not completely sure what to say, but luckily Oliver gave me a question to follow up the conversation. "What made you want to be a chef?"

"My parents. Kind of. They weren't around a lot during the week, because they worked at the church in my small town, and a lot of their time was spent there, super early in the morning and super late into the evenings for Bible studies. I came from a very religious town, where it was Jesus twenty-four seven. Not that there's anything wrong with that, but it would've been nice if my parents came home a bit more. So, while they were gone, I was responsible for making the meals for my younger sister and me. That's when I learned that I kind of loved cooking."

"How old were you?"

"Seven."

"Your parents left you alone at the age of seven to take care of your sister?"

"Let's just say their morals were a bit out of order."

"Do you still keep in touch with them?"

"Gosh, no. I haven't spoken to them in five years."

"Since Reese was born?"

"Yes."

"Did they not approve of you having her at such a young age?" He cleared his throat. "If I'm asking too many personal questions, you can tell me to stop."

"No. It's fine. My parents didn't really approve of anything I did. I never understood why they were so hard on me over my sister, but it is what it is."

"They were very religious?"

"Extremely," I laughed, thinking about the number of crosses that lived within my parents' house. Then I glanced around my apartment, which had just as many crosses.

"Did that make you less religious?"

"No, surprisingly. I rebelled against almost all of my parents' beliefs, as a way to show my teenage angst. But not when it came to God. My faith always stayed intact. What about you? Do you believe in God?"

"I want to," he confessed, "but it doesn't come easy for me to believe in a thing that seems so far away from me."

I understood that. But for me, when God felt far away, that normally meant I was straying myself.

We talked for hours more, about anything and everything, about nothing, about life. Within those hours, Oliver's hard shell began to soften. He even chuckled once when I told a poor joke. When it was time for us both to fall asleep, he thanked me for the call, to which I said, "Call me again tomorrow."

And he did.

# 16

## OLIVER

Emery allowed me to call her each night. When I didn't call, when I felt a bit too disconnected from reality, she'd dial my number to check in on me. From our late-night conversations, I was learning more and more about her. But when she showed up the next morning, I froze up. It was as if I didn't know how to talk to her in person. As if I was able to be more vulnerable with her on our calls than face to face.

I hated it. I hated how awkward I'd appear sometimes, not knowing how to communicate with her when she walked into a room. Mainly because she took my breath away. Everything about Emery was remarkable. From the way she cooked, to the way she dressed. To the way she loved her daughter, and the way she spoke with such a softness to her tones. Being around her made me uncomfortable, because a part of me didn't want her to leave. She felt like a safe place, and I'd never had that in a woman. I'd never had someone who'd stay up late on the phone with me just to make sure I was all right, outside of my family.

Emery did it with so much care too. She never seemed tired by our conversations, and I swore I could almost feel her light through the phone when she spoke about her life.

Whenever we hung up, I instantly missed her voice.

Then, when she showed up for work, I'd freeze up in front of her. She never seemed to care, though. She just remained her bubbly, kind self and made me some of the best meals I'd ever tasted in my life. I was thankful for that. For her ability to make my awkwardness less . . . awkward.

"You're staring at her," Kelly remarked as we sat at the dining room table eating our lunches. The more often I could get Kelly to sit down and eat her meal with me, the better. She was looking a bit better lately. The bags under her eyes were slowly fading away, and she laughed a lot more too. That was also due to Emery. Emery had that personality. The moment she and Kelly had connected, they'd become great friends. I was happy about that too. Kelly needed someone to lean on, and I knew I wasn't that person for her.

She was smiling more each day, which was a good thing. Emery had that effect on people. She made the saddest souls want to feel better.

"Staring at who?" I grumbled, looking back down at my salad. Out of the corner of my eye, I could see Kelly beaming ear to ear.

"You know who!" she whispered, leaning in toward me. "Oh my gosh. Do you like Emery?"

"Like Emery?" I pushed out a sarcastic laugh. "I don't even know her." That was a lie; I was learning more each day. She liked Scrabble; she hated Monopoly. She loved all genres of music, except for heavy metal. She'd had a goldfish named Moo that her mother flushed down the toilet when she was ten, and ever since then, she'd avoided seafood. She hated Reese's camp friends. Her favorite color was yellow, and her favorite season was autumn. And when she smiled with her lips, a faint dimple would appear on her left cheek.

She didn't tell me that; I just happened to notice.

"Then why are you blushing?" Kelly asked.

"I'm not blushing. Men don't blush."

"The lies!"

133

"It's true. Besides, even if I did like Emery—which I don't—it would be too soon. I just got out of a long-term relationship."

Kelly huffed. "Are you seriously calling what you and Cam had a relationship? I've had better relationships with stray cats on the road."

True.

"So, be honest. Do you like Emery?" she asked. Her lack of true whispering skills was making me nervous that Emery could overhear the conversation. "I won't tell. It's our little secret."

"There's no secret, because there's no truth to your question."

"Okay. Well, I guess you won't mind if I invited Emery to eat lunch with us," she said. She was acting just like an annoying little sister. Before I could oppose the idea, Kelly was calling Emery's name. "Did you eat yet, Emery?" she asked.

Emery peeked her head into the dining room, and a knot formed in my stomach. Then she smiled, and another knot joined the first one.

"No, I haven't yet."

"Great! Come join us." Kelly smirked as she looked my way with a guilty grin.

"Are you sure? I don't want to intrude," Emery said.

"No. You wouldn't be. Come sit right here, between Oliver and me." Kelly patted the seat right beside me, and within a few seconds, Emery was entering the room and sitting down. Right beside me. With her salad. And her smile. Her smile that was smiling toward me.

Oh fuck.

Maybe men did blush.

I turned my stare back down to my plate and started stuffing my face.

Kelly glanced down at her watch. "Oh, man! I forgot I have to shoot off some emails. I'll be back in a bit."

I sat up straighter. "Shouldn't you finish your lunch first?"

"No, no. I'll get back to it in a few. You two go ahead and eat and enjoy each other's company. I'll be back." She began to walk away, and

Emery's back was to her as I shot Kelly a death stare. *Talk to her!* she mouthed before slipping away.

Silence filled the space, and I didn't know what to do with myself. I kept overthinking every topic that I could bring up to her, so I went back to stuffing my face as Emery ate like a normal human.

I looked up toward the kitchen and saw Kelly peeking around the door toward us. She once again mouthed, *Talk!* So I swallowed the too-big chunk of chicken and began choking on it like a damn fool.

"Oh my gosh!" Emery gasped. "Are you okay?"

"Yeah, it's just"—I coughed, feeling the piece of meat sitting tight in my throat—"I'm"—the coughing grew worse and worse—"fine." I choked the last word out before the coughing became overpowering. Well, fuck. I was choking.

"Oh my gosh, here!" Emery said, standing to her feet. She walked behind me and pulled me up from my chair and began patting me on the back before she wrapped her arms around me and started giving me the Heimlich maneuver. Her small body flung my massive body around the room like she was an Olympic weightlifter.

"Okay, okay, hold on," she said. Then she began singing, yes, singing, "Stayin' Alive," by the Bee Gees, as she pumped her palms into my gut. She did it repeatedly as I searched for a breath of air, and on her final pump, the lodged piece of poultry came flying out of me and landed across the dining room table.

All of my pride went flying, too, with the piece of meat.

"Oh my gosh, Oliver, are you okay?" Emery asked, rubbing my back in circular motions, and oddly enough, I didn't want that movement to come to a halt.

"I'm fine. Yes. Sorry about that."

"Don't worry about it. Gosh, you scared me. Here, let me go get you some fresh water." Emery hurried into the kitchen, and Kelly was now standing in the dining room with her jaw dropped open in shock at the events that had taken place all within five short minutes.

"Well, that escalated quickly," she said, a small smile on her face.

"You think this is funny?"

"Kind of. Yes. All I wanted you to do was talk to her, and, well . . . that didn't happen at all. You seriously froze up there." She walked over to me and patted me on the back. "You okay?"

"I'm fine."

"Okay, good." A wicked smile fell over her. "Remember that time when I tried to get you to talk to Emery and you choked—both literally and figuratively?" she joked.

"Kelly?"

"Yes?"

"Shut up."

Needless to say, Kelly's matchmaking skills didn't go as she had planned, and I escaped to my studio to avoid any more embarrassment. I was still licking my wounds even after Emery left that afternoon, overthinking how idiotic I must've appeared as Emery thrust me around like a potato.

The only thing that disrupted my thoughts was Tyler coming over in a complete flurry of emotions.

"Did you see this?" Tyler barked, marching into my living room. He held his phone out toward me as he wiped sweat from his forehead. "Un-fucking-believable," he grumbled. "She's a freaking snake! I've always known she was a snake, but this is bullshit."

His nose flared as I took the phone from his hand and read the headline.

*Cam Jones Tells All about What It's Been Like Living with Oliver Smith*

Oh boy.

"You read that? Don't read that," Tyler said, snatching the phone from my grip. "It's trash. She's trash. Why would she even do that? What would make her go out to do that kind of interview?"

"I broke up with her a few days ago."

He looked at me, and his eyes flashed with glee. "You broke up with her? There is a God! You broke up with her!" he repeated, jumping up and down with bliss. Then, his joy seemed to dissipate as another reality set into his head. "Oh no . . . oh no, oh no, oh no . . ."

"What is it?"

"What is it? Dude. Cam is crazy. And now she's out there getting exposure on your breakup. Who knows what she's going to say?"

Before I could reply, my phone had started ringing. Kelly's name popped up across the screen, and I answered. "Hey, what's up?"

"Oh my goodness, she's insane!" she exclaimed—speaking of Cam, I assumed.

"Yeah, I saw the article."

"The article? No. She's on Channel Five right now doing a sit-down interview."

Within seconds, Tyler had switched the television on, and there she was, holding a tissue in her hand, speaking to the interviewer through her sniffles. Screw her singing career: Cam should've gone into acting.

"So, you're saying living with him was like living with darkness?" the interviewer asked her.

"Yes. It wasn't always like that. I knew Oliver suffered from depression, but I never thought he'd go to the level of belittling me in the way he had. He was cruel with the name-calling, saying I was worthless, putting me down on the regular."

"That's awful," the interviewer said, reaching out and placing a hand of comfort on her knee.

"Yes, it's . . ." Cam paused her words and turned to look away, seemingly emotional. "I'm sorry, it's just so hard to talk about. I did everything I could for him. We were all mourning the loss of Alex. I wished I had someone to lean on during all of this, but Oliver was so cruel."

"Did he ever hit you?"

"What kind of fucked-up question is that?" Tyler shouted, gesturing out of frustration at the television.

Cam looked up from her tissue, and the pained expression in her eyes signaled exactly what she wanted it to be seen as—as if I were abusive. As if I were a reclusive monster who'd made her life a living hell.

She didn't answer the question with her words, but oddly enough, her silence gave all the viewers exactly what she wanted them to receive. They'd think I was a monster. An abusive one at that.

Tyler shut off the television and kept cussing beneath his breath. "Shit, shit, shit, shit," he muttered, marching back and forth. "This is complete bullshit."

I didn't say a word, because what exactly could be said? My mind was spinning fast, coming up with all of the opinions that were being formed about me. I felt the heaviness of it all. I felt the disgust of others thinking that anything that Cam said held an ounce of truth. They thought I was abusive. They thought I was cruel. They thought I was the monster, when truthfully, I had just rid myself of the beast.

*I don't want to be here.*

"She's the fucking devil!" Tyler hissed. "How could she say any of that? I'm gonna get on the phone with PR and see how we spin this bullshit. Dammit. It's going to go viral. Fuck, fuck, fuck. I gotta get to work. You good, Oliver?"

*No.*

But of course, I lied. "I'm fine."

"Okay. I'm going to head off and do damage control. Keep your phone close and stay off-line, okay? Don't read any of that shit."

After Tyler left, I tried to turn to music to quiet my thoughts, but it didn't work. I was spiraling deep into my mind, so I turned to my next fix: alcohol. At that time in my life, I was trying to drink away reality for a short period of time. I'd started drinking by myself to find a numbness, because my thoughts were growing wild. But instead of being a smart drunk, I was an idiot.

I went online and googled articles about Alex & Oliver. I read people's comments on Cam's interviews. I looked up old YouTube videos of our concerts. I watched Alex do some of the best guitar solos in the history of forever, and I fucking hurt.

The alcohol that night didn't bury my emotions; it released them like a river of sorrow. I felt the pain of Alex's loss tenfold, and then I found comments on Twitter blaming me for his death. Blaming me for being an abusive asshole. Blaming me for being me.

It was bullshit. They didn't know me. How dare they throw their judgments from behind their keyboards as if they were saints. How dare they diminish the most important relationship in my life down to rumors and lies. How dare they hurt me without having a damn clue about how damaging words could be.

If humans knew how damaging words could be to someone's mental health and stability, then maybe they would've chosen them differently.

Then again, maybe they liked the outcome. Maybe some sick fucks enjoyed hurting others in a way to make themselves feel better about their own shitty lives.

Emery tried to call me a few times, but I didn't answer. I wasn't in the right mindset to talk to her. She would've given me comfort, and I didn't think that was something I deserved that evening. It wasn't until around ten that night that my doorbell rang. I stumbled to answer it, and when I peeked out to see who it was, I was surprised to see Emery standing there.

Shit.

What was she doing here?

She couldn't see me like that. I was drunk and in no state of mind to be dealing with her. She didn't deserve my heavy mind that night.

"Oliver? I hear you moving around. Can you open up, please?" she asked.

I sighed as I took a step away from the door. I brushed my hands over my black T-shirt and raked my hand over my face, as if that was going to make me appear less intoxicated.

I opened the door, and there she was. Little Miss Sunshine, holding a bottle of wine. The moment she saw me, her smile turned upside down.

"Hi," she breathed out.

"What are you doing here?"

"When you didn't answer my calls, I wanted to check in on you. I've seen the news about . . ."

Her words wandered off, but I knew what she was talking about. By this time, the whole world knew what she was talking about.

"I thought I'd bring wine, but it seems that you already found something to take the edge off."

I wasn't proud of it. The last time I'd had a drink was when I woke up in a Disney princess bed. Luckily I wasn't that far gone yet. If Emery hadn't come over when she had, there was a chance I would've ended up at that same level of drunkenness.

"Can I come in?" she asked.

I grimaced. "I'm not the best company right now."

"It's okay. We don't even have to talk, not really. I just want you to not be alone tonight."

"What about Reese?"

"My neighbor is watching her for the night. So . . . can I?" she asked again. I stepped to the side of the door, and she walked in. "Maybe instead of wine, we should shoot for water, eh?"

"I'm not really feeling up for water," I said, wanting whiskey.

"Well, we can do sparkling water and make it fancy. Did you know that if you add MiO to sparkling water it tastes just like Diet Dr Pepper? Random hack of the day," she said, as if everything was normal. As if Cam hadn't made some outrageous claims against me all over the internet and television today.

My throat felt tight as she wandered to the kitchen and came back out with two bottles of sparkling water. What did she think of me? What did she think of the rumors?

"Emery."

"Yes?"

"I . . ." I looked down at my hands and rubbed them together. "I never hit Cam. I would never do that. I would never lay my hands on a woman." The words burned as they fell from my mouth. I couldn't think of a worse rumor to be spread around about me. The thought that people were thinking such things, tweeting those kinds of comments, made me sick to my stomach.

"I know," she said, nodding, as if she didn't even need me to confess that truth.

"I feel like I need to make it clear that everything she said was—"

"A lie." Emery rested her free hand on my forearm and shook her head. "Oliver. I know. She lied about everything. I watched her lie straight to you when she spilled that drink on me. I watched her cruelness for days on end. I know what kind of person she is. You don't have to explain yourself to me. I know your heart. At least I'm slowly beginning to learn it, from what you're showing me."

"That's not how people see me online. They are saying the complete opposite of that, judging every part of me. They even brought up the idea that it was my fault that my brother died again."

"Which is all lies. You know that, right?"

I didn't reply, because my brain seemed to love to jumble up my thoughts, making it hard to know what I believed anymore.

Emery set the bottles of water on the coffee table and walked back over to me. She put her hands into mine and squeezed. "Oliver, those people who judge you the most are the ones who have never been close enough to you to hear your heartbeats. Their opinions don't matter at all. They don't get to define who you are with their lies. And every time you feel as if they are getting to you, I'm going to remind you of the truth."

"That's not in your job description."

"You're right, it's not. It's in my human description. That's what humans are supposed to do. We're supposed to look out for one another."

I wondered if she knew she was too good for the world we lived in. Not many people like Emery Taylor existed. Especially in my world. The entertainment business was built around the concept of people looking out for themselves.

"You don't really think that Alex's death was your fault, do you?" she asked me.

I tilted my head to lock eyes with hers, and I knew she saw it, because she slightly gasped. She saw my hurts, my demons that were sitting at the forefront of my eyes. She then turned to face me fully, crossed her legs, and squeezed my hands again. She linked our fingers together, and her warmth melted the frozen pieces of me.

"Oliver, it wasn't your fault," she whispered. As if she'd known the story I'd been telling myself for over seven months now. As if she saw my guilt-ridden soul and knew the words I needed to hear.

I was so close to falling apart, but I didn't want to do that in front of her. I didn't want to turn into any more of a pathetic fool in front of the first woman who'd made my heart feel things that I hadn't known hearts could feel.

"If you want, I can give you the name of my friend. She's a retired therapist, and she helped me through the lowest points of my struggles. Without being able to talk to her, I would've crumbled completely."

I swallowed hard and cleared my throat. "She helped you?"

"Yes."

"You trust her?"

"With my life." She squeezed my hands lightly. "How can I help right now, though?"

Every time she spoke, I felt a wave of comfort. Every time she touched me, I felt somewhat okay.

"Just stay with me for a while?" I asked, feeling stupid for saying it. Feeling insane for wanting it. But knowing I needed it.

"Of course. But can I ask you something?"

"Yes."

"Why don't you talk to me during the day? I know we've been having our nightly phone calls, but it feels different during the day. Almost as if you try to make yourself more distant."

"Sometimes I don't know how to be in the same space with you," I confessed. "You make me nervous."

"Why?"

"Because somehow you make me feel better, and I'm not certain if I'm allowed to feel better."

"Oh, Oliver," she sighed. "If there was one person on this planet who deserves to feel better, it's you."

I gave her a sloppy smile, unsure what to say. So, like an idiot, I said the first thing that came to my mind. "It was supposed to be 'War,' by Edwin Starr."

She arched an eyebrow at me, confused. Of course she was confused. My thought made no sense.

"You sang the Bee Gees when you were giving me the Heimlich. I believe you're supposed to sing 'War,' by Edwin Starr, and thrust at the word *Huh*."

Her smile grew ten sizes bigger as she covered her face in embarrassment. "Oh my gosh, I knew something was off!"

"I think the Bee Gees is for CPR."

"I'll keep that in mind when I give you mouth to mouth next time," she joked.

Even though it was a joke, the thought sat in my mind as my stare fell to her lips. Those full lips . . .

"So, uh, maybe we should move to the couch. Watch some television or something?" I said, tearing my thoughts and my stare away from her lips. She agreed, and we took a seat.

She sat close to me. As time went by, it felt as if she was growing closer. We watched a few movies. Well, she watched them, and I watched her. Every time she'd laugh, it felt like a burst of sunlight.

I didn't know when she fell against me. I didn't know how long we stayed pieced together. I didn't know how long my arms lay against hers and how long hers were wrapped around me, but I did know that I liked it. I liked the feeling of her smooth skin. I liked the honeysuckle smell of her hair. I liked the way she held on as if she had no plans to let go.

I liked the way that she stayed.

# 17

## OLIVER

Dr. Preston wasn't what I expected her to be. When she showed up to my house, I was expecting to find a woman in a business suit with a briefcase. Instead, I got a very vibrant woman with a wildly bright outfit. She wore thick-framed glasses, and I could almost feel her energy bursting from her being.

"Hi, Oliver?" she asked, holding her hand out toward me. "It's very nice to meet you."

I shook her hand. "Yes, Dr. Preston, it's nice to meet you too."

She waved a dismissive hand at me. "Oh, no. No 'Doctor' needed, really. Just call me Abigail. Can I come in?"

I stepped to the side of the door and welcomed her inside. I didn't know what to expect from the experience. I had my doubts that Abigail would be able to help me work through the mess that was my mind.

"Do you want to work in my office? Or . . . ?" I started.

Abigail gave me the warmest smile and shook her head. "Oh, we can go wherever you want. I'm flexible. Whatever makes you comfortable. This is about you, not me."

I chose the living room. She sat in the oversize chair, and I sat down on the sofa. My anxiety started to build up, and I was almost certain

Abigail had some sort of sixth sense, because she shook her head. "Don't worry, that's normal."

"What's normal?"

"Feeling like you don't know what's about to happen."

I snickered and pinched the bridge of my nose. "That's exactly what I'm feeling. I'm sorry, I'm new to this whole thing. I tried once, and well, the paparazzi kind of ruined that for me. I honestly don't even know why I decided to reach out to you. I don't know much, truthfully."

"Well, I do," she said matter-of-factly as she crossed her legs and leaned forward toward me. "You know why you reached out to me, Oliver?"

"Do tell."

"Because you got to the point of being tired of being tired. You are at the edge of despair, and you are looking for light. And when you start looking, it's good to know that the light is always there for you. My job is to help you get to it sooner rather than later. Now, I'm going to be honest with you: some days you're going to think I'm your best friend; other days I'm public enemy number one. But regardless, I'm on your team. I'm here to help in any way I can. Healing doesn't walk a linear line; it takes the messy route. I believe that healing comes during both the dark days and the bright ones. It's not all rainbows. Sometimes healing means slicing open the scars that made you hurt so much before and examining them to fully understand yourself. Why did the cut hurt you in the past? How did it change you into who you are today? What can we learn from the pain of your yesterdays to better your tomorrows?"

"It seems like a lot to unpack," I confessed.

"It is. But luckily, there's no rush. We get to unpack each bag as slowly, as carefully, as we choose. We're on your timeline, Oliver, not the world's."

That brought me a comfort that I didn't even know I needed to have.

Abigail leaned back in her chair and straightened her glasses. "So, you're a musician, correct?"

"Yeah, I am."

"Successful?"

"Yes."

"Did that make you happier?" she asked.

"No."

She nodded. "So, what you're saying is, outside success doesn't define a person's happiness?"

"Exactly." For a long time, I believed that money and fame would make everything okay. Truth was, there wasn't a dollar amount that could make a person happy if their soul was sad.

"So you already know the truth that so many people miss out on. True success comes from within. And that success is defined by being able to wake up and have gratitude. That's the goal. Now, that's not saying that everything is perfect when you are happy. That's not what happiness is. Happiness, gratitude, is the ability to wake up and say, yes, some things in my life are hard right now, but I still get to feel good about one or two things. You get to choose joy, even when times are tough. That's where we are going to get you."

"That sounds too good to be true."

"It always does in the beginning. So," she said, opening her colorful notebook. She grabbed a pen from behind her ear and began scribbling. "Tell me your truth."

"My truth?"

"Yes. Tell me the thing that you think more often than not. No matter how good or bad it is."

I parted my lips and felt ashamed of the thought that was sitting there on the back of my tongue. The thought that had haunted me for months now. "I don't want to be here."

"Here as in on Earth?"

I nodded. "I mean, I don't want to die either. But I have those thoughts. Sometimes it doesn't even feel like it's my own thought."

"Not every thought you have is yours. We live in a world where outside noise pollutes our minds. With you being a celebrity, I'm sure people are tossing thoughts and commentary your way all the time."

"Yes, exactly. There's so much noise in my head, and I don't know what belongs to me."

"We're going to figure all of this out, don't you worry. Regardless, that's a good thought to work with. I'm glad you shared that. Speaking that thought out loud gives it less power. And we are going to work through that thought over the next few weeks, okay?"

I nodded and she smiled. I didn't even think she knew how her smile worked, but it was powerful. The way she smiled my way made me feel as if I wasn't completely damaged goods.

"So now, tell me about your mixtape," she said.

"My what?"

"Your mixtape. I figured as a musician, this would be the best way to get to know your story. Every person in this world has a mixtape of sorts, a collection of tracks that defines their lives. Each memory is a song, and they all come together to create a masterpiece. So, tell me about your story. What lyrics, what melodies, live on your mixtape?"

In that moment, I knew I was in the right hands.

I took a deep breath, clasped my hands together, and began to speak about one of the most important songs on my mixtape. As the words sat in my throat, they burned, but I managed to push them out of me. I managed to share that painful song. "I had a twin brother named Alex who passed away almost seven months ago."

"I'm sorry to hear that, Oliver." Abigail looked up at me with sincere eyes and comforting tones. "Go ahead. Tell me a little about him."

# 18

## EMERY

Each day, I felt closer to Oliver. Not only did we have our nightly phone calls, but now during the day we also ate our meals together with Kelly. He asked me questions about my life, and I asked him questions about his. He never talked about his brother, and I didn't push for him to do such a thing. I figured he'd bring Alex up when he was ready to talk about him. But he told me a million other things.

He told me about his struggles with fame. He told me about his favorite book growing up. He talked about his fears of how he thought his music wasn't going to be good enough, and how he doubted fans wanted to hear it.

He opened up to me day by day, and every time he revealed a new piece of his story, my heart fell for him a little more. He was a beautiful man with a beautifully scarred soul, and the best part about it was that he didn't even know how beautiful he was. The broken pieces of his story were exactly what made him shine.

"Mama, do I really get to swim in Mr. Mith's pool today?" Reese asked me as we drove to Oliver's house for the Fourth of July party. I had all the food prepped and ready to be cooked up later that afternoon, but I was heading over to Oliver's early before anyone else arrived so I could set up a little more.

Even though fewer than ten people were going to be attending the get-together, I had enough food for an army. I didn't know why I felt so nervous about it all. Maybe because I was going to be meeting Oliver's parents. Not that it meant anything. Oliver and I weren't involved with one another. But still, my mind felt entangled by the idea of meeting the parents.

Reese's mind, however? She was focused on one thing and one thing only—the pool. She'd been going on and on about the swimming pool ever since I told her about it.

"Yes, but only when I finish cooking. You can't go in by yourself, since I'll be working."

"But Mama!" she cried.

"Don't 'but Mama' me, Reese. Those are the rules, and if we don't follow them, there will be no pool time at all."

She grumbled and whined the whole ride over, until we pulled up to Oliver's home. By that point, her eyes widened from shock, and her jaw dropped to the ground. "Oh my gosh," she whispered, staring at the mansion. "Can we just move here?" she asked, making me laugh.

"Probably not." I put the car in park and turned to look at her. "Now, remember what we talked about. Today, you're going to meet some new friends, do some of your coloring activities, help me make a few meals, and what else?"

She sighed and slapped her hand against her face. "And not ask Mr. Mith why his mirrors are covered in his house and not tell Mr. Mith that his music is garbage even though it is garbage because calling someone's music garbage isn't a nice thing to do."

I smiled. "Exactly. Now, come on. Let's get inside."

She was quick to unbuckle her seat belt and then hopped out of the car, pretty much sprinting toward the front door. The moment Oliver opened it, he gave Reese a stern look. "You here to give me a hard time, kid?" he asked with a smug look on his face. A sexy, sexy smug look.

Reese placed her hands against her hips. "Depends. Are you gonna give me a hard time, Mr. Mith?"

"It's Smith."

"That's. What. I. Said," she sassed, and goodness, those two together were going to be the end of me.

"Whatever, kid. How about you head straight back to the kitchen and see what my assistant, Kelly, got for you. She's in there waiting."

"You got me a surprise?" Reese said with narrowed eyes.

"I guess you'll have to go see for yourself," Oliver replied.

In an instant, Reese disappeared down the hallway toward the kitchen. The minute she made it in there, she gasped. "Oh my gosh, Mr. Mith! This is amazing! Mama, you have to come see this!" she screamed.

I smiled toward Oliver. "You really didn't have to get her anything."

"It's not a big deal. I figured she could use some things to keep her busy." He slid his hands into his pockets and gave me his halfway grin. "You look nice today."

I glanced down to my teal sundress and smiled. Then back to him in his dark slacks and smooth black crewneck that hugged every muscle on his body. "You don't look half-bad yourself."

We stood there for a moment, taking one another in, and I wondered if he felt the butterflies that I felt too. I wondered if his heartbeats raced at the speed of light like mine did whenever I was near him.

"Mama!" Reese screeched, demanding my attention at that very moment.

We walked into the kitchen to find a full-blown display of female superhero action figures and dolls, along with a cape that had Reese's name on the back of it. Kelly was already helping her tie it around her neck.

On the table were doughnuts that had small capes drawn on them too.

"Look, Mama! I'm a superhero!" Reese remarked, striking her power pose.

I snickered at her happiness as she jumped up and down. "This is too much," I told Oliver.

"No, it's just enough!" Reese exclaimed, picking up two of the action figures. "Look! It's Wonder Woman and Captain Marvel. There's even Gamora!"

"Wow, that's amazing. And what do we say to Oliver?"

Reese looked up and got a bit bashful. It wasn't every day that the very loud, energetic girl quieted down. She walked over to Oliver and wrapped her arms around his legs, giving him a hug. "Thank you, Mr. Mith, for being nice to me even though I told you your music was garbage before."

"Reese!" I scolded.

She looked at me with widened innocent eyes. "What, Mama! I didn't say it was trash again, even though it kind of still is," she explained. I didn't know what was worse—her words or the true confusion sitting in her eyes.

Oliver snickered and bent down to start tickling her. "Oh, you really think it's garbage, huh?"

Reese giggled nonstop as the two of them went back and forth. The sight of them interacting, the sight of Oliver playing and letting loose with my daughter, was the oddest turn-on to me.

*And that, kids, is how I met your father.*

Pregnant on the spot.

Kelly took Reese off to the dining room to enjoy their doughnuts and to play with the action figures while I began pulling out some of the things I'd prepped the day before.

"Wait, you can't cook without your gift," Oliver said, reaching for something hanging on the back of one of the stools. He held it up, and I started instantly cracking up at the apron in his hands.

"A superhero chef apron?"

"Seems fitting enough." He walked over to me and slightly nodded in my direction. "May I?"

"You may."

He slid the apron over my head, and when I turned my back to him for him to tie it, butterflies began to somersault in my stomach as he pulled the strings around my waist. For a second his fingers stilled. For a moment, his fingers brushed against my hips. His fingers then rested against my lower back. I shut my eyes and held my breath, feeling his proximity that close to me. I swore I felt his breaths brush against my neck. I swore, his body slightly pressed against mine. I swore, I wanted more . . .

"There you go," he said, knotting my apron in place and taking a step away from me.

I released the inhalation I'd been holding.

"Thanks." I smoothed out the apron and turned to face him, hoping he wouldn't see how flustered he'd made me.

His hands slid into his slacks, and he stood tall. He looked different today. Still handsome, still dreamy, but maybe . . . happier? There was something about him that seemed different. I couldn't quite put my finger on it, though.

"Everyone should be getting here in about three hours. So how can I help you?" he asked, rubbing his hands together.

I arched an eyebrow. "Help me? In the kitchen?"

"Yeah."

"Do you cook?"

"I can make a mean grilled cheese. I know you might use your fancy cheese and whatnot, and add avocado and fancy bacon, but my grilled cheese cannot be topped."

"Is that so?"

"It is. You'll be begging for seconds."

I laughed. "You'll have to make it for me one day, then."

"I look forward to that. So, what can I do in the meantime to help?"

153

"Uh, nothing."

"What?"

"I'm sorry, Oliver. I'm not letting you near any of the food I'm pre-paring for today. It's too important for me that everything be perfect."

"It doesn't have to be perfect. It's just a few close friends."

"And your parents," I added.

He raised an eyebrow. "You're trying to impress my parents?"

"Maybe."

"Why?"

"Uh, I don't know . . . maybe because they're your parents?"

He gave me a sly grin, and the amount he'd been smiling over the past few days made me want to wrap my arms around him and hold him close. Maybe that was what was different. He was smiling.

"You're smiling more," I commented, allowing my thoughts to leave my head.

"Am I?"

"You are."

"I must be in good company."

*Oh, Oliver. Don't make me blush.*

"Why are you single?" he asked, throwing me completely off.

I turned to him and raised an eyebrow. "What?"

"Sorry. I've just been wondering. You're a good woman. I mean, not that being single means you're not a good woman. What I mean is, do you?"

"Do I what?"

"Date."

*Oh.*

"Well, after Reese, I had a hard time even getting dressed in the morning. Then, as she grew older, I was always working two jobs at least. Time wasn't really on my hands to be dating. Plus, growing up, I never really saw decent relationships. So it hasn't been at the forefront of my mind."

"So you have no interest in it?"

"In dating? If it were the right person, I guess."

"What makes a person the right person?"

I was surprised at all the questions he was shooting my way. Each day it seemed as if Oliver's words flowed easier when he was around me. As if he were getting out of his own way with his thoughts.

"Oh, I don't know, someone who's caring. And romantic. And kind. Loves kids, obviously. Someone who listens. Someone like . . ." *You* . . . "Someone like that. Someone who makes me feel like home."

"I see." His brows lowered. "Someone who makes you feel safe."

"Exactly. Who makes me feel like I belong."

"You do that to me," he confessed. "Make me feel like I belong. No one has done that since my brother."

His brother.

He'd finally brought up Alex around me.

Before I could ask him anything about it, a voice burst into the kitchen, breaking into our conversation.

"Oliver, we need to talk before the get-together tonight!" Tyler said, barging into the room. "My wife said I'm not allowed to bring up work stuff today, so I came over early to get work stuff out of the way!" He paused the minute he noticed our proximity to one another. "Uh, am I interrupting something?"

"Mama, I dropped my doughnut and ruined my shirt!" Reese exclaimed as she shot into the room just as quickly as Tyler had. "Can I have another doughnut?"

"How about we get you cleaned up first," I said, taking her hand into mine. I looked back at Oliver, who was looking my way. A sad smile crossed his face as he turned to go talk to Tyler, leaving our conversation unfinished at the most important part.

# 19

## OLIVER

"Do we have to do this today?" I asked as we sat in my office with the door shut.

"We most definitely have to do this today. I've been working with the PR team for the past few days trying to figure out how we dig ourselves out of this mess with Cam. And the best thing that we could come up with was you doing a live sit-down interview with one of the biggest stations. You know everyone will want to talk to you. You haven't done an interview since . . ." His words faded. Since Alex passed away. Tyler shifted in his chair. "Anyway, we need to put you out there. We need to show your face to be put out there. Otherwise, it paints you in a terrible light."

"I don't do interviews," I said. I hated interviews. I bombed most of the interviews I'd ever done. The only reason they seemed semidecent was because Alex had made them great. For all my flaws, he showcased his talents.

"You have to, man. These type of allegations against you can ruin your career, and even more so, your life. You can't let someone like Cam ruin your life. You deserve to tell your side. The truth."

"Even if I told the truth, would they believe me?"

"I don't know." He shook his head. "But if you say nothing, they'll definitely believe her. Just think about it for a minute, all right? I know it's the holiday, and I won't bring it up again, but this is a big fucking deal, Oliver. We have to handle it sooner rather than later. Especially if you're thinking of dropping new music."

I knew he was right, but that didn't ease my anxiety about it. I had a history of having interviewers twist my words and take things the wrong way. I knew for a fact that if I spoke, some questions would build up in my anxious mind, and I wouldn't have my other half there to pick up my slack.

Tyler headed out to pick up his family for the gathering, and a few hours later my house was packed with kids running around and diving in and out of the swimming pool, with Kelly supervising them as Emery finished up the final touches on setting up her serving table. Everything smelled delicious, and I wasn't surprised.

The only thing left to do was grill some of the meat, which Emery wasn't allowed to do. My dad had a rule that only he could grill, since he was a Texas man and knew a thing or two about making meat tender.

When my parents finally arrived from the airport, I met them in the driveway. Mom beamed with excitement when she saw me. "Ollie! Come here, oh I missed you!" she said, wrapping me into a tight hug. "How's my babe doing?"

"I'm good, Mom. I thought you would've been here sooner. I sent the driver a while ago."

"Well, you know how this LA traffic is. It's bullshit," Dad stated.

"Richard! Do you have to use that language around our son?"

"Oh, hush, woman. Oliver writes songs about oral sex; I think he is grown enough to hear me say 'bullshit.'"

"He does not write songs about that!"

"What do you think 'The Falls' is about?" Dad asked her, and hell, only a few minutes had passed, and my parents were already talking about the sexual lyrics of Alex's and my songs. My brother was lucky to be missing out on that moment.

"The Niagara Falls!" Mom exclaimed, making me chuckle at the idea. She was so sincere and honest with her reply.

"Woman, that's a sexual innuendo," Dad told her, shaking his head in disbelief. He'd grown a beard since I'd last seen him, and it looked good on him. He'd put on some weight, too, which also looked good.

"How is that a sexual innuendo?" she asked.

"You really want to know?" he questioned.

"Yes, I really want to know."

"Okay, well, remember when we were in college and you came over for a study date, and I did that thing with my fingers to your—"

"Whoa, whoa, whoa, oversharing much?" I barked, knowing exactly what he was talking about and wanting to delete the image that had formed in my brain forever.

Mom's mouth dropped open, and she slowly nodded. "*Ohhh*, the Niagara Falls!" She grinned bright and shimmied a little. "I love the Niagara Falls. We should take a trip there tonight, Richard."

Oh dear God.

"If you both could stop talking, that would be wonderful," I begged.

"Don't act like you're innocent, Oliver. You did write the song, after all." He moved toward me and patted me on the back. "Happy Fourth, buddy. Please tell me there's food inside, because I am starving."

"We just need to get you on the grill, but there's enough food for a football team in there," I said.

"Or for your growing pop," he said, rubbing his stomach. "I start Weight Watchers on Monday."

"He said that last week, too," Mom chimed in. "Then we ordered pizza."

"Deep dish and delicious. But I'm really starting next week. Scout's honor."

"Mm-hmm, we'll see when Taco Tuesday comes around and you want margaritas," Mom said, smacking Dad's stomach.

"You're right, I should start next Wednesday," Dad agreed. "Now come on, let's get a move on so I can get the grill started."

We headed inside, and my parents greeted everyone with big hugs, because that's who they were—huggers. I swore, they'd hug every stranger they met if they could. We walked into the kitchen to find Emery finishing up the spread, and she looked up with a big smile on her face.

"Oh my goodness, it looks like a Thanksgiving feast in here," Mom exclaimed.

"Smells like one, too," Dad said as he grinned. "You must be Emery."

Mom was already rounding the corner to pull Emery into a hug, and without any thought, Emery fell into her arms. "I'm Michelle, and this is Richard. We're Oliver's parents."

"It's so nice to meet you both. I'm so glad you made it."

"Me too. Oliver has told us so much about you!" Mom said.

Emery looked my way with a sheepish grin. "Is that so?"

"Not *so* much," I countered. "I may have mentioned you in passing conversation."

"Are you kidding me?" Mom gasped, shaking her head. "Oliver went on and on about how you have made some of the best food he's ever had. Why, just last night he was telling me all about you and how—"

"Mom," I groaned, shooting her a stern look.

Her cheeks flushed over. "Oh no. There I go talking too much. It's nice to meet you, Emery. How about I just leave it at that."

"Mommmm!" Reese screeched, racing into the kitchen from the backyard, wrapped up in a towel and dripping water from the pool throughout the house. "Mom! Mom! I made two new friends Catie and Garrett and they are so much cooler than Mia and Randy and and and

159

their mom said I could go to their house sometimes and make cookies and stuff and and and, who are you?" Reese breathed out as she looked toward my parents after rambling off a million words a second.

Mom smiled to the little girl and bent down to meet her at eye level. "I'm Michelle, and this is my husband, Richard. We are Oliver's parents."

Reese's eyes bugged out. "You made him?"

"That's right," Mom said.

"Like, he was in your stomach?"

"Yup, yup."

"How?" Reese questioned. "He's so big." We all laughed, and she looked confused as to what was funny. "That's my mom over there, and I was in her stomach when I was a baby, too," Reese said matter-of-factly.

A flash of despair washed over Emery's face as those words left her daughter's mouth, and no one else caught it, because they weren't looking her way. It disappeared as quickly as it had shown up.

"Anyway, Mom! Can I go to Catie and Garrett's house sometime?" Reese said, coming back around to her main point.

"We'll see, honey. But how about you get back outside. You're dripping water all over the house."

"Okay, Mom, thanks." She dashed out of the room as fast as she entered, yelling, "You guys! My mom said yesssssssssss!"

"And that right there is my daughter, Reese," Emery said. "The energetic bunny."

"She's adorable and looks just like you," Mom said.

Emery simply smiled and didn't say anything else.

Dad rubbed his hands together. "So, I'd better get a quick bite before Oliver and I get the grill going." Without any hesitation, he dived straight into the meatball sliders, groaning in pleasure as he bit into one. "Holy moly, this is good. You weren't kidding, son. She is amazing."

"Amazing, huh?" Emery asked with a smirk. "You think I'm amazing."

"Yeah, they were. You said she's freaking amazing. I have a memory like no other," Dad argued.

"All right, how about the two of you head outside and get the grill fired up. You're talking too much," I ordered, shooing my parents away.

"I can tell when we aren't wanted. Okay. We're going. It was a pleasure meeting you, Emery. Hoping we get some time for some girl chat later on," Mom said, winking her way.

*Why the wink, Mom?*

The two of them took each other's hand and danced their way to the backyard, because that was what my parents always did with one another—they danced and joked and loved on each other.

The only time they'd ever stopped dancing was when Alex passed away. I was happy they'd found their rhythm again.

Emery was still smirking my way with her hands on her hips.

"What?" I asked.

"You think I'm freaking amazing, huh?"

"Oh God. Don't let it go to your head." I dramatically rolled my eyes as I popped one of her apps into my mouth.

"Too late. The ego has been inflated. I am freaking amazing, and no one can tell me differently."

I shrugged. "You're average at best."

Her jaw dropped open. "You're lying."

"I'm lying."

She smiled.

I smiled.

My gosh, I was beginning to fall in love with that woman's smile.

"I should go ahead and help my dad with the grill. But yeah." I rocked back and forth in my shoes. "We'll talk later."

"Wait, before you go." She leaned forward and rested against the countertop. "Can you tell me how freaking amazing I am?"

# 20

## OLIVER

"Well, I'll tell you what, that Emery girl can really cook," Dad said as he and I sat in the studio while everyone else was outside waiting on the fireworks to begin, although they wouldn't start for a few hours. We'd spent the past few hours celebrating the holiday outside, and I wanted to share some of my new music with him to try to get his input.

"She's a very nice girl, too," Dad added.

"She's a hard girl not to like."

"Based on her cooking skills, I see why you like her, too," he joked. "So, is she?"

"Is she what?"

"Your girlfriend?"

"What? No. We are just . . ." What were we? Associates? Friends? Were Emery and I friends? "No. She's not."

"But you like her, and don't go lying to me trying to deny it. I'm your father, and I know when you're lying. All those years dating that Cam girl, and I ain't ever seen you look at her the way you look at Emery. She must mean something big to you."

I agreed. I knew it had only been a few short weeks since I'd met Emery, but she was the first woman I'd ever found myself opening up to be with. I knew if I was going to be hers, I had to crack open the layers of myself that I normally kept to myself.

"She showed up at a time that I felt extremely alone."

"I believe that," Dad said with a nod; then he clasped his hands together and cleared his throat. "Which brings me to my next point, a point I want to make really clear to you. It wasn't your fault, son."

"What?"

"What happened to Alex. It wasn't your fault."

I went to respond, but Dad shook his head and placed a hand on my shoulder. "I know you, son. I know how you work. And I know you've placed that blame on yourself. I know the media spun that story, and it probably came back to you more than it ever should've, but I'm here to tell you it's not your fault."

I clasped my hands together and looked down. "I know that's true. It's been hard. I don't know how to explain it. If it wasn't for me, he wouldn't have been in that car."

"You can't think like that. The fault of the accident were those idiots speeding down the road like psychopaths. I blame them for what happened to your brother, not you."

"You don't blame me?"

Dad sighed as he pinched the bridge of his nose. "Never. I'm here to say that thought never for a second crossed our minds. Also, you have to reach out to us when you're struggling, Oliver. You are never a burden to your mother and me. We are always here for you, through the shitty days especially. It's easy to have people who ride for you during the peaks, but we want you to know that we are here during the valleys. Especially during the valleys."

I clasped my hands together again and stared down at them, my mind connecting the dots to exactly what my father was saying. "It wasn't my fault?" I asked with a hoarse tone splitting through my words.

"It wasn't your fault."

A relief that I didn't think I deserved hit me. I slowly began to let go of the guilt that I'd been hanging on to since the day Alex left my side.

I wiped my hand beneath my nose and cleared my throat. "Thanks, Dad."

"Welcome. Now, play me some of your new music, and let me make it better."

It was a long time ago, almost ten years, since my dad had helped me with the music in my studio, but I'd never forgotten that he was the man who'd made Alex and me fall in love with music. He introduced me to the greatest artists of all time when we were children, making sure every classic was in our lives, from Sam Cooke to Frank Sinatra. Our house was always lit up with the sounds of the greats.

Dad worked in the music industry for a while as a technician, and he was the one who'd built Alex and me our first studio when we were teenagers.

Without his guidance, none of our dreams would've come true.

I played the tracks for him, and he listened with an attentive ear. He usually didn't give me feedback until a song had finished, and then he'd sit back, purse his mouth, and nod. "It's good. It's good."

"But?"

He didn't go into the buts at first—he never did. Dad wasn't one to criticize a piece of music before pointing out all the good within it. That went for any and every song. He said every piece of art held ounces of beauty.

I was thankful for that. I needed some good feedback. "But . . . ?" I said again, after the compliments had come in.

"What if we tried this?" he asked, standing up and tweaking with the equipment. We stayed in there for hours, creating. We took pieces we'd made, broke them apart, and stitched them back together. We had . . . fun.

When we finished a song, once it had turned into something that made me feel proud, we stood in silence for a minute, almost in shock.

Dad patted me on the back and grinned. "Alex would love this."

I smiled, because I knew he was right.

"Play it again," Dad told me. "It's too good not to hear again." So I did as he said.

"Mr. Mith! Mr. Mith!" Reese chanted, racing into the studio to get my attention. She was out of breath as she waved me over. "Come on! Hurry!"

"Hurry for what?" I questioned.

"The fireworks, duh."

We headed outside to the backyard, where the display of fireworks could be seen over our houses. Everyone was sitting on the ground around the pool, looking up at the colorful sky in complete awe at the beauty. The three kids were jumping up and down with excitement screaming oohs and aahs, giggling with one another at how big, bright, and loud the fireworks were.

I took a seat on the ground beside Emery, and it didn't take Kelly long to give me a stupid smirk about that fact. I tried my best to ignore it. Emery turned toward me with her knees bent and her arms wrapped around them. Then she looked back up to the sky.

"Beautiful, right?"

"Yes. Stunning."

*Say something to her.*

*Something that makes sense, though.*

*But something that matters too.*

*Just talk.*

*Say something!*

"I'm sorry," I sputtered out.

"Sorry? For what?"

"For having you cook on a holiday. I've been overthinking it since I asked. I should've just invited you over and hired a caterer. It was rude of me to ask. Sometimes I don't think things through until I overthink it and—"

Her hand fell on my forearm. "Don't overthink this one, Oliver. Today was so fun, and it gave me a chance to do what I love the most. Being able to cook for you has reminded me so much of who I want to be. This is my passion, and because of you I'm able to make it come to life."

I sighed, relieved. "Good. I'm glad."

"Are you okay?" she asked me, posing her normal question.

"I'm all right today."

Her eyes flashed with emotions, and her hand, which was still on my arm, squeezed so gently. "Really?" she asked, getting emotional. You would've thought I'd said it was the best day I'd ever had.

"Yeah, really. Today was good." The tears that were sitting at the back of her eyes began to fall, and I lightly chuckled. "Don't cry, Em."

"Sorry, gosh, it's all the wine your mom has been giving me, I swear," she laughed, taking her hand away from my arm and wiping her eyes. The moment her hand left my skin, I missed her touch. "It's just . . . since I've been asking you how you've been, that's never been the answer. That makes me so happy, Oliver." She was overly emotional about it, which made me feel bad for making her that way.

"I didn't mean to make you cry."

"Happy tears," she said, laughing a little. "Just happy tears. I'm really happy for you. You deserve good days."

"Emery?"

"Yes?"

"Are we friends?"

Her brown eyes smiled more than her lips. "Of course we are."

"Okay, good." I felt myself becoming uncomfortable, feeling stupid for even asking her that question. But ever since my father asked me what Emery and I were, I truly wanted to know. Because in my mind, we were friends, but sometimes my mind lied to me.

"I like that about you, you know," she commented.

"What's that?"

"How shy you get at times and how you overthink things. I mean, let's be honest. You might be thinking just enough, and the rest of the world is underthinking. Perspective," she joked.

I gave her a half smile, and she gladly gave me the other half.

"I like when you do that too. Smile."

Seemed as if I'd been doing more of that ever since she'd come around.

Shortly after, Reese came dashing toward me. "Mr. Mith! Can I sit in your lap to watch the fireworks?"

I shifted around and held my arms out toward her. She hopped into my arms and rested against me as she looked up to the sky. I noticed that Catie and Garrett were sitting in Tyler's arms, and I was certain that was where Reese got the idea.

I held her tighter as she laid her head on my shoulder. I could tell she was getting tired, which wasn't shocking after the active day she'd had with her new friends. Her eyes were somewhat open as she tried to watch the fireworks overhead. She yawned with her mouth wide open before snuggling against me.

"Mr. Mith?" she whispered.

"Yeah, kid?"

"The music I heard you playing with your dad didn't sound like garbage."

Within seconds, she was asleep in my arms, not knowing how much those words touched me. That little girl was adorable in every way possible. From her dark hair to her bright smile. I swore she had Emery's eyes too. And her button nose, and her heart. I had no doubt that Reese had her mother's heartbeats.

After the fireworks show came to an end, I placed the sleeping Reese in one of the spare rooms of my house. Kelly and Tyler both headed out, exhausted but with smiles on their faces. Mom and Dad were still drinking and dancing outside with one another, because that was who they were, and they'd dance all night if their feet allowed it.

Emery was in the kitchen trying to clean up the mess that had piled up throughout the evening. I walked over to her by the sink and placed a hand on her shoulder. "You don't have to do this tonight. I'll handle it in the morning."

"Oh gosh, no way. I can get it all cleaned up. It's not a big deal."

"It's been a long day. I'm sure you're exhausted."

"I'll get to sleep in tomorrow. It's really okay."

"Let me help you," I offered.

"Don't tell me you two kids are in here cleaning," Mom said, coming into the kitchen with an emptied glass. "You should be outside with us drinking up some wine and dancing! Come on," she said, waving us in her direction as she went to pick up another bottle of wine.

"Oh, I would love to, but I'm already still a little tipsy, and I have to sober up to drive Reese home."

"That's nonsense. Just stay the night. Oliver has more than enough space for you both. Isn't that right, Ollie?"

"Of course. I have some extra pajamas you can borrow too. It's probably best not to be driving this late at night on the holiday too. You're more than welcome to stay."

Emery hesitated for a moment, nuzzling on her bottom lip.

"Come on, Emery. We only get this one life. We might as well make some good memories with it," Mom said, sounding very carpe diem. It must've been the wine talking.

"Well, okay. If I stay I can clean up a bit better in the morning when I'm sober," Emery said, before turning toward me. "Are you sure it's not a problem?"

"Of course he's sure," Mom said, waving me off and grabbing Emery's hand. "Now, come on—let's get outside and dance. That way Richard and I can teach you both about the good ol' music from the old days."

The two of them walked off, leaving me with a strange feeling in my chest.

For the first time in a while, my heart felt full.

# 21

## EMERY

The energy of the day was so wonderful to take in. Exhaustion was present, but it was the good kind of tiredness. An exhaustion that came from an outstanding time. Watching Reese find two friends who weren't bullies felt like the highlight of the day for me. The second highlight was hearing that Oliver was having a good day. And the third highlight? Oliver's parents.

Watching Oliver's parents felt like watching an old romantic movie. His parents were the most caring and attentive people in the world, and the way they looked at one another and laughed together was what dreams were made of. I wanted that someday—a love that lasted throughout the decades.

Those two loved in a way that made other humans swoon in their presence.

The four of us were gathered in the backyard, listening to old-school music, and I swore we laughed more than I thought possible. Oliver seemed more himself than I'd ever witnessed, and I could tell it was because his parents meant so much to him.

"I swear Oliver has the most intense favorites playlist on his phone," Richard commented, shaking his head. "What number is it at?"

"Six hundred and sixty-eight," Oliver remarked.

*"Six hundred and sixty-eight!"* Richard repeated. "Those aren't favorites. Those are just songs! A favorite list should have a max of ten, tops. Otherwise, it's just a list of songs."

I pulled out my phone and opened my music app. "Well, I have eight hundred and ten on my favorites list," I said. I smirked over to Oliver and arched an eyebrow. "Step up your game."

"You two should exchange playlists to see if you have any favorites in common," Michelle said. "It might take days to get through the lists, though."

"I'm still stuck on the over eight hundred songs of favorites." Richard's jaw was wide with disbelief. "You youngsters are doing too much. I could listen to the same ten songs over and over again and be a happy man."

"You do listen to the same ten songs every day," Michelle groaned, rolling her eyes.

"You act like you don't like them just as much as me, woman. Speaking of, Oliver, come help me put my top-ten playlist on the speaker. I'll show you all good music in under ten songs." The two men headed off to the sound system to hook up Richard's phone.

"You two have the greatest bond," I said to Michelle as her husband danced around to Biggie Smalls while he scrolled through the playlist on his phone with Oliver.

"We're just a bunch of nutjobs. It's how we stay sane. I swear, if I hadn't had Richard by my side these past few months, I would've crashed and burned."

"I can't imagine how tough things have been for you with your loss. I'm so sorry. I'm glad you had Richard."

"I'm glad too. He's my anchor. My weird, oddball anchor. What about you? Are you close with your family?"

My whole demeanor shifted, and she witnessed it happen. I shook my head. "No. My parents and I are the complete opposite of close. And my sister . . . we grew apart." Sammie had actually reached out to me earlier that day. She wished me a happy Fourth of July, and I didn't reply to her message. That was the first time she'd gotten in touch since hanging up on me during my time of need. I couldn't for the life of me bring myself to respond to her message. I was still too hurt by the way she'd shut me out. Then, she had enough nerve to text me as if nothing ever happened.

That was the thing about Sammie: she disappeared and reappeared on her schedule. That wasn't fair to me, though.

Michelle frowned. "I'm really sorry to hear that. I come from a disconnected family, too, so I know how hard that can be."

"Yeah, it's hard. But at least I have my little girl. She's the only family I truly need."

"She's beautiful. Truly your twin. Seeing how Oliver and her connected was so touching. Gosh, it's good to see him like that. Smiling."

"Isn't it? I'll be honest, it took a bit of time before he shared his smiles with me."

"Why do I get the idea that you might be responsible for some of those smiles?" she asked, making cool chills race across my arms. "You have a great spirit, I can tell. I'm good at reading people."

"I wish my own mother felt that way about me," I muttered. It hadn't even been eight hours since we'd met, and Michelle had given me more compliments than my mother ever had. "I'm actually very envious of watching you and Richard with Oliver. My parents and I are nothing like that."

"I know that feeling well. I wasn't close with my parents, either," Michelle said, sipping her glass of wine. "Well, at first I was, but after I brought Richard around for them to meet, they had very strong views against it because he didn't really come from money. I grew up with wealth like no other. My father and mother were both very successful lawyers. Richard's family was the complete opposite, living on food stamps. My parents hated the fact that I was dating someone lesser than me."

"I'm so sorry. I can only imagine how hard that would be. To be torn between two worlds."

"Yes, it was. I was only sixteen when I met Richard, and I was smitten right away. My father told me he'd disown me if I kept seeing him, and my mother told me I'd be alone forever, because she had no doubt that Richard would never be able to provide for me. They told me to make a choice, Richard or my family."

"They wanted you to decide that at age sixteen?"

"Yup. Either I walk away from Richard, or I walk away from them."

"What did Richard say about it?"

She smiled a sad grin and shook her head as the memories came flying back to her. "Sweet Richard said, 'Don't you dare walk away from your family.'" A few tears danced down her cheeks as she wiped them away and locked her eyes with mine. "Which is exactly why I stayed with him."

"He was your family."

"My heart family. The only family that truly matters. Not for a second did he tell me to choose him. He sacrificed his own happiness in order to protect mine. If that's not a man you hold on to, I don't know what is. That was when I learned that true love is unconditional. It doesn't set guidelines for how you have to act in order to be loved. His mother and father took me into their home without question. They raised me; even though they already didn't have much, they made enough space for me to exist within their home. When I think of my parents, I think of them."

"I felt crushed when my family turned on me. I still do, honestly."

"Yes, and that doesn't really go away—not fully. But you now have a beautiful daughter that you can begin again with. You get to start from the ground up, building a family set with values that serve you. From new traditions, to new love stories—you can break generational curses based on how you love one another."

Generational curses were something I'd thought about for a long time in my life. I never knew my grandparents, because Mama had had a falling out with her parents, and Dad never knew his. Now I felt as if I was repeating that same pattern of disconnect, because Reese didn't know her grandparents, either.

If I had it my way, my children's children would know me, and know of my love. They would never feel a disconnect from love, because it would surround their souls. One day, that family curse set against the Taylors would be broken. I was more determined than ever to make that true.

"Sometimes family isn't what we were born into—it's what we choose," Michelle explained.

Those words were so important to me. Sure, perhaps I wouldn't have the connection to my own parents that I'd craved, but that didn't mean I wouldn't get to create something even more powerful down the line.

"How old is your daughter again?" she asked.

"Almost six, and sassy as ever. She and Oliver bicker like no other, but they have a connection that they can't deny."

Michelle smiled brightly. "I always thought Alex would be the family man. Oliver looked so far away from settling down. Alex always seemed to connect so well with kids." Her smile slowly faded away as she stared off in the distance, thinking about Alex.

Sometimes the world didn't make sense. No parent should ever have to bury their own child. I couldn't even imagine that kind of pain that raced through her heartbeats on a daily basis. If I could offer up only one set of prayers for the remainder of my life, it would be for the parents who had to say goodbye too early to one of their own.

Those hearts would always beat a little slower in my mind.

"I'm so sorry, Michelle."

"Thank you, sweetheart." She reached out and patted my hand, and I knew it was because she needed a hand to hold. So I wrapped both of mine around hers. "The mourning doesn't get easier. It just gets quieter. Some days, I still cannot get out of bed, but I'm blessed. Because Richard stays in bed with me and my quietness. Then, when it's time for me to get up, he pulls me to my feet, and we dance. A piece of advice—find yourself a man who will dance with you even when your heart is broken." Her eyes flashed with tears, and she held my hands tighter. "You want to know a secret?"

"Yes."

"I thought I was going to lose Oliver too. He kept everyone so far away, even Tyler and Kelly. So, when I flew out here, I prepared myself for the worst. I thought he'd be in a drunken stupor, or worse . . . so much worse. Last time I came, a few weeks ago, he wasn't doing too well. But this time? This time I came back and he's smiling."

"That's so good."

She smiled brightly up at me as tears freely danced down her cheekbones. "So thank you."

"I didn't do anything," I swore.

"You're the only difference in his life since I came back. Plus, there's the way he looks at you when you're not looking. Now, sweetheart, I don't know what you did, but I'm almost positive that you helped bring my son back to life after he was holding death's hand. Call it my mother's intuition. So, thank you for helping him. Even if it's just by being his friend."

Now I was tearing up, and I pulled her into a tight hug. "You're an amazing mother," I whispered, and she began to cry harder.

"You have no clue how hard it is to believe that each day."

All mothers probably thought that. The ones who doubted their mothering skills were sometimes the ones who were trying their best, day in and day out. I didn't expect the conversation with Michelle to go the direction that it had, but I was glad it had taken that path, because it was clear we both had some healing corners of our hearts that had to have been touched that evening.

"Oh, don't tell me you two are wine drunk and emotional," Richard cut in, walking in our direction. "We were just picking out a song for two seconds and we turn around to find you both moping."

"Oh hush, Richard. Can't us girls have a moment every now and again?" Michelle said, standing to her feet.

"Yes, but for now, we dance to the Spinners, my lady." Richard reached out for his wife and took her into his arms as they began swaying to the song "Could It Be I'm Falling in Love." Richard serenaded Michelle as she smiled and melted into him like a perfectly fit puzzle piece.

Oliver came to stand beside me as we both watched his parents fall more and more in love with one another.

"This was their wedding song," Oliver said. "Dad recorded it, and they danced to it for their first dance."

"Oh my gosh, how sweet is that," I said, swooning. True romance.

"They dance to it every single night. On the good days and bad days. Especially on the bad days."

"They're what I want my love to look like," I confessed. Oliver gave me a tight smile but didn't say anything. I shifted around for a minute before looking toward him once more. "Do you want to dance with me?"

Butterflies filled my stomach, and maybe it was the liquid courage that had brought me to even asking Oliver to dance with me. Everything I knew about him told me that his answer would probably be no. From his shyness to his discomfort in certain situations. Yet, to my surprise, he took my hand into his and pulled me into his chest.

My heartbeats picked up speed as I fell into him the same way Michelle fell against Richard. As if we were missing pieces for one another.

My head rested against his shoulder as he swayed back and forth with me, holding me close. He smelled so good, like a smoky oak forest. It was in that very moment when I realized that one of my favorite things in the world was being that close to Oliver. He held me as if he wasn't going to let me go. And after a few seconds of swaying, he mindlessly began singing the lyrics to the song he'd heard throughout his whole childhood. His voice was so smooth, the voice that I fell for at a young age. There was a reason he was my favorite musician. He sang so effortlessly. Sometimes when he spoke, his words became entangled, but that never happened when he sang. It was as if singing was his first language, and speaking was his second.

As he sang the words to the Spinners song, he held me closer to his toned body.

And I secretly pretended he was singing the lyrics to me.

# 22

## Oliver

"I hope these work," I told Emery, handing her a pair of sweats and a T-shirt to wear for pajamas. We stood in the hallway, right outside her room for the night, where Reese was sleeping. Mom and Dad had headed to their bedroom for the night, and it was well past midnight.

"This is the second time I'm wearing your clothes," she joked, taking them from me. "Soon I'll just start shopping in your closet. Thank you, though. I really appreciate it. And I swear your kitchen will be spotless when I clean in the morning."

"I'm not worried about that at all. I just hope you had a good night."

"It was fantastic. Your parents are amazing. They are relationship goals. Honestly, they got me so lively that I'm not even tired yet."

"Same." I slid my hands into my pockets and swayed. "You want to exchange playlists until we get tired? Unless you wanted to be by yourself. I'm just curious about what some of your favorite songs might be."

"I'd love that. I'm going to change, and I'll meet you in the living room?"

"Sounds like a plan."

I headed to the living room and gathered a few items for the impromptu listening session, including a couple of snacks, some drinks, and a deck of playing cards. I sat down at the coffee table, and the moment Emery turned the corner, my chest tightened. Even though she was drowning in my clothes, it somehow looked as if they fit her perfectly.

"Your clothes are more comfy than mine," she said, cozying up against the fabric of the T-shirt I'd lent her.

Her locks were pulled up into a large messy bun on top of her head, except with two strays hanging on each side of her face. All the makeup had been removed from her skin, and somehow she looked even more beautiful than when she'd arrived that morning.

She took a seat beside me, and when her leg brushed against mine, I thought about what it would be like if her lips brushed against mine too.

She wiggled around a bit as she crossed her legs and grew comfortable; then she looked to the deck of cards and raised an eyebrow. "We're playing games?"

"Sort of." I picked up the deck of cards and started to shuffle them. "I used to do this with Alex when we were on the tour bus for hours. We set out a deck of cards, and each symbol stood for a theme. Then, we'd have to pick out a song for said theme based on what card we pulled. We can use our favorites list to pick out the song. All we need to do is pick four themes. But if you get the joker, it's a wild card, and you can play whatever's on your mind."

"Oh, this is going to be amazing. Okay. Can I pick the themes?"

"Go for it."

She rubbed her hands together with a devilish grin. "So, hearts will be love songs. Clubs will be songs that hype you up. Diamonds are songs that make you emotional. And spades will be wishes and hopes. How's that?"

"Great." I finished shuffling the deck and set it on the table.

"I'm going to add a rule to the game, though. We have to somewhat explain why we pick the song, and then at the end of playing, each person gets to ask one question during the game. It can be any kind of question. Nothing is off the table."

The anxiety in me began to skyrocket at the idea of any type of question, but the bigger part of my brain wanted to ask her a question that had been passing through my mind over the past few weeks.

"Deal. Ladies first."

Emery reached to the stack of cards and pulled out a card. Diamonds.

"Going straight to the emotions," she laughed, and my God, I loved the sound. She picked up her phone and started shuffling through her playlist, swaying back and forth as she smiled at the songs in front of her. "Okay, got it!" She started playing the song, and I knew it right off the bat, probably because it was on my playlist too. "Trying My Best," by Anson Seabra. "This one is for all the times I feel like I'm failing at being a mom. Reese looks at me as if I'm the best person in the world, but I fail her so many times. But at the end of the day, I really am trying my best."

"You're a great mom. And trust me, I know great parents."

"I wish I could be half as good as your parents."

"But you are. My parents' love is loud when my own love for myself is quiet. That's how you love Reese. You are her loudest love."

Emery smiled, and I thought about kissing her. Leaning over, wrapping her in my arms, and tasting her lips against mine. "Well, we're just trying to get me to cry now, aren't we?" she joked, pushing the deck of cards my way. "You go before the tears flow."

I picked up a club. First song that I noticed on my playlist: "Tha Crossroads," by Bone Thugs-n-Harmony. I couldn't hear that song without vibing to it. Clearly Emery couldn't, either, because she tossed her hands in the air and started dancing to the beat.

"My dad introduced me and my brother to Bone Thugs when we were around ten. This was the first song, and still, it gets me."

"Gosh, it's a classic, that's for sure. My parents would never let me play this music, though. Honestly, if they heard me listening to this, they would've flipped the house upside down and brought out the holy water. Funny how different we were raised."

"My dad always thought music was a way to teach. Every song had a story—good or bad—and he thought that was a good way to teach us about human nature."

"You officially have the coolest father."

She wasn't wrong.

We pulled more cards, and the realization hit that so many of our favorite songs were the same. Yet, the ones I didn't know, I was happy to learn from her. "Two Ghosts," by Harry Styles, for example. Worth the listen. When she brought up Jhené Aiko and HER, I knew I liked her more than words. My favorite thing about Emery was how diverse her playlist was. It went from Frank Sinatra to Erykah Badu without a moment of hesitation. You couldn't box Emery Taylor. If you tried to, she'd just break out of the restraints.

Great personality, and great music choices.

"Spades," she sighed, laying the card in front of me. "Wishes and hopes, eh? I'm going to mix it up and go with my country heart. 'My Wish,' by Rascal Flatts."

"What's a rascal flats?"

Her mouth dropped open and she swatted my arm. "Are you joking? Only one of the best country bands of the early 2000s. My sister was in love with them. When we would sneak in listening to music, she would always play this song or 'God Bless the Broken Road.'"

I wrinkled up my nose. "A little too country for me."

"It will grow on you, just wait and see." She yawned, and it was clear that we were getting to the end of the game as true exhaustion began to settle into both of us.

"One more for me, and then our questions," I said, reaching for the card. Diamonds. I'd been pretty lucky to avoid the emotional card for most of the game, but there we were on the last song of the evening.

Emery sat up straighter as she listened to the first chords of the song. "Oh, what is this?"

"It's called 'Godspeed,' by James Blake." I rubbed the back of my neck as I tried to keep my emotions in check. "My brother and I would share a song with one another every single day, no matter what. This was the last song he shared with me."

Her eyes watered over, and she didn't even try to keep the tears from falling. Her hand landed against mine, and she squeezed it lightly. "I'm so sorry, Oliver. I know you hear that a lot from so many people, but I am so deeply sorry."

I gave her a tight grin and shrugged. "It's all right."

"No. It's not."

She was right.

She closed her eyes as she listened to the song, and the tears kept streaming down her cheeks as she felt it. I saw it happening—she wasn't just listening to the words; she was feeling them. They were being imprinted on her soul, the same way she was being imprinted on mine.

When the song came to an end, she opened her beautiful eyes and took both of my hands into hers. "Can you play it again?"

And I did.

It was crazy how life worked. For the past few months, I hadn't been able to play that song without feeling as if my heart was being ripped out of my chest. But having someone to listen to it with me, having Emery there to experience the song, the lyrics, the story behind its meaning to me, made it hurt a little less. As if she was sharing the burden of it with me.

When I was with her, I felt less confused, less sad. Less lonely.

"Thank you for sharing that, Oliver. It means a lot to me."

"Thank you for listening."

She wiped her emotions away from her eyes and cleared her throat. "So question time? Should I go first?"

"Yes."

"Why do you keep your mirrors covered?"

I grimaced and shifted a bit, but I didn't drop my hold of her hands. I wouldn't dare drop her touch. "It's hard to look in mirrors. Because it feels like I'm looking at my brother."

"I figured that was it. I get that . . . but . . . and I don't mean to be offensive or anything, but I feel like that could be a bit of a gift. You know? To see your brother every time you look into your own eyes. It's as if a piece of him gets to keep living on within you."

"I've never thought of it that way."

"Yeah. Maybe that's stupid. That's just how my mind works, though."

"I like how your mind works."

A slight squeeze to her hands.

She tilted her head and didn't break our stare. "Okay, now your question."

"Does Reese not know her father? Is he not in the picture anymore?"

Within seconds, Emery sat up straighter, and a somber look found her eyes. Her hands slipped away from mine, and I realized that maybe that was the one question I shouldn't have asked about.

"I'm sorry, I didn't mean—"

"No, no. It's fine. I did say any question," she laughed. "That came back to slap me in the face."

"You don't have to answer."

"No. It's fine. I just don't talk about it a lot, so it's hard. But, no. She doesn't know her father. I don't know him, either. I have no clue who he is."

My chest tightened as I narrowed my eyes. "Was it a one-night stand or something?"

She shook her head. "No. I mean, I've never met him. I have no clue who he is, what he looks like, or anything about him."

How was that possible? What was I missing?

Emery must've seen the confusion in my eyes, since she gave me the saddest frown she'd ever produced. "Reese isn't my biological child. She's my sister's."

# 23

## EMERY

*Five Years Ago*

They were going to disown her before she even parted her lips. I knew
that the moment Sammie told me about her pregnancy. She knew it
too. That was the truth about who our parents were. They set their
judgmental opinions down before they offered compassion, no matter
what. Theo and Harper Taylor weren't millennials, by any means, but
they were well versed in cancel culture. They'd canceled my aunt Judy
for getting a divorce. They shunned the gospel choir director for having
photographs online of herself at a Drake concert.

They'd belittle children who celebrated Halloween.

I'd never met two souls who placed judgment like they placed
prayers—every morning and night.

Sammie's hands weren't shaking, because she was frozen still as I
sat beside her on the sofa in Mama and Dad's living room. I'd gone off
to college two years before and had felt a heavy amount of conflicted
emotions the day I left home to attend a culinary school in Los Angeles.
I cried two sets of tears the first night I'd stayed in my dorm room.
First, tears of relief from the fact that Mama couldn't place her words of

disappointment over me every single day for random reasons, and Dad couldn't hold his hand of disapproval up in front of my face.

The second set of tears I shed were for Sammie. She was left alone with our parents now, with no safe haven to escape to when she needed to hide away. In the past when our parents were too harsh, Sammie would sneak into my bedroom and we'd listen to music on my laptop, sharing earbuds. Mama didn't like when we listened to anything other than gospel music—so we always made sure to listen at night, when our parents were fast asleep.

Our current favorite artists were Alex & Oliver. They were soul music mixed with pop with not a drop of clichés. Sure, they only had two albums out, but those albums were the cure to every broken piece of our hearts.

I didn't know what my sister would go through without me being home with her. Unlike me, Sammie was sensitive. While our parents' judgments didn't affect me, because I had thick skin, I knew how their words slithered beneath my sister's skin, infecting her thoughts and mind.

From a young age, I'd understood how thoughts created outcomes, so I tried my best to keep my mind clear. Sammie wasn't like that, though. She cared so much about what people thought of her. She was a people pleaser through and through, doing anything and everything to be loved by the world—mostly by our parents.

The worst part was that she craved love and acceptance from two people who were unable to give her what she was looking for. My parents were two narcissists who hid their true, heartless colors behind their religion. They strove with their religious beliefs to condemn people, instead of showing them love.

Dad's face was grim after Sammie spoke her truths to him and Mama. My little sister had come to me first when everything unfolded. She called me to her side, and I drove all the way from California back to Oregon to help her during her storms.

She was pregnant at eighteen years old. Even if my sister was deemed an adult by age, Sammie was merely a child herself. There was such an innocence to her that she seemed too gentle for a world as harsh as ours.

She waited a week before she told our parents about the pregnancy. Seven days passed before she felt comfortable enough to share the news that had taken place in her life. I hated that she'd told them, thinking our parents would give her the comfort her soul was begging for. Instead, she received disgust.

"You're a statistic," Mama commented. "We raised you well and pushed you hard to make you the complete opposite of this. You were on your way to an Ivy League school, and you threw it away. For what? For this mistake?"

"Mama, be easy—" I started, but I was instantly cut off.

"Stay out of this, Emery. Lord knows you are probably the one who influenced your sister to act out this way."

"Wait, what?"

"You think I didn't find the pack of cigarettes under your mattress after you moved out to college? You've been a troublemaker from the beginning, and poor Sammie's probably taken after some of your sinful ways."

"This has nothing to do with Emery, Mama. Really," Sammie said, defending me. She was wasting her breath, though. It was no secret that my parents saw me as the troubled child and Sammie as the saint. I'd come to terms with that many moons ago.

"It's Devin's?" Mama asked. Dad was standing behind her with his arms crossed and a look of coldness behind his eyes. Most people feared when their parents spoke, but it was quite the opposite for me with my father. His silence terrified me more than any words ever could. My father could make a person feel like nothing, simply with a blink of his eyes.

I'd been nothing to that man more often than not.

It was scary that those looks of coldness were now being directed toward Sammie—his pride and joy.

Sammie didn't answer Mama's question, but it was the only thing that made sense, for it to be Devin's child.

Devin was the pastor's son, the one who would someday take over the church down the line, and he and Sammie had been high school sweethearts. Out of everyone in the world, Devin was the only boy my parents approved of Sammie being with. I wasn't allowed to date in high school, but Sammie could, because she found Devin. A boy of God.

If anyone would've been more upset about the pregnancy than our parents, it would've been Devin's. They were the definition of strict. I would've been surprised if poor Devin even knew what sex was. My parents' reaction was probably tame compared to his parents'.

"Do you know what that will do to that boy's life? You'll ruin his whole future," Mama scolded, and in that moment I hated her a little. My parents were more loyal to the church than they were to their own children. "What will people think of us?"

"I-it's not his," Sammie said as her voice shook.

All of our eyes widened in shock. That was a surprise to me, to say the least.

Mama cocked an eyebrow. "Then who's the father?"

Sammie lowered her head and didn't speak.

That only made things worse.

Mama cringed from the silence. "You don't know, do you? You went out running around town like a little hooker—"

"Mama!" I cried out, disgusted.

"Stay out of this, Emery. I don't even know why you're here. You're not wanted during this conversation," she said so coldly. "You haven't been wanted for a very long time."

A rush of air left my lungs. I felt that one. It felt as if Mama had slammed her fist straight into my chest.

Where Dad abused with his stares, Mama's power was through her words. Mama spent her whole life working inside a library, and it was as if she'd learned how to use her words to hurt others. If only she'd learned a few words from her Bible, then maybe things would've been different.

Calling her daughter a little hooker? Telling her other child that she was unwanted?

Seemed a bit unholy to me, but who was I to say?

"Don't talk to her like that," I ordered.

"Watch your tone, Emery Rose," Mama demanded right back.

"Watch your words," I replied as my hand rested against Sammie's shaky forearm. I wanted her to feel my closeness to her. I wanted her to know that she wasn't alone.

Mama's black-as-coal eyes locked with mine. I hated how much I looked like that woman. From our doe eyes to our full lips and kinky hair, we were identical. She aged slowly, too, and often looked as if she could've been an older sister to me. I hated that when I looked into mirrors, I saw my mother's face. That face had disapproved of me and my sister for so long, to the point that the way she pouted triggered something tragic in my chest.

Mama narrowed her stare. "Don't give me that slick college mouth, Emery. You may not live under my roof anymore, but you will not step foot into this house and act as if you are some independent woman who's out there taking the world by storm. Don't you forget who's paying for that free life of yours in California."

I went to argue with her, because unlike Sammie, I wasn't afraid to speak up to my mother. Yet, before words could leave my mouth, my father held up a stern hand toward me, silencing me.

Within seconds, I was quiet. Even though Mama wasn't scary, in my eyes, my father had a way of intimidating me with a simple wave of his hand. He hadn't even needed to say anything to me. That simple hand raise to quiet a situation always sent chills down my spine in the most disturbing way.

My father never liked me. Sammie always disagreed whenever I'd say that, but that was simply her being nice. It was clear as day to me that my father didn't have a drop of love for me, but he did love my sister.

While I looked like Mama, Sammie was Dad's twin. They had the same nose, same ears, and same dimples. They were both tall and slim too. Their brown skin was shades lighter than mine and Mama's. It wasn't only physical features the two had in common; they also shared many hobbies together. They loved watching sports together. I was almost certain Sammie had joined the basketball team simply to appease our father.

One night, after a victorious game where she was the leading scorer, Sammie told me that she didn't even love playing. When I told her she should quit, she laughed, saying Dad would never forgive her if she walked away from the court.

My sister was so obsessed with pleasing our parents that she never took a second to please herself.

Except for four months ago.

Except for when she'd finally put her hair down and allowed herself to be free.

And that was when everything took a turn for the worse.

"Explain yourself," Dad commanded of Sammie.

Sammie's gaze rose from the carpet she'd been staring at for the past ten minutes. Her lips parted to speak, and I hated how they were looking at her as if she was anything less than their daughter.

How were we both born from two people who were so cruel?

I stood close to Sammie and squeezed her hand, letting her know that still she wasn't alone. "I'm here, Sammie," I whispered. She lightly squeezed my hand back, and then she began speaking as we all listened closely.

"I went to a party with a few girls from the basketball team. I knew I shouldn't have gone, but I wanted to be a normal kid for one night. So,

I let loose. I . . . there—there was this guy . . . ," she softly whispered, her voice trembling.

I stood up straighter and tilted my head. "What happened?"

"He asked me if I wanted to hook up. I said no to him. I know I was a little bit not myself, but I said no to him. Over and over again, I said no as he pinned me . . . as he undressed me . . . as he . . ."

Raped her . . . ?

*No. Not Sammie. Not my baby sister.*

"Do you know who it was, Sammie?" I asked as rage simmered beneath my skin.

"No . . . it was some college guy. That was how we got to talking. He was telling me how he was a big shot at his college, how he loved living away from home, and how I'd love it too. I-I never thought he'd—I thought . . ."

Her words faltered, and the pain in her brown eyes was deeper than the ocean.

"Did you get tested?" I asked. "Did you go to the hospital?"

She shook her head. "No. I . . . I didn't mean for it to happen—"

"Were you showing off your body?" Mama asked.

"Mama!" I snapped, rage shooting through my whole system. My entire mind twisted at my mother's question. What in the world did that have to do with anything that Sammie was telling us?

"Answer her," Dad ordered.

Sammie shook her head. "No, I wasn't. I was hanging out with my friends, Susie and Ruby."

Mama huffed. "Those sinners who don't do anything but play on their phones during church services. Of course. Were you drinking at the party? What in the world would make you think you should've even been at a party? Do you have any clue how this is going to make Devin look? How it will make us look? Goodness, I doubt we'll even be able to step foot inside of that church again."

"Are you fucking kidding me?" I snapped. "Did you not hear what happened to Sammie? What she just told us?"

They both ignored me. Looking past me as if I didn't exist. Instead of being worried about the church, they should've been horrified by the trauma their daughter had experienced.

"I—I . . ." Sammie took a deep breath as I laced my fingers with hers and squeezed her hand slightly. *Still here, Sammie. You're not alone.* "The girls from the basketball team threw me an eighteenth birthday party. It was a surprise. I didn't know it was happening until I showed up."

"Did you drink?" Mama asked.

"No, ma'am."

"Did you do drugs?"

"No, ma'am."

"But you were stupid enough to let a boy take advantage of you because you were running around like a little hussy with your whore friends. I mean, seriously, Samantha Grace, what did you expect to happen? You were pretty much throwing yourself into these men's faces and—"

"Shut up, Harper," Dad cut in, scolding his own wife. I wasn't shocked that he'd told her to shut her mouth, because my father was a professional at putting my mother down. He belittled her all the time whenever he got the chance. If dysfunctional was a love story, it would be Theo and Harper Taylor's. "I'm getting sick of your monologues today."

Mama didn't say a word. Embarrassment flashed across her face. The only person in the world who could make Mama feel worthless was Dad, and he made sure to make her feel that way every chance he got. She took his verbal beatings too. Almost as if she didn't know anything else. Mama never seemed the type to be afraid of anyone. I swore, sometimes I thought she could stand up to the devil and not break a sweat. Yet with Dad, she always fell submissively to her knees before him.

Toxicity at its finest.

At least he was stopping her from putting down Sammie. At least it seemed as if he was doing the right thing, until he spoke again.

"You need to leave," Dad said as he stared my way.

I raised an eyebrow, confused. "I think Sammie needs me here."

"I wasn't talking to you, Emery. I was talking to your sister. Samantha, you need to pack your bags and go."

"What . . . but Daddy . . ." Sammie's eyes welled with tears. She always called him Daddy, because she was his little princess.

"Don't call me that," he snapped at her; his eyes that often looked on her with pure love were filled with nothing but distaste. "Go pack some bags and leave. I will not sit here and have you showcase your mistakes in front of me, in front of this town, and ruin our reputation. Leave."

Mama's eyes softened for a split second before they iced over just like Dad's.

When did it happen?

What year was it when my parents became monsters who pushed their children away?

When did they give themselves to the darkness and pretend that they were praising God?

"Where . . . where will I go?" Sammie asked as her voice cracked with fear.

"How about to the house of the boy who did this to you? It's not really our concern, now, is it?" Mama snapped, her words filled with disgust. She turned her body away from Sammie, as if the simple act of looking at the child she'd brought into this world was too hard for her soul to handle.

It wasn't long before Dad turned his back on her too. Without thought, Sammie crumbled as she rushed over to Dad's side. She threw herself at his feet and wrapped her arms around his legs, begging, pleading for him to reconsider. Praying that he'd change his mind about disowning the one child who seemed to never have let him down.

"Daddy, please, you don't understand. I'm sorry. I'm sorry, it's just—"

"Let me go, Samantha," he ordered, his tone smoky and harsh. My father never smoked a day in his life, but his voice held a grittiness as if he'd smoked a pack a day for the past forty years.

"No. I won't let go. Please, Daddy. I'm sorry. I love you, Daddy, and we can fix this. We can do whatever it takes. Please. Please," Sammie cried, and with each plea, my heart ached for her.

Dad didn't show any signs of pity, just disgust.

I walked over and wrapped my hand around Sammie's forearm. "Let go, Sammie. Come on. Let's go."

"No. I won't let go. Look at me, Daddy. Please," she said, but he wouldn't. What kind of monster could be so cruel?

"Get up, Sammie, please." I yanked on her arm. "You don't need to ever beg for anyone's love. Not even his."

"You should leave, too," Dad told me.

"Trust me, I am. I don't want to be here to begin with."

Once I was able to get Sammie to let go of Dad's leg and pull her to a standing position, Dad finally built up enough nerve to look her way. "You did this to yourself." With that, he and Mama exited the room.

There was something so disgustingly vile about the two humans who'd raised us.

Sammie's whole body broke into uncontrollable shivers. A weighted cry broke from between her lips as she covered her mouth from shock and despair. If I wasn't there, she would've crumbled to the ground and shattered into a million pieces of brokenness. If I wasn't around, Sammie would've hit rock bottom before her mind had had a chance to catch up with the fact that she was falling.

Yet I was there, so into my arms was where she fell.

"I got you, Sammie. I got you," I promised. She held on to my shirt and began sobbing into my arms.

"Where will I go?" she cried. She was so young, so innocent, at only the beginning stages of her life. She was supposed to be going off to college in the fall and getting her breath of freedom away from our parents. She was supposed to become a doctor. She was supposed to succeed in ways that I never could've.

Sammie did everything right, as far as giving Mama and Dad exactly what they'd expected of her. She showed up to church every Sunday and Bible study on Wednesdays. She volunteered at food shelters on her weekends and had received straight As throughout her whole school career. During the summers, she went on mission trips. My little sister was exceptional in every way possible. Even though I was older than her, I looked up to Sammie and her ability to succeed with nothing less than a smile against her lips. My sister was always the definition of success. She was our parents' golden child, and in her moment of need, they tagged her as fool's gold and tossed her back into the stream.

"With me," I promised, holding her close to me as I comforted her the way our parents should've. "You'll come stay with me in the dorms. Then, when the time is right, we'll get an apartment together. Don't worry, Sammie. You're not alone in this. You're never going to be alone in this."

She didn't reply, because her tears were too consuming. Her body shook as I walked her to her childhood bedroom to gather the essentials that we'd take away with us. I packed her bags for her, because she was too much in a state of shock to do much of anything.

When I was finished packing up her things, I walked her to the car and placed her in the passenger seat. "I'm just going to get your last bag. I'll be right back," I told her.

She didn't reply as she stared forward into the darkening sky before us.

I walked back inside the four walls that had witnessed me grow up and paused at the front door when I saw Mama pulling the suitcase to the front door. She had a scowl sitting against her lips that made her appear ten years older than her actual age.

"Here," she said, shoving the suitcase my way.

I didn't say a word, because I knew if I spoke to my mother, nothing decent would fall from my lips. I was standing before a woman who had no love inside her heart. I knew it was pointless to try to argue with her.

"You did this to her, you know," Mama stated, making me turn back to face her.

"Excuse me?"

"You did this. You were always a bad example to your sister. You were always the troubled child, and she had to watch you grow up. Your sins infected her."

I narrowed my eyes, baffled by her words. "I'm sorry—are you somehow finding a way to blame me for Sammie being pregnant?"

"If the shoe fits. If it weren't for you, she wouldn't have even known about these kinds of things."

I laughed. "You mean parties? Sorry, Mother, I'm pretty sure she would've found out about parties with or without me."

"Your sins are what led her here. You did this. I bet whatever outfit she wore that night she found in your closet."

My jaw slacked opened as shock skyrocketed through my system. "What does that have to do with anything?"

"If she was showing off her body in a provocative way, that would make boys—"

"What is the matter with you?" I snapped, cutting her off. I couldn't take any more of listening to Mama's radical beliefs. Was she victim-shaming? Was she blaming my sister for the horrific act that had happened to her body? That had happened to her soul?

How dare she.

"The truth is, Sammie could've walked into that house party completely butt naked, and it still wouldn't have given that animal enough reason to put his hands on her. He raped her, Mama. A disgusting boy took advantage of my sister, and he raped her body. He raped her heart.

And somehow you are saying she's to blame for the acts that happened to her, due to her outfit? Are you insane?"

"It wasn't only her outfit. She put herself in that situation by showing up to a party. She made herself prey. If she didn't—"

"If she didn't what? Exist? Would you rather her live in a bubble? Would you rather she wore a potato bag? You are fucking insane and—"

*Slap.*

Mama's palm flew across my cheek, making me stumble backward. My heart raced in my chest as shock filled me up inside. Even though my mother was cruel, she'd never laid a hand on me. She'd never crossed that line until that very moment.

"Mama," I choked out as tears formed in my eyes.

"Don't come to my house cussing like you ain't got no sense. How dare you, Emery. This is a house of God."

She was batshit crazy. Delusional to the truths that surrounded her.

"I hope I never see you again," I whispered before walking away with my hand still on my stinging cheek. I couldn't listen to her anymore. Hell, I couldn't look at her. Besides, Sammie needed me. I didn't have time to deal with my abusive mother.

We drove back to California, and the ride was completely silent, because I didn't have the right words to give to my sister. It was late into the night once we arrived at my dorm, and Sammie refused to eat anything. I skipped dinner too. We were close in that way—when her stomach was in knots, my stomach ached too.

We lay in the small twin-size bed beside one another, staring at the ceiling and not speaking a word. I reached for my cell phone and headphones and handed one of the earbuds to Sammie as I placed the other in my ear. Without question, I began playing Alex & Oliver's first album, the one that had gotten me through some of the hardest times in my life. Alex and Oliver Smith's voices had a way of healing through the headphones. Their words fixed parts of my soul that I hadn't even known were broken.

We still weren't speaking, but tears were rolling down Sammie's cheeks as her eyes remained closed and the powerful duo soothed her.

She fell asleep in my arms, but I couldn't do the same. Not after learning what had happened to my innocent little sister. Sammie's breaths fell from between her slightly parted lips. I studied the swollen bags sitting beneath her eyes from crying.

In that moment, I promised myself I'd never abandon her like our parents had done.

I'd be by her side throughout every storm, no matter what.

# 24

## EMERY

*Present Day*

I'd never shared the truth about Reese with anyone, outside of Abigail. My chest felt as if it were on fire as I told Oliver all the history of what went down with Sammie. He listened closely, without any judgment in his eyes.

When I grew emotional talking about it, when I needed comfort, he gave it to me, wrapping me in his hold. He felt like the safest place I could reside in that very moment.

"Sammie hasn't been the same since she left. We talk every now and again, but I know it's different. She went off to find herself, and I can't even blame her for that. I'd want to escape too. But I hate it. I hate that when I need her, she closes herself off. Then, like today, she reaches out to me as if nothing's happened at all. As if I'm just supposed to pretend that everything is dandy when it isn't. I hate it."

"That's a lot on your shoulders."

"I'm okay," I said with a smile, wiping my face. "Gosh, I did not expect to end up crying so much tonight."

"It's fine. I don't mind."

"It's probably all the wine. Speaking of, I should probably get some sleep before I tell you my whole life story." I stood up from the ground, and Oliver followed after me.

"I'll walk you to your bedroom," he offered.

I nodded, not wanting to pass up the offer. When we reached the room, I paused and turned his way. "Reese doesn't know about me not being her biological mother. So, if you can keep everything between us . . ."

"Your secrets are safe with me, Emery."

His words soothed the aching parts of me.

He slid his hands into his pockets and gave me a slight frown. "Are you okay?"

I should've lied, but that wasn't something we seemed to do with one another. "No."

"Can I hold you again?"

I sighed and whispered, "Please."

His large arms wrapped around my frame, and I relaxed against him, breathing him in. We stayed there for a few minutes. Maybe five. Maybe ten. Long enough for me to gather myself. Long enough for me to fall into loving the idea of being in Oliver's arms.

As he held me, his mouth moved to the edge of my ear, and he spoke words that sent chills down my spine. "You're the greatest mother that she could ever have."

That only made me hold him more.

When we separated, he gave me his broken smile, and I gave him mine.

"Good night, Em. I hope you sleep well tonight."

He turned on his heel and began to walk away as I slightly parted my lips and muttered, "Good night."

I awakened as the sunlight beamed into my bedroom, shaking me from my night's rest. As I opened my eyes, I remembered that I wasn't in my bed, but the guest room at Oliver's. I rolled over in the bed, expecting to see Reese still sleeping beside me. When she wasn't there, I shot up from my bed as anxiety hit me quickly.

I rushed out of the bedroom, on a mission to find my daughter.

"Mr. Mith! We need more chocolate chips!" the familiar voice said, giving me a flash of comfort as I headed toward the kitchen. There, standing in front of me, were Oliver and Reese, covered in flour and hovering over a mixing bowl.

"Hi, Mama!" Reese exclaimed, waving my way as she popped chocolate chips into her mouth instead of the mixing bowl.

"Good morning." I smiled, looking around at the spotless kitchen that I was supposed to be cleaning that morning. Well, almost spotless, except for the flour and cracked eggs from their morning cooking ventures. "What are you two up to?"

"Mr. Mith wanted to make you your favorite breakfast. So we're making you chocolate chip pancakes!"

"Oh, how sweet." I sniffed the air. "Is something burning, though?"

"Oh shit!" Oliver remarked, rushing over to the oven. He pulled it open as a cloud of smoke filled the space. He tossed on an oven mitt and pulled out the tray of bacon. Crispy, black, burned-to-a-crisp bacon.

"That's a quarter for the jar!" Reese replied. "Eww, Mr. Mith, that stinks."

He placed the pan on top of the stove and gave me a goofy grin. "Reese said you love bacon, but I doubt you'll love this."

I laughed and walked toward them. "Let me help you guys out."

"No!" they said in unison, shaking their hands in my direction.

"Mama! We wanted to make it for you and bring it to you in bed. So go back to bed."

"But—"

"Bed!" Oliver commanded, pointing toward the direction I'd come from.

"Okay, okay," I said, tossing my hands up in defeat. "Fine. But I'm not eating that bacon."

He picked up a piece and bit into it to make a statement. The way his face cringed as he chewed it made me snicker. "I'll make some new bacon."

I headed back to the bedroom and waited for another twenty minutes or so for the breakfast to come. When it was ready, both chefs entered the room with a tray that had a vase with flowers, a cup of coffee, and a plate with the oddest-looking pancakes I'd ever seen in my life. A bottle of syrup sat next to a bowl of fresh fruit.

"Here you go, Mama." Reese helped Oliver hold the tray, and then she placed it on my lap.

"Oh my! It looks amazing," I said, beaming. "I've never had breakfast in bed."

"I picked the flowers outside! And Mr. Mith made you better bacon."

"I see that." I picked up a slice of bacon and bit into it. "Perfection. Perfectly crisp."

Oliver patted himself on the back. "Third time's a charm."

"Third time?"

"We don't need to go into details," he joked.

"Mr. Mith, I'm gonna go eat my pancakes with your parents and tell them about how you burned the bacon," Reese said, hurrying out of the room. That girl was always rushing off.

"Breakfast in bed? What did I do to deserve this?"

"You deserve so much more than that. But fair warning: if you find eggshells in the pancakes, that's my fault."

I laughed. "You should've just made me a grilled cheese."

"Next time."

He moved in closer and sat on the edge of the bed. "Are you okay?"

"Yes. Sleep helped. Thank you for listening last night. I didn't know how much I just needed someone to listen to me."

"I'm always here to listen to whatever you need to say." He brushed his thumb against his nose, and I was getting to the point where I was learning when he had thoughts in his head that he wasn't speaking out loud.

"What is it?"

"It's not my business, but last night you mentioned that your sister had reached out to you, and you didn't respond. After hearing what you told me, I'm sure it's due to a lot of trauma. I can't imagine what she's been through, and it's not my place to do that. But, I do know that if I had a chance to speak with my brother again, even if we were at odds, I'd take it. Life is short. Each day isn't promised. So, if there is a chance to fix what's broken, don't pass it up."

That sat heavy on my heart as the reality of it all set in. He was right. Each day wasn't promised, and Sammie had been through a tragic situation. It wasn't my place to judge her. It was my place to love her—even if it was from a distance.

After I finished my meal, I thanked Oliver and headed into the bathroom to wash up. To my surprise, I noticed that the mirror wasn't covered with a sheet. I checked the other rooms, and I noticed that all the coverings had been removed.

Healing came in waves, and it seemed as if lately Oliver was learning to ride the current. I guessed I would do the same with Sammie and called her while I still had the chance.

I picked up my cell phone and dialed her number.

"Hello?"

"Hey, Sammie. Sorry I missed your call."

There was a small sigh on the end of the line, and she sounded emotional as she spoke. "Thanks for calling me back."

Later that afternoon, I headed home with a very happy Reese and three of the action figures that were allowed to leave Oliver's home. When I put her to bed later that night, we did her nightly routine of saying our prayers.

When we finished, I leaned in and kissed her cheek. "Get some sleep."

"Okay, Mama." She placed her hand against my heart and stamped it, and I went ahead and stamped hers back. "Love you," she yawned.

"Love you too. Good night."

I stood to walk away, and Reese called out to me once more. "Mama?"

"Yes, Reese?"

"Mr. Mith is really nice. I like him."

"That's good. I think he likes you too."

"Maybe next time he'll let me swim in his pool again."

I smirked. "Maybe. Good night."

"Night." A few seconds later: "Hey, Mama?"

"Yes, rug rat?"

"Do you like Mr. Mith, too?"

I chuckled to myself at the innocence of her voice and the depth of her question. "I sure do."

"Good, because I think I'm gonna ask him to be our friend the next time I see him, and maybe he can play with the superheroes with me when I go over there too."

"That sounds like a good plan. Now, get some rest, okay?"

"Okay, Mama." A brief pause. "Hey, Mama?"

I sighed, pinching the bridge of my nose. "Yes, Reese?"

"Do you think Mr. Mith is hot?"

My eyes bugged out of my face. "What?"

"Kelly asked me to ask you if you thought that, and she said that if you turned red and made a big reaction, that meant yes. So, I guess it's a yes."

There was no question in my mind that I was going to kill Kelly the next time I saw her.

"Good night, Reese Marie."

"Night, Mama." I took a few steps before I heard, "Hey, Mama?"

"Yes?"

"Love you."

A happy sigh this time released from me. "Love you too."

# 25

## OLIVER

Emery and I began sending each other two songs each day. Songs to show how we were feeling early in the morning. Songs that summed up how we felt when nightfall came. I listened to every single one she sent, because it made me feel close to her even when she was far away.

The more songs we played, the stronger our connection grew.

Emery: I had to cuss out the camp instructors for allowing some kids to bully Reese today. Song of the day: Last Resort

Oliver: Is Reese okay?

Emery: She's fine. I don't think she even knows that they are bullying her. I just so happened to walk up when the kids were picking on her for her hair. I told the parents . . . they said it was kids being kids.

Oliver: Kids learning from their shit parents.

Emery: Facts. What's your song of the night?

# The Mixtape

Oliver: This City, Sam Fischer. Read some bad comments on the internet. Got to me a little.

Emery: Stay. Off. The. Internet. Or at least only read the good things.

*I know, I know.*

Oliver: Kelly keeps asking me to ask you a question, but I haven't talked myself into doing it yet.

Emery: What's the question?

I started typing, then deleted, then typed, and deleted.

Emery: Don't do that. Don't leave me on a cliffhanger. Tell me.

Oliver: Do you think about me the way I think about you?

A few seconds passed before she started typing again.

Emery: Depends. How do you think about me?

Oliver: Like you're every single good thing in the world wrapped in one person.

She started typing, then stopped, then started and stopped. Those ellipses were going to be the end of me.

Emery: I think of you how you think of me.

The biggest sigh of relief fell from the depths of my spirit.

Emery: You know what's weird?

Oliver: What's that?

Emery: I think I start missing you each day before I even leave your side.

While Emery and I were slowly falling into one another, my breakup with Cam was getting messier and messier due solely to her and her dramatics. It turned out that breaking up with one's crazy, narcissistic ex-girlfriend wasn't good enough when she was a celebrity and had the ability to trash your name in the tabloids. I figured Cam would grow tired of the interviews, but they seemed to be getting her the exposure she so desperately craved.

Her favorite new pastime was bashing my image to highlight hers. The rumor mills were getting so out of control that even my team was getting slammed with hate mail, claiming I was an asshole for hurting America's sweetheart and that they should be ashamed that they worked for me.

It was at that point when I decided I needed to do something about it. I needed to do an interview. And fuck me, I didn't want to do an interview.

"Are you sure this is the only way?" I asked Tyler as I sat in the dressing room of one of the biggest local entertainment channels.

"The only way, man. I know how hard these are for you, but I want you to know that we're all in your corner. Okay?" He turned to the clothing designer who'd dressed me that morning. "Also, can we get him out of the dark-gray top? Put him in light blue. It's more welcoming." Tyler turned back to me and patted me on the back. "Remember, Oliver. You just gotta tell the truth, all right? Cam and her bullshit lies have nothing on the truth. I'll be out there cheering you on with Kelly and Emery."

"Emery?" I said, surprised. "She's here?"

"Said she wouldn't miss it." He glanced at his watch. "Switch shirts, and I'll see you out there in five minutes."

He hurried out of the room, and once I was given the shirt to switch into, I was left alone in the room. Me, myself, and my overactive brain. After a quick change, I sat in front of the mirror and looked at myself. Something I was just recently getting used to again, thanks to Emery. Some days it brought me pain; other days there was comfort.

Abigail had been teaching me that all people had days like that. Days that were up, and days that were down. It was all just part of the human experience.

I reached into my pocket for my wallet, opened it, and pulled out the other half of the necklace that was paired to mine. Alex's heartbeats. I'd been carrying them around with me for the past seven months, holding them close to me, wishing that the necklace was still sitting around his neck. Wishing that he was there to do the interview with me.

"Stay close, brother," I whispered, closing my eyes and holding the piece of jewelry next to my half.

"Oliver?" a voice said, with a knock on the door.

I went over and opened it to find an intern of some sort standing there with a smile on her face and a gleam in her eyes. "They are ready for you."

"Thank you."

"Of course, and can I just say, I'm a huge fan. I know some people are saying some shitty things about you, but I don't believe it at all. Your music saved me and helped me through my depression. I just—it's an honor to meet you," she said, stars in her eyes and shakiness in her hands.

I gave her a small grin. "You have no clue how much that means to me."

Funny how when you took your depression and created art, it could help someone else who was struggling with their own demons.

We walked to the set, and the closer I got, the more nerves began to grow in the pit of my stomach. The interviewer, Brad Willows, introduced me and welcomed me to the stage. I took my seat in the oversize cushioned red chair and felt as if the lights were going to blind me.

*I don't want to be here.*

It happened pretty quickly. The shaky hands, the sweaty palms, the words getting tangled up in my mind. This was all before Brad had even asked me a question, other than how I was doing.

I felt stiff when I answered. "I'm fine," I choked out. I blinked a few times, feeling as if the word had come out too aggressive, too cold, too much like myself and not enough like Alex. What would Alex do? He would've been personable. He would've greeted the audience as well when he walked onto the stage, waving toward everyone. Asking how they'd all been.

I didn't do that.

I didn't greet the audience.

*Fucking idiot! You should've greeted the audience. Now they are all thinking that you're an asshole and you don't know how to properly engage, which makes what Cam said seem more true, and now you're sweating under the stage lights like an idiot and oh shit—*

Brad was staring at me. As if he was waiting for a reply.

Did he ask me something?

He must've asked me something.

What did he ask me?

I blinked a few times and shifted in my chair. "I'm sorry, can you repeat that?"

"I said I'm sorry for your loss. It must've been a hard one for you to handle."

Brad wasn't a big asshole. That was exactly why Tyler set it up for me to go on his late-night show, which was filmed during the daytime. The sun was still out, the birds were still chirping, and fuck. *Reply, idiot!*

I cleared my throat. "It hasn't been the easiest year."

"Understandable. But, I've been informed that you've been in the studio. Maybe working on some solo pieces?"

"Yes. Slowly but surely it's coming together."

"Is it hard creating music without your brother?"

*Is it hard creating music without the one person who talked me into doing music in the first place? Is it hard learning how to be a solo artist when you've always been part of a duo? Is it hard not hearing Alex's vocals and guitar on the songs when they come to a finish?*

*No, Brad. It's insanely easy.*

*Don't say that, Oliver. You'll sound like a dick.*

Damn, it was hot in here. Was there no air-conditioning? I bet Tyler was sweating buckets in the audience. Cursing under his breath about how I was bombing the interview.

The interview.

*Answer Brad!*

"Uh, yeah. It's difficult."

"It's probably even tougher with the allegations that have come out about you and your relationship with Cam."

Brad seemed so calm as he spoke. Almost as if he wasn't speaking about how some lunatic was out to ruin my life after my life had already been extremely damaged from losing Alex.

*I don't want to be here.*

I shifted in my chair. I felt everyone staring at me, but I couldn't figure out what to say. I didn't know how to speak up for myself. I didn't know how to sit there and tell my truth to combat Cam's lies.

"I, uh, I'm," I started, but I began to get choked up. I grimaced and then scolded myself for grimacing because that would be picked up on camera. "I'm sorry, Brad. Can we take a break?"

Brad looked at the cameras, then to the producers off in the wings of the stage, who were furiously shaking their heads. But before Brad could reply, I was walking off set toward my dressing room. I yanked at the collar of my shirt, trying to take in deep breaths.

I swung the dressing room door open and cussed at the top of my lungs the moment the door shut behind me. *"Fuck!"*

*"Fuck!"* was echoed behind me as Tyler walked into the room. His face couldn't have been redder if he tried. I couldn't tell if he was pissed off, scared, or felt bad for me. Maybe a little of all three.

He paced for a minute before he stood still and took in a deep inhale. Then he looked to me. "Okay. It's okay. Shit," he muttered before taking a few more deep breaths. "Okay. I'm going to go talk to the producers, apologize, and let them know we'll have to reschedule."

"This is going to make me look worse," I muttered in return, sitting down and rubbing my hands against my face.

Tyler didn't respond, because he knew it was true.

He cleared his throat and patted me on the back. "Don't worry, buddy. We'll get it figured out. Not a big deal."

Translation: a big fucking deal.

I bet the moment this news got out, Cam would be smirking with pride, knowing she'd kicked a dog that was already down.

There was a knock at the door, and Tyler called out, "Yeah, give us a minute!"

"Sorry," a calm voice said. "I'll wait."

Emery.

"Let her in," I said with a nod.

Tyler moved to the door and opened it. Emery stood there with a sad smile and Kelly's backstage pass around her neck. That explained how she'd gotten past security.

"Hi," she breathed out.

I couldn't even form a word to greet her.

Tyler looked to me, then to Emery, then back to me. "Okay. I'm going to do damage control. Emery—don't let anyone else come in here unless it's me. No pop-up interviews, all right? You stay here with him and guard this door until I'm back."

"Will do."

Tyler left and closed the door behind him. Emery walked over to me and sat down in the chair beside mine.

"You okay?" she asked.

"You really need me to answer that?"

"No. But still . . . at least you almost did the interview. That's a step closer in the right direction."

"I was never good at this. I don't do well under that kind of pressure. That was Alex's ball game, not mine. I've just made everything that much harder for my PR team too. I keep fucking up, which in turn fucks things up for other people."

"It isn't your fault. This is too much pressure for anyone. I couldn't imagine going out there and having to defend myself to garbage statements that were being made about me. It's not fair that you even have to deal with this petty stuff after the year you've had."

I shut my eyes and placed my hands on the sides of my temples. "I just need the world to slow down for a minute. I need my brain to slow down. It feels like I'm spiraling."

"Okay," Emery said. "Come here."

She moved to the floor and sat down, patting the spot beside her.

"What are you doing?"

"We're going to take a minute to slow down. Now come on." She lay down and grabbed her phone. Within seconds the song "Chasing Cars," by Snow Patrol, began to play. She tilted her head in my direction and gestured for me to join her.

I did as she said, lying down beside her as the music played. We lay shoulder to shoulder, and she laced her hand with mine, sending that wave of warmth through my system.

How did she do that?

How did she help make me slow down my madness?

The song played on repeat, over and over again, as my thoughts began to slow.

She tilted her head to look at me, I tilted my head to look at her, and I swore somehow I felt her heartbeats.

"Thank you, Emery."

"For what?"

"Existing."

# 26

## OLIVER

"What were some of your victories this past week?" Abigail asked at our next meeting together. I took comfort in knowing that after my meltdown on the set, I'd be able to work through some of the bullshit in my head with Abigail. It helped knowing that each week, I had someone assisting me in unpacking my heavy baggage.

Each week, before we dived into my mind, she asked me that. She said it was a way to switch the narrative in my head that every week was a bad week. It was a way to rewire my mind. Some weeks it was easy to come up with the good things that had happened to me. Other times, like said week, that felt almost impossible.

"I don't know," I muttered.

"You do. So tell me."

I blew out a cloud of hot air and sat back on the couch, searching my thoughts for any positive thing that had happened in the past week. Still, I struggled.

"I finished a song."

Abigail's eyes widened with joy as she wrote that down in her notebook. "That's fantastic. What else?"

"Nothing."

She smiled warmly and shook her head. "No. What else, Oliver?"

She never let me get away with simply one good thing. It was kind of annoying, honestly. "I left the house and didn't have a complete panic attack when I went to the store, thinking people would spot me."

"Even bigger than the first thing. What else?"

"Kelly has been eating regularly. Something she hadn't been able to do since Alex passed away."

"Good. This is so good, Oliver. What else? Just one more victory."

"Emery."

Abigail's eyes flashed with instant comfort as she paused her pen. "Anything specific about her?"

"No . . . just her as a whole."

"Beautiful," she breathed out as she wrote down Emery's name. She sat back in her chair and reread the good things that had happened to me. My miniature victories. "See? No matter what, there's some good. Even in the worst times, we have some victories."

"Can we talk about the failures of the week now?"

"No failures. Just opportunities to learn about yourself and your triggers more. But yes, do tell me."

I told her about the interview. About how Cam had made it her mission to ruin me out of spite due to me ending our already failing relationship. How I was making everything harder for everyone on my team. How I felt like every time I tried to step forward, I'd stumble back.

"Alex would've handled it better than me," I told her as I reached into my wallet and pulled out his heart necklace. "He would've never gotten himself into that situation to begin with."

"Maybe. Or perhaps, he would've handled it worse. Who's to say? Regardless, it's not your job to compare yourself to your brother. You shouldn't be comparing yourself to anyone, because at the end of the day, even though we are all human beings, none of our situations are close enough for us to even compare. Not even you and your brother's lives were the same, because you were both living uniquely different realities based on perspective. It's like comparing Picasso to Van Gogh. They might both be artists, but their work is solely theirs. The good, the bad, and the painful. And one doesn't cancel out how great the other is. There's space in the world for everyone to be extraordinary."

"But with Alex—"

"How many times a day do you do that?" she asked, interrupting me. That was the first time Abigail had ever cut me off.

"Do what?"

"Compare yourself to him?"

Too many times to count.

She shifted around in her seat and crossed her legs. "Do you think your brother was better than you?"

"Yes, of course."

"Why?"

"Where do I even start?" I snickered sarcastically. "There's a million reasons."

"Just give me a few."

"He was good with people. He always knew what to say and how to handle a situation. He never twisted his words or thoughts and fumbled them during interviews."

"Do you think you were a burden for him?"

My brows knitted as I sank deeper into the couch cushion. "Sometimes, I think he would've been better off as a solo artist, instead of feeling as if he needed to carry me alongside him."

Abigail did that therapist thing where she stared at me as if she was examining every inch of my being. Then she reached into her oversize purse and pulled out her laptop. "I need you to watch something for me."

She pulled up a video and set the laptop on the table in front of me. Then she hit play.

It was a video of Alex being interviewed by some person. Whenever Alex did solo interviews, it was normally because I couldn't manage to bring myself to join him because my anxiety was fucking up the situation. Still, he went and performed by being the charming person he'd always been.

"What was the question again?" Alex asked as he puffed on a cigarette, sitting relaxed in a director's chair.

"Do you think your brother's social flaws have damaged your success as a duo?"

"First, thank you for the question. Second, that's a fucked-up question," Alex remarked, making me smile a little. "Oliver is the true talent of this duo. Yeah, maybe he's quieter, and he stays a bit behind the curtain of success and fame, but that's because that shit doesn't matter to him. To him, the main importance is always the music. So, yeah. People see me as more lively, more engaging, more quote unquote 'normal,' but they are missing out on the truth."

"And what's that truth?"

"I'd be nothing without my brother. Oliver has more depth in the tip of his pinky than most people have in their whole body. He cares about others more than he cares about himself. He pours everything he has into our music, into the lyrics, into the songs that everyone loves. Maybe I do better in certain situations than he does, but it goes both ways. He has more heart than me. He feels deeper than me, he understands people more than I do, even though he'd never admit it. I might be the hype man of Alex & Oliver, but Oliver is truly the mastermind. He is the magic behind us. The true wizard behind the curtain, and it pisses me off that you people don't see it. The truth of the matter is, without Ollie, there is no music. He's my better half, and I'd give my life for that guy without a moment's hesitation, because I know he'd do the same for me. He's the light to my shadows. He's my best friend, end of story." Alex flicked off the ashes from his burning cigarette and sat back in his chair. He gave the interviewer an award-winning smile and said, "Next question."

The clip ended, and Abigail shut the computer down. Alex's words kept moving through my head as she continued the conversation. "There are dozens and dozens of interviews like that online. Have you watched any of those ones since he passed away?"

"No."

"But you've watched and read the negative commentary?"

"Yes."

"And you've done the same with the commentary surrounding the situation with Cam, correct?"

"Yes."

"Why is that? Why do you turn to the negative opinions of others rather than the positive ones?"

I shrugged and clasped my hands together. "I don't know."

"You do," she disagreed. "You just don't want to admit it. You turn to the negative because that's what you've spent so much of your life believing. So these individuals, these naysayers, are somewhat enforcing a flawed thought process that's been on repeat probably since you were a child. Probably leading back to the first time you felt that you didn't fit in. That led you to navigate through life dealing with people and situations that then pushed that anchor of self-doubt deeper into the ground of your soul. You were just following the narrative that your brain was creating. But you know the cool thing about this narrative? It's never too late to change it. If you hear a song on the radio that you hate, do you just continue to let it play? No. You change the station. So, go ahead, Oliver. Change the station."

"How?"

"By shutting off the outside noise for a while—the good and the bad—and creating your own original song for your mixtape. You get to decide the good and the bad, and you get to now start surrounding yourself with things that make you feel good about yourself rather than bad. Luckily, I believe you've already begun to do this."

"With Emery?"

Abigail smiled. "That's for you to decide. It's not about the songs you've played in the past to yourself. It's about the songs you want to play from this point out. So, what song are you going to play?"

------ ❧∽✲∼❧ ------

"I missed your morning song this morning," Emery said as she chopped some vegetables two days after my therapy appointment. I'd been working through so much of the homework Abigail had assigned me, which meant trying to change the narrative of my normally negative mindset, and that shit was hard to do.

But, I wanted to do it, because I wanted to feel better.

Each day it helped that I was able to see Emery and be around her good light.

"Yeah, I wanted to play it to you in person. There's a bit of back story to it."

"Oh?" She placed the knife down and gave me her full attention.

"Yeah. I don't know how to start this, so I'm just going to say it. I like you, Emery. I like you so fucking much. I like the way you care for others. I like the way you don't judge. I like how when you're happy with the meals you cook, you do a little jig. I like how you listen. I like how you love your daughter. I like how you stay around when I'm at my lows. I like how you laugh. How you smile. How you exist. I. Like. You."

Her eyes were wide and filled with wonderment as she walked over to stand in front of me. She looked down at her hands before locking her stare with mine. "You like me?"

"I like you," I swore.

"Good," she breathed out as she linked our fingers together and held my hands against her chest. "Because I like you too. I like how you interact with Reese. I like how you love your parents. I like how you look after Kelly. I like how you didn't give up on your music. I like

218

when you're deep in thought and your forehead wrinkles. I like how you burn bacon. I like how your smile feels like a secret prize that you share with so few. I like how you smile toward me. I like your laugh. Your good days. Your bad ones too. I. Like. You."

We were close together, her body heat falling against mine. I couldn't stop staring at her face. Her eyes, her nose, her cheeks, her lips. Those lips.

I rested my forehead against hers. "I'm a mess," I confessed. "Even with Abigail, I don't know how long it's going to take me to work through my troubles. I fall apart and struggle through normal activities. I am the complete opposite of what normal is. Some days I struggle to get out of bed, and others I struggle to breathe. But you make it easier. You make it better, even without doing anything. Before you, I didn't want to try. Some days, I still don't want to, but I'm going to keep trying because I want to be good enough for you. I want to be someone whole so you don't have to deal with my broken pieces."

"Oliver," she sighed as she placed a palm against my face. "Don't you get it? So much of your beauty comes from those broken pieces. In those cracks is where you shine."

I swallowed hard and closed my eyes for a moment. "Can I play the song for you now?"

"Please."

I reached into my pocket and pulled out my phone, where the song was already set up. I hit play and placed the phone on the countertop.

"Can I Kiss You?" by Dahl.

Emery's eyes flashed with emotion as I took my place back in front of her. My hand wrapped around her waist as I pulled her in closer to me. Her hips pressed against mine. Her body melted into my hold. I couldn't stop staring at her, at her lips, wondering how it was that she tasted. Was it her body that shivered or was it mine? Was it her nerves or mine that were skyrocketing through the space? I didn't know where her fears began or where mine ended. I hadn't a clue what her thoughts were, and truthfully, I was working my damn ass off to not believe the negative ones rolling through my head.

It was easy to sound them out when she placed her hands against my chest. My heartbeats flooded her fingertips as she felt what she'd done to me. She'd made my heart beat after months of being inactive.

The song lyrics kept playing, about a man asking permission to have that first kiss, the first moment when their lips crashed into one another. The first time they'd become something new.

And then, she smiled, and said yes.

I didn't hesitate. My lips crashed against hers, tasting every inch of her being against my mouth. She kissed me back, falling into me just as passionately as I fell into her. She tasted like strawberry ChapStick and new beginnings.

Her arms wrapped around my neck as our kiss deepened. I could have kissed her forever. Her lips were soft; her kisses were full. I liked how she kissed me as if she were searching for every single piece of me. The whole pieces and the shattered corners of my soul.

I kissed her back, searching for the same thing.

Each day, I had to work on changing the dial on the station of my mind to better-feeling thoughts. It wasn't always an easy thing to do, but that day? In that very moment? I loved the song that was playing.

# 27

## OLIVER

"Thank you again for passing Abigail's name on to me," I told Emery one afternoon as we drove to the grocery store in town. Normally, I hated shopping due to the paparazzi, but any chance I got to spend with Emery, I took.

As far as the weather went, it was a perfect California dream. The sun beamed overhead, the sky clear of clouds and a nice shade of blue. It was days like today that made me happy to live in California.

"She's really special, isn't she? I've never met someone as special as she is. She genuinely cares about the well-being of others. She's saved me during some of the hardest times over the past five years."

"I'm hoping she can help do the same for me. The other day, she asked me what I wanted to do for that day. Not what I wanted to do in the next five years, or what I wanted to do in the future, but she asked me right then and there what I wanted to do, and I didn't have the answer. But if she asked me what I wanted now, I'd know what to say."

"What do you want to do today, Oliver?"

"Be around you."

She smiled the warmest grin my way, and I wished I had enough nerve to tell her how much I wanted to kiss her too. How much she stayed on my mind. How much I loved being around her.

We stopped at a farmers' market to pick up some fresh vegetables and fruits—per Emery's request—and my stomach knotted up the moment I saw a paparazzo tailing us a bit. I looked over to him and frowned, but I realized he was lowering his camera the minute he saw me.

Emery didn't even notice that we were being followed. She was too excited about being in fresh fruit and vegetable heaven.

"I'll be right back, all right?" I said. "Just going to go check out that stand over there."

Emery agreed and squeezed my hand before she turned back to the sweet potatoes in front of her. "I'll be here, feeling up the eggplants," she joked.

I walked around the corner, noting the guy following me like the snake he was, and when he grew close enough to me, I finally snapped.

"Can we not today, man?" I asked, almost in a begging tone. For a few seconds with Emery, I'd almost forgotten that I was famous.

He grimaced and nodded. A flash of embarrassment filled his cheeks. "Yeah. I'm sorry, man. I was just trying to help."

"Help?" I huffed. "How so? How is this helping me?"

"I wanted to show you in a good light, you know? In good spirits. I've seen all the bullshit that Cam has been putting out about you, and I know it's all lies."

I arched an eyebrow at him, confused by his confession. I never engaged with the paparazzi, because for the most part I saw them as annoying vultures, but something about him seemed . . . genuine?

He shifted in his shoes and cleared his throat. "I lost my brother earlier this year too. Cancer," he muttered.

In that moment my distaste for him lessened.

"I'm sorry to hear that," I said. "It's not easy."

"No. Not at all." He scratched at his wild blond hair and shrugged. "Listen, I know what we do for a living is shit, but honestly I'm just trying to feed my family. We took in my brother's kids, and things have been tight. I'm not proud of this, so I was trying to do something good, you know? Maybe help you. I was hoping to use these pictures to spin your story into a good light. I'm a fan, after all."

I didn't know what to say, because I never looked at people like him as being human. With families. With struggles. With pain. "What's your name?"

"Charlie," he said, nodding slightly. "Charlie Parks."

I held my hand out toward him. "Nice to meet you. But don't worry about me. I'm good. Just take care of your family. If selling these pictures helps you, go for it."

He grimaced and shook my hand. "I know it might not seem that way, but a lot of us are rooting for you, Oliver. You got a team of silent supporters."

He headed off, leaving me a bit in disbelief at what had unfolded.

"Is everything okay?" Emery asked, walking closer to me after seeing the interaction that had taken place.

I took her hand into mine and kissed her palm. "Yeah. Let's head to our next stops."

As we walked into the grocery store, I tossed on my cap and sunglasses. I knew it was a terrible disguise, but the more I could avoid people spotting me, the better. Emery pulled out her shopping list, and I gladly added as much junk food to the cart as possible when she wasn't looking.

Everything was going smoothly until I heard a gasp take place. "Oh my gosh!"

I looked up to see a woman staring directly our way, and my chest tightened at the idea of being recognized. That feeling settled away pretty quickly when the woman clapped her hands together. "Emery Taylor, as I live and breathe!"

For the first time ever, it wasn't me who was being recognized—it was Emery.

The woman darted over to Emery and pulled her into a tight embrace. "Jeez, how long has it been? Five years or longer?" she said.

"Eve, hi. Oh gosh, it's been so long. Since I left Randall, I guess. What are you doing here in California?"

Eve held up her hand, showing off her sparkling ring. "Kevin and I are honeymooning! We got married last week and came to California to do Universal and Disneyland. It's a cheesy honeymoon, but it's who we are. Wow. How have you been? What have you been up to? I cannot believe it. Emery, you look good! Real good." Her eyes moved over to me and danced up and down my body before she nudged Emery. "You got a cute one on your arm, too, I see. Has anyone ever told you that you look just like Alex Smith? You two are an adorable couple."

Emery nervously laughed. "Oh, no. We aren't—"

Eve cut her off, and it was clear that she was one of those people who talked a lot and listened very little by the way she went on and on. "Oh my gosh, I gotta text Sammie and let her know that we ran into one another."

Emery's eyes widened. "Wait? You've been in touch with Sammie?"

"Are you kidding? Of course. I see her every week at Bible study. She even stood up in my wedding. I figured you knew. Anyway, I'd better get going before Kevin wonders why I'm still in this store. I was just meant to get a few snacks. If you ever make it back to Randall, let's have a girls' night! It's been too long!" She paused and looked over to me and raised an eyebrow. She snapped her fingers. "No! Not Alex Smith. Michael B. Jordan. That's it! You look like Michael B. Jordan. Well, okay, good seeing you, Emery! See you soon!" Eve hurried away as if she hadn't rocked Emery's world upside down with the information she'd just revealed.

I walked over to the pale-faced Emery, who was staring forward as if she'd seen a ghost. "Are you okay?"

"My sister's been back in Randall all this time? No. That doesn't make sense . . ."

The longer we stood in the store, the more I noticed people staring our way, and this time I knew they were staring at me, based on the cell phones in their hands as they snapped photographs.

I placed my arm around Emery's and leaned in to whisper. "We need to get going."

She didn't say anything but simply took steps forward as we abandoned our cart in the store. I got her into the car and drove for a few blocks before pulling over to talk to her, to make sure we were far enough away from paparazzi or fans snapping pictures of us.

"It doesn't make sense. She told me she was off finding herself. My mother said she hadn't seen Sammie when I called. Why would they lie?"

I didn't know what to say to her, because it was a messed-up situation.

"I have to go back to town," she muttered to herself. "But I can't take Reese to talk to them, and I definitely can't leave her alone. But I need answers. Oh my gosh." Her eyes watered over as she began to become overwhelmed with every word she spoke. "What does this even mean? Why would Sammie go back to Randall?"

"I can go with you, if you want. I can watch Reese in town as you confront the situation."

"What? No way. I can't ask you to do that, Oliver. Besides, you need to be focused on your album. I don't want to take your time."

"Emery, please." I took her hand in mine and squeezed it lightly. "Take up my time. I want to do it for you. You deserve answers after all this time. I want you to get those answers. We can go as soon as possible."

She hesitated for a moment before agreeing. "Okay, and I'll head home tonight with Reese and pack our bags. Do you want to pick us up in about two hours from my place, and we can hit the freeway? I'll book us two rooms at the bed-and-breakfast in town."

"Sounds good."

I drove us back to my place, Emery picked up her car, and then we went our separate ways.

As I packed, I felt like a damn fool for being somewhat excited about a weekend getaway with my girls.

My girls.

Fuck, they weren't mine, but that thought felt good in my head.

# 28

## EMERY

*Five Years Ago*

"I can't do this," Sammie sighed as Reese screamed her lungs out at two in the morning. "I can't do this, Emery. I can't," she cried along with the little one as she aggressively rocked her daughter in her arms.

"Hey, hey, it's okay. Here, hand her over."

I took Reese into my arms and began to soothe her the best I could. "Did you warm up a bottle?" I asked. Sammie wasn't able to breastfeed no matter how hard she tried, so we were working with formula. I knew that was hard for my sister. She blamed herself so much for not being able to nurse her child.

I tried my best to convince her it had nothing to do with her skills as a mother, but I knew she didn't believe me. I never would've been able to understand her pain through it all, either. I wasn't a mother. I didn't have the same struggles of trying to feed my daughter. Every time Sammie tried, she'd burst into tears from feeling like a failure. It wasn't until the doctor recommended going to formula that Reese began eating.

Even then, Sammie had a hard time getting the little girl to take a bottle from her.

"Here," she said, handing it to me. "She wouldn't take it. It's still kind of warm, but I don't know. Maybe I gave it to her when it was too warm? Oh gosh, what if it was too warm and I burned her? What if—"

"Sammie. It's fine. She's fine. Don't worry."

She paced back and forth, raking her hands through her hair. She looked a mess. She'd been wearing the same clothes for days and hadn't showered in who knew how long. Her eyes were swollen from lack of sleep, mixed in with her constant flow of tears. It was clear each and every day she was getting closer and closer to her breaking point, and I couldn't blame her.

I didn't see Reese's father in that little girl's face. I didn't see his eyes, or his nose, or the crooked smile that he might've had. I didn't see the way she resembled the man who'd stolen something away from my sister to create this beautiful child.

But Sammie did.

She saw him in her waking dreams and her nightly nightmares. She saw parts of him in Reese's eyes, in her smile, in her everything. It was a daily reminder of the tortured situation she'd been placed in. It was a reminder of what had happened to her all those months ago, when she'd finally allowed herself to take a break and let loose.

I begged her to go to therapy, but she swore she was fine without. I begged her to talk to me, yet she told me she was fine. I prayed she'd open up to someone—anyone—because I knew she wasn't doing okay.

Reese began to fuss while I was feeding her, and as the baby's irritation started to rise, so did Sammie's.

"I can't do this, I can't do this," Sammie kept saying, kept reciting as she moved back and forth across the small space. Her hands were pressed against her ears as her annoyance grew more and more from the noise that had shaken us awake in the night. "I can't . . . I . . . just stop crying! Shut up!" my sister hollered at the top of her lungs.

My heart shattered in the moment as Sammie paused her movements and looked up at me with tears sitting on the forefront of her eyes. I knew she was seconds away from a breakdown. Seconds away from spiraling further and further into the pit she'd been falling in for months now.

"I hate her," she confessed, and in that very instant my heart split into two. "I hate her so much, Emery," she said before covering her mouth with her hand and breaking down into uncontrolled sobs.

I held Reese to my chest and gave my sister a small smile, trying my best to hide how much she scared me in that moment. "Hey, how about you go take a shower, Sammie? Clear your mind and regroup. Then go to sleep. I got Reese. Don't you worry, okay? I got her."

Sammie opened her mouth to speak, but no words came out. Only an involuntary nod of agreement as tears streamed down her cheeks, and then she walked away toward the bathroom.

The sigh I'd been holding inside me for so long evaporated as I listened to the water start running. My main task now was to soothe Reese.

I rocked the little girl in my arms and got her to take the bottle after a few moments. When she stared up at me with those doe-brown eyes, I could tell she was exhausted too.

"I know, I know, sweet girl. It's okay. I know you're just doing your best. We're all trying our best, okay? You're okay. You're more than okay. You're so good," I promised her, rocking her slightly in my arms as she kept her stare on me. "And you know what? Your mama is good too. She's so, so good, Reese. And she loves you so much, no matter what. Okay? I just need you to know your mama loves you. She's trying her best. I promise you, she's trying her best."

After a while, Reese faded back to sleep, and I laid her back in her crib. Once she was asleep, I went to head back to bed, but I noticed that the shower was still running.

"Sammie, you okay?" I asked, knocking on the door. My chest tightened when I didn't get a reply. I knocked louder this time. "Sammie? Are you good?"

I heard mumbles, but still, no reply.

When I turned the doorknob, I witnessed my sister sitting in the bathtub as the water poured overhead. She was rocking back and forth as she scrubbed her arms up and down with her hands, to the point that her arms were reddened from how hard she was scrubbing.

"Sammie . . . ," I whispered, taking steps closer to her.

"I can't do this, I can't do this, I can't do this . . . ," she said on a loop, shaking as her tears intermixed with the water droplets shooting down from the showerhead. "I can't do this, I can't do this, I can't do this . . ."

"Sammie, come on, get out of the tub," I said, turning off the water.

"I c-c-can't do this," she repeated. She stared forward as if she couldn't even see me. As if she wasn't even aware that someone was in the same space as her. She looked so far gone that I worried she didn't even know where she was in that very moment in time.

I couldn't get her to climb out of the bathtub. I couldn't get her to snap out of the trance that she'd somehow entered. So I climbed into the tub with her and wrapped my arms around her shivering, naked body. "I want to go home, Emery. I don't want this life. I need Mama and Daddy. I need them. I can't do this. I can't," she kept repeating.

I pulled her close to me and held on for dear life as she kept her chant going, her whispers stinging my ears.

I didn't let go until the sun rose the next morning.

# 29

## EMERY

Taking Oliver and Reese to my hometown terrified me. I had a horrible feeling in my gut, and I wasn't sure how to shake it off. But I tried to look for the silver linings in the situation. I was able to show the two most special people in my life the place that had shaped me. Sure, my parents hadn't been the best at raising my sister and me, but the small town where I grew up had a few gems.

When we got to town, it was already late into the night, so we checked into the bed-and-breakfast—getting two separate rooms. So when morning came, we were fully awake and ready to hit the town full speed ahead.

First stop was my old stomping ground: Walter's Diner. Home to the best hash browns a person would ever taste.

"I worked here for three years. I started when I was fifteen, even though I was supposed to be sixteen to officially have a job, but the owner, Walter, let me slide, and he'd help me learn cooking skills in the kitchen with him. By the time I was sixteen, I was the head chef back there, flipping burgers faster than anyone around. It was in this place where I fell in love with cooking," I said, looking around in awe.

Walter's Diner was set up as a 1950s spot. From the red-and-white booths down to the old-school glasses that the Coca-Cola and sundaes were served in. The decor was posters of classic sports cars and models and actors from the fifties. They still even had the old jukebox that was spinning tunes from that time period. It was as if we'd walked into a time capsule and taken a seat to enjoy some food and history.

"This is the place where you found your passion," Oliver commented.

"Not only that . . . this is the place that raised me. When my parents were in their moods and they'd take it out on me, I'd come here. Walter lives in the apartment right upstairs, and he'd always let me in, no matter what time it was, day or night, to teach me some cooking skills."

"Sounds like an amazing man."

"I owe so much to him."

When Walter came out with menus in his hand, I grinned. He was the one who brought each table the menus every single day, because he wanted to know the people who were showing their support to his business. He didn't only want to feed the people of Randall; he wanted to know how they were doing.

As he walked closer, still staring down at the menus, he began to speak to us. "Hey, hey there, folks, welcome to Walter's Diner. I, Walter, am so happy you're—" His words came to a halt when he looked up and saw me staring at him. His smile stretched so wide that I was almost certain my heart was going to explode from happiness. "Emery Rose," he breathed out. "As I live and breathe."

I leaped up from the booth and wrapped my arms around the older gentleman, holding him close to me. "Hey, Walt. Long time."

"Too long," he said, shaking his head in disappointment. "But I'm glad you're here. Are you staying for a while?"

"Just the night. We'll head out tomorrow, actually."

"Shame, I wanted you to cook me up one of your random dishes like you used to do."

Walter placed his hands against my cheeks and squeezed lightly, smiling at me as if he was a proud grandpa. In many ways, Walter was a grandfather figure to me, and I was a granddaughter to him. He never married. His business was his family, and as far as I went, I never knew my grandparents. So, we had each other. He even called me his grand-daughter when people would ask. He claimed me as his family with the biggest amount of love and pride when he spoke about me to others.

"Well, who do we have here?" he asked, turning to Oliver and Reese.

"Oh, this is Reese, my daughter." I almost hesitated saying the word, knowing that I was back in the town that knew Sammie. I wondered if they'd ever found out that she was pregnant. Then again, probably not. Mama and Dad never would've spread that news around. It would've brought too much shame to their image.

"Your daughter?" Walter exclaimed with excitement as he bent down to be eye level with Reese. "Well, how do you do, sweet thang?" he asked, holding a hand out toward Reese.

"I do good, sir," she said, shaking his hand.

Oliver huffed. "I wish I got that kind of greeting from her."

Walter's eyes moved to Oliver, and he gave him a stern look. "And you're the father?"

"Oh, no, Walter. This is Oliver. He's my—" My what? My friend? My employer? My person that I daydream about kissing on the regular?

"Good friend," Oliver answered, reaching out to shake Walter's hand. Even though Walter was wary about accepting the handshake, he did place his hand in Oliver's.

"I feel like I've seen you around before," Walter said, narrowing his eyes as he tried to put a finger on how he knew Oliver.

My heart began to beat harder as worry overtook me. The whole reason to bring Oliver out to Randall was for him to be a normal human for a day, and now Walter of all people was trying to pinpoint how he knew him. Walter took his hat off and slapped it against his knee. "Gosh darn it, aren't you Bobby Winters's cousin from Oklahoma?" he asked.

The relief that washed over our faces was identical as Oliver replied, "Nope, not me."

"Aw shucks, okay, my mistake. You got his ears, that's all. Here's the menu for you all. Oliver, I bet you'd like to know that this menu is the same exact one that Ms. Emery here created for me six years ago. All of the favorite dishes are hers."

"You're kidding me," I laughed. "You haven't changed the menu in all that time?"

"Of course not. You don't mess with perfection. I'll only change it when you come back to upgrade it."

"Well, I'll have to do that sooner rather than later," I said.

"Good. Okay, well, let me get you some time to look over the menu while I go get this sweetheart a slice of red velvet cake," he said, winking in Reese's direction. Of course, her eyes lit up with excitement.

"Oh, I don't know about cake at nine in the morning, Walter," I argued, being my daughter's worst enemy in that very moment.

Walter waved me off, dismissing my parenting. "Oh hush, girl. I remember feeding you cake in the morning more often than not. You know what they say: 'A slice of cake a day keeps the grumpy away.'"

"No one says that, Walter."

"Well, they should."

"Yeah, they should!" Reese chimed in with spirit.

Of course she'd agree; she was getting sugar.

When I sat back down, Oliver was grinning at me. "What is it?" I asked.

"I'm just wondering if you know how amazing you are. You created a whole menu that's being used in a restaurant today. Do you know how amazing that is?"

I blushed and shrugged. "It's a small-town diner. It's not that amazing."

"No, it is. It's amazing. You're amazing," he said, and the butterflies flipped upside down in my stomach. "This is only the beginning for you. I cannot wait to be sitting inside your restaurant someday."

"Me too!" Reese turned to me and placed her hands on my cheeks very tightly, smooshing my face together. "Mama. You are somebody, and you will do great things."

I gave her a peck on the forehead and then snuggled her nose against mine. "Love you."

"Love you more."

After a while, Walter returned with Reese's cake in hand and set it down in front of her. "There you go, sweetheart. Are you all ready to put down your orders?" Walter asked.

"Definitely are." I gave him the orders, and he wrote them all down, then paused for a second and looked my way.

"You sure you don't want to hop in the kitchen and whip these up on your own?" Walter offered, and for a moment a spark of excitement shot through me at the opportunity to work in the first kitchen I'd ever stood in.

"Seriously?"

"Of course, get back there," he said, waving me in the direction of the kitchen.

I looked over to Oliver, and he gave me a knowing look. "Don't worry, I'll just eat this cake with Reese," he told me.

"No way, Mr. Mith. You'd better get your own cake," Reese said with a mouthful of food.

I left the two of them to fight over the dessert and headed to the kitchen to get to work. The moment I slid on one of the diner aprons, it was as if my body went into muscle memory. Without even thinking about it, I knew what to do. Luckily, Walter had kept almost everything in the same exact place. I began preparing our breakfasts, and the excitement I felt came rushing back to me.

I knew cooking was my passion. I knew I had to finish my degree at some point soon, and I couldn't thank Oliver enough for giving me the chance to be his personal chef to relight that fire in my soul.

After our meal, which Walter refused to let us pay for, we walked over to the town square to explore the farmers' market. Oliver sported a nice baseball cap and sunglasses to hide his appearance the best he could, and luckily for us, no one really called us out, even though I ran into a few familiar faces.

I loved watching Reese and Oliver explore everything together. I loved how free they both looked, how free Oliver seemed to be. At one point, he lifted Reese onto his shoulders as they bought me flowers.

Each passing day, I was falling more in love with the man standing in front of me, and I doubted I'd ever be able to stop that fall.

The day was smooth throughout, without a hitch in sight. We explored all day and made our way back that night for some food trucks and street music.

Everything was going better than I thought it could, up until I came face to face with the people I feared most in Randall.

After we finished the slushie drinks that Reese had to have a part in, I tossed our cups into the trash can, and when I looked up, I met a pair of eyes that matched mine.

"Mama," I muttered, stunned to see her standing in front of me with Dad right by her side. They were holding bags from the local grocery store, and they were clearly just as stunned to see me as I was to see them.

"What are you doing here?" Mama snapped at me. "I thought I made myself clear on our last call that I didn't want to hear from you again, let alone see you."

Her stare was intense and cold. For a moment, I felt as if I were that same little girl who'd taken on so much of her verbal abuse. For a moment, I went back in time and stood frozen in fear as my father stared at me as if I were a monster.

Then, a hand landed on my lower back. Oliver approached me with Reese, and he gave me a small smile. "Everything okay?" he asked.

"Who are you?" Mama asked, her eyes going directly to Oliver, and in that moment, I found my confidence again.

"None of your business," I said, standing up straighter.

"Mama, who is that?" Reese asked as she moved to stand behind my leg. She was hiding behind me, which was so outside of her normal. My little girl wasn't one to be bashful. My protective instincts went up the moment I realized she was afraid.

My mother's eyes widened with surprise. "Is that . . ." Her words trailed off as she shook her head back and forth. "It can't be . . ."

I stepped backward, moving Reese back with me. Already I could tell where the direction of the conversation was unfolding, and I didn't want my daughter to take in anything that my mother was going to toss out at her.

Dad hadn't spoken one word at all, but his stare was on Reese's every move. Studying her entire existence. I hated how it felt whenever I was around him. I hated how we could have been so close, yet he felt so far away.

"Well, I'll be damned, if it isn't Emery Taylor. It looks like it's a Taylor family reunion," a voice said with excitement. I looked over my shoulder to see Bobby, my high school friend, walking in my direction. If only he knew how bad his timing was in that very moment. "It's been too damn long, that's for sure," he said the moment his eyes locked with mine.

He went straight for a hug, and I let it happen, mostly because I was in a state of shock. He completely missed the uncomfortable situation unfolding before us, probably due to the alcohol in his bloodstream. "How have you been?" he asked. "It's been too long."

Before that very minute? Pretty great. In that moment? Awful. "I've been good, Bobby. It's good to see you."

"Shit, you too, Emery. This town's sure missing your face—and your cooking. Sammie has been cooking the meals down at the church after services, but it's nowhere as good as your cooking. Maybe before you go, you can whip up some of that mac and cheese you used to make for—"

"Where is she?" I asked, turning straight to Mama as my stomach dropped. It felt as if boulders were sitting heavy in the pit of me, weighing me down from shock.

Mama shifted uncomfortably in her shoes as Dad looked away from me. They didn't say a word. Guilt sank in Mama's eyes, yet Dad didn't show a blink of remorse for the news that Bobby had revealed.

"Where is she?" I asked again. A rage was building up inside me, and I didn't know how it was going to explode from my system with the news my parents had been hiding from me. "I called you, Mama. I asked about her, and you didn't say a word."

"I don't have to tell you a thing," she said, crossing her arms as if her stance made any sense.

I turned to Bobby. "Do you know where Sammie is staying, Bobby?"

"Don't answer that, Bobby," Mama ordered, scolding him as if he were a child.

"Bobby." I took a deep inhalation and locked my eyes with his. "Do you know?"

Bobby's stare dashed back and forth between Mama and me, and his aloof persona was completely drained away as he began to read the seriousness of the situation at hand. "Oh man, look, I didn't mean to cause any trouble," he explained, ruffling through his curly hair.

"It's fine, just tell me," I said, trying everything to keep myself from shaking him out of fear. Oliver stood behind me with his hands on Reese's shoulders. He leaned in and whispered that he was going to take Reese off to play a game to give my parents and me space to talk. I nodded in agreement.

As they began to walk away, Mama's eyes widened in shock. "You're just going to allow a strange man to walk off with my granddaughter?"

A strange man?

Her granddaughter?

She couldn't have been serious in that moment. She couldn't have been questioning my parenting skills, when she'd been lying to me about the whereabouts of my sister for who knew how long.

I didn't even give her question the answer she was in search of. My eyes stared into Bobby. "Bobby?" I asked again.

He grimaced and rubbed his hand over his mouth and then shrugged. As he was about to speak and give me the information, Dad jumped into the conversation.

"I think it's about time for you to walk away, Bobby," he ordered.

Bobby took the command and ran with it. Literally. He jogged away and didn't look back once.

Acid began to burn at the back of my throat as my panic rose. My little sister had been living in our small town for so long and had never reached out to let me know. She'd made it seem as if she was going off to find herself, not to return to my parents' chains.

"How did you get that child?" Mama asked, her voice harsh. Her forehead was dripping with sweat, and it was the first time in a long time that I remembered seeing Mama nervous—outside of Dad yelling at her.

"Excuse me? Sammie left her with me five years ago. She said she was going off to find herself."

"No. That can't be. Sammie said the baby didn't make it. She said she lost it, and that's why she came back," Mama said, shaky.

"Why in the world would she leave a child in the hands of someone like you?" Dad barked, disgusted by the idea. That hurt me more than he'd ever know.

I couldn't grasp what was happening, or why it was happening. "Why didn't you tell me she's been living back here?" I asked Mama.

"Why would I tell you anything? We don't speak. Besides, Samantha is fine."

"No, she isn't," I said, shaking my head. Nothing about the situation felt right, and I couldn't believe that Sammie was okay after everything she'd been through. "She can't be okay if she's back in this town."

"You watch your tongue, talking about my daughter," Dad cut in.

Same ol' Dad.

*I'm your daughter too.*

"Why? It's true, and you both know it. She can't be okay after what she went through."

"That's why we take care of her. That's why we see her, because that's our baby. She came to us when she needed us. Not that any of that is your business."

I stood flabbergasted by the words that were leaving Mama's mouth. "You're insane if you think—"

I flinched the moment Dad's hand landed against my forearm and he held on tight. His dark eyes locked with mine, and I swore I felt a darkness race over me. "Don't you dare talk to your mother like that," he scolded as he squeezed my arm.

My mouth parted as my body began to shake uncontrollably from his grip. "Let me go," I ordered, even though my voice shook as the words left me. It was no secret that even to that day, I was afraid of my father.

He held on tighter, and I cringed from the pain. "Apologize to your mother."

Mama's eyes softened for a split second as she looked down at his grip on me. "Okay, Theo, I think that's enough."

Dad squeezed harder. I gasped.

Mama placed her hand against his and shook her head. "Let her go, Theo."

"Stay out of this, Harper," he ordered. The hatred that painted his eyes terrified me. "Apologize for speaking to her like that."

"What?" I cried. "No."

Harder.

"Apologize," he commanded.

The pain shot up my arm, and I was almost to the point where tears were ready to release from my eyes, but I didn't want to cry in front of him. For some reason, I felt that if he saw me weak, he'd feel strong.

"What the hell are you doing?" a voice barked. I looked over my shoulder to see Oliver standing there, with Reese beside him. He marched directly toward my father and ripped his hold from me. "Don't ever put your hand on her."

Dad stood tall, but unlike me, Oliver didn't shiver with fear. He stood eye to eye with the man who'd raised me and stepped in front of me, protecting me from the first man who was supposed to be my protector.

"Who the hell do you think you are?" Dad snarled, fury sitting against his face. His hands were rolled in fists.

"Someone who will never watch a man put his hands on a woman and do nothing about it. If you ever touch Emery again, it will be the end of you," Oliver said, cold as stone.

"You don't know the person you're defending," Dad said with spite.

"You think you have the right to put your hands on a woman? Any woman? Why, because they're smaller than you? Because they make you feel big? Come on, then. Do it to me. See what happens," Oliver ordered, stepping straight into Dad's space. "Show me what a tough guy you are."

"Oliver," I said, placing a hand against his arm. "Let's go."

His stance was firm, and he didn't seem to be stepping down, so I pushed between him and my father and looked Oliver in the eyes. "Hey, right here."

He lowered his head to make eye contact with me, and the fire that swam in his stare softened once he was staring my way. "Let's go. Please."

His shoulders relaxed, and he nodded slightly.

Reese looked as if she was confused and horrified all at once. I hated that fear that she was feeling. I rushed over to her and lifted her into my arms. "It's okay, baby. You're okay."

She curled into me, and I held on tighter than ever.

"That's right. You need to get to leaving," Dad said, trying to be strong, but I swore when Oliver stepped up to him, I saw something I'd never seen in my life—I saw Dad flinch.

I felt defeated as I looked toward him and asked him the one question that had been sitting on my mind almost my whole life. "Why do you hate me?" I whispered, sounding like the hurt child I used to be.

Without hesitation, he blinked once and answered. "Because you've always been a disappointment."

My heart.

It shattered.

"Let's go," Oliver softly spoke, placing a hand on my lower back.

I looked toward my parents and wanted to say so much, yet nothing was strong enough to leave my lips; instead, I turned on my heel and began to walk away.

"You okay, Mama?" Reese asked, wiping away the tears that fell down my cheek.

"Yes, baby, I'm okay."

"She shouldn't be calling you her mother," Mama called out, but I kept walking, even though her words felt like stabs to my soul. "She's not yours," she said, making every inch of my body shake with heartbreak. How could she say something so harsh? How could she be so cruel?

I felt as if my knees were going to buckle beneath me any second, and right before I almost fell apart, Oliver was there, linking his arm with my free one. He kept me standing when I felt like falling.

"Keep walking, Em," he whispered. "Just keep walking."

We moved on autopilot until we reached the car. I buckled Reese into her car seat and then moved into the passenger seat. Staring forward, I tried my best to control the anger and pain rushing through me.

"Hey, Mama?"

"Yes, Reese?"

"Why did she say I wasn't yours?"

I shut my eyes as tears rolled down my cheeks. "I don't know, sweetheart. She was just a crazy woman."

"Oh, okay." She accepted it easily as ever, before saying "Hey, Mama?" again.

I sniffled. "Yes, sweetheart?"

"I don't think you're a disappointment."

My head lowered as the tears kept falling from my eyes. "Thank you, baby." I tried my best to still the shaking of my body so Reese wouldn't see my poor reaction.

"Are you okay?" Oliver whispered.

With a deep inhalation, I said, "Just drive, please."

He did as I requested, and I kept my eyes closed the whole time as we drove toward the bed-and-breakfast. I didn't pull away when I felt Oliver's hand fall against mine. With a gentle squeeze, a splash of comfort hit my soul.

"Thank you," I whispered.

"Always."

Reese was asleep within seconds of falling against her queen bed once we made it to our room. I moved slowly as my mind was spinning fast. After washing my face and putting on my pajamas, I heard a knock at the door.

I opened it to find Oliver standing there with his hands in his pockets. "Hey."

I tried to force a smile, but it wasn't there. "Hey."

"Let me hold you?" he asked.

I shook my head. "It's okay, you don't have to; I'm okay. I'm fine. It was just a long day, that's all. I should be getting to sleep."

"You don't have to do that, you know."

"Do what?"

"Be strong all the time."

"Yes," I said while nodding, "I do. Because if I'm not, then I'm not able to be what my daughter needs me to be. She needs me to be strong in order to take care of her."

His eyes moved to the sleeping girl in her bed, and then he looked back to me. "Right now she's good, she's safe, she's okay, Emery. So, now it's time for you to be taken care of."

"I . . ." My words faded as I crossed my arms and shook my head slightly. "I've never had anyone take care of me before. I don't even know what that looks like."

"It's different every time, but tonight it's me holding you."

I bit my bottom lip and nodded slightly, giving him permission to take me into his arms. The moment he wrapped himself around me, I melted into him, feeling at home in an instant. He moved us to my bed, and we lay down beside one another. His arms felt like the greatest weighted blanket that my soul needed that night.

He didn't push for conversation; he didn't try to understand what had unfolded before him that evening. He simply gave me comfort, he took care of me, and I kept falling, falling, falling . . .

*I love you,* I thought.

*I love you,* I felt.

*I love you,* I knew.

I couldn't say the words, though, because love scared me. Every person I'd ever loved had always let me down. I couldn't allow myself to verbalize my feelings for Oliver, because once I did, I knew there was no going back for me.

My body turned to face him, and I looked into those brown eyes that had been the source of sparks of happiness over the past few weeks, and then my stare fell to his lips. My heart began racing; my mind began to spin.

"Oliver?"

"Yes?"

"Do you feel for me what I feel for you?"

"More," he whispered, inching his face closer to mine, resting our foreheads against one another. "I feel more."

"Does it scare you?"

"No."

"It scares me," I confessed. "I'm not used to people caring about me, and the ones who were supposed to are the ones who left. So that scares me. Getting close to you freaks me out, because what if you change your mind? What if one day you decide that you don't want me anymore and you leave?"

"I can't erase your fear, Emery, but I need you to know that you did this to me," he said, taking my hands into his and laying them against his chest. "You found me when my heartbeats were hardly there, and you stamped them. You stamped my heart, and that's why it's still beating."

The way my body filled with love was almost overpowering. "Oliver . . ."

"Ask me to be yours, and I'll be yours. If you let me stay, I'll stay forever."

I moved in closer to him and slightly brushed my lips against his, and the small graze sent a ripple throughout my whole system. My lips crashed against his. I kissed him hard at first, and then a gentleness fell over me. His lips tasted like every dream come true, and I loved the way he kissed me back. He kissed me as if he'd missed me for decades before we'd met. His kiss felt like a promise that I needed to feel. As he pulled back, I met his stare and gave him a small smile.

"I'm yours, please stay, and please kiss me again," I whispered, and then he did.

I didn't know how long our lips stayed together, or how long it was until exhaustion fell over us. All that I knew was that in his arms, I felt comfort; in his arms, I felt safe.

As my eyes faded shut, and his closed, too, I dreamed of him saying he loved me.

In my dreams, I whispered back that I loved him too.

# 30

## EMERY

The next morning, I knew I needed to talk to Sammie, and I knew exactly where I'd find her—down at the church getting ready for morning Bible study. It didn't take much effort to find out where she'd be in a small town like Randall. All I had to do was ask around, and I quickly received my answers.

I arrived before the church service had begun, and I found Sammie in one of the classrooms, preparing for her lesson. She hadn't noticed me, as she was busy flipping through paperwork, so I stood in the doorframe and knocked on the wall.

The moment she looked up, she dropped the papers in her hands, which went scattering across the room.

"Emery," she whispered, her voice in pure shock. She looked as if she'd seen a ghost, and in some ways, she had. "Wh-what are you doing here?"

"Are you kidding me, Sammie? What are *you* doing here?" I barked, stunned. I hated the fact that a part of me wanted to hug her, to embrace her, to cry, knowing she was alive and well. Another part of me wanted to cuss her out. "You told me you went off to start a new life. You didn't tell me that you came back here. Each time we talked, you were somewhere new. How could you do that? Why would you keep it from me that you came back here? Did you ever even travel at all?"

Her eyes showed the truth. She hadn't. She'd run straight home all those years ago. I was going to be sick.

"I . . . it's . . ." She swallowed hard and glanced over my shoulder as if she was afraid of someone overhearing our conversation. "It's complicated."

I closed the door behind me and walked into the room in her direction. "You ran back to Mama and Dad right away, didn't you?"

"I had to, Emery. You don't understand. I had nothing."

"You had me!"

"Not really. And I get it. It was easy for you to walk away from Mama and Dad, but I'm not like you. My relationship with them was good before I made a mistake."

"You didn't make a mistake—you were raped, Sammie."

She cringed at my words before breathing in deeply. "Yes, well, that was a long time ago, and it's something we don't talk about anymore. So, yeah. I have to get ready for class." She went to pick up the paperwork, and I was so confused. What was going on? She was acting like a weird Stepford wife, moving as if she had no real emotions and acting as if her abandoning me and Reese five years ago wasn't a big deal.

"Sammie, you left Reese. You left me. We struggled for years trying to keep our heads above water, and you walked away and came home. You could've reached out and told me. You could've given us help somehow."

She blinked a few times before shaking her head. "I made the best choice I could, Emery. That's all I could do."

"And Mama and Dad were fine with you abandoning Reese?"

Her brown eyes glassed over before she went back to picking up the pieces of paper. "It doesn't matter what they think."

"Well, they seemed pretty shocked when they saw Reese in town yesterday."

"What? They saw her?" Sammie gasped. "No . . . no . . ."

"Yes. And they were stunned. They said you told them you lost the baby. They didn't even know she existed."

Sammie wasn't listening to me. She wasn't taking in the words that I was saying. "Reese is here? In Randall?"

"Yes . . ."

"No one can know I had that baby, Emery. Do you understand? No one can know. It would ruin my world. Mama and Dad would flip out. I told them I lost the baby, and that's why they took me back in. They said it was God's way of healing me."

That alone made me want to vomit. The only way my parents would take my sister back was by believing she'd had a miscarriage? And they believed something so horrific was a sign from God?

What was wrong with those people?

What was wrong with Sammie for telling such a terrible lie?

"Well, now they know Reese exists. So you'll have to deal with that," I warned her. "Not that you're good with dealing with things."

"You don't get to scold me," she started.

"The hell I don't!" I snapped.

"Watch your language—you're in a church," Sammie muttered, sounding a bit too much like Mama.

"Is this all you wanted? To be a carbon copy of Mama? To pretend that things are fine when they aren't? You abandoned me, Sammie, after I took you in, and you have nothing to say about it? No remorse?"

She parted her lips as her body shivered a little. "It . . . it was in God's will to end up this way."

God's will?

What a fucking cop-out.

I couldn't believe it. I couldn't believe the woman who was standing in front of me saying these things. I didn't know that woman. I didn't know the girl who stood there speaking the words that she had. My sister wasn't that person. My sister could never be so cruel and heartless.

No . . . the woman in front of me was a product of our parents. They'd shaped her solid during the most traumatic times of her life.

And the sister I knew, the Sammie I loved, was no longer anywhere to be found.

"It's a sad day when a person needs to use God to cover up their guilt for harsh choices in life," I muttered, turning away, knowing there wasn't anything else left for me to say.

As I went to open the door, Sammie called out.

"Emery?"

"Yes?"

I looked back to find a teary-eyed girl staring my way. Her bottom lip trembled as she said, "Please don't tell anyone about Reese and me. It would ruin my life. I can't deal with that. I have a new beginning. People can't know."

I didn't say another word to her as I walked out of the building. I'd never tell a soul about what Sammie did all those years ago. But that guilt on Sammie's heart?

That was something she'd have to deal with for the rest of her life.

My days felt heavy as memories of my trip to see Sammie kept coming up and pounding me with emotions. I did my best to distract myself with spending extra quality time with Reese and coming up with new recipes to try for Oliver. Cooking and my daughter were my two saving graces. Without them both, my mind would've run wild.

One afternoon, while I was making a grocery list for the week at Oliver's, I heard sniffling coming from the pantry.

Alarmed, I headed over quickly, where I found a crying Kelly falling apart, with her palms over her face.

"Oh my gosh, Kelly, what's wrong?" I asked, rushing to her side and pulling her straight in for a hug.

"I'm sorry, Em." She sniffled and tried to control her emotions. "I just saw the cereal up there, and it reminded me of a night that Alex and I stayed up late into the night eating cereal, and it's stupid but it hit me hard, and now . . ." She couldn't finish her words, because she began sobbing again.

It was the first time I'd witnessed Kelly showing any kind of sadness. Oliver had told me that she and Alex had had a past together and were falling in love, but I'd never brought it up to her, because I figured it was a hard topic to tackle. She always seemed so upbeat and composed, so seeing her crumbling from having a memory come rushing back to her broke my heart.

"I'm so stupid. I'm sorry, I'm fine," she said, wiping the tears that kept falling.

"You're not stupid, and you're not fine. You don't have to be fine, Kelly. I cannot even imagine what it is you're going through."

She looked at me with the most heartbroken stare and shook her head. "You don't know how awful I feel. I feel so guilty."

"Guilty? Why?"

She sniffled and covered her face with the palms of her hands. Through her muffled sounds she said, "A man asked me on a date at CycleBar today, and I gave him my number," she cried. "How could I do that? How could I give another man my number after losing the best man I've ever had?"

*Oh, Kelly . . .*

That moment was a complete realization for me. While I'd been dealing with my own demons, Kelly had been facing hers. I hadn't even known how deep her scars ran until that very moment. It was then that I realized that everyone had struggles that they tried their best to keep to themselves.

"You can't be that hard on yourself, Kelly. You deserve to be happy again."

"I don't even know what that means anymore!" She cried, even harder, and I held her tighter in my arms.

"You know what you need?" I whispered, trying my best to soothe her.

"What's that?"

I pulled her back a little and smiled at her as I brushed away some of her tears. "You need a girls' day."

After some convincing, Kelly agreed to have me take her on a spa day, to help clear her head and heart from the mess that was sitting inside of her.

"Are you sure it's okay?" I asked Oliver as Kelly went to clean herself up a little.

"Yes, of course. She needs it. Plus, I can get by feeding myself for the day," he joked. "How can I help?"

"Actually, I was wondering if you could do me a huge favor and pick Reese up from camp today? I asked Abigail, but she already has plans."

"Of course, not a problem. What time?"

I gave him all the information, and he was more than willing to help me out.

"Thank you, Emery . . . for being there for Kelly. I know you're going through your own stuff, but it means a lot to me that you're helping her out."

"I think we both need a day to get away," I confessed. "The world's been a lot lately. I just feel as if it's time to unplug for a second."

"Take all the time you two need. I'll be here with Reese when you're ready to come home."

*Home.*

He said it as if his home was mine. That made me smile more than I knew possible.

# 31

## OLIVER

Reese's camp looked like a scene from the cartoon *Recess*, where the kindergartners ran around in their playground like wild animals. All the kids were shouting as they chased one another around. In that moment, I was so damn happy I'd never attended summer camp. It probably would've fucked with my anxiety more than anything else.

I stood leaning up against my car, waiting to spot Reese to take her home. Emery had already called the camp instructors to inform them that I'd be the one picking her daughter up, so now was the waiting game.

Kids dashed past me as they hurried to their cars to head home for the night. When I spotted Reese, I stood up straighter and studied the interaction that was taking place. She didn't look like her bubbly self that I'd grown to love. She looked . . . sad?

Then, my concern turned into rage as I witnessed a young boy poking her with a stick, and then he pushed her down to the ground.

"Hey, what the fuck!" I hollered, rushing over to the scene, shocked by what had just happened. No camp instructors seemed to notice what had taken place, which only made me more livid.

"Dude, don't ever put your hands on her again," I snapped at the kid.

He looked at me like he was the toughest kid on the playground, and he rolled his eyes. Yeah, that's right. The little shit rolled his eyes at me.

"Whatever, you're not my dad. You can't tell me what to do," he huffed.

I helped Reese up, and she hurried to stand behind me as embarrassment settled in.

"Yeah, I'm not your dad, but I will tell on you," I threatened.

"My dad could kick your butt," the kid said, leaving me shocked. What kind of demon child was this? Was his mother Cam? He had way too much in common with her.

I looked around and shouted, "Hey, whose kid is this? Somebody'd better tell me whose little shit this is!" I hollered.

"That's a quarter for the swear jar," Reese whispered.

I'd gladly put the coin in the jar for this situation.

"What's going on over here?" a deep voice said. I turned to see a guy who was twice my size marching my way, but I wasn't going to step down. Not when it came to having Reese's back.

"What's going on is your son pushed Reese to the ground, and he wouldn't apologize."

"It's not true, Dad! He's lying!" the jerk lied.

Must've been Cam's kid.

"He said he didn't do it, so he didn't do it," the man said, standing tall.

"Well, your kid's a liar."

He puffed out his chest. "You getting slick? Don't talk about my son."

"Then tell him to keep his hands to himself, and we wouldn't have a damn problem."

Before the huge giant spoke again, he narrowed his eyes at me, taking me in. "Wait a fucking minute. Aren't you Oliver Smith?"

Oh shit.

I shifted in my shoes. Not wanting to answer that.

"Yeah, he's Oliver Mith, and he's my friend!" Reese chimed in, finding her voice again.

"Holy shit! I'm a big fan," the scary giant said, taking my hand into his and shaking it nonstop. His whole demeanor shifted as he came to the realization of who I was. "Man. Your music is the best. Sorry about your loss, dude. My condolences."

It was as if he was a brand-new person. He even seemed a bit smaller somehow too.

He turned to his kid and gave him a stern look. "Did you push that girl, Randy?"

"Yes! He did! I even scraped my knee!" Reese said, showing her leg.

"Why did you push her?" his father asked him.

"Dad! 'Cause she's a weirdo," Randy whined.

His father gripped him by the arm and pulled him closer to Reese. "Apologize."

"What? No way! I didn't even do—" Randy's father gave him a cold, hard stare that made him shut up in an instant. Sure, I couldn't get the kid to act right because, as he'd stated, I wasn't his father. Yet the big dude *was* his father, and he clearly had that power.

Randy groaned. "I'm sorry," he muttered.

His dad nudged him. "Say it with meaning. And look her in the eyes."

"Dad!"

"Do. It. Now."

Randy walked closer to Reese and looked her in the eyes. "I'm sorry for pushing you, Reese."

She grinned with pride. "Thank you."

"Sorry again, man," the dad said, taking my hand yet again and shaking it. "Again. Huge fan. Can I get a picture?"

Awkward situation, but I took a picture with him.

The whole camp had slowed down as everyone took in the interaction that had taken place. So I took it as an opportunity to express my thoughts on the whole situation.

"Let this be a lesson to all of you. If you pick on this girl, you're picking on me, and you definitely don't want to pick on me. Otherwise, there will be trouble."

"Yeah!" Reese chimed in. "Because he's Oliver Mith, and he's a rock star and rich and famous and he will kick all of your butts and take you to court to sue you, because he's rich and he has a lot of money and he'd win!"

"Easy does it, kid," I mumbled. "No need to threaten lawsuits."

"Sorry, Mr. Mith," she whispered back.

We headed to the car, and Reese seemed to have found her light again as she jumped into the back seat, where her booster seat had been placed. I went to make sure she was buckled in safely, and she leaned in toward me, placed her hands on my cheeks, and said, "Mr. Mith?"

"Yeah, kid?"

"You're my best friend."

———— ❦ ————

Emery and Kelly's girls' day faded into the night. Reese fell asleep in the guest room after our second time watching *Frozen 2*. When Emery showed up, I welcomed her with a tight embrace.

"I hope Reese didn't give you too much trouble," she said.

"What? No way. We're the best of friends. She's asleep in the back room."

"Thanks again for watching her."

"Anytime. Is Kelly okay?"

Emery frowned. "She'll get there. One day at a time."

She didn't know what a phenomenal woman she had been. Even when she was going through her own storm, she always made time to help others. I'd never met a woman who gave so much of herself without asking for anything in return.

I slid my hands into my pockets and swayed. "At my first meeting with Abigail, she made this analogy about how everyone's life story is a mixtape, and each track is a chapter of their life. Some chapters are happy, and others are sad, but they are all entangled to create that person's mixtape."

"I love that concept," she said, snuggling in against me. The warmth of her skin heated me up too.

"I do too." I rested my head in the nape of her neck, trailing kisses down her skin. "Can I tell you a secret?" My lips fell against her earlobe as I nuzzled against it gently.

A light moan escaped her as she opened her eyes to look my way. "Yes."

"You're my favorite song on my mixtape."

She placed her hands against my cheeks and pulled me in for a kiss. I kissed her slowly, enjoying every second I was able to spend with her by my side.

"Stay the night?" I asked.

"Okay."

"Come to bed with me tonight?"

She bit her bottom lip before leaning in and kissing me gently. "Okay."

I took her to my bedroom, and I began removing her clothing as she removed mine. My lips fell against her skin as I laid her on my bed. I took my time at first, tasting every piece that I'd craved for weeks. I spread her legs wide and lowered myself down to taste the heaven I'd been dreaming about.

Each time my tongue swept against her core, she moaned in pleasure. I sucked and licked every drip she gave me. I loved the way she tasted against my mouth, and fuck, I couldn't wait until I felt my cock sliding in and out of her.

We made love that night, making a song that was ours, and ours alone. Every time she moaned, I fucked her harder, pulling on her locks as her fingers tangled up in my hair. Her wetness made me want her more. Each time I slid inside I wanted to live inside her even longer. She rode me hard, rolling her hips against me, coming over and over again as she cried out my name.

"Em, I'm going to . . . I'm gonna . . ." *Shit.* I went to pull out, and she stopped me, gripping my neck in her hand, forcing me to lock eyes with her.

"I'm on the pill," she whispered, and that was the only confirmation I needed before I sighed, unable to say any more words as the orgasm overtook me.

I released inside of her, and I felt her tremble against my skin. My body dripped in sweat as she breathed heavily from exhaustion.

"That was . . . ," I said, breathing intensely and resting my forehead against hers.

"Exactly," she sighed.

Perfection.

It was perfect.

We stayed there for a few moments before we made love again.

Our bodies mixed together the same way that our hearts were intertwined. I placed her on top of me and watched in amazement as she rode me in what felt like slow motion, her hips rising and falling to a tempo that was created solely for us. My hands sat against her waist as we moved as one, me sliding into her deep as she fell deeper against me every few seconds.

I groaned in pleasure and she moaned in desire. Her moans were the most beautiful sound in the whole damn world, and I loved it. I loved the sound of us, the taste of us, the rhythm of us. I loved the way that when she climaxed, I felt every piece of her shiver against me, making my own body grow closer to completion. I loved how she begged me to let her keep riding me. I loved how she owned my body, my mind, my soul.

I loved her.

I was falling in love with her so fast that it should have scared me, but instead I felt happy.

*Happy...*

I didn't know I still knew how to feel that way.

Our songs that night tangled together, creating a remix of sorts. Her heart beat with mine, and as we fell asleep in one another's arms, I felt as if we were creating something new. A brand-new mixtape, one that held our story.

I loved the sound of that.

# 32

## EMERY

"We need to talk," Mama said as she stood at my apartment door. I had no clue why she was standing in front of me, let alone how she knew where I lived. I'd only arrived home with Reese about an hour ago after leaving Oliver's, and now Harper Taylor was there to dampen my mood.

"There's nothing that we have to talk about," I said, crossing my fingers. "How did you even find out where I live?"

"I've known where you've lived for years. Sammie told me ages ago. I just didn't have a need to come to your doorstep until now."

Reese came out of her bedroom and walked over to the front door. "Mama? Who's that?" she asked, looking at the door. Then her eyes widened, and she hid behind my leg. "Is that the crazy lady again?"

*Yes, Reese. Yes it is.*

Mama leaned down so she was eye level with my daughter and gave her a big, fake smile. "No, sweetheart. I am your grandma."

Reese's eyes widened with excitement. "I have a grandma?"

I pushed Reese farther behind me and shot Mama a hard look. "Don't speak to my child."

Mama stood back up. "She's not your child. Which is why I'm here."

"You need to leave."

"Not until we talk."

"We have nothing in this world to talk about. And I will not have you disrespecting my daughter in front of me. So, if you don't leave—"

"Sammie's in the car downstairs," Mama said, cutting me off. "With Theo."

"What?"

"She's downstairs, waiting in the car. She wants to talk to you, and I figured an arranged meeting at the diner down the street might be best so we can speak about our family issues."

Family issues?

I snickered.

*What family?*

I moved over to the window facing the street, and to my shock, there Sammie was, sitting in the back of my parents' car, with Dad sitting in the passenger seat. I walked back over to Mama, shaking my head. "What do you want to talk about?"

"It's about Sammie's mental health, and getting her what she needs. Can you stop with all the questions, Emery, and just listen for once in your life? We will discuss everything once we get there."

I looked over to my daughter. "What about Reese?"

"What about her? Bring her along. I think it might be good for everyone."

Over my dead body.

"I don't want to talk about anything in front of her. Let me drop her off at my neighbor's. Come on, Reese." I took my daughter's hand and took her over to Abigail's apartment. I felt awful for even having to ask Abigail to watch my little girl again, but I didn't know what else to do. I had a feeling in my gut that the conversation with my family wasn't going to be all rainbows and roses, so I wanted to keep Reese as far away as possible from the conflict.

Of course, Abigail was more than willing to help out.

"Is everything okay?" Abigail asked, raising an eyebrow as she looked down the hallway toward Mama.

"I don't know, honestly. But I don't want Reese to be involved in the conversation I'm about to have with my family."

Abigail's eyes widened a little. "Oh my. Is that your mother?"

I nodded. "Yeah. I'll be back as soon as I can to pick her up."

"Of course, no rush. She and I will be just fine," Abigail said, placing her hands on Reese's shoulders.

"Thank you."

"Hey, Mama. Is that really my grandma?" Reese asked. My chest tightened from the question.

I bent down and kissed her forehead. "I'll explain everything later, baby. You just stay with Abigail until I get home." I stamped her heart, and she stamped mine back.

I walked over to Mama, and she was grimacing, like usual. "Do you always leave your child with strangers?"

I rolled my eyes and kept walking toward the elevator. "You're more of a stranger to me than anyone in this building is. Let's get this over with."

"We will drive together, to the diner on the corner," Mama stated, taking control of the situation, like she always had. I didn't complain or argue, because my focus was zoomed in on Sammie.

I opened the back passenger door and looked at my sister, who was fidgeting with her fingers and looking down at her lap. I sat down in the car and took in a deep breath. "Hey, Sammie."

She turned my way with the saddest eyes I'd ever witnessed and gave me an upside-down frown. "Hey, Emery."

She was sitting up with perfect posture, as if she'd never slouched in her life. Her sundress was smooth as ever, without a wrinkle to be found, and her hair was in perfect curls. She looked remarkable from the outside, but I saw it—her truths within her eyes.

As we walked inside and took our seats, I had a million and one questions swirling in my head to ask Sammie. I wanted to know what the plans were to get her on the up-and-up again. I wanted to know how I could help her, because I would. I'd do whatever it took to help my sister.

But then, the conversation started off in a completely different direction, throwing me for a loop.

"We want full custody of Reese," Mama said, clasping her hands together calmly, as if she'd only asked for a glass of ice water. As if she hadn't just said the words I'd feared most in my whole life.

"Excuse me?" Did they really just bring me to a restaurant to tell me that kind of information?

"After talking to Sammie, and going through the process of research on the subject, I think it is in the best interest of that little girl that she comes back to Randall with your sister, father, and me, and we take over raising her."

I laughed.

I laughed out loud because what she was saying was beyond ridiculous and out of this world. What kind of request was that for her to even consider making? When I realized they weren't laughing along with me, my chuckles turned into rage.

"You're joking, right? This is some kind of joke?" I choked out, staring at my family members and wondering how there was any possible way that the blood that raced through my veins was the same blood that flowed in theirs.

"We think it's best that—" Sammie started, but I cut her off.

"'We'? What is this 'we' you're speaking of? Because you can't be talking about our parents. They abandoned you, Samantha. And if you recall correctly, you went ahead and abandoned me and Reese too. Like mother, like daughter."

She shifted in her seat, looking down at the tiled floor of the restaurant. "That was a long time ago, Emery. We want to give Reese a shot at a family."

"What family?" I shouted, not caring about every person who was looking my way. "These two abandoned you at your lowest point, Sammie. They turned their backs on you after something horrific occurred. These people are not your family."

"Lower your voice, Emery Rose," Mama hissed, becoming flustered as she patted her cheeks with a napkin. "The whole point of coming to a restaurant to talk was so you wouldn't have an outburst. So, calm yourself."

"No. I'm a grown woman and I can be loud if I want to, Mama. You don't get to order me around like I'm still a child."

"I will not put up with your outbursts in a public setting. Now, calm yourself or remove yourself."

"I will do no such thing. Not until Sammie realizes what a mistake she's making."

"See, Samantha? Do you see how unstable your sister is? Having Emery raise Reese after all this time is a terrible idea. She needs to be in a more structured household, with your father and me. That little girl needs to be raised in a God-fearing household with two parental figures. We can provide more for her than Emery can. What do you think it will do to a little girl growing up without a father figure around her?"

I sat back in my chair, completely baffled. "Did it bother you that much?"

"I beg your pardon?"

"Seeing me that day in the marketplace with Reese. Did it bother you so much, seeing that we were okay without you? That we didn't have to be controlled by your unrealistic demands?"

"We're not doing this, Emery. We came here to allow you to have an idea of what's to come with Reese's future. I don't think you even deserve that privilege."

"You know what's funny?" I asked, shaking my head in disbelief. "How you judge us so hard when you made the same choices when you were our age."

"You have no clue what you're talking about, little girl."

"I'm not a little girl anymore, Mama. I'm grown. I have my own little girl now. But how old were you when you had me?"

She tensed up. "Like I said, we are not doing this."

"Seventeen," I said, ignoring her as she tried to change the subject. "And if I recall, you weren't married at that time, either."

She shifted around in her chair and shook her head. Dad held up his controlling hand as a way of silencing me. The number of times I'd seen that hand raised in my childhood to shut me up whenever I had a comment, or a question, or even a random thought, was staggering. That hand had wielded so much power over me, for so long, that even after all these years I slightly flinched from the sight of it.

"That's enough, Emery," Dad said, his voice low, smoky, and controlled. "I will not have you making your mother feel guilt for past sins she'd taken part in that she's already asked forgiveness for."

I laughed, trying to hide my fear of the man who raised me. "Her sins? Last time I checked, it took two to tangle up together and make a baby, Dad," I snapped. I hated him. I hated what he stood for, how he looked down on women, how he'd controlled not only Sammie and me for our whole youth, but also how he belittled Mama right in front of her face.

How was it her sins that had gotten her pregnant before marriage, but not his own? Why did Mama have to ask for forgiveness, but Dad simply had to put a ring on her finger to fix his actions? It wasn't right.

Nothing about their story was right to me.

"You shut your little mouth, will you not?" Mama snapped, waving her napkin in my direction. "Your disrespect will not be tolerated, and your assumptions are out of line. Do not ever speak to your father in that fashion again, or so help me—"

Dad held his hand up to her.

She fell quiet.

And the abusive cycle of control continued.

What would it be like for Reese to grow up in a household like that? What would it mean for her special mind that was filled with wonder?

Her favorite superheroes were women.

Dad would quickly stomp that out of her system.

I turned to my sister, the girl who looked as if she'd been drained of her spirit completely, and I placed my hands in hers. "Sammie, you asked me to be her mother. Don't you remember? All those years ago, you left, and you asked me to raise her. I did as you requested. Do you know what this will do to me? Do you know how much this would destroy me? How much it would uproot Reese's life?"

Sammie wouldn't look me in the eyes. I couldn't help but feel as if she was under some kind of spell. All I knew was that the person in front of me looked nothing like the girl I grew up with. She looked nothing like my best friend. She was hollow inside, and my parents didn't seem to care at all.

"Drop her hands, Samantha," Dad ordered.

Sammie's shaky grip in my hold released as she placed her hands into her lap. She'd always been an obedient child, never speaking back, never causing trouble, and that didn't bode well for me in the current situation. I needed her to crack. I needed her to scream. I needed her to have my back the way I'd always had hers.

Instead, nothing.

Silence and emptiness.

I wanted to cry, but not in front of them. They didn't deserve to see the way they were hurting me. They didn't need to witness my pain.

"Well, while this has been a great family reunion, this is where I exit." I stood up and pushed my purse up my shoulder and turned to my sister. She was fidgeting with her short fingernails, but I knew she was listening. "Sammie, if you need me, I'm always here for you. But don't think for a second what they are doing has anything to do with making a better life for you. They don't even know who you are. But I do. So when you need me, I'll be there. No matter what."

"Samantha's life has been wonderful. Reese's life will be better, too, without you. She will be raised better and have more opportunities—you'll see," Mama said.

"I hate you," I hissed, disgusted by the woman sitting there staring at me. With eyes that matched mine. Skin as dark and smooth as mine. She was my look-alike, yet our heartbeats had nothing in common.

"You think being hated by someone like you could affect me?" she said, her words dripping with coldness.

I walked away before they could utter another word. I walked away from the ones who were supposed to know me the best but truly didn't know me at all.

# 33

## Emery

*Five Years Ago*

"She doesn't like me," Sammie confessed as I laid Reese down for another nap. She was officially a month old today, and I thought it would've been fun to do a photo shoot for her, so we'd have the memories. Sammie seemed less than interested, and when I set up the shoot, she decided she'd rather go for a walk.

She'd been taking daily walks now, sometimes two, three times a day. I was the only one working and still going to school. When I came home, I was the one caring for Reese while still trying to complete my schoolwork, so my exhaustion was at an all-time high. I was trying my best to not complain, because I knew whatever I was feeling, Sammie was feeling tenfold.

"That's not true—she loves you," I said to comfort my sister.

"No, she loves you. She hates me. It's as if she can tell how she was created when she looks at me."

"That's ridiculous."

"Don't tell me what's ridiculous. I know what I see. You're better with her."

"I'm not better with her; we just have different connections to her, that's all. There's nothing wrong with that."

Sammie sat down in the glider chair I'd bought two months before, and she grimaced. I felt like she was always frowning. It had been so long since I'd seen her smile that I was almost certain she was turning more and more into Mama each day.

I almost forgot what my sister's smile looked like.

"There's everything wrong with that. I'm supposed to feel something for her, but I don't. I see the way the two of you bond . . . that's not me."

"I think you're overthinking it. These things take time."

"It didn't take time with you."

"That's because I'm not her mother. I'm just an outside figure."

"Which is why you shouldn't be closer to her than I am. But you are."

I sighed and pinched the bridge of my nose. "Maybe it's postpartum depression. I looked into it, and I think—"

"I don't have postpartum depression! I just want my life back!" she snapped, her words stinging as they hit my ears. "Stop saying I'm weak. I'm not weak, Emery."

I narrowed my eyes and shook my head. "No, I'm not saying you're broken, Sammie. People with postpartum depression aren't weak; they're just going through a lot with the changes in their systems. You brought a life into the world. There's nothing weak about that."

She began biting at her nails and shaking her head. "Mama said she doesn't believe in things like postpartum. She said it's just an excuse for women to be lazy."

"Yeah, well, Mama doesn't know what she's talking about."

"Yes, she does," Sammie said, standing up for Mama as if she wasn't the one who'd turned her back on her own daughters. "She does know."

"How could she, if she's never experienced it before? Look, I researched it, and I think it's worth looking into. We can get you on some medications—"

"I'm not crazy, Emery!"

She was extremely defensive about everything, and I felt as if no matter what I said, she was going to snap at me over it. I could say she was fine, and she'd tell me she wasn't. I could say she needed help, and she'd call me a liar. Nothing I said was good enough.

But still, I kept trying.

"Taking meds doesn't mean you're crazy, Sammie. It's just trying to get your hormones in check, is all. Or, you can talk to a therapist. That could help too. Especially with what you went through with—"

"Ugh!" she cried out, rubbing her hands against her face. "You don't get it! No one gets it! I just don't want to do this, okay? I just don't want to deal with any of this anymore."

My heart was breaking, and I wasn't exactly sure what to do about it.

I glanced at my watch and then back to my sister.

Her anger-flooded eyes were now filled with sadness, exhaustion. Pain.

"I'm sorry, Emery. I'm just having a time, that's all."

"It's okay. I can miss school today and stay with Reese. You can take a break."

She stood up from the chair and rubbed the palms of her hands against her eyes. "No, really. It's fine. I have her. You can't miss school. I'm going to shower fast and then make some coffee. I just need to wake up more."

"Are you sure?"

"Yes. I'm sure. I'm fine."

I moved in and hugged her, wrapping her tight in my grip so she could feel the comfort that her mind seemed to be missing. "I love you so much, Sammie."

"I love you too. And I'm sorry for snapping at you. I'm just tired."

The whole day while I was at school, my mind thought back to my sister. I wanted so much to get her the help she needed, but I wasn't exactly sure how to go about it. She refused to acknowledge everything she'd been through.

When I finished my classes for the day, I rushed home to take Reese off Sammie's hands to give her a break for her nightly walk. As I stepped inside, I heard Reese howling, and my stomach began to flip. I couldn't help but think of the day that she and my sister had had. I bet they were both emotionally exhausted.

"Sammie, I'm home. I know she can get fussy around this time, so I can take her off your . . ." My words faded as I walked into the house to find Reese lying in her crib, screaming her eyes out. "Sammie?" I called out as panic rolled through my stomach.

I rushed over to Reese and picked her up. Her face was bright red from her burst of emotions.

How long had she been lying there unattended to? How long had she been alone? Where the hell was Sammie?

"It's okay, sweetheart. I got you. I got you, you're okay," I said, hurrying to the bedroom to change Reese's diaper. As I began to change her, I noticed a note sitting on the gliding chair. I couldn't force myself to read the note right away—not until the sweet little girl had calmed down.

After Reese was changed, I went and warmed up a bottle. Then, as I fed her and tried my best to soothe the troubled girl, I picked up the letter. A letter that broke my heart with every single word that was written in black ink.

Emery,
I only left five minutes before you're reading this. I saw you pull up from work and went out the back way. I just hope you understand that I can't do this. I can't look at her without seeing him. I cannot hold her, without remembering him holding me down. I cannot be the woman that she needs, I cannot be her

mother. I tried, and I know you might think that this is something that's going to pass, but it's not. I can't do this. I can't. I got some paperwork filled out to leave you as her guardian. You're the right one for this job, and I wouldn't trust her with anyone else. As far as me, I'm going off to make a new life for myself. I'm going to find my footing in a new city, and I'm going to begin again.

Please take care of her.

Raise her as your own.

You're the mother she deserves.

That's not my daughter. She is yours.

I'm sorry for leaving, but you both are better off.

—Sammie

My teardrops hit the wrinkled paper as I stared down at the words that shattered every piece of me. Then, I went through the apartment and realized that all of Sammie's things were gone—including her suitcases.

I called Mama to see if she'd gone home.

She hadn't. Mama told me to keep her out of whatever issues Sammie and I were going through. I told her that Sammie was gone, and then she told me it was probably my fault before she hung up the call.

Sammie didn't come home that night, or any of the nights that followed. She never came back, leaving me with a child to raise on my own and forcing me to drop out of school. Each night, Reese wailed, almost as if she knew Sammie had abandoned her. Late one sleepless night, as I tried my best to soothe the upset child, I cried along with her.

Around two in the morning, I heard a knocking at my door, and my heart skipped a beat. I hoped it was Sammie, finally coming back to her senses. Since she'd left, I'd found a list of organizations that could help her through her struggles. I'd made many calls and gathered a lot of information for both victims of rape and new mothers.

I wanted to give it all to her, I wanted to help her heal, I wanted to do whatever I could to bring my little sister back to me.

Yet when I opened the door, it wasn't Sammie standing there. It was a woman I'd seen a few times in the building before.

"You're having trouble keeping that baby quiet," the woman said.

I was flustered, knowing that Reese had been quite vocal the past few days and that the walls of our apartment building weren't the greatest.

"I know, I'm sorry. I promise I'll do whatever I can to—" I started, but she cut me off.

"Oh, sweetheart, I'm not here to complain," she said, shaking her head with a genuine smile against her lips. "I'm here to help. I noticed that your roommate moved out a few weeks ago, and I figured you were struggling. My name is Abigail. Can I come in?"

I nodded slowly, beyond my breaking point. "I am sorry about the crying, though. This hasn't been the most normal situation."

"You have a newborn. There's nothing normal about newborns. I think you're doing great, truly, but I just wanted to reach out and offer my help if you needed it."

"Thank you, I appreciate it," I said, still trying to soothe the panicked child.

"May I?" she asked, nodding toward Reese.

I was hesitant at first, but something about that woman seemed so gentle and caring. I handed Reese over, and within minutes, the woman had calmed her down.

A sigh of relief rippled through my system as the crying came to a halt. In response, I began to cry. The flood of emotions escaped my body as I covered my face, humiliated by my inability to keep myself together in front of a stranger.

"I'm sorry," I said as I took the now-sleeping Reese from her arms and laid her in the crib. "I'm normally not like this."

"You are today, and that's normal too. There's no wrong way to feel," she told me. "So, go ahead. Feel it all."

That allowance, that gift of being told that every feeling was valid, sent a wave throughout my system, and I began to truly fall apart. I covered my face with my hands and began to break. For so long, I'd been trying to hold my sister together, trying to keep Reese in one piece, that I hadn't had any time to fall apart myself.

Abigail came over to me and wrapped me in her arms, soothing me as I cried like a fool against her shoulder. "That's right, sweetie, feel it all," she repeated, and I did.

I felt it all. I felt the fear, I felt the anxiety, I felt the sadness. I felt anger, too, and resentment toward my sister. I felt hurt. Abandoned. Lost.

I felt it all, and Abigail was there to help me through it.

"You probably have no clue what's happening right now. You probably feel like you're falling apart, but in truth, this is you falling together, sweetheart. Sometimes, part of the healing journey involves falling apart. That doesn't make you weak; it makes you strong. So, fall apart tonight, and you'll be stronger for tomorrow. You're doing great."

To hear someone say I was doing great as I sobbed against her shoulder felt untrue; it felt like the biggest lie in the world, but I did as she said. I felt it all.

# 34

## Emery

Oliver: Do you need me to come over?

Emery: No. I'm okay.

Oliver: Do you need me to come over?

Emery: No. I'm probably just going to fall asleep.

Oliver: Do you need me to come over?

Emery: Oliver. I'm fine. Really.

Oliver: Okay.

*Knock, knock, knock.*

I looked up from my cell phone as I sat in bed. Then I headed to the front door and opened it to find Oliver standing there, leaning against the doorframe.

"Hi," he whispered.

"Hi," I replied.

He took my hands into his and stepped in closer to me. His forehead rested against mine, and he closed his eyes as mine faded shut too. "Do you need me to come over," he softly spoke, his hot breaths brushing against my lips.

I nodded slowly, releasing a weighted breath that I hadn't even known I'd been holding in. "Yes."

He stayed with me as I cried against his white T-shirt. Over and over again, he told me Reese was my daughter and I was her mom, reasoning away the demonic thoughts that were flooding my system. When my body became too exhausted, when no more tears could be cried, he held me close throughout the remainder of the night.

The next morning, it wasn't the sun that pulled me from my slumber. It was a little girl, screaming at the top of her lungs. "Mr. Mith! What are you doing in Mama's bed?" she shouted, jumping on the bed.

"Reese, volume, lower," I muttered, only able to get out a few words due to my exhaustion. Then I yawned and focused a bit on Reese. Who was on my bed. Right beside Oliver.

Oliver.

In my bed.

Reese.

In my bed.

*Oh hell.*

"Reese!" I said, sitting up straight. Oliver was rubbing his eyes and trying to piece together what was going on. "What are you doing up so early?"

"It's not early; it's late," she said before turning to Oliver and then back to me. "Why is Mr. Mith in your bed?" She smiled from cheek to cheek. "Are you two in love?" She went back to jumping on the bed, shaking both Oliver and me from our slumber.

Her question shook me, and I felt my cheeks heating up from the comment.

274

"Reese, no, we are—"

"Yes, I love her," Oliver cut in, giving Reese his smile that made me feel everything all at once. I turned his way, my eyes widened from shock. He gave me his dopey, tired grin and took my hands into his and squeezed ever so lightly. "I love every part of you, Em."

My heart flipped, kicked, and leaped inside my chest. I wasn't ready for that, but truthfully, was anyone ever ready to find out that the person they loved, loved them back? It felt like the biggest dream coming true.

"I love you, too," I said, feeling as if my cheeks were going to burst from happiness. I wanted to lean in and kiss him, but I knew that might've been too much to do in front of Reese. Especially since she'd just found us in bed with one another.

"What about me, Mr. Mith? Do you love me, too?" Reese asked.

Oliver smirked big and pulled Reese into a hug. "Yeah, kid, I love you too."

Reese began to giggle as Oliver tickled her, making her wiggle all over the place. "Okay, okay, stop!" she screamed out, twisting and turning. This was one of those moments in life when I forgot all my troubles. Moments when the world seemed to stand still and every good thought aligned as one. As the three of us rolled around in bed, this was one of those moments. A moment that would forever live in my heart.

It was funny how those moments could make me forget about all the other troubles I was facing in my life. For a second, I'd forgotten all about the drama that my parents and Sammie had laid at my doorstep.

It felt as if Reese, Oliver, and I were creating our own family, with our own rules. We were creating one of my favorite songs on my mixtape. Just the three of us, and our happiness.

After a few seconds of lying across both Oliver and me, catching her breath, Reese said, "Hey, Mr. Mith?"

"Yeah, kid?"

"Does that make you my dad now?"

Welp.

That seemed a little too much for that morning's conversation. Oliver's mouth was agape, and it was clear he didn't know what to say, so I wrapped Reese into a tight hug and snuggled her. "How about we talk about this at a later time, and for now we go make some waffles?" I offered.

Reese's face lit up. "With chocolate chips?"

"Yes, with chocolate chips. Let me get up to get started and—"

Reese shook her head and hopped out of bed. "No, Mama. I want Mr. Mith to make me the waffles this time."

I raised an eyebrow. "I thought you loved my waffles."

"I do, but I want to love Mr. Mith's too," she said matter-of-factly. She held her hand out toward Oliver and pulled him out of bed. "Come on, let's get started."

Without another word, the two were walking off toward the kitchen to get started cooking. I could hear their voices as I lay in bed. "I'm going to be honest, kid—I don't know the last time I cooked waffles."

"It's okay. Even if they are nasty, I'll still eat them because I love you now," Reese said.

Oliver chuckled. "Well, that's very nice of you."

"I know, I'm a good person. And Mr. Mith?"

"Yeah, kid?"

"Stop calling me 'kid.'"

The following two days came and went without any incidents from my parents and Sammie. For a minute, I thought they'd come to their senses and realized they needed to back off, but I wasn't that lucky.

After Reese and I came home late one afternoon after spending time swimming in Oliver's pool, I found a thick envelope sitting outside my door. Picking it up, I noticed the word "Emery" scribbled across the front of it. It was definitely in Mama's handwriting, and that fact alone made acid start to rise from the pit of my stomach.

"What's that?" Reese asked.

I smiled her way and patted her behind. "Nothing, sweetheart. Go pick out some pajamas so we can get you ready for bed, okay?"

Thankfully, she did as I said, and I headed into the apartment, nervous about what I was going to uncover in the envelope. After I ripped it open, my heart dropped as I read the letter:

> Is this the man you are raising Reese around? This won't look too positive for you in court. Make the right decision, and hand Reese over before things get messy.

Inside the envelope was article after article of Cam's interviews about Oliver and the terrible made-up story lines she'd created. They spoke about Oliver's spiral over the past few months. They spoke about his drug usage, which didn't exist, and his cruelty toward her. They highlighted every false subject that Cam had made up about Oliver, and it made me sick to see those words lying against the page.

Mama had grabbed every fake article she could find on Oliver, and she was now throwing it all in my face as a way to get her way. The worst part of it all? The articles seemed real, since Oliver had never voiced his side of the story. I couldn't believe this was happening.

I was going to be sick.

"What are you looking at, Mama?"

I quickly put the papers down. "Nothing, sweetheart. Let's get to bed." I stood up with shaky hands and tried my best not to reveal my panic in front of my daughter.

My daughter . . . she was mine, and my mother was trying to take that fact away from me. What kind of woman would do that? What kind of person would ruin someone's life? Reese had been mine for over five years. I'd spent five years raising her, teaching her, loving her, and now my parents were threatening to tear her away from me.

# 35

## OLIVER

"Slow down, Em. What are you talking about?" I asked. She wasn't making any sense as she stood in front of me. She'd shown up to my house with puffy eyes and a shaky voice.

"I can't work for you anymore." Her eyes were swollen, and I couldn't imagine the amount of crying she'd done the previous night. I didn't know what had brought her to spend the evening crying, but I hated that I hadn't been there to comfort her.

"What happened?" I asked, concern overtaking me as I stepped in her direction.

Her shoulders dropped and rounded forward. "It's a long story."

"I have time."

"I don't. I'm sorry. I just wanted to tell you face to face instead of over the phone. I figured you deserved that much."

"What aren't you telling me?"

Her lips parted, and her body began to shake. She was trying her hardest to keep herself together, but she was failing every single second that passed by. "It doesn't matter, Oliver. I'm handling it. Which means I can't work for you."

"That doesn't make sense."

"It does. I know it's probably a lot to hear, but I have to do what's best for my daughter. I have to put her first."

"Is it about your parents?"

She nodded.

"What does that have to do with me and this job, though? I mean, hell, if you want to quit, that's fine, Em. But what I really want to know is how I can help you. I need to know what I can do for you."

"Nothing. You can't do anything for me." She glanced down at the tiled floor in the foyer as tears rolled down her face. "Oliver, I can't be with you anymore. After this, we can't see each other again."

That sent a shock of panic through me. "What the hell are you talking about? What does that mean?"

"It means exactly that. I don't have time for a relationship right now, not with everything going on with my family and Reese. My main focus has to be on her and keeping her safe."

"Of course that makes sense. But I don't see why you won't let me help you. I can do whatever it takes to make sure Reese stays in your custody. I can get you the best lawyers. I can—"

"Oliver, stop. Please. You're making this harder than it has to be."

"You're breaking my fucking heart, so please excuse me if I am making this hard," I snapped, and I instantly felt like an asshole for doing such a thing, but dammit. My heart felt as if it was going through a fucking paper shredder. I couldn't think straight.

She wiped away the tears that kept streaming down her cheeks and locked her brown eyes with mine. She didn't say anything, though; she just stared my way, and with that simple stare, I felt her worry, I saw her fears. I couldn't help but step toward her and wrap her into my embrace. "Em, come on. It's me. You don't have to do this alone."

"I do," she disagreed, shaking her head. "I do. You don't understand, Oliver. My father is a powerful force in our small town, and he has connections with people in the law system, and he will use this against me. He will use you against me."

"How?"

She sniffled and tilted her head up toward me. "They sent me all these articles from Cam about you. They said it shows proof that you being with me is an unhealthy environment for Reese. What's worse is there's no interviews or anything from you to counter the assumptions. So it makes you look guilty."

Son of a bitch.

How could someone shoot so low to hurt another person?

Did they really think they were doing what was right?

Did they think this was the best way to go about everything? By ripping a child away from the one parent she'd known her whole life?

I didn't know what to say. I didn't know how to comfort her over this issue, because I knew how Cam's comments appeared. She'd painted me as a sick devil.

"I'm sorry," I muttered, not knowing what else to say, because shit. I was so fucking sorry. And sad. And hurt.

She pulled me in closer and laid her lips against mine, kissing me hard. Her kisses didn't taste like new beginnings anymore. Her lips tasted like goodbyes, and that broke my fucking heart.

"Please," I muttered against her mouth, not even knowing what I was begging her for. Because I knew it was too much to ask her to stay. I knew it was too much to beg her to give us a chance. I would never want to be a roadblock in Reese's life. I would never want to be a cause of Emery losing her daughter.

But damn it, it hurt.

"I'm sorry," she whispered, her lips still grazing mine. I didn't want her to pull away. I didn't want her to walk away from me, because I needed her more than I'd realized. I loved her. I loved her so much, and the thought of losing her was killing me second by second. And that was exactly what was happening. I was losing the woman who'd saved me.

"This is just a bad track," I said, my hands against her lower back, holding her to me as I shook my head. I rested my forehead against hers and closed my eyes. "This is just a bad song on our mixtape, Em. This isn't the end of us. Okay? This isn't the end, and I will wait as long as it takes for everything to work out for us. I'm not giving up on this, I'm not giving up on us," I told her.

She gave me one last goodbye kiss as she slowly removed my touch from her. With one big step backward, she let me go.

"I'm so sorry, Oliver," she repeated, turning to walk away. "I love you," she whispered, walking out of the front door quickly, almost as if she had to run away; otherwise she might've thought about staying.

She didn't even hear me tell her that I loved her too.

The next several days all felt like night. Even though I wanted to turn to my familiar demons, I didn't do it. I wanted to drown in the whiskey and wake up with vodka in my hands. I wanted to shut off my brain and forget how I'd lost the two girls who meant the world to me.

But I couldn't do that. I couldn't spiral, because that would prove that Emery's parents were right about me. That would prove that I wasn't good enough for the two girls I loved.

I missed Emery. Every second, every minute, and every hour of every day, I missed her. I turned to the only thing that kept me sane in the darkness: I turned to my music.

I wrote nonstop, almost in a manic state. The words poured out of me until my studio floor was littered with paper. Then I wrote some more.

When my mind felt emptied, I called Tyler over to come listen to a few of the tracks I'd created that week. I wasn't even sure if they were any good, but I wanted him to hear them, because it felt like the first time in ages I'd been able to truly tap deeply into my emotions. I was learning to use my pain to create beauty.

I didn't only write about Emery and Reese. I wrote about my brother. I wrote about the pain and sorrow that flooded through me. I wrote about hurts and happiness. I worked through every single emotion that hit me because I was no longer pushing everything down within me. I felt it all and didn't criticize myself for the need to feel. When anger built up in my system, I wrote it down. When love was heavily in my heart, I created from that place of being.

I created a mixtape and set it in front of my friend to hear.

Tyler's jaw sat on the floor after I played the tracks for him. He raced his hand over his head. "Holy shit," he muttered. "You did all of this over the past two weeks?"

"Yeah, I did."

"Holy shit," he repeated, running his hand over his mouth. "Oliver, this is the best music you've ever created. It's raw and real, and holy shit," he huffed, shaking his head in disbelief as he pushed the palms of his hands against his eyes.

"Don't tell me you're crying," I joked.

"Fuck off, will you? There's nothing wrong about a grown man expressing his emotions."

"So, that means you like it?" I asked.

"That means I think you've created your comeback album."

"I don't really care if the world hates it," I started to argue, but he cut me off.

"Nobody's thinking about the world right now, Oliver. I'm talking about *your* world. This is the comeback album for you and your soul." He clapped his hands together. "So what about Emery? Did you figure out how you're getting her back?"

I grimaced, because I wished it was that easy. I wished I could just play her a few songs, and everything would fall back into place. But I knew better than to give myself that false hope. Emery had too much to lose in order to keep me. I wouldn't get in her way.

"I can't have her back, Tyler. She can't be in my life."

"Wrong." He clasped his hands behind his head and gave me a smirk as if he knew something that I didn't. "I saw you with her, Oliver. I saw how she was with you. It's not that she made you better . . . you made her better too. You're stronger when you both are together. So, now's not the time to respect her wishes, because these aren't her true wishes. Now's the time to fight for her. To fight for each other. We only get this one shot at life. Please don't stop fighting for Emery's love."

"What do I do?"

"Don't play dumb, Oliver. I think you already know, and you're just too much of a little bitch to do it. So go ahead. Just do what you think needs to be done."

I hated him, because he was right. I knew what I had to do, but I also knew I would be crossing some lines.

But for Emery and Reese?

I'd cross every border, if it meant I could keep them in my life.

"Thanks, Tyler."

"Yup. Always here," he said, repeating the words my parents often said to me. "Alex would love this, you know," he said, waving toward the soundboard at the tracks I'd played for him. "This is what he wanted from you all along. To go back to the basics. Now, figure out a way to let those two girls hear this too. Don't let your music die in the studio."

After speaking to Tyler, I knew I had to do something for Emery, even from a distance. So I went to the last person I wanted to see in order to try to protect Emery from losing Reese.

"I'm surprised you called," Cam stated as we sat down at a table outside a restaurant. I wanted to meet in private, but of course, Cam wanted to go somewhere public. Probably for the opportunity of the paparazzi to get their photographs of us together. "Now, what do you want, Oliver?"

"We need to talk."

"Oh, now you want to talk? You sure didn't when you broke up with me for your bullshit reasons."

"They weren't bullshit, Cam. We both knew that we weren't compatible."

"Yeah, but I was sticking it out because I saw the opportunities that could've come from being with you. You could've really helped my career."

"Don't you see why that's a shitty reason to stay in a relationship?"

She rolled her eyes. "What exactly do you want, Oliver? If you're here to just waste my time, congratulations. I'm already bored."

I clasped my hands together and placed them on the table. "I need you to tell the truth to the news outlets about our relationship. I need you to tell them that I wasn't the monster you made me out to be."

She huffed. "Yeah fucking right. You think I'm an idiot? That would make me look insane in the public eye."

"Don't you care about how you made me look?"

She laughed. No shit, she actually laughed. I couldn't for the life of me believe that I'd been so low in my past that I'd settled for someone as cruel as her.

"I couldn't care less about how it makes you look. Haven't you seen? Ever since those interviews, my career has taken off. I've had the number one single for the past three weeks. Not to mention, I've been on almost every magazine cover."

"You've also ruined my life."

She smirked and shrugged. "That's show business, baby. We're in the entertainment industry, Oliver. This is what we do. We tell the world a story. The story I'm telling is that I'm the country sweetheart, and you're the dark, damaged musician who lost his way."

"You don't feel remorse for doing that to me?"

"Not a lick. The truth is, the only reason I stuck around with you was because of the payoff I was supposed to get. The fame and celebrity-couple status."

And there it was.

Cam's true colors.

"What you've done is affecting other people's lives, though, Cam. In a very serious way. I don't care about me anymore. You're hurting people that I love."

"Like who? It's not like you have anyone in your life that actually cares for you, except for your pathetic parents. Is it Tyler? Kelly? Whose life?"

"It's not them."

She cocked an eyebrow. "Then who?" Her lips pursed together as she released a low whistle. "Don't tell me it's that chef?"

"It doesn't matter who it is."

"But it does," she disagreed. "Oh my God, of course it's her. Were you fucking her when we were together?"

"No. The only one who was ever unfaithful in our relationship was you."

She snickered. "Can you blame me? Why would anyone want to love someone as damaged as you?"

I didn't have anything else to say to her. Honestly, I'd heard everything that I needed to hear. She wasn't going to go back on what she'd said to the press; therefore I had no reason to stay around Cam for a second longer. Her and her toxic ways weren't a lifestyle I lived in anymore. I'd worked too hard on my healing to crumble at her feet.

# 36

## Emery

Each passing day, in the morning I received a text message from Oliver. They were simple messages with songs attached to them. Simple messages that got me through the hardest moments in my life.

Oliver: For when you need to laugh—Fuck You, by CeeLo Green

Oliver: For when you need to cry—Trying My Best, Anson Seabra

Oliver: For when you need to remember your strength—Girl on Fire, Alicia Keys

Oliver: For when you need any emotional girl power time—Any Lizzo or Taylor Swift song

Oliver: For when you need to remember my love—You Are the Reason, Calum Scott

The last song made me cry, but it wasn't sad tears. It was tears of love. So, even though I knew I couldn't be with Oliver now as I worked through my issues, I sent him a song as a reminder of my love for him.

Emery: For when you need to remember my love—Heart Stamps, Alex & Oliver

Each day the songs kept coming my way, and I played every one on repeat. Even though for now Oliver and I had to keep our distance, I swore I could feel his love as the lyrics of the songs danced within my soul.

# 37

## OLIVER

I didn't know if what I was doing made any sense, but in my gut, I knew I had to try my best. As I pulled into Randall, Oregon, I was determined to track Emery's sister down. It didn't take long for me to find out where Emery's parents lived, and once I'd learned that, I was able to find Sammie.

It was midday when I pulled up to their house, and I was thankful when I knocked that Sammie answered the door instead of Emery's parents. Don't get me wrong: I would've stood up to their father again, but he wasn't my target for the day—Sammie was.

"Oliver Smith," she muttered, looking stunned as she stood in front of me. "What . . . I . . ."

"You're Sammie?" I asked, holding my hand out for her to shake. She took it, and shook, allowing me to feel the trembles in her grip. "It's nice to meet you."

She stared blankly, shocked, as if I were a ghost or something.

Her fingernails scratched at her forearms for a bit. "What are you doing here?"

"I think you know why I'm here. I came to talk to you."

"To me? Why would you do that? I'm nobody."

The way the words fell from her mouth hurt me, because she'd spoken the word "nobody" as if she truly believed it.

"You're somebody to a lot of people. Especially your sister, Emery. I'm here because she probably believes she can't be. I just didn't want to do nothing while her world was falling apart."

"What do you have to do with Emery?" she asked, looking baffled. "I mean, I know she works for you, but . . ."

I narrowed my eyes. "Your parents didn't tell you?"

"Tell me what?"

"Emery and I have been dating for a while now. Your parents were planning to use me against Emery to take her to court over Reese."

"You're . . . Emery's dating you? You as in Oliver Smith? No way."

I smiled. "We were dating, until your parents, well . . . you know . . ."

Her eyes glassed over, and I noticed so many parts of her sister that lived in her features. "I don't get why they would do that, though. They promised they wouldn't fight dirty. They just wanted what they thought was best for Reese. They promised . . ."

"How many promises have they broken to you?" I asked.

She remained quiet.

"How many promises has Emery broken to you?"

Her head lowered. "None."

I crossed my arms and narrowed my eyes. "Sammie . . . do you want Reese back in your life? Do you want to be her mother?"

She glanced around the streets as if she was afraid of someone listening, before she shook her head. "I'm sorry, I need you to go. I can't be talking to you. This is too much. I can't do this." She turned to reenter her house as I called out to her.

"It wasn't your fault." She paused her footsteps yet didn't turn to face me again. Her shoulders deflated, and I repeated those same words once more. "It wasn't your fault."

With the slowest movement, the broken girl had enough strength to turn around and face me. Her shoulders were rounded forward, and the heaviest part of her soul sat right there in her eyes, which matched Emery's. I didn't know how, but I knew right then and there that guilt had been the thing eating her alive each day. I knew that she'd been swallowed whole by demons.

I'd been swallowed, too, yet nowhere near as long as she'd had to face the darkness. I was lucky to have stopped falling before I spiraled too far. But Sammie? She'd been spiraling for five years. Her life had been stolen from her, and then she was told that she was to blame by the ones who were supposed to protect her, by the ones who were supposed to cover her with love.

I would've spiraled hard too. I'd lose myself in ways I couldn't even imagine. I'd fucking snap and hate the world to its core.

Yet that wasn't what I was seeing when I stared at Emery's sister.

No.

I saw guilt.

I saw blame.

I saw her holding on to shame that never should've been placed against her shoulders.

"What did you say?" she whispered, her voice coarse and cracking.

I slid my hands into my pockets as I took a few steps toward her. "I said it's not your fault. What that man did to you—it wasn't your fault. What he took from you—it wasn't your fault. Everything that took place afterward wasn't you playing the victim card. You *are* the victim of a disgusting act, and I know your parents have told you that you could've avoided what happened to you, but that's not true. You are not to blame. You were abused. You are the victim, and none of this is your fault."

Her shaky hands moved to her face, and she covered her mouth as her slim body began to tremble. Tears flowed down her face, and she shook her head. "I was wearing—"

"It doesn't matter what you were wearing. It doesn't matter what you said. It doesn't matter what hour of the night it was, Sammie. What that man did to you was unacceptable and evil, and I am so sorry that you went through that, but you aren't to blame for what happened to you. It wasn't your fault."

"Maybe what happened to me wasn't my fault, but I abandoned Reese . . . I left Emery to handle it all on her own. I made so many mistakes."

"Still, not your fault. You were dealing with a trauma, and you didn't know how to handle it, so you did what you thought was best in that moment. That's not your fault. Someone broke you, and fucked you up. I can't say that I know what your mind went through, but I can only imagine the damage it caused. That's why I want to help you. Let me get you set up somewhere so you can find yourself—really find yourself. I have some property in Texas by my parents that you can stay at, and there's a great women's center down there that helps with mental health due to trauma."

"Why?"

"What do you mean?"

"Why would you want to help me? I'm nobody," she repeated, shaking as she rubbed her hands up and down her arms.

I stuffed my hands into my jeans pockets. "You're the girl who sings poorly. You're smart. You're kind. You care so much that sometimes it can feel overwhelming. You hate feeling like a burden to anyone. You eat tacos with ranch, and you dip your Doritos in blue cheese. You wanted to go to college to be a therapist—to help people. You cried during *The Notebook* and laughed during *The Hangover* movies that you watched behind your parents' back. You used to write your prayers out each night and placed them beneath your pillow. You can't whistle, and you hate the pink Starburst—which, frankly, I find highly disturbing—and when you laugh, it lights up the room. You're not nobody, Sammie. You're somebody important."

"How . . ." She took a deep breath. "How did you know all of that?"

"Because your sister told me. She talks about you all the time. She loves you and misses you more than you'll ever know, and she needs you right now. She wants to help you too."

Sammie's eyes flashed with sadness. "I don't deserve her help. Not after what I did to her."

I snickered, shaking my head. "But you know she would still want to help you. She would take you in with arms wide open, Sammie, because that's how she loves. Unconditionally."

She shut her eyes and placed her hands against her chest. "I'm broken."

"Who isn't? It's okay."

"How is that okay? I don't even know who I am anymore. I look in the mirror and don't see myself anymore."

"Everyone breaks sometimes. It's a part of life. Sometimes we have to fall apart before we can fall back together. I couldn't look in mirrors for a long time. I couldn't face my demons because they were reminders of my mistakes and mishaps. But Emery walked me through them. I didn't have to get through it on my own. So, please . . . let me walk with you. We're all just trying to breathe, Sammie. It doesn't make you weak to reach out for help. That's actually what makes you strong. So, what do you say? How about we breathe together?"

That night, when I got home, I opened my email to find a letter from an insider whose name seemed very familiar to me.

The title of the email read: "Just In Case You Need This."

## The Mixtape

Hey Oliver,

I'm not sure if you remember me, but we met at
the farmer's market. I was the asshole following you
and taking your picture. Well, I was also the asshole
who saw you when you were having a conversation
with Cam at the outdoor diner, and I was able to
record it. The clip is attached above, and I wanted
to let you know that I can pass it on to media outlets. It might help clear your name.

I know you might be against this, or not trust me,
but again, a lot of us are your supporters. I won't
share it, unless you ask me to do so. I don't want to
cause you any more struggles.

—Charlie Parks

I sat back a bit, completely baffled by the email sitting in my inbox.
My mind raced back and forth as I tried to figure out the best thing
that I could do with the information he'd given me. I didn't care about
clearing my name as much as I cared about making life easier for Emery,
and maybe having a chance to have her come back to me.

So, I hit reply.

Dear Charlie,

Please send the video out.

—OS

# 38

## EMERY

"I miss Mr. Mith," Reese stated for the fifty millionth time in the past two weeks. Every time she said it, I felt like an awful mother. I'd brought Oliver into her life, only to have him ripped away from her days after she was questioning if he was going to be her father. I hated the guilt that was building up inside of me every single day, yet what I hated most was how much I missed him too.

I missed him to my core. At night, he'd show up in my dreams, and come morning he'd live in my thoughts. Even though I knew I was making the right choice for my daughter, it didn't make things any easier. I wished I could've figured out a way to make our love work. I wished I could've been able to keep him by my side during my hardest days, but I didn't see any way that it was possible.

"I know, baby, I miss him too." I sighed, rubbing my hands against my eyes. I hadn't cried in a few days, so I took that as a win. I knew I had to stop my tears from coming when Reese began asking me why I was sad. Hiding my sadness from my little girl was probably the hardest thing for me to do. Appearing strong when I felt weak was harder than anyone could've ever believed.

There was a knock at my door, and I hurried over to answer it. Kelly was standing there with two bottles in her hand. One was red wine, and the other was sparkling grape juice.

I cocked an eyebrow. "What are you doing here?"

"It's good to see you too," she joked, barging into the apartment without an official invitation inside; not that she needed one. "I figured tonight was a great night for a girls' night out!" she exclaimed. "Reese! Do you want to have a girls' night out?"

"Yes!" my daughter shouted, making me shake my head.

"No," I said back. I didn't have the energy to get up and go out. Most days, I was just trying to make it from morning to night. I didn't have an ounce of extra energy to put anywhere else but within my daughter.

"Oh, gosh. Don't be a party pooper, Emery," Kelly said.

"Yeah, don't be a party pooper, Mama," Reese echoed. I gave her a stern look, and her eyes widened as she whispered, "Is 'pooper' a bad word?"

I couldn't even hold my smirk in from her comment. But she wasn't the one I was supposed to be scolding in that moment. Therefore, I turned back to Kelly. "I can't go out tonight. I have to keep trying to find a job."

"Jobs will be there tomorrow. A girls' night is needed. And I bet you'll feel even more inspired to job search tomorrow after a great time. You were there for me when I needed a girls' day, so let me be there for you when you need one. Please, Emery?"

"Yeah, pleeeeeeease, Mama?"

I wanted to say no, go crawl into bed, and surrender to my sadness, but the spark of hope in Reese's eyes wasn't something that I could let fade away. Ever since Oliver had stopped coming around, I'd noticed how sad Reese was about it. If me going out for a girls' night would make her smile, I'd do it.

"Okay. What do you have in mind?"

"It's a surprise. Just go get dressed, something cute! I'll help Reese pick out something to wear. Meet out here in about twenty minutes, okay?"

I snickered. "I don't need twenty minutes to get ready."

Kelly scanned me up and down with her blue eyes. "Oh, sweetheart. I'm sorry to say, but you do need twenty minutes to get ready. You've been running around looking like a zombie for the past few days."

"She's right, Mama. You look like a zombie with fifty billion bags under your eyes," Reese agreed. Then the two of them began walking around the living room like zombies.

Well then.

That felt like the confidence boost I was searching for.

Before I could reply, Kelly was patting me on my behind, shooing me in the direction of my room.

"And wear a nice pair of heels!" she shouted.

Heels? Yeah, right. She was going to get a pair of sneakers, and she was going to like it too.

It took me fifteen minutes to get dressed and do my makeup, but I hung out in my bedroom for those extra five minutes, giving myself a pep talk. I needed to put on my superhero cape in order for the girls to not notice how sad I felt. From zombie to superwoman in twenty minutes or less.

"There our lady is!" Kelly cheered as I emerged from my bedroom as a butterfly. Well, maybe more like a moth, but they were getting what I had to give that night.

Reese was wearing an adorable pink dress that flared at the bottom, and her kiddie heels. Her wild curly hair was tamed and pulled back into a perfect bun. I had no clue how Kelly had managed to do that in less than thirty minutes. It normally took me five hours to tame my daughter's hair.

"You look beautiful, Mama," Reese gasped, looking my way. "Like a princess."

When my girl was sweet, she was the sweetest. "You look like a princess, too, sweetheart."

Kelly poured two glasses of wine, and one of sparkling grape juice, and handed them out to both Reese and me. Then she held her glass in the air. "A toast to Emery Rose Taylor. The best mother and friend that a person could ever have. We're better with you, Emery. And nothing is ever going to keep us apart."

Reese hadn't a clue how important and meaningful my friend's words were to me, but I needed to hear them. To hear that my life as Reese's mother wasn't going to come to a standstill. I'd been overthinking it all. How would I explain to her the truth about what had happened? How I wasn't her biological mother? How her real mother had abandoned her?

I couldn't answer those questions at that time, so I went ahead and pushed them to the back of my mind the best I could.

We finished our drinks—well, after another glass of wine each—and we headed downstairs to the Uber that Kelly had called for us. I still had no idea where we were going, but she wouldn't give me any clues at all. "Just enjoy the ride," she said, smirking.

When we pulled up in front of an arena with a massively long line wrapped around the building, I cocked an eyebrow. "What in the world . . . ?" I muttered, climbing out of the car.

Then, when I looked up at the sign flashing on the building, my heart stopped beating.

**LIVE** TONIGHT **OLIVER SMITH'S** RETURN TO THE STAGE.

Oliver's return to the stage? Oliver was performing tonight? How hadn't I known this? How hadn't I been aware of him getting to the point of where he'd perform again? Would he be able to perform? Or would he relapse and spiral again, like he had all those months ago when I first met him at Seven? Was he okay? Was he nervous? Why were we here?

"Kelly," I started, but she linked her arm with mine and cut me off.

"Come on. We'd better get backstage before the show starts," she said, giving her other free hand to Reese to hold.

"Backstage?"

"Yes. For the meet and greet."

"Meet and greet?"

"Geez, Emery, are you going to echo everything I say? Less yappin', more trackin'," she said, yanking me along. With ease, Kelly flashed a few passes to a few security people, and before I knew it, we were backstage at the arena, standing beside Oliver's dressing room.

My stomach was in knots, and I felt as if I were going to pass out any second. Kelly still hadn't explained herself, and honestly, now that we were standing in front of Oliver's door, I didn't even need an explanation.

I just needed him.

Kelly knocked on the door, and before anyone answered, Reese took the doorknob in her hand, turned it, and pushed it opened. "Mr. Mith? Are you in here?" she called out.

The moment the door was fully opened, we saw Oliver standing there, fussing with his microphone pack in his back pocket. He dropped his hands quickly, and his eyes lit up the moment he saw Reese. She turned into the brightest light when she saw him too. "Mr. Mith!" she hollered, dashing in his direction, and he was there to catch her in his embrace with arms wide open.

"Kid!" he exclaimed, spinning her around.

She snuggled closer to him and held on tight. "I missed you, Mr. Mith."

"I missed you, too, kid."

"Mama missed you too. She'd been crying a lot since you left." She moved her mouth toward his ear and whispered—but a loud whisper because my daughter didn't know how to lower her voice. "But she pretended she had allergies."

Oliver moved his stare from my daughter over to me.

It happened.

I looked at him.

He looked at me.

And still, he controlled my heartbeats.

His sweet yet somehow sinful lips turned up into a smirk that made my thighs tremble.

"Hi there," he said as my heartbeats drummed away in an erratic pattern.

"Hi there," I replied.

He placed Reese down on the ground, and before I knew it, his arms were around me. Within seconds, I was melting into him, because I didn't know how to do anything but. He felt so warm against me, he felt like the missing piece to my small family puzzle, and I knew he fit perfectly as Reese wrapped her arms around our legs.

We were the perfect trio, and all I wanted to do was love the two of them for the rest of time.

"I missed you so fucking much it hurt," he said, holding me close.

"That's a quarter in the swear jar!" Reese remarked, making us both laugh. "Hey, Mr. Mith. Is it true that you're performing tonight?"

"It is. At least, I hope so. I'm going to be honest: I'm really nervous. I haven't performed in a long time without my brother, and I'm not sure how it's going to go."

"Well, can't he just watch you from heaven?" she said. Her question seemed so matter of fact, and it made everyone in the room tear up. "So don't worry, he's still here. Come here." She pulled on his pants and made him come to eye level with her. She then placed her hands against his shoulders and gave him a stern look. "Mr. Mith, you can do anything because you're my best friend, and that means you can do anything."

My little girl was giving him a pep talk, and my heart just about exploded from hearing it.

My love for her was like a wild garden. It blossomed more every single day.

Oliver's eyes glassed over, and he bent down and kissed her on the forehead. "Thanks, Reese."

"Welcome."

Kelly cleared her throat. "Okay, well, how about I get Reese some snacks and we make our way to our seats so Emery and Oliver have a second to talk before the show."

The two headed out of the room, leaving me standing there, still stunned and confused about what was happening exactly. But also, happy. I couldn't deny the happiness that was running through my veins.

The moment the door closed behind Kelly and Reese, Oliver's lips were pressed against mine, and I fell into my safe place. His tongue swept against mine, and I bit his bottom lip lightly as he moaned into me. "I'm so glad you're here," he said. "I was nervous Kelly wasn't going to be able to get you here."

I pulled away a little, still baffled. "You're really performing tonight?"

"Yes. I think it's time. I've been working on a lot of new stuff these past few weeks, and I feel like it's time to get back out there."

"I'm proud of you, I just . . . are you sure you're ready?"

"No. Not at all. But I'm learning in life that you don't have to be ready for every situation. You just have to be brave enough to try. So, I'm going to try tonight, and I think it will be better if I'm able to look out into the audience and see you sitting there looking back at me."

"I believe in you," I told him, kissing him again.

We kept kissing until it was time for him to go put on a show.

# The Mixtape

So I made my way to the audience, to make sure I was there for him when he needed a boost of love to go his way. I didn't know what any of this meant for us, because the situation with my parents and Reese was still a mess. I knew I couldn't be with Oliver yet, but I also knew that I was going to go into that arena and be his biggest fan.

The lights were already dimmed when I made it to my seat. Reese was standing on her chair as she and Kelly talked about their favorite songs from Alex & Oliver. When the light show began onstage, I could sense that the whole audience was feeling butterflies. There seemed to be a nervous energy about Oliver's arrival. Many wondered aloud if he was going to be a no-show again. Many were skeptical that he was going to actually perform. But even with their doubts, they'd still shown up. Because their love for Oliver was still there, even with the letdowns.

He made his way to the stand and stood there for a moment as the crowd went wild. Every time he opened his mouth to speak, the crowd cheered louder, shouting their love for him. I saw the moment it hit him too. When his eyes glassed over and the emotions flooded in.

Oliver cleared his throat as he adjusted the microphone in front of him. "To be honest, I wasn't sure if anyone was going to show up tonight after my last failed attempt of a show. Then, with how the last few months have gone with me in the tabloids, I considered staying hidden. But there was something bigger than my fear that made me want to come out of hiding. Something worth fighting for," he said as his eyes looked toward me.

Butterflies.

A million butterflies.

"We always believed in you, Oliver!" someone screamed.

"We'll always be here, Oliver! We love you!" someone else shouted from the crowd.

"I love you too," he apprehensively snickered. "I, um, to be honest I've been going through a very rough patch lately. As many of you know, I lost my best friend a few months back, and I didn't handle it in the best way possible. But I was lucky enough to have a team who didn't give up on me. I want you all to know that you are a part of that team. Thank you for showing up for me, even though I'm flawed."

He brushed his hand beneath his nose, and I could almost feel his nerves tingling through my system. "I went over and over how to start this show tonight. I thought about coming out here with insane energy and performing like a madman up here. I thought the bigger, the better, like my brother. My brother was a force on the stage. His energy was magical, but that wasn't who I was, and that's not who I am now. Truthfully, I've been feeling pretty small these past months. So, in the spirit of being authentic, I figured we'd start that way tonight, and build up. Is that okay with you, Los Angeles?"

The City of Angels cheered him on.

"Okay, so this is my brother's guitar. I figured I should play it as a way of having him here onstage with me. But a sweet little girl reminded me that he's always with me, even if I can't see him. So, we are going back in time with the first song that Alex and I ever recorded together. If you're an ancient fan, you know it. If you're new, here's a part of me. And I apologize ahead of time if I get lost in myself. I'm trying my best. This is 'Heart Stamps.'"

My hand flew to my chest as Reese and Kelly began jumping up and down as Oliver began to play the song that saved me during so many of my darkest days.

As he began singing, his voice filled the arena like magic dust. The words rolled off his tongue as if they were a part of his soul, and he was sharing it all with us. Everything was going fine, until he looked out into the audience when he got to the chorus, and he stumbled over his emotions.

"And I'll keep your heart stamped," he began, but the overwhelming feelings overtook him, and he stepped away from the microphone as tears began to roll down his cheeks. I wanted to rush up to hold him. I wanted him to feel my comfort, that he wasn't alone in that very moment. But I quickly realized that he didn't need my comfort in that very moment.

He had ten thousand people surrounding him with love, singing the lyrics that his voice struggled to push out.

I'll keep your heart stamped
Right against mine, every beat, every time
I'll keep your heart stamped
Through the dark days you face, and the shadows you've chased
Your heart stamps with mine.
Your heart stamps on mine.
Everything will be fine
Because your heart beats in sync with mine.

It was the most powerful moment I'd ever witnessed. Oliver stepped closer to the microphone, tears still falling, but I could tell they were now from the love that filled that arena. He began strumming the guitar again and singing as the chorus came back around.

When love met pain, beauty could be created.

My lips moved to the lyrics as a woman came toward the empty seat beside me. I was completely thrown off when her hand took mine in her hold. I snatched it away quickly before turning to see Sammie standing there beside me. Her eyes were washed with tears, and she gave me the most broken smile.

I didn't understand. I didn't know why she was there, or how she knew where I was going to be. Yet the moment I looked up at the stage to find Oliver singing the chorus once more, I knew he'd had a hand in this.

I turned to Sammie, and I wanted to yell at her. I wanted to tear her apart and snap for what she and our parents were putting me through with Reese.

But "Heart Stamps" was our song.

It was us for so very long, and Sammie looked so broken, so I did the only thing I could think to do. I took her hand in mine and held on tight.

I felt her trembles intensify as I gripped her hand. She began falling apart as tears rolled down her cheeks. Her eyes shut, and I watched as her lips slightly mouthed the words of the song. Then, I sang along with her.

Your heart stamps with mine.
Your heart stamps on mine.
Everything will be fine
Because your heart beats in sync with mine.

# 39

## Emery

After the concert, Oliver drove Sammie and me to his house so we could have the conversation that needed to happen. Kelly took Reese to her place for a sleepover, because I wanted to make sure she had no interactions with Sammie. Honestly I wasn't sure if Sammie was still on our parents' side.

If anything, we had to have the heart-to-heart that we should've had years ago.

"I'll be in the studio if you need me," Oliver said, kissing my cheek. "But take all the time you need."

He gave Sammie a broken smile as he walked out of the living room, leaving us to ourselves. The silence was heavy, and I hadn't a clue where to even start with her, but I knew we had to start somewhere.

"I—" we both said in unison.

Uncomfortable laughter fell from both of us, and Sammie gestured toward me. "You go first."

I sat down on the couch, and she sat across from me. My mind was spinning wildly as I tried to control my thoughts. "Why did you leave?" I asked. "All those years ago, why did you leave?"

She lowered her head. "I didn't know how to stay. I was losing myself, Emery. I was in a dark place and didn't see a way out of it. And when I looked at that baby, the thoughts I had were even darker. I left because I felt as if I was going to hurt her. I left because I didn't know how to stay."

"You left her alone in an apartment, Sammie!" I argued, tossing my hand up in irritation. Every now and again, I'd think back on that day, on the screaming child, and my heart would break all over again.

"I know! I know! Okay. If you're just going to yell at me, I can just go—"

She began to stand, and I reached across to her and grabbed her arm.

"No," I said sternly. "You have to stop running, and I'm guessing you came because you're tired of that."

"I don't need to be yelled at and hear how you hate me."

"Me yelling isn't because I hate you, Sammie. It's because I love you, and you hurt me! You hurt me to my core. And then, finding out that you've been seeing our parents and not me broke me even more. And now the idea that they are pushing to have custody of Reese is insane. You have to know this. Don't you remember what it was like for us growing up? Why would you even want that for her? They are toxic, Sammie."

"Mama said she could do better this time . . . better than she did with us," she whispered, shaking her head. "And she said she'd let me back into their family completely, not just once every now and again. That's all I want, Emery. I just want things to go back to how they used to be."

"Nothing is ever going to go back to what it used to be. That's impossible, and truthfully, you shouldn't want it to be the way it used to. Our parents controlled us and belittled us, Sammie, making it hard for us to trust anyone or anything."

Her lips parted and her trembles returned. I hated how nervous and fragile she seemed all the time. Even though I was upset with her, it still broke my heart to see her so damaged.

"I just want them to love me."

"You should never have to beg for anyone to love you. You should never have to do as they say for them to deem you worthy of their love. That's not how love works."

"I don't know how it works," she confessed. "I've never known how it works."

"Yes, you do. You loved me, and I loved you unconditionally for all of our lives, Sammie. That's what love is. It holds no chains attached to it. But Mama and Dad's love doesn't work that way. It holds you down and suffocates you. You can't really want that for Reese. Or for yourself."

She stayed quiet for a few moments before sniffling. "Oliver talked about getting me into a clinic down in Texas that deals with women's mental health. It's in the town that he's from. Said he would cover all the costs."

That sounded like the man I loved. "Are you considering it?"

She nodded. "I'm supposed to go out there next week, but there's something I have to do first, and I need you to do it with me, if you can?"

"Anything."

"I need you to confront them with me, Mama and Dad. I need you there with me."

I was a bit wary about the idea, because I knew how our parents could corner Sammie and make her shift her thoughts. Yes, in that moment she seemed strong and sure, but I knew how my sister's mind worked. It flipped back and forth between hope and despair. I never really knew who I was going to get, but still . . .

"I'll be there for you, no doubt about it."

She hugged me, and I held her so tight.

"I'd visit you and Reese sometimes," she confessed, wiping her tears away. "I'd come to your neighborhood throughout the years and see you with her. I'd see how happy you both got over time, and it was clear to me that she was never mine, not really. That's your daughter, Emery.

And I'm so sorry for all the hurt I caused you. I'll do everything it takes to keep her with you. I promise."

Hearing her say that Reese was mine meant more to me than she'd ever know.

We still had a lot more to talk about, a lot more baggage to unpack, but I knew we'd done enough that evening.

Oliver set up a guest room for Sammie to stay in, and when it came time for me to go to bed with him, I thanked him a million times for getting Sammie to come around and not only drop the conversation with my parents, but to also get my sister the help she needed.

"Should we talk about us . . . ?" I asked, feeling nervous that I'd ruined the chance we had after breaking up with him all those weeks ago. I wouldn't have blamed him if he didn't want to take me back with arms wide open. "I mean . . . is there an us still?"

Oliver walked over to me and wrapped me in his arms. "There will always be an us, Emery."

"You have no clue how much good you've done for me," I said as he held me.

"I'll do anything for you. From this point on, I'm always here."

I smiled and kissed his lips gently. "It's been a wild ride with you these past few months, but I wouldn't change a thing."

"I love you."

"I love you," I echoed.

His mouth danced against my earlobe as he whispered into me, "Can I show you? Can I show you how much I love you?"

He led me to his bedroom, and it didn't take him long to lay me against his mattress and pin me down, hovering over my body. His eyes glassed over, and he repeated his words. "I love you, Emery," he said again, and I knew I'd never tire of hearing those words fall from his mouth.

My lips pressed against his, and I muttered into him, "I love you too."

He took one hand and traveled it down to the hem of my dress and pulled it up slightly.

First, he slipped one finger inside me, sliding it in slowly; then he added another, spreading me wide. The speed picked up as my hips began rocking against his hand. Then, another finger, and I moaned out from the feeling, turning my head toward the pillow, not wanting to make too much noise as he finger fucked me hard and deep.

The deeper he went, the harder I moaned, until I released against his hand. He pulled his hand from my panties and licked his fingers before pressing his mouth against mine.

"Make love to me," I whispered, wanting to feel his hardness inside me, wanting every piece of his love to rock my world. He didn't deny my request. As he slid into me that night, as he made love to every inch of my body, I felt our hearts healing together. As he made love to me, I felt the promise of tomorrow he was giving me that night. As he lost himself inside me, I knew I'd found my home. I knew I was going to be his forever.

And he'd be mine.

# 40

## EMERY

Going into the conversation with my parents, I had one thing on my mind and one thing only—breaking generational curses.

"You're joking, right?" Mama snapped in the same diner where she'd told me she was going to try to take my daughter from me. Only this time, Sammie sat beside me, holding my hand under the table, so we could squeeze each other's hands whenever we needed a push of comfort. "You cannot think you can keep her. You are not the right fit to have that child."

"I have been for five years, and I plan to be for the rest of my life," I said, disagreeing.

"Samantha, tell your sister that she is wrong. You already spoke to us about this situation, and we agreed that what was best for your daughter is—"

"She's not my daughter," Sammie said, sure as day.

Mama's mouth dropped open. "You are wrong. We had a plan. Your father and I were going to raise that little girl and give her a real shot at life, at a family."

"She has a family," I said. "I'm her family."

"You're a single mother; you could never be enough for that girl. You've never been enough. You run around with drug-addict musicians who sleep around with any- and everything. You think he's going to look after you? Good luck. He's going to throw you to the side like you're nothing," Mama huffed. Her words stung me, but only a little.

Because I knew no truths lived within them. "You have no clue who Oliver is, and you have no clue who I am. You don't know who Samantha is, either, I'm sure."

"Oh, shut your mouth, Emery Rose. I know who my daughter is."

"What's my favorite song, Mama?" Sammie asked quietly.

"Excuse me?"

"What's my favorite song? What song did I listen to over and over again growing up? Who's my favorite musician? What's my favorite color? What did I want to be when I grew up? How do I like my eggs?"

"Samantha, I don't see how this has anything to do with anything. Those are stupid facts that don't matter at all," Mama snapped. "Now, tell Emery that we are going to move forward with the custody case."

"'Heart Stamps,' by Alex & Oliver—who are her favorite musicians. Her favorite color is teal during the summer and yellow in the winter, because she believes the dark days need some bright color. She wants to be a therapist to help people, and she likes her eggs scrambled with two slices of American cheese," I said, because I knew my sister.

Sammie squeezed my hand.

I squeezed hers back.

"This is ridiculous!" Dad finally snapped, speaking up for the first time since we'd arrived at the restaurant. "I cannot believe I even wasted a second of my time going through this bullshit, anyway, Harper. This is all your fault to begin with."

"No, I—"

"I should've never even given you another chance after you got knocked up by that asshole all those years ago. You should've gone ahead and aborted her anyway," he said, gesturing toward me. "Instead I've been forced to deal with your mistakes."

Wait, what?

Mama's eyes teared up as she looked at her husband, stunned. "Theo. You promised you would never bring this up."

"Well, obviously it needs to be stated. I've dealt with too much of your bullshit over these years. And now I've watched the same thing unfold with my daughter because of your flaws. Same mistakes, same story. And now, I bet the same shit happens to that little girl because this family is cursed."

"What is he talking about?" Sammie asked.

"I'm talking about this family's sins! The same thing that happened to you happened to your mother, which is why I'm so sick of watching this story unfold the same way. Yet somehow I ended up raising her bastard child."

"Mama . . . ," I started, but my words faded. What was he saying? I wasn't his? My father wasn't my father? How?

Mama wiped the tears from her cheeks as she tried to keep her composure. "I was young and went to a party. I made mistakes, and a boy took advantage of those mistakes. My father found out and kicked me out."

Déjà vu.

We were living in a loop.

Everything Mama had gone through, she'd put Sammie through too. And if the generational curse stayed in place, if we didn't change our future by speaking and healing from our past, we'd keep that loop going.

Everything was beginning to make sense. It made sense why my father never seemed to love me the way he loved Sammie. It made sense why they were so hard on us, so overly protective. Because they didn't want what happened to them to happen to us.

Yet still, life happened. And there they were again, trying to control the outcome by taking Reese in as their own, so they'd have another shot at molding her into something they thought was right.

"We failed with you both, but we can do better with Reese. I knew it the moment I lay eyes on her," Mama said, falling apart in the diner. "I can be better with her. I know how to fix her."

"She's not broken," I said, shaking my head in disbelief. "She's not yours to fix."

"You have no clue what you're doing," Dad told me with coldness in his stare. "You don't know how to be a parent."

"Sure I do. I'll just do the complete opposite of everything you've ever done to me." I turned to my sister, feeling sick to my stomach as the revelations unfolded before me. "Are you ready to go?"

She nodded.

Mama huffed. "Really, Samantha? You're going to choose her over your own parents?"

"She is my family, Mama. She's the best family I've ever had," Sammie confessed, squeezing my hand. We headed out of the restaurant and went back to my apartment. The whole ride over, Sammie kept holding my hand, and I was thankful for that. I needed the comfort.

I think she needed it too.

"Are you okay?" she asked me as we stood in the hallway in front of my door.

"Not now. But I will be. Everything makes a bit more sense now, that's for sure. I always thought I wasn't enough for them both, but truthfully, they were dealing with their own demons. It had nothing to do with me." I smiled at her. "Or you. Parents can be broken, too, it turns out."

I looked down toward Abigail's apartment and nodded once. "Do you want to meet her? Reese? I'm going to be honest: I don't know how we move forward with this. I don't know where we go from this point with her."

Sammie placed her hands over her heart and nodded. "I'd love to meet her, but only if you're comfortable with it."

I nodded and headed over to grab Reese. The moment we walked back to my apartment, I could see the nerves shooting through Sammie. They were running through me too.

"Mama, who is that?" Reese asked with narrowed eyes.

"That's my sister, Reese. Her name is Sammie."

Reese's mouth dropped open. "You have a sister?"

"Yes, I do. And she's a very strong person."

Reese smiled at Sammie, who began to cry. Reese frowned at the sight, walked over to Sammie, and hugged her. "Don't be sad. It's okay," she said, giving her comfort.

"Thank you, Reese," Sammie said, bending down to meet her eye to eye. "Oh my gosh, you're beautiful."

"You're beautiful too. You look like Mama. So, if you're her sister, does that make you my aunt?"

Sammie looked up to me, and then back to Reese. "I think that does make me your aunt."

"Oh great!" Reese's eyes lit up once more, and she hugged Sammie again. "I always wanted an aunt."

# 41

## EMERY

"When is Mr. Mith going to get back?" Reese groaned as I picked her up from school. Summer had come and gone, and Oliver was back to work with his band, traveling around the US doing interviews for their newest song release. It turned out Alex & Oliver may have come to an end, but Oliver Smith was finding himself day in and day out. Watching him find his footing in a new world without his brother was inspirational and, truthfully, empowering.

I'd missed him a lot during his travels, but our FaceTime calls were enough for me.

Reese, on the other hand? She was missing her best friend.

"He'll be back next weekend, sweetheart, don't worry. You'll be annoying one another again in no time."

"Good," she said as we parked the car and headed upstairs to our apartment. Her eyes widened more when we reached our floor and she saw Oliver standing outside my apartment, holding a houseplant in his hand. "Mr. Mith!" she screeched, running in his direction with her backpack on.

I pretty much ran, too, the moment I saw him. "What are you doing here?" I asked, leaning in to kiss him.

"Took an early flight home. Figured I'd stop by to see my girls. Plus, I wanted to get you another houseplant to add to your collection." I laughed a little but grew silent as I looked down at the plant. Staring back at me was a huge diamond ring.

"Oliver," I muttered, stunned by what I was seeing.

He got down on one knee in front of me and held the ring in his hand. "I love so many pieces of you, Emery Taylor. I love the quiet parts, and the loud ones too. I love how you give your all to everyone around you, and also save some love for yourself. I love your cooking, and I love your laugh. I love the way you love your daughter. I love her too. I love your daughter. And if you'll allow it, I'd love to spend the rest of my life being able to shower that love on you both from this point on. Marry me, Emery. Marry me, and I'll keep you forever," he swore.

I was stunned, unable to say anything. All I could stare at was the ring, and then I turned around to look at my daughter, who had a devilish smirk on her face as she held up a sign in her hand from her now-opened backpack.

### Say yes, Mama!

She was in on this, too, the sneak.

I turned back to Oliver and said the word that mattered the most in that very moment. "Yes." He stood to his feet and wrapped his arms around me, pulling me in close. His lips crashed against mine, and as he slid the ring onto my finger, we both laughed nervously with one another.

Once he'd finished proposing to me, Oliver turned to Reese and got down on one knee in front of her. "I wanted to propose to you, too, kid. Now, I don't have a ring, but I have this." He reached into his back pocket and pulled out a half of a heart necklace. Alex's heart. "This was my brother's, and it means the world to me, so I wanted to give it to the little girl who means the world to me too. I wanted you to know that you have half of my heartbeats, and I'd spend forever protecting you if you'll have me."

Reese was cheesing so hard, I was almost certain her cheeks were going to pop. "Yes, Mr. Mith! Yes!" she shouted, jumping up and down. He placed the jewelry around her neck and then gave her a tight hug. "Does this mean I can call you 'Dad' now?" Reese asked nervously.

"Yes, Reese. If you want to, you can call me 'Dad.'"

She hugged him tighter. "I love you, Dad," she cried, breaking and healing my heart all at once.

In that moment, I knew the truth about family. There wasn't one cookie-cutter way to create love bonds. Families came in all shapes, forms, and sizes. Some were tied together by blood, and others by heartbeats. At the end of the day, it didn't matter how you came together; it only mattered that you stayed together. That you looked out for one another and loved in an unconditional way.

There were no limitations on my love for Reese and Oliver.

Which was exactly why it was going to last forever. Before, they stamped my heartbeats, and those stamps would last forever.

# EPILOGUE

## EMERY

*One Year Later*

"It's too tight," I breathed out as Sammie finished lacing up my dress.

"I told you not to eat those extra cheese fries last night," she joked as she finished. "Anyway, it's not too tight—it's a perfect fit."

Sammie had come back to California a few weeks before to help me prepare for the wedding between Oliver and me. She'd been in Texas for the past few months getting her life together—with the help of Oliver's parents, who looked after her. Even though I was trying my best to get her to move back to California, she seemed to be finding her footing down in Austin. I couldn't have been happier for her. She looked healthier, too: not only physically, but mentally. Emotionally. I knew my sister still had so many things to work through, so many demons to still slay, but she was doing it day in and day out.

And I couldn't have been happier to have her by my side during the happiest day of my life. I often used to dream about my wedding day, and it was always my sister who was standing by my side in those visions. I was so happy they'd come to fruition.

"Hey, Emery, wow," Tyler said, coming into the dressing room. "You look amazing. I was supposed to come here and tell you that the photographer needs Reese and Sammie for solo pictures. They just finished up doing mine and Kelly's. They are right down the hallway to the left," he said.

Sammie thanked Tyler as she walked away with Reese's hand in hers.

Tyler turned to me and gave me a tight smile. "You look amazing, Emery, truly. My best friend is a lucky bastard."

"Thank you. Now, if only I could get my nerves in check," I joked.

"Nothing to be nervous about. I've never seen two people who were more meant to be. Listen, I just wanted to take a moment to say thank you . . . for loving him. You gave him a shot when the rest of the world had counted him out. You're a phenomenal woman, and he's so damn lucky to have you."

"He's not wrong," a voice said, interrupting us both. I turned around to see Oliver's father, Richard, standing there. "Not to jump in uninvited, but do you think I can have a moment with Emery quickly?"

Tyler nodded and headed out of the space.

Richard stood back for a minute with his hands stuffed in his pants pockets. "Wow," he muttered. "Completely breathtaking."

"Don't make me cry too soon, Richard. My makeup artist is MIA."

"Sorry, I just . . . my son is very lucky. I won't take up too much of your time. I'm going to be honest: I don't know much about wedding traditions. Michelle and I ran off to Vegas for a shotgun wedding, and to this day my parents are still pissed about it. But I heard this thing about something old, something new, something borrowed, and something blue. I only got one of those pieces, but I figured I'd offer something borrowed to you, if you'd like." He reached into his pocket and pulled out a watch.

"This was Alex's favorite piece. He, um, always had a watch, no matter where he went. He hated that his brother was always late, so to make up for it, Alex was always right on time. And I think that's fitting for you, because you were right on time for Oliver with your love. Now, I know this might not go perfectly with your outfit, but—"

"Please," I said, cutting him off as I held my arm out toward him. He smiled and nodded as he began putting the watch on my arm. I stared down at the beautiful piece that held the history of a beautiful man. "I wish I could've met him."

"He would've loved you. Just like the rest of us." The way the Smiths had welcomed me into their world seemed so unreal. I didn't feel worthy of their love sometimes, but they always gave it to me and my daughter without thought.

Richard stood in front of me as if he had something else to say but wasn't sure how to get it out.

"Is there something else?" I asked.

"Yes, I mean . . . you're allowed to say no, because you're your own person. But I realized you have no one walking you down the aisle, and I wanted to say that if you needed a father figure to hold your hand, I'd gladly offer mine."

The tears fell down my cheeks, and Richard held his hands up, trying to stop their flow. "No tears! Your makeup."

"It's fine, we'll find the makeup person again," I laughed, pulling him into a hug.

When the time came for me to walk down the aisle toward my favorite love song, I linked my arm with Richard's. When the officiant— Abigail, of course—asked who was giving me away, Richard gave me off to his son. It was the most touching moment, and I felt more love than I'd ever felt in my life.

Everyone who meant anything and everything to both Oliver and me stood around us, supporting our happily ever after. Oliver stood tall, looking like a dream that I'd never thought I'd receive. Thinking back on life, I realized that I wouldn't change a thing. I wouldn't trade in a tear, a struggle, or a broken heartbeat, because all those pieces had led me to where I was right then and there. I stood beside the love of my life.

Right there, in front of our family and friends, we recorded the best song to exist on our mixtape of love.

That night we danced to the Spinners' "Could It Be I'm Falling in Love," Oliver's parents' first-dance song. We were creating a new story. Breaking generational curses and making new traditions. And from that point on, Oliver and I would be dancing together for the rest of our lives.

# OLIVER

*Two Years Later*

It had been a long time since I'd felt lost. Don't get me wrong: I still experienced sadness, but working with Abigail, I'd learned better ways of coping with my emotions over time. There was a point in my life where the bad days outweighed the good, so coming to the place where I was now, I was overwhelmed by how many great days I'd experienced.

Thank God I didn't give up on my life. Thank God I kept fighting through the darkness. If I'd given up all those years ago, when I was at my lowest, feeling as if death was closer to me than life, I never would've made it to this very moment. I never would've discovered my true happiness.

As I breathed in the autumn air, the breeze brushed against my face, and Emery laughed with Reese as they lay in the grass staring up at the fading sunset. My little boy, Alex, lay on his stomach, trying his best to figure out how to crawl, wiggling his body back and forth repeatedly. On the speaker, music blasted loudly. It was smooth music, with a calming characteristic to it.

It was my birthday. Each year on my birthday, the family went to Alex's grave site, and we'd play him our favorite songs of the current year and talk to him. We'd tell him the ups and downs of life and celebrate him. Every time a breeze passed, I knew he was there with us. Even though we couldn't see him, I felt his spirit surrounding me.

It was also tradition to sing "Godspeed," by James Blake. This year, Reese sang along with me before she wished her uncle Alex a happy birthday. A song that had once brought me heartache now stood for something beautiful.

I stood to my feet and held my hand out to Emery, who, without question, placed her hand into mine. I pulled her up, and we began swaying back and forth against one another. We danced to the music as my daughter sat beside her brother, rocking back and forth, trying to help him figure out how to move forward to his new life of discovery.

Emery laid her head against my shoulder, and I held her as close to me as possible.

Her lips touched my earlobe as she whispered against my skin, "Are you okay?"

"Yes."

No day was perfect. Not every day ended with slow dances and laughter, or smiles and happiness, but each day was worth it. Each day was worth living because it led to the better tomorrows, the brighter days, the happily ever after. This was our life. It had its ups and downs, but without question, it was ours. This was our mixtape, and I was damn proud of it.

I was overwhelmed in that moment with the best truth I'd encountered. A truth I hadn't thought I'd ever achieve, but I was so happy that it had finally found its way to me:

*I want to be here.*

# ACKNOWLEDGMENTS

Firstly, I would like to thank you, the reader, for taking the time to meet Emery and Oliver. Their story was a labor of love, and it means the world to me that you've given this story a chance. Without you all, these characters never would've come to life. Your support never goes unnoticed.

Up next are my extremely talented and kind editors from Montlake, Alison and Holly. Without your patience, support, and brilliant ideas, this story would still be unfinished. From our emails to our phone calls, thank you for helping me take these characters to the next level. Your creativity and allowance for me to explore have been a gift. Working with you both has been such an honor. Thank you.

Thank you to my amazing agent, Flavia, who held my hand the whole way and talked plot with me day in and day out. You've always been in my corner, and I am lucky to have you by my side.

To my family and friends who understand that sometimes I disappear for a while to finish a book, or I randomly start talking to my characters at dinners out—thanks for not calling me weird. And thanks for allowing me to still go out to dinner with you, even if I'm not always there mentally. You give me the space to be creative, and I hope you know I'll always give you that same love and respect back.

Thank you to Amazon Publishing for taking a chance on me. From the editing team, to the PR group, to the cover designers—I am so grateful.

And once again, we are going to end this the same way we began. Thank you, readers. Your love and support keep me going. Thank you for stamping my heart. You are my favorite songs on my mixtape.

—BCherry

# ABOUT THE AUTHOR

*Photo © 2018 Keith Gasper*

Brittainy Cherry has been in love with words since she took her first breath. She graduated from Carroll University with a bachelor's degree in theater arts and a minor in creative writing. She loves writing screenplays, acting, and dancing—poorly, of course. Coffee, chai tea, and wine are three things she thinks every person should partake in. Cherry lives in Milwaukee, Wisconsin. When she's not running a million errands and crafting stories, she's probably playing with her adorable pets.